FACE THE SUN

BY
ROBERT DAVIS
TAMMY MERRITT-DAVIS

First published by Dog Ear Publishing
4010 W. 86th Street, Ste H
Indianapolis, IN 46268
www.dogearpublishing.net

ISBN: 978-145750-496-9
eBook ISBN: 978-145750-662-8

This book is printed on acid-free paper.

This book is a work of Fiction. Places, events, and situations in this book are purely Fictional and any resemblance to actual persons, living or dead, is coincidental.

Printed in the United States of America

CHAPTER

ONE

OUTSIDE THE HOUSE, beyond its warmth, the daylight hours were passing into memory. The night was seeping through the cracks in the sunlight and rushing to fill in the spaces between the shadows that stretched across the floor from the edge of the windowsill. The intricate pattern of grandmother's lace swayed in the wind, poking inky black fingers through the lace and vibrating the screen against the frame as darkness stalked the house. The shadows stretched black arms from the underbrush as the wind raced through the window, looking to snatch the last bit of sunlight between its dark fingers and snuff it out.

Shadows danced across the dirty gray floor, competing with the darkness in the pale light of a single bare bulb hanging from a cord in the ceiling. A solitary figure sat at the table by the window as he watched the last of the sunlight melt and die across the surface of the lake. He slowly dragged the worn heel of his boot through the dusty lines on the floor. The moon would be rising soon, and a sudden brilliance would silently kiss the lake, turning the black water into a shimmering bone-white glare disturbed only by the circles drifting away from small baitfish breaking the surface as if for gulps of warm, heavy air.

The night began to invade the emptiness of his mind with dreams and grief, an amalgam of bliss and misery. He dared to let these harsh memories rise as fear settled across his soul like sweat across the skin. Emotions swelled in the fetor of his mind overrun with murky faces and blinding colors, a throbbing headache slipped like a thief behind his eye, blinding him to the moment and completely blocking the flow of tolerance, clearly marking the end of the day.

The sound of the slamming screen door on the back porch slid across the wet surface of the evening air, and his footsteps echoed from the warped planks leading to the copse of woods surrounding the lake. The image of a man emerged from the seam where shadow and darkness joined, a tall man with lanky limbs and a round, gentle face. He was average, not unattractive, with his plain features thin and delicate, not quite masculine yet not feminine either. He had his father's eyes, and there was slackness to the jaw; a head full of mousy brown hair with just a hint of red hung over his shoulders in waves. An instinctual gait to his stride allowed him to glide silently through the shadows. He was not an intruder here; this was his element, and as he stood hand in hand with loneliness, it was as if he stood hand in hand with a lover. What mattered, however, was not what the world saw, the world never noticed anything, its glance ricocheting off the rough and sharp edges, and missed the shadow following the obvious. The man settled like fog across the land, seen but not noticed, nothing more than a hollow ditch, void of spirit, void of soul. The world never let its glance touch him for more than a second or two before feeling the icy cruelty and deciding not to linger.

Darkness tolerated the distraction and found humor in watching him stand perfectly still in the pine thicket, listening to the voices screaming out words not known as language in the dark at the setting sun. However, he could not dawdle, not tonight. It was time to go. There were people to see and important matters waiting for him. The moon was already full and directly overhead. He took a deep breath, filling his lungs, and headed across the glen toward the lake.

The agony and twisting torture of the voices grew beyond vicious and cruel. They became one with the screams united with all that is obscene and abusive, stripped bare of hope and rescuer to become nothing less than death's beloved griffin's lonely wail, crying to the insouciant moon as black wings spread across the face of the distracted sky. The night talked to no one, but everyone listened to its loneliness, the desperation calling across the divide that separated terror from composure, superstition from piety. There was no one who did not hear it, none could ignore this wailing and they had no choice but to listen to the maelstrom of deranged shrieking. There was a melody in the air, a flow of disjointed notes not quite connecting, a temptress singing harmony with breaking glass. A sound that forced mad men, saints, mothers, and gods alike to hanker after the sound, chasing illusions and specters into the chilling embrace of nightmares born from childhood fears and death's last lamentation.

He had come, gone, and done what he had wanted with no thought to cost or effort or to how hideous, irreversible, and senseless the actions were to those who lived outside his world. Nathan had no regard for those who might come after him, who might venture into his world of darkness and shadow, and when he slipped away, he did so as quietly and completely as he had come. All he left behind was an enigmatic message, an incomplete token of his scorn for those men who must come after him to stand as witnesses to his efforts. It is misunderstood by the invited, let alone easy to explain to the uniformed, that this enigmatic message was Nathan's language. The message was in plain view for those bold enough to look, there with the blood and gnawed bones, and in the artistry of the scattered corpses so tastefully displayed for the unprepared. Yes, the message was revealed as the layers of shock were peeled back, exposing the sheer terror found beneath.

Establishing terror in the hearts of sane men, as they look upon the casual dismissal of life, helpless in the face of not understanding the reason for the violence was the point of the act for Nathan. He was capable of sharing his talent so selflessly with the rest of the world, but Nathan expected payment for such altruistic efforts. The panic of his victims and those who had to view the scene was his reward for the moments of self-denial were the risk of being so open and personal. There was always the chance of Nathan being denied the admiration of the garbage collectors, those who came after too must clean the mess that is left behind. Rejection is always a cruel experience for an artist, and if repudiated with anxious disdain, so be it, he had nothing to prove to the audience.

Nathan would stand back like a proud papa to watch his hard work, his child, step from the bowels of creation and stand naked, unprepared, before the world. There would be the shuffling of nervous feet between the stale jokes spoken from dry lips, and then abruptly, a hush would settle over the appalled, paralyzed audience. This would mean he had achieved nothing less than total success.

Tonight, as he had done so many nights before, Nathan danced with his dreams. He laughed at old jokes, shouted old hellos, and peeked into the forbidden chamber of the dream maker's secret room. After just one glance, the dream maker had him by the throat, dancing, swaying, and twirling him about. He moved and breathed in rhythm with the dream maker. It collected his wild thoughts and put them in a glass box with a diamond lock. The ashen, bloodless hands grabbed only the best thoughts, disregarded those too small, too white, or too pale. The dream maker murmured soothing words inflated with emotion and mystery to accompany those dreams found to be just right. The chosen dreams filled his being with racing panic, with distraction jammed full with confusion and fear. The dream maker belched a hollow laugh, with a curt nod hitched a ride on a moonbeam, and soared upon ragged black velvet wings. The departure left a sour taste in Nathan's mouth, and a small voice giggled as sanity slithered through the wasteland of his mind, abandoning him to wallow in stagnated hopes as the smell swallowed his soul, saturating it with a foul stench.

The wind moved through the sand at the edge of the lake, and dust swirled around his ankles like a cat. The sky was beginning to turn a lighter shade of night as the morning hours approached from the far side of the lake. This time always seemed lost to him as the hours bridged the darkness to the dawn. For Nathan, these were the hours when time dragged to the doorstep of a new day, anticipation lurking between the afterthoughts of night, when time itself sulks, drifts and sometimes sits down. Hours that often go unnoticed by the rest of the world, hours that first crawl and strain to their legs, which wobble before stumbling into an all-out run. These are the hours that launch another new dawn with bleeding knees and injured spirit, the hours that reach for the stars and search for buried treasure down moonlit patches

4

of mystery that tempt those who dare to tag along to places where cat screams go to die in the dark. These hours chase after ghost-colored shadows in shades of spoiled milk dancing upon wasted aspirations and slipping past wide-eyed stares from faces strange yet familiar. These hours smile in slow motion and with mechanical precision until all thoughts fade like overexposed film memories left bared to the noonday sun.

Old times, bad times, slapped Nathan hard across his face and he thought of her. He tried hard to remember the time they had first met. She had been just nine, but she had looked twelve, and what they had shared was true love. Was it she who had first said hello and started the decline of ever-tightening spirals of inward emotional descent? There was a time when everything had glistened, when everything had been just right. But the memory collapsed almost as quickly as it rose, to become just another fleeting moment that slipped like sand through his mind. "I saw her dancin' in the air, the music did not sound right, and the light was dim. I sat there with other wanderers of the night and shared the sight."

The silence hummed a familiar song, skipped and filled in the blanks as Nathan clung to the image, the perennial refugee escaping a history of regret. "It was late and it was early," he whispered to no one. "All the minutes run together for one last try." He grinned and held tightly to his loneliness.

Everything was soft and warm, but not as warm as before. The softness was showing signs of slowly stiffening, and the warmth had begun to cool. The seconds were ticking in his mind like hot metal cooling, clicking, winding down, and the world delivered itself into the hands of darkness.

"It is time to go home." The words dripped from the edge of lips painted egg blue, spitting contempt into the air. The pretty boys were laughing with their polished nails and matching lipstick-smeared desires, dragging themselves by with sleepless, vacant eyes that harbored the look of death. Nathan watched and picked at the blurry edge of his dream with fingers that drank the cool silence through cracks in the skin.

He spoke to his demented mind in a voice filled with sharp edges. "Prior lovin' left the bed sheets sweat-wet with yielding wants and misunderstandin's that have turned joy into tears, and the fear now lays weeping. Yes, there was blood on the mattress, but there is more in the heart and it's cloggin' the arteries to the soul. But wait; now she claims rape! The greatest assault to all womanhood! Cut the bastard's balls off, the jury would scream. Yet, had she not done that already?" Nathan sat crying, bleeding in his mind and confused. A sound drooled past his pale trembling lips, and he babbled a whisper, "Mama." And the moment had passed.

The solitude of the moment was spoiled as spilled words came rushing, climbing over each other's backs. The voices took a ride on the wind, and he sat in the darkness with his ears twitching. There were only two of them left sitting at the lake's edge. They were close enough for their legs to touch and for desires to ignite. Nathan watched for a moment. He loved to watch, a skilled and practiced voyeurism, and he passed the time spending himself into his sweaty palm. He licks the skin clean and goes crazy from the pungent taste dancing on his tongue, getting lost in the desire and losing track of what it was he had come to do.

Nathan would run the razor-sharp edge of his knife across tender skin to bring him back to the immediate task. He laughed at himself in silent, violent gulps and remembered a Chinese proverb. He watched the two lovers, and he watched the memory of the proverb slide through the thin film running along the top of his brain. He saw a scorpion nervously approaching the river's edge. Nathan could clearly see the little thin barb at the tip of the tail and the pincers like a crab snapping in the air. The little scorpion was crying, pleading for someone to help him get across the water, for he could not swim and would surely drown.

Nathan closed the door on the memory for a while as a sudden flash of light illuminated the face of the man. A match ignited the tip of a dangling cigarette, and Nathan could make out pale eyes squinting through the smoke. The match light faded, the tip of the cigarette faded to reddish embers, the distraction passed, and Nathan returned his attention to the tittering little scorpion. Nathan smiled when he saw the bright green frog approach on thin, cautious legs. The frog offered to help the scorpion but pleaded with the deadly creature not to sting him, for then surely, both of them would drown. Nathan wiggled with pleasure and smirked because he knew what was coming. "Stupid frog," he whispered.

The frog received the scorpion's promise and allowed the segmented fellow to crawl atop his bright, slick skin. The frog pushed off mightily, and inevitably, as he proceeded toward the distant bank, he felt the sharp pang of the scorpion's sting. "Oh, Mr. Scorpion, why did you sting me, for now we both will drown," the bewildered and trusting little frog cried out just before they began to sink. The scorpion clicked his pincers nervously, dancing away from the advancing water slowly consuming his ride, and replied, "Because it is in my nature, Mr. Frog. Because it is my nature." And they both sank to the bottom of the river.

"Smart fuckers, them Chinks." Nathan spoke in a small, one-sided voice as he watched the couple becoming more comfortable with the sounds of the deserted lake beach and more familiar with each other. Nathan heard muffled laughter, watched their exaggerated gestures, and waited. He waited for the moon to break through the ink-black clouds and send iridescent angles of light racing to puncture his eyes like burning darts.

The woman's voice was shrill against the summer air, and Nathan sat upon his haunches, alone and barefoot, with emotions twitching and swirling in his anxious empty stomach. He watched her push down the new white jeans and kicks them aside. The man reached up to pull down the sheer panties. The woman straddled her lover and settled into his lap with a sudden groan.

Nathan pleaded in his mind for the woman to shut up, to get on with it, have a go at being a slut, "but just shut the fuck up."

He knew he had to settle down or they would hear him. The game would most certainly be over if they knew he watched from the grassy edge. He told himself a poem, mumbling softly, "I am insane, or so I am told by those who speak so brazen and bold. With tongues that wag

7

and chatter on, until all words are dead and gone. Bright eyes stare into my world, better to see dark corners of theirs. I'll let them in to occupy their time, and then I will break the rhythm of their minds. What fools they are to think black and white. I dream in color late at night. Like robots all standing so straight in line, they stare at me yet they are blind. But I am insane, or so I am told by those whose minds are bought and sold."

Nathan watched as the woman collapsed to the ground in sated pleasure and stretched against the warmth of the sand. The moonlight radiated across the sweat pouring from her skin. Nathan sneered and fought to keep from rushing the moment, but he grew bored and impatient with this fat, indolent whore.

The woman wallowed like some crippled sow fallen in a hole, unable to do anything more than bellow. She was apparently comfortable now that her companion had scratched her itch, but she was still not completely satisfied. Nathan bit his tongue in anger because he was forced to watch the man reach out and grab hold of the woman again, pulling her down and taking hold of her breast. Nathan tasted the blood in his mouth as he watched the woman pull the man's hands tight against her, her flesh bulging between the man's fingers. Nathan imagined that she whispered a private joke about someone from the party they had left. She fingered the corrupt flesh between her legs, and then her plump hands shoved the man's legs apart. She gobbled him up as a fish would a worm, sucking him hard, working him into rigid attention. With fat fingers moving fast between the folds of her thighs, she jerked her hips forward and screamed with satisfaction.

Groans from behind the couple attracted their attention, and the woman yelled out, "Pervert." But the man laughed and told her that it was only the spirit of the lake come to gaze upon her beauty. He stopped laughing when Nathan stepped into the light of the moon. The woman grunted approvingly and walked over to him. Nathan looked down at the sand between the toes of his boots. She stopped just a few feet away and did not attempt to cover her nakedness.

"I met a friend starin' down at the ground with a face of stone and eyes like burnin' embers. He spoke of men in endless strife, wasted years, bein' fascinated by the lips movin' more than the words sailin', missin' a word and findin' it floppin' about like a minnow out of the water. Other words buzzin' that senseless buzzin' like high-tension wires and others still fallin' tall-tree dead in the forest. Timber! Swoosh! Flat to the earth, but no one hears—or do they? Yes!" The woman repeated the lines from a play in a mocking, shrill voice.

Nathan recognized her. She was an actor from the local theater, and he spat on the ground at her feet. "You are the Devil's own whore, with fat legs and sagging tits. You ain't any beauty, just some sweating heap of rotten shit."

The woman sputtered with indignation and took a defiant stance with her hands resting on her massive hips. The man would be easy, Nathan thought as he carefully let his eyes drift over the woman's soft, bloated shoulders to look at her companion. Nathan took the liberty of a glance down her body and fought the urge to vomit. He returned his eyes to the ground, the bile burning his throat as he listened to the voice he would soon silence.

"Who are you, some filthy little animal?" she screamed unexpectedly, and Nathan looked hard into her eyes. Then the man on the ground jumped up because he thought that Nathan had struck his companion.

"I was born from somethin' like you, squeezed from a stagnant cunt like pus from a wound," Nathan growled.

"You're just some fucking little monkey beatin' off in the bushes. Watchin' us fuck, are ya? I bet you ain't ever had any real woman, have ya? I bet you can't even get it up."

The man applauded, and the naked woman took a bow toward him. Nathan stepped back to avoid the woman's ass and grimaced at the sight. The man yelled at Nathan, "Go ahead, ol' boy, take her. I don't mind. I've shared before."

The actor walked closer to Nathan, and he automatically took a step back. She shouted at him, "Fuck me, asshole," as she bounced her breasts. "Are you afraid, afraid you can't get it up with a real woman? Come on, let me see it. I can kiss it and make it feel real good, I promise. Come on; show big mama what's in them pants." The woman squeezed her breasts together, holding them high so the nipples pointed directly at Nathan. "Do you want to lick them, or maybe suck them?"

Nathan watched the woman's antics as the need churned inside him, building with each second that passed. The woman pulled her sagging tit up to her lips and smiled at Nathan as her tongue ran across the dark nipple. "You see, it ain't so hard. I'll even help. Just come suck it for a while. I promise you will like it." The woman offered her tits to Nathan one more time before laughing, then yelling, at the rejection.

She finished taunting him, and Nathan watched her turn abruptly toward the man, who smiled and reached out for her hand as she approached. He did not see Nathan move, and neither had seen the glint from the edge of the knife. Nathan issued a hard, low growl, and the flash of the blade turned the air crimson. The woman staggered and looked back over her shoulder with a strange expression before collapsing to the sand. The man froze with fright and mumbled incoherently while Nathan brought the blade around for one more pass. The man's head fell gently to the side. The wound to his neck stretched by the weight, and he settled slowly to the sand. Nathan left the man's body alone and concentrated his efforts on the woman.

Nathan gave a long loving, look at his work, felt the tightness growing in his pants, and giggled silently as he walked back to the man. The shriveled cock came off with one hard chomp of Nathan's teeth. Nathan could still smell the filthy woman's juice on the man's body as he unzipped his own pants. He showered the violated body with liquid gold. "One more thing and my work is done."

Nathan carried the severed manhood to where he had left the woman's head, then opened her mouth and placed the penis inside. He could feel his desire growing as he gazed at the now perfected bodies, the face of the actor transformed into a beautiful masterpiece. Nathan kneeled down in front of the head and, with warm, gentle hands, stroked her hair; his blood-soaked fingers traced her lips. He straddled the head and shoved his hard cock deep into the hole that taunted him, pumping violently, feeling the severed cock rub against him with each thrust. He exploded and filled the void. Now that he was truly done, he took a swim in the warm embrace of the lake to wash away the blood and gore.

As he stared at the moon, he shouted, "Who would believe a whore and her lover in my graveyard? Oh, yes! I have walked through yonder glade and heard a thousand silent tongues. I've kissed the lips of pretty girls, filled private holes with my essence, and watched the crows help themselves when I'm done. Who am I, you asked, you slut—I am but a shadow. I ain't nothin' special, but I am doin' a damn sight better than you. Got here just like y'all, in a burst of blood. I ain't nothin' but a driftin' memory. It is here that men are born and mere gods die. Ain't it pretty to think so? Yes, siree!"

CHAPTER
TWO

NATHAN WAS BORN a long time after his family had done their part in the Civil War, supporting the northern effort to restore the Union. The Pomeroy family branded traitors after they blazed the trail for Sherman's famous march through the south. Spies were dealt quick justice, Sandra Pomeroy, Nathan's ancestral grandmother, had paid with her life, and her family had been shunned. Sandra had fallen in love with a young, handsome Union soldier. She had given him her love and her life, but he had given her nothing but sweet words and promises. The town her family had so proudly founded, originally called Pomeroy, but soon after it was discovered that young Sandra had forsaken her people, the place had been renamed Caulking, for reasons no one can remember.

Sandra's last living decedent would one-day stand amongst the towering pines where once she had lain with her seductive Yankee. Sandra had given to her soldier those things that a woman can give only once in her life. He had taken them easily, with grace and treachery. He had stolen her love and her trust, and he had taught her well the bitter lesson of betrayal. Sandra had given all, including the essence of her life, and as she had fallen to the ground with a gunshot wound to the chest, she had seen laughter in her lover's eyes while the smoke drifted from the barrel. Sandra Pomeroy bled twice for duplicity.

Nathan Pomeroy heard stories but knew very little of the history or infamy of his family, and no one living today remembered the name of

Sandra or her Yankee beau. Nathan did not dwell on ancient family history; instead, he occupied himself with watching a man unload suitcases from the top of a van. The man would stack the various pieces of matched luggage on the ground, and a tall, black-haired woman would direct their three children to carry them into the house.

The woman was slim and attractive, and she issued orders in a voice that fell across the surface of Nathan's face like acid rain. Nathan stood still in the high thicket, watched as another group of tourists prepared to violate his space in the world. Gritting his small, even teeth with muscles straining along his jaw, he turned to face the lake, and that was when the woman noticed him amongst the dark brown shadows running away from the tall, majestic trees.

"Wonder who that is," she called to her husband, and the man stopped to follow his wife's stare in the direction of the trees.

"Don't know, probably just someone looking at the lake."

Nathan did not look back until the barking of the family's Rottweiler ricocheted between the ancient tree trunks. He spun around in fear and searched wildly for the dog. He hated dogs, loathsome creatures that served only to lick the hands of masters that beat them into obedience. The beast was straining against the leather lead tied to the bumper of the van, and Nathan watched the animal throw back its massive head, discharging a shower of spittle in the air with every rumbling bark.

"Fucking dog," Nathan sneered as he slithered away. He had a history with dogs.

The family was on a vacation of sorts and planned to spend the rest of the summer in the area. They had rented the house until the end of August, when the kids had to be back in school. Harold Thornton was from Boston, an associate professor who had been granted a sabbatical to conclude his last effort in publishing research sponsored by the university. His wife, Phoebe, was thrilled to spend a couple of months in the country. She had been born in Oklahoma and raised on a farm. Phoebe missed the open spaces and the smell of the earth. She hated Boston but was devoted to Harold. They had met in college and fallen in love during a fast-moving summer romance. They had promised to marry right after graduation, but neither had been able to wait that long. Harold had graduated first and found work at the local power plant as a first-line engineer. The pay was good and the hours long, but Phoebe had made all the difference in the world.

Phoebe had landed an excellent job just prior to her graduation and helped Harold make it through graduate school. Their first child, Harold Jr., was born during the week of his father's final exams, but Harold Sr. graduated in spite of the distraction, with the reassurance from his wife that she would take care of everything, as she always did. The first university Harold applied to had hired him. He stayed there ever since. He was an avid cyclist, had been since his freshman year, and found a brisk ride to work every day exhilarating, even though they lived better than fifteen miles from the campus. Phoebe had had to give up the position of her dreams, but she had always placed Harold and her family first. Harold had become her life, and Phoebe would follow him to Hell. She tolerated Boston by becoming totally involved in motherhood, and although she kept aware of developments in her own profession, she slowly lost track of the outside world. She resigned her-self to being a professor's wife and the adoring mother of three chil-dren. Phoebe never complained, but on occasion, she still found herself daydreaming about those things she had given away but never forgot-ten.

Their second child had been born without ceremony. Deirdre Terry Thornton had come into the world on a blistering-hot day in late August and had been the perfect baby from her first day on earth. She had been picture-perfect beautiful, with big eyes, an easy disposition, and a penchant for sleeping all night long.

Phoebe drove the obligatory Dodge Caravan, British green with the proper camel interior and equipped with dual child seats in the back and sporting a luggage rack across the top. Phoebe had demanded the minivan after Sarah, their third child, had been born. The Thornton's bought a new van every other year and was the perfect middle-class baby-boomer family with all the trimmings and attitudes.

Phoebe drove to the downtown area after she opened the windows to air out the rental house and put away most of the clothes. She wanted to become acquainted with Caulking. The city had grown from a collection of mom-and-pop–type stores to strip malls, contributing greatly to the urban sprawl. There was now a gas station on every corner, a dozen banks, and the ever-necessary video store. Caulking had grown up and out in all directions. The population had tripled in less than ten years, and the old-timers sat around talking about the good old days. The downtown section alone now covered an area twice the size of the town's entire boundary a decade before. Modern buildings reached for the clouds drifting in the clear blue sky. One of the few remaining original structures used to house the local government center, police station, and courthouse. The three-story building also had a jail in the basement and stood in the center of Main Street, which forced the road to split. A town square appeared over the years, and the people of Caulking had their first park.

Phoebe laughed aloud when she heard about the park. The town was surrounded by forest and had a beautiful view of a lake; she could not imagine what on earth the townsfolk would want with a park. She eased the van into a parking spot in front of the grocery store and had started to unload Sarah when she heard a booming baritone voice. The sudden sound scared her half to death, and she jumped, spilling the contents of her purse all over the sidewalk.

"Beg yer pardon, ma'am. Didn't mean to have you jump out of your skin," the voice continued, and Phoebe turned to face Sheriff J.C. Chandler, whom everybody called Buddy, as he explained when he introduced himself. The man was three hundred pounds stretched over a six-foot–five-inch frame and had a baby face that never stopped smiling.

"That's okay. I just wasn't expecting anyone," Phoebe apologized and started picking up her belongings from the ground.

"Let me, ma'am. It's my fault you dropped everything," the sheriff told her, giving her one of his famous smiles.

Phoebe could not help but giggle girlishly, taken with the man's southern charm and easy manner. She let the sheriff snatch up the purse with a single swipe of his hand and return it to her. He stood back up with a grunt, his face now quite red, but he was still smiling.

"Just wanted to welcome y'all to Caulking, ma'am. You and your family have rented the old Joseph's place out on Rock Creek Road, right?"

"Yes, we will be staying until the end of August. It is so beautiful out here. Does it ever snow in the winter?" she asked, feeling very comfortable talking with a man she had just met.

Buddy loved to talk about his town and gave Phoebe a brief history of everything, from the first settlers to plans for building a new elementary school next fall. Sarah became restless and began to fuss a little. It does not take much to bore a healthy four-year-old, and soon she was whining. Phoebe gave Sarah a consoling pass of the hand through her long blonde hair and kept on talking. It had been a long time since she had had a conversation with an adult that was more than just pretext, and she did not want it to end. Sarah complained a little louder, but her voice suddenly stopped. The abrupt halt gave Phoebe pause, and she turned to see what the distraction was.

At first, Phoebe was unable to see what that had attracted her daughter's attention, but then she saw a man standing across the street. Phoebe felt uneasy under his stare and pulled Sarah close to her side. He looked familiar, but Phoebe could not place where she had seen him before.

Nathan looked hard into the bewildered face for a second but could not bear to let her eyes touch his for long. He looked at the ground, searching for something, anything to hold his attention until the moment passed. "*Whore,*" he hissed in his mind. "*How I would love to lick the shit-city stain from between the cheeks of her ass. Yeah, I can smell her dripping pussy from here. Give it to her up the ass, I would. Grunt and groan until they ain't no more. Yes, siree, I would.*"

Phoebe was visibly uncomfortable, and the sheriff quickly looked toward the store. "Nathan Pomeroy," he said quietly, but she heard part of the name.

"Nathan, did you say?"

"Yes, ma'am. It's just ol' Nathan. Folks 'round here pretty much ignore him. He's kinda slow, if you know what I mean. His family has been in these parts from the beginning. Far as I know, he's the last of the Pomeroy clan. He's harmless, ma'am. Just a little special, if you get my meaning. I'm sure coming from the big city, you can relate."

Phoebe searched his face for a moment and then looked back at Nathan. Nathan stole another glance but quickly returned his attention to some crack in the street.

"Oh, I get it," she said in a straightforward, innocent way. "You mean that his parents were a little too closely related, like brother and sister maybe." Her conclusion was so honest and genuine that the big sheriff burst out laughing.

"That's 'bout right, ma'am—three-fingered and web-footed, we like to say 'round these parts. Kinda sad, though. Poor soul ain't got nobody in the world to care about him. Oh well, that's the nature of some folks, I guess."

Nathan pierced the back of the sheriff's head with a hate-filled look and had visions of stripping the skin from the man's body. He shuddered with the pleasure, but the thought gave way to his other desires. "*Shit, she's looking at me,*" he screamed in his mind. "*Oh, just to run my hands across that body, to beat it and use it like the piece of trailer trash she is. Just to spurt my juice all over that prissy little face, get it matted up in her long, blonde hair, and listen to her scream as I carve my initials between those delicious thighs.*"

The sheriff did his best to sidetrack Phoebe. He did not want certain locals to scare the tourists—that would be bad for business. He asked if she had visited the souvenir shop inside the post office and explained that the local Indians sold some items along with hand-painted pictures of the lake. Phoebe listened politely, but the sudden appearance of the strange man across the street had put her in a different mood. Sarah was still quiet and held tightly to her mother's leg. Phoebe turned again, but she did not see Nathan. She felt her body relax, and then her heart went out to him. The first signs of a headache were now tapping at the back of her head.

Nathan had not left; he was inside the store, watching her from the window. He would be leaving by the back door soon, but he would not be far. He smiled and tapped long fingernails on yellow teeth. He licked the tips of his fingers and absently rubbed his crotch with the other hand.

"She is a beauty, mysterious. Just look at them eyes and all that hair." He sighed. "I might jus' fuck her mother too, so she won't be so stuck-up-ass jealous, yes I would," he said in a low voice as the clerk behind the counter turned.

"Can I help you, sir?"

Nathan gave the clerk the finger and walked through the door toward his home.

Nathan went home to a rambling structure of solid wood. It was a place that had grown as family had come and gone through the years, growing a room at a time when the family expanded and later growing a porch when the elders had decided to sit themselves down to wait on eternal darkness. The house had stretched itself to the limits to accommodate the family. This old unpainted house, his house, was a living creature, as much a part of Nathan as the very blood running in his veins.

Nathan loved the house, spoke words of endearment to it, words of anger—and why not? Who better to listen to the words from the soul than your own flesh and blood? He knew that the spirits of his ancestors, recent and ancient, still roamed within these walls. Nathan would call their names and listen to their whines of regret, whispers of sorrow, and screams of torture. A family tradition, he assumed. He would cry with them; laugh at their suffering; coax them to sleep with tales of terror, promises of pain; and watch them slip back into the shadows one by one until, once again, he was alone.

He hated the wails of the women more than those of the men, but not nearly as much as he hated those of the children. Little bastards, maggot piss from filthy whores. Nathan would pound the walls until his knuckles bled and the buzzing stopped. He would remember his own life at times like these, and he would try to shove the memories back behind the pain. The thoughts would spit pus across the open sores of his memory, split the skin beneath the unfocused eyes, and the past would escape. Once again, she was dancing in the air and he had to watch.

"Mother..." he moaned, and he heard the scurrying feet of demons racing to the very edge of time, kicking minutes down into the pit of Hell itself. Not long to go now, no siree, not much time left to dance. Wet, fleshy lips would part and whisper, "I have to go," and plain brown eyes would dance in tempo with the beating of hearts. There would be a rush of time and noise, and soon the wait would be over—no time left and he would have to go. A touch seared his flesh with an explosion of joy, happy feelings dancing in the pit of his empty stomach, the end of a long struggle building. It was over for now, no images left dangling over cold thoughts, no identity recognized as he stood by the edge to watch.

Nathan would hide in the corner because he liked to feel the walls vibrate when the rats fought. He would wait until the crowd started to grow bored with the show and leave just before sunrise. Drunken men would stagger home to loving wives, and Nathan would find him sitting alone at the bar. The crowd was thinning, the smoke-filled air clearing, and he would be grinning like a lunatic. Nathan would watch him pound the polished wood with open palms and wipe the beer foam from his mustache with the back of his hand, and he would hear him shout filthy names at the dancer.

"Daddy," Nathan called aloud to the silence of the house.

"Come here, my little baby. Come to Mama," the dancer called. Nathan would try to run, but he could never get past the man at the bar. The man would grab him anywhere he could, tear him from the ground with powerful arms, and throw him across the stage at the feet of the dancer. Nathan would lie on the filthy floor and stare into the painted face. He would follow the pits and hollows of the skin as she leaned close enough for him to reach out and lick the nipple hard with an outstretched tongue and tear the tender flesh with bared teeth, and he would hear the man at the bar scream with delight.

"Do the bitch, boy," he would yell to Nathan.

"Let Mama see the little baby," the dancer would whisper, and Nathan would cry out for the dancer to stop, to please don't do it again, to leave him alone. She would cackle, the man at the bar would laugh, and Nathan would stand in the spotlight while she pulled down his pants. He would feel her hands grab his little-boy cock and massage the skin until it was taut. Nathan could hear the other dancers snicker behind him, and he would watch the man at the bar fall from the stool, roaring with laughter.

Nathan lost the memory for a moment and fell hard to the floor as the room swirled with confusion and his stomach lurched, and then the moment passed. He had time to crawl to the sofa before it came again and he found himself once again back in time. His mother was finishing her shower, and the water was a rainbow going down the drain. The colors slid from her face, and soon all that was left were the scars from a hard life. She liked Nathan to stay in the bathroom with her while she showered and played her little games.

His father was still at the bar, asleep on the floor, rolling around in the spit and vomit. He would be home sometime before noon, or maybe a little after, and he would look for Nathan. Nathan's old man would beat him senseless before raping him. Nathan had killed his father when he had turned thirteen and was strong enough. He strapped his father to the dining room table after smashing a perfectly good bottle of corn liquor on the side of his head. His father had come around with a howl and a flow of obscenities. Nathan had grinned, picked pieces of glass from his hair lovingly, and decided to let his father die slowly and in pain.

Nathan had cut the clothes from his father, stood back in deliberation, and then jabbed the tip of the skinning knife into the little eye of the shriveled cock. He had brought the tip up sharply and cut the flaccid flesh in two. *"No different than guttin' a fish,"* thought Nathan as the old man fainted from the pain. Nathan sewed the old man's lips shut while he moaned. The rest of the work went quickly, and Nathan was careful not to let him die right away. He wanted to prolong this father-and-son moment of bonding a while longer—dear old Dad had always been there for him, and now he wanted to return the favor.

He marveled that the human body was an amazing thing, running his bloody hands over the bulging belly and down to the ruined flesh. Licking his lips, he slowly lowered his head and kissed his father's inner thigh as the leg quivered in pain. Smelling the fear leaking from his father made Nathan's dick grow hard, and he could feel it pressing against his pants. "Bastard," Nathan whispered as he stroked himself. This gave him pleasure beyond dreams at the peak of his release. The white liquid filled his hand as he shoved the blade between the old man's cheeks. The knife turned and dug deeper with each burst of ecstasy, digging wider and deeper into the hole until the blood flowed across the table and dripped to the ground.

The old man heard the laughter fading as the darkness closed in around him.

Well, that was done and it was time to find Mama.

The woman was hiding in the bathroom with her hands held tightly to her ears. She was crying hysterically, trying to keep out the sounds of the screams and the horrible laughter. She knew it was only a matter of time before her baby came to find her, but the waiting would not be the worst part.

The door burst into splinters, and the woman screamed and pleaded as her little boy stood over her, smiling. "It's time to play, Mama. Come dance with me," he whispered. "Would you like to take a shower, Mama? You remember all the fun things we done in the shower, don't you, Mama." Nathan had adjusted the temperature on the tank earlier that day and determined that it should be just about right.

He tied his mother to the showerhead and slowly turned on the water. The steam filled the shower closet as her screams filled the air and the blisters stood out red and bloated across the skin. The blade was sharp, and the incisions were deep and swift. The water again was a rainbow going down the drain, but today it was a rainbow of a different color. Nathan carefully collected every piece of his beloved mama to be placed in a plastic bag along with the two lumps of flesh that had been her breasts. He sucked the edge of the blade clean before carefully cutting away the legs and arms.

Hours later, Nathan sat at the edge of the lake and talked softly in words of love to the bodies of his parents. He had taken the liberty of reassembling them in a fashion he thought more appropriate. The panoply was a display of genius, and Picasso would have been jealous.

He did have some trouble determining what to do with the fingers from his mama's left hand. Nathan had run out of openings, and so he had tossed them in the water for the turtles to eat.

The animals took care of the evidence and by the time the Welfare people discovered Nathan several years had passed. He had played the part they expected, appearing disheveled, confused, and untrusting. He had cried, and begged to keep the family home and property because it was all he had left in the world from his family. They had bought his story about being abandoned, of having to steal food from neighbor's' garbage cans to survive, and they had promised that the state would take care of him. Everything was going to be all right, yes, siree. Wasn't it pretty to think so?

Time reached with fingers of curled rage from beneath Nathan's private Hell and hit him hard with a closed fist. The token visit of his childhood days ended without as much as a good-bye. He slept like a baby on the verge of death until the early afternoon and woke with a raging hunger. It was time to go a-visiting, to be neighborly.

CHAPTER

THREE

SARAH PUSHED PAST her father. She wanted to be the first one through the door. This was a game with them, a mock race filled with laughter, squeals of joy, and youthful energy. "Hey, not so fast. You could slip and hurt yourself," Harold called after his daughter. Seconds later, he heard her fall and a burst of crying erupt, but the noise stopped as quickly as it started. Harold dropped the bag of groceries to the floor as he came through the door to young Sarah's aid. He instinctively pushed the rest of the children back to the porch when he saw the smear of blood and his little girl's stunned expression. His mind could not immediately comprehend what he stared at, but, thinking she was hurt, he picked up his child and held her close.

Phoebe peered through the crack in the door and gasped at the sight. She rushed to enter the house, thinking her daughter was hurt, but the look on Harold's face stopped her. He held up his hand, and she stayed with the other children outside the door.

"Wait, stay with the children. Sarah is not hurt. It's not Sarah's blood, and there is a lot of blood in here," he whispered to his wife, not wanting to alarm the children any further. He handed Sarah to Phoebe and proceeded inside.

The smear of blood led across the foyer, through the hallway, and up the stairs. He called for Champion, but the dog did not respond. "Oh my God," he whispered as he followed the trail of blood up the stairs and down the hall where the bedrooms were. The blood trail led him to Sarah's bedroom.

Harold slowly turned the knob on Sarah's bedroom door, absent-mindedly wiped the blood on his shorts, and pushed open the door. He immediately let out a gasp. He had found Champion. The dog was lying on Sarah's bed in a pool of blood with his stomach torn open and what looked like stab wounds across his neck and back. His head was resting on a silk Tinker Bell pillow. With so much blood, it was hard to determine what exactly had happened. Harold immediately thought Champion must have gotten into a horrible fight with a wild animal and come into the house and into Sarah's bed after suffering terrible injury. Even the dog's eyes were punctured, and his right rear paw was missing; Harold figured something had bitten it off. "Champion," he called as if the dog might rise and come back to them.

The sheriff responded in record time and determined that the animal had been dead for several hours. Harold and Buddy wrapped the dog in the blanket and carried the carcass down the stairs. They took it out the back door, and Harold dug a deep hole to bury the animal. Champion had had his fifth birthday the previous week and the family had celebrated with a cake made of dog food. There had been presents also: a new collar, a three-foot rawhide chew bone, and a box of liver-flavored snacks.

Champion was one of the family, and the children were devastated by the loss. What if they had been there, Phoebe thought, and with that realization, she was scared to death. The only one to have seen the blood and gore was little Sarah. Phoebe cleaned the house twice before she let any of them inside. She poured bleach on the tile floor and scrubbed the carpets, crying the whole time as terror stabbed at her heart like an ice pick.

Who or what could have done such a terrible thing? Champion was one hundred and ten pounds of muscle and teeth. He would never have let anyone in the house. Phoebe collapsed on the floor and cried until she could not cry any more, until the tears refused to flow. She remembered Champion the bundle of black fur with a tan mask that Harold had brought to her in a wicker basket.

Harold let the kids put flowers on Champion's grave. They said prayers in quiet voices and vowed never to forget the faithful dog. Harold cried silently and watched Sarah place stones around the outside of the fresh red dirt.

"I'll be goin', Harold," Buddy whispered, and Harold nodded. The tears embarrassed Harold, but the sheriff understood. He was a dog man himself, with a pack of good Walker hounds back at the house. Hell, that one bitch was about to drop a litter any day now, he remembered, and he wondered if these folks would appreciate a new puppy to help the kids with their sorrow.

The sheriff settled his bulk behind the wheel of his marked squad car with a grunt and searched his mind. What was it that he could not think of completely but that was chewing away at his thoughts from the first glance at the scene inside that house? Just as his mind was about to pull up a memory from a long-ago incident, the dispatcher raised him on the radio.

"You go ahead, dispatch," Buddy answered, and he released the button on the microphone.

"Sheriff, you fixin' to clear that call?"

"Yeah, Ed, what ya got?"

"I don't know, Sheriff. You best get out to the west side of the lake. I got a call from some kids that say a pack of dogs are chewin' up people. The kid on the phone said they're findin' body parts all over the place!"

Buddy got a sick feeling in the pit of his stomach. He hoped it was just kids overreacting to some animal torn apart by other animals, but after what he had just seen at the Joseph' place, somehow, he doubted it.

"Did ya say the west side, Ed?"

"Yeah, seems like it's next to that big stand of pines where the kids go swimmin'," the dispatcher advised.

The sheriff slid the microphone back in the clip on the side of the radio and slipped the selector into drive. The roar of the big engine startled Harold, and he looked back to watch the dust swirling behind the sheriff's car.

Buddy saw the group of kids jumping and waving their arms in the middle of the road over a mile from the stand of pines. Buddy was complaining about Ed to himself when he brought the car to a halt next to a tall, dark-haired boy he estimated to be about thirteen. There was a look of horror on the boy's face, and Buddy reached down to unsnap the holster of his service revolver.

"Come quick, mister…I mean Sheriff. There's a piece of somethin' over here," the wide-eyed boy yelled. Buddy now recognized him as one of the Thompson kids from Hickory Lane. His daddy ran the crop-dusting company, when the plane was able to fly.

Sheriff Chandler pulled at his pants, yanked up the thick, black leather utility belt, and trotted after the boy. The rest of the kids were standing around in a semicircle and pointing to what looked like a piece of rotting meat about four feet long by the side of a dirt path. The smell of decay was strong, and the flies had already had a field day, along with the ants. Buddy could see that some kind of animal had also had its fill. The boys had found what was left of a human leg.

"Sheriff," a small voice called from behind him.

"Yeah, hold on, boy," Buddy answered. He could not take his eyes away from the blue-and-green–colored piece of meat.

"Sheriff, there is somethin' else over here," the voice continued.

"And over here, Sheriff," a second voice added.

The sheriff was on the radio for a long time, issuing instructions to an excited Ed. This was the biggest thing to happen around these parts in a long time, and Ed made copious notes as Buddy spit orders into the microphone. Buddy wanted every available deputy and fireman to respond immediately. He told Ed to call the next town and get all their extra men out to the scene as soon as possible. The sheriff thought he was going to have to search an area larger than a hundred acres, but all he actually had to do was walk over to the stand of pines.

Buddy collected the kids together and had them tell him step by step what had happened. They all started to talk at the same time, and it wasn't until the first backup unit arrived more than twenty minutes later that the sheriff got a rough understanding of what had led to this grisly discovery. David Thompson became the spokesperson for the group, and he told Buddy that they had been swimming over by the pines. The kids had tied a rope to a limb and used it to swing out over the water. Johnny McLaren had caught a glimpse of something behind the group during his turn on the rope, and the group set out to explore.

The sheriff waited until he had a dozen men assembled before he began his official briefing. He had told each man what was happening as they had arrived, but he wanted to bring a touch of professionalism to the search. He ordered Ed to contact the coroner's office and the local branch of the Georgia Bureau of Investigation. The sheriff knew he was out of his league on this one. This was not a barking dog call or a drunk needing persuasion to head on home after a fight with the wife. This was big; it had been a long time since he'd had a call about human remains.

"Men, we will search in teams of two, spread out in a line and work our way to that stand of trees over there."

Buddy pointed toward the pines growing on the edge of the lake about a mile away. He cleared his throat. Suddenly, he was thirsty and wanted to clear his head. A deputy had brought a cooler filled with drinks, as ordered by the sheriff, and a thirty-gallon container of water used by road crews. The sheriff helped himself to a long drink of cold water before he continued talking to the search party.

"Okay, let's spread out, and remember, don't touch anything. Yell if you find something, anything. I have these here long poles with pieces of bright orange tape on the top. Stick 'em in the ground when you find something. I want you to mark clothes, shoes, beer cans, cigarette butts, anything, and everything. Is that understood?" The sheriff looked at the men and women before him with grim faces and set jaws. With the nodding of a few heads, they were off. No one said a word, and only nervous glances were exchanged between the searchers.

The day was hot, and not a hint of a breeze stirred the grass or leaves on the trees. The dust was thick on the paths, and the faces of the search teams were streaked with dirty sweat within minutes. Buddy looked out across the field leading to the trees. He could already see eight poles marking the ground. He rubbed his right eye with a sausage-sized thumb and sighed. The sounds of approaching trucks could be heard, and Buddy shaded his eyes against the glaring sun. He saw two vans from the Georgia State Police Department bouncing over the ruts in the dirt road. A third van, painted appropriately black, was from the medical examiner's office.

The vans rumbled to a stop, and Sheriff Buddy Chandler was again the center of attention. He explained briefly, what had happened between the time the boys had called Ed and the arrival of this new group of investigators. Doctor Peeples from the coroner's office had separated himself from the group and was examining the leg. He had started to interrupt Buddy with a question when loud shouts were heard from a member of the first search party to reach the pines as other body parts were being discovered.

The area was now buzzing with activity while a race waged against the setting sun. A four-mile grid was cordoned off to secure the crime scene, with deputies posted at each corner. A mobile command post was established, and a helicopter flew over the area, taking photographs. Doctor Peeples determined in a matter of minutes that there were two bodies involved, a male, and a female, both in advanced stages of decomposition.

They had found most of the female but were still missing a hand and the lower portion of the left leg. The torso showed evidence of evisceration and extensive mutilation. Dr. Peeples looked closely at the clean edges of the cuts. The edges were not torn or ragged, indicating that someone used a very sharp instrument and that whoever had used the instrument had some knowledge of how to butcher a human body. They had known where the joints were, where to insert the blade without having to cut or break the bones. A chill ran up Doctor Peeples's spine with the realization that whoever had done this had lots of experience.

The body of the male victim did not have damage as extensive as that of the female. In fact, the second body had been recovered almost completely intact. Doctor Peeples noted that the penis had been removed and that the organ was still missing.

Peeples took the bodies along with the cameras and other equipment back to his laboratory in Albany for a more thorough examination. A complete autopsy might help answer the hundreds of questions already being asked by the police. The doctor knew that he would not be able to answer most of the questions, that, indeed, his investigation would only create more questions for investigators to answer.

The autopsy was performed the following day. It had taken most of the night to unload all the body parts, develop the crime-scene film, and lay out the victim's' personal effects found scattered around the area. The clothes did not reveal much to the medical examiner or the GBI investigators other than the fact that the victims had not been wearing them at the time of the attack. There was no evidence of the clothing being ripped or cut, and none of it had evidence of blood.

Doctor Peeples's first report stated that death was from multiple stabs, punctures, and slash-type wounds from a sharp instrument like a scalpel or a skinning knife. An individual with some workable knowledge of human anatomy had wielded the instrument, and both victims, especially the female, had experienced considerable damage prior to death. This conclusion was based on the amount of blood loss in the tissue and muscles. He estimated that the victims had been tortured prior to dying and the bodies mutilated after death. Most of the major organs from the female victim had not been recovered at the crime scene. The penis of the male victim had been located lodged deep in the throat of the female. Peeples also noted neither breast of the female was recovered. A serology report indicated that traces of marijuana discovered in the tissue of both victims.

"Pretty straightforward boring stuff, a little sicker than most, but still boring," admitted Doctor Peeples as he handed over a copy of his report to Sheriff Chandler.

"This may be everyday stuff to you, Doc, but we damn sure don't have this sort of thing happen in Caulking every day," the sheriff answered with a grimace as he continued to read.

"The boys from GBI picked up their copy already. Are they going to be handling this, Sheriff?" asked Peeples.

"God, I hope so. I pray they will. I don't want no part of all this," announced the sheriff as he shoved the inch-thick report into a manila folder. "Did they tell you that we think we know who those poor folks were?"

"Yeah, some actors from a theater group out of New Orleans. My investigator has already sent a fax to Louisiana requesting information from the next of kin," responded Peeples as he answered the telephone on the first ring. "We need someone to make positive identification if they can," he said before saying hello into the receiver.

"It's for you." Peeples handed the phone to the sheriff and excused himself. He had not had a cigarette since before noon, and if he could not sneak one in within the next ten minutes, he would have to wait until after his lecture. He was scheduled to give a talk to a group of forensic pathologists on mutilation murders, a coincidence that seemed ironic even to this man of science. He wanted to go over his notes and, being a pragmatist, hoped to include the murders from Caulking in the lecture.

Peeples had spent hours photographing the torso of the female victim and made careful notes describing the wounds. He created a carefully worded report describing the crime scene in detail, and forwarded the package to FBI headquarters in Virginia.

Now he needed this country sheriff to shuffle on home. "If you'll excuse me, Sheriff Chandler, I have something that needs my immediate attention," explained the doctor as he made a hasty departure.

"Yeah, you go ahead, Doc. I'm fixin' to leave shortly anyways," Buddy said to Peeples's back as the doctor disappeared out the door, and then he said into the telephone, "Hello, Sheriff Buddy Chandler speaking."

"Buddy, thank God. This is Ed. We have them newspaper people all over the place," the voice screamed from the receiver. The sheriff jerked his head away in time to save his hearing.

"Calm down, Ed. Just give them that press-release thing the state police prepared and tell them we ain't got nothin' else to talk about, okay?" the sheriff shot back.

"No, it ain't okay! You are sittin' in Albany, and I am here in Caulking having to deal with all these people," Ed screamed again. "Just when are you getting' back here?"

Sheriff Chandler calmed his dispatcher to a degree just beneath panic and explained he was leaving within the hour. He also advised that he wanted all the people who had participated in the initial investigation at the scene of the murders to be available for a meeting when he got back to the station around eight o'clock. Ed assured the big man that he would have it under control by the time he got back. The sheriff couldn't help but snicker as he hung up the phone. The day Ed had anything under control would be a day for celebration.

CHAPTER

FOUR

NATHAN SAT IN front of the television and stared in fascination at the blonde woman who was explaining in a prim and proper way that the town of Caulking was front-page news. She was reporting the grisly discovery of two murdered visitors from a Louisiana theater group. There was not a great deal of information available at this time, but they knew the nude victims had been stabbed to death.

"Is the shit hot from the ass of the Devil's bride? You bet your sweet little ass, darlin', that them fuckin' bitches were nakeder than jay-birds. Yes, siree," Nathan shouted. He clapped with uncontrollable excitement.

A couple of miles away, Phoebe Thornton was chewing the thumb-nail on her right hand down to the skin. She had chain-smoked a pack of cigarettes and screamed when Harold shut the front door. "What the hell is wrong with you, Phoebe?" her husband asked as he dropped a towel to the floor. He had just finished a five-mile run, and the eighty-five–degree temperature and the humidity had made it like run-ning in a sauna.

"Sorry, have you seen the news report about the murders? It is just awful, and right around here." Harold heard the quiver in her voice.

"No, but I did see several helicopters flying out over the lake on my way home," Harold answered as he peered over his wife's head at the television set. He told her that the area the camera was panning showed a part of the lake only a few miles from the back of the property line. Phoebe ran over and immediately turned off the television.

"Harold, I want to go home now! Where are the kids? I want them here in the house." She was on the verge of panic. Harold had never seen his wife act like this before today. Phoebe was always the calm one, always the one in control.

He sat down quietly next to her and pulled her close. Phoebe buried her face in Harold's neck, and he felt her shaking. The death of Champion had shaken her emotionally—such a brutal and senseless thing. Harold wondered what the hell the sheriff was doing to find out what had killed their dog and why. He then remembered the murders and chastised himself for being so selfish.

Phoebe cried herself to sleep, and Harold fixed dinner for the kids. There was nothing fancy on the table, but everyone loved macaroni and cheese with those little Vienna sausages. The story about the murders was still being carried on all the local channels. Harold was glad Phoebe had planned by bringing a dozen videos in case the kids got bored with the country. He glanced over at the couch and watched Phoebe sleeping.

Phoebe jerked suddenly and gave a short cry. Harold kneeled in front of her and stroked a strand of hair from her face. The unexpected touch woke her with a start, and she stared in confusion for a few seconds at Harold's surprised face. Sweat formed immediately on her skin, and the bad dream she had been having drifted all around her. "Where are the kids?" she almost screamed.

"They're in the kitchen. Damn, honey. What's wrong with you?" She was sweating profusely, but she was cold, ice cold, and her teeth chattered. Harold held her tight, felt her shiver, and rubbed her arms to try to warm her. He rolled his eyes in irritation as she cried and trembled in his arms. Harold depended on Phoebe for everything, and he knew that he was extremely selfish when it came to his needs. He knew his faults, but Phoebe did also, and in fact, she allowed him to exercise his egocentric nature to the extreme. He could not function with her like this. He needed her to run the family and allow him to exist like a special visitor when it was convenient. This vacation was *his* vacation, his opportunity to detach himself, to savor his self-centered posture, not her chance to go off the deep end, to lose control.

Sheriff Buddy Chandler had also been watching the television reports, as was most everyone in the state. He had mixed emotions. For the most part, he was excited because of the attention and because everyone being afraid would help his budget request, but this terrible crime made his town look like a bad place to live, and he didn't like that at all. Buddy loved Caulking. He had been here all his life, just like his daddy and his granddaddy. He was as much a part of Caulking as the big oak standing in the middle of the town square.

He had finally knocked the receiver to the floor, growing tired of answering the telephone and being asked if he was watching the television. Of course, he thought with a smirk, he was the damn sheriff. Who would know more about this thing and what they were saying on the tube than him?

Ed walked into the sheriff's office, and Buddy waved for him to just sit down and be quiet. Ed noticed the telephone disconnected and absently returned the receiver to the cradle. The telephone immediately rang, and Buddy shot an angry expression at Ed.

"Doggone it, Ed," shouted the sheriff as he picked up the phone. Ed shrugged and settled himself into the chair close to the television.

"It ain't my fault you're so famous," Ed mumbled as he watched the blonde woman talk about the murders with a fake look of concern.

Doctor Peeples was examining a fax his secretary had just dropped in the middle of his desk.

"I think you should have a look at this. It looks pretty damn interesting," she advised before blowing across the fingernails on her left hand. She had just applied another coat of bright red acrylic nail polish to both hands.

"Thank you for screening my mail, Ms. McNickles," the doctor shot at the back of the woman as she waddled away toward the front desk.

"You're welcome, Doc," she answered while switching her attention to the right hand.

The fax was from the Behavioral Unit of the FBI in Quantico, Virginia. The first page was marked confidential and urgent in bold letters. The report was only three pages long, but each page contained five similar homicides reported over a three-year period that matched the general description of the Caulking murders. The dismemberment was the same, as was the placement of the bodies near a large body of water. The rest of the description of the crime scene was similar too, and the female victims had all been eviscerated. The other female victims were also missing breasts and internal organs, and all victims had been killed with a sharp weapon. The cause of death was listed as slashing or cutting resulting in excessive blood loss. The assailant had let the victim bleed to death and then severed major body parts, only to sew them back on in a reverse arrangement. Doctor Peeples closed his eyes and tried hard to block the mental image this report had created.

"Ms. McNickles, could you call Detective Waters over at GBI homicide?" the doctor asked in a strained voice.

"You bet, and you are receiving another stack of papers from the FBI guys," she yelled back.

The doctor explained the similar traits in each of the listed homicides from the FBI report in detail to Detective Waters. Waters listened without interruption and only grunted when Doctor Peeples had finished.

"Detective, did you hear me?" the doctor had to ask.

"Yeah, fascinating stuff, Doc. What made you call the feds on this?"

The doctor was amazed that the detective found it necessary to ask. He asked again if the detective had heard what the report stated, and Waters only grunted a second time. "Detective, don't you find it the least bit curious that there have been over a dozen similar deaths in the last couple of years within a one-hundred-mile radius of the Caulking murders? We are talking about a serial killer here, Detective. Are you listening to me?"

"Yeah, there may be something to that, but Doc, just let us handle the investigating and we will let you handle the autopsying. Is that a deal?" Detective Waters asked, or rather he told the doctor that this was how the investigation would go, and he hit the release button on the phone. Peeples was beyond amazed, and he continued to read the last report faxed by a special agent assigned to the profiling section of the FBI.

The agent wanted details and the latest reports from Peeples. He explained in the cover letter that he was the agent assigned to assist the local police investigation and to assimilate information to be used by all police departments across the nation. He had listed the names of seven detectives, including Detective Waters, who were handling similar homicides. He also requested that Peeples get in touch with Doctor Janice Southern of the Medical Examiner's Office in Atlanta.

The last page of the report gave Peeples information regarding three additional homicides in two other states. One case was concerning the murder of twin girls in Alabama, and the other was down in Florida—a Latin female, twenty-six, found dead near a lake in a new housing development not far from a suburb of Tampa. The Latin woman, like the two twin girls, had been cut to pieces, reassembled, cut open, and sewn shut with some type of blue-waxed string.

Doctor Peeples realized that if the FBI had included Detective Waters's preliminary investigative reports, someone in Waters's office was communicating with Quantico already and Detective Waters was just being an asshole.

CHAPTER

FIVE

PHOEBE WAS BECOMING increasingly paranoid with every passing day, and Harold began to withdraw from the family emotionally. His resentment was obvious, and the more Phoebe tried to reach out for help, the further Harold distanced himself. She was flustered and frightened, but Harold demanded a return to the way things were before Phoebe started acting so strange. He never considered why she was afraid, what had scared her so, nor did he think to ask.

The children clung to their mother, for they too felt the loss. She'd had the flu the previous year, and she had still put the needs of the family ahead of her own. She had always been a mother and wife first and an individual last, but she needed something from them now. The children clung to her. Harold sulked and spent even more time with his bicycle. He locked himself in the spare bedroom when he was home and worked on his book. Harold often slept on the couch, and Phoebe never bothered to call him to their bed.

Phoebe was afraid to go out of the house, and this forced Harold to do all the food shopping. He was angry most of the time and treated Phoebe with contempt. She started to lose weight, and by the end of the month, she had lost close to twenty pounds.

The sheriff stopped one day on his way to a routine call. He had passed Harold on the road to town and the man had not bothered to return his wave. That was not very neighborly, Buddy had thought, and he had decided to stop by to see if everything was all right. He found Phoebe collapsed on the floor just inside the front door, crying to herself.

"What's the matter, ma'am?" the big man asked. He expected Phoebe to look up at him with a busted mouth or the beginning of a black eye.

"I really don't know, Sheriff. Maybe it's just that time of the month," she said with a forced smile. Buddy was much relieved to see her face undamaged.

"I'm sorry. I didn't mean to pry. Mama always said to stand back when 'Granny' came a vistin'."

"Beg your pardon, Sheriff?" she asked.

"Oh, well, you see that was what my mama would say when, well, you know, the woman thing, and all," he explained, his face red with embarrassment.

Phoebe laughed for the first time in a long time, and it felt good. "Yeah, I guess that's it." She enjoyed talking with the sheriff; he was so different from Harold. The kids had come out of their rooms, and Harold Jr. asked Buddy a thousand questions about shooting people and locking up bad guys. Deirdre was her normal, quiet self, studying Buddy from the edge of the sofa, while Sarah crawled up into his lap. The sheriff enjoyed the attention and liked playing with the children. It had been a long time since he had held a child and heard that special carefree laughter.

He stayed longer than he had expected, but he got up to leave when Harold returned in the van. Buddy watched Phoebe's face change and felt the tension fill the room. The kids felt it too, and the older one's disappeared, back to their rooms and the video games. Little Sarah stayed with her mother, and Phoebe held her close. The sheriff said good-bye and nodded to Harold as he stepped off the porch. The sheriff shook his head as he was getting into his car and thought that Harold was a stupid man.

"What the hell did he want?" Harold asked, but Phoebe did not answer. "Did he find out anything about the break-in, or what?" Harold sounded almost angry.

"I didn't ask. I figured he has enough to worry about right now with everything else. I am sure he will get to it," she said and promptly left the room. She walked out the back door.

She had been gone only a few minutes when her screams brought Harold running. He thought she had found a wild animal or maybe a snake in the garden. Harold flew through the screen door and found Phoebe standing against the wall with a rake in her hand.

"What's wrong now, Phoebe?" Harold yelled, but he spun around when he saw the shadow pass behind him.

"I'm sorry, folks. Really I am. Didn't mean no harm," spoke a tall, slim man, maybe thirty-something, gaunt, with mousy brown hair that flickered in the sun, showing the red highlights except where the hair was thinning on the top. It was Nathan, and he had a paper sack full of fresh-shucked corn in his arms.

"I am real sorry, ma'am. Didn't mean to scare ya none," he said in a boyish voice. He then explained that he had not been very neighborly, that he had been busy, but that he wanted to welcome the Thornton's to Caulking. He stared at the ground between his boots the entire time he talked. He talked for five minutes, rambling, mumbling sometimes and stuttering other times. Phoebe looked at Harold, and her eyes softened with pity for the lonely man. She remembered him from town a while back. She also remembered that the sheriff said that this poor soul was all alone in the world, and Phoebe could relate to that feeling now more than ever. She felt as if she had discovered a kindred spirit.

"Just why the hell are you sneaking around back here?" demanded Harold. Phoebe could tell by the tone of his voice that he was afraid. Phoebe almost laughed out loud at her husband's reaction to such a harmless man.

"Really didn't mean anythin'. I'll be goin'." Nathan turned to leave, stopped a few feet away, and turned back toward the couple. "Oh yeah, this here is some corn I got fer ya. Just wanted to say hey and welcome y'all." Nathan smiled a crocked smile and set off again. His disarming manner angered Harold, which pleased Phoebe to no end.

"Its okay, Harold. He just scared me. Everything is scaring me these days; you said so yourself. He didn't mean any harm." She turned away from Harold and in the direction the stranger had walked. "Nathan," Phoebe called after him.

Nathan felt the blood slamming through his heart. This was going to be easier than he'd thought. *The stupid bitch likes me*, he thought, and he giggled to himself. It seemed like everything would be anticlimactic after their introductions. Phoebe was a sucker, and the asshole was just the husband of a sucker. *But let us not forget the lovely Sarah.*

Nathan spent the rest of the afternoon talking with Phoebe. He used his little-boy looks, his little-boy charm, and his little-boy voice to soothe her doubts and fears. He verbally patted her on the ass every chance he got, and he watched Harold stomp around like the spoiled asshole he was.

Nathan stayed for dinner that night, enjoying his first real meal sitting down at a table with a real family. He'd never had a meal with his mom and dad. They had drunk most of the time, and Nathan had just looked after himself. The holidays had come and gone, leaving no aromatic memories of fresh ham, roasted turkey, or homemade sweet potato pies for Nathan. No, siree. Just bad breath and booze, a slap across the face, and a hard dick up the ol' Hershey highway, a soothing kiss from Mama, and a quickie. Those were Nathan's memories swirling around in the wasteland he used as a mind.

Nathan had to stay in control. He had to avoid touching the children and had to not appear too nervous. He was testing himself, pressing himself to the limits of resistance, and loving the denial. He was building the desire, feeling the pressure expanding in his stomach like a frozen ball of shit rolling around and around. Yes, siree, it would be worth the wait, he thought, and he stole a glance at Sarah when she bent over to grab a toy from the floor.

Harold Jr. was another story. Nathan did not like the boy—too much like his old man. The kid never smiled, always stared, and never said very much. Yeah, he would be quick and done. Junior would be fast. A slice here, a cut there, and the kid would be history, yes, siree. Maybe he would spend more time with Deirdre, who looked a lot like her mama. Nice little tight ass, yeah, and he wouldn't mind dumping a load between those cheeks. But he could not concentrate on other matters with the lovely Sarah around; she stole his attention, his heart, and his desire.

"So, Nathan, you live by yourself?" Phoebe asked, being polite. She was nervous because Harold was so angry, and consequently, she chattered endlessly about polite little topics. Mental piss, verbal vomit to pass the time and to keep Nathan from leaving. Harold was seething with anger, for he could not be himself and run away with a guest in the house. He was upset with Phoebe and gave her ice-water glares when he thought no one was looking, but Nathan saw everything. He watched Harold and decided that this was the enemy; this one would have to go first, but how?

"Yes, ma'am, I live in my great-great-granddaddy's house, out in the woods. He built it back when there weren't no one "round these parts. Course, it done growed up with the rest of us over time." Nathan told her about his house with little detail, but a sense of pride came through in his words that surprised him. He looked automatically over at Harold, but he did not let the man's eyes touch his—just a glance and back to the floor.

Phoebe loved to talk about history, and Nathan's comment about the house being so old stimulated her interest. She asked about his parents, but Nathan let the question drift around the room like a bad odor, ignored but not forgotten. Phoebe let the question go, embarrassed for reasons she did not understand, and went on to ask about the town of Caulking and its history. She asked about little things that meant nothing, just polite and safe conversation.

Nathan answered her questions with whatever came into his head. He had never known much about his family, never cared to ask, and there was no one to ask anyway. Harold grew bored and excused himself, saying that it was beyond Sarah's bedtime.

"*No,*" Nathan screamed in his head, and the sound bounced back and forth in his skull. "*Don't touch her! Don't take her away!*"

"Maybe Deirdre is tired too, honey," Phoebe said. Her words came out a little stiff, and the use of the word honey felt like a blister forming in her mouth. Harold smiled at Phoebe, but she felt his eyes drill holes in her face.

"Sure, honey, I'll take care of her too. Why don't you just sit here and talk with your new friend about the wonders of Caulking."

Harold sneered and stomped out of the room. Nathan laughed out loud, excused himself, and looked genuinely mortified at his outburst. "I'm sorry. I reckon I done overstayed my welcome. I best be gettin' home. It's late and all."

Phoebe scowled at her husband and tried to apologize. Nathan said that it was nothing. He said that Harold was right and he should be going. Harold had already started up the stairs, carrying little Sarah and dragging Deirdre along by the hand.

"No, let go of her! Take your filthy fucking hands off her!" Nathan wanted to howl. He was in anguish and followed the thin, dangling legs hanging over Harold's arm. Sarah was gone for now, but he would be back, yes, siree.

"Thanks for the vittles, Mrs. Thornton. I'll be seeing ya."

Phoebe walked him to the door and said good-bye, and she added, "By the way, Nathan, you can call me Phoebe." She felt a slight pang in her chest as she watched Nathan disappear into the night, swallowed whole by the darkness. She liked the man. He seemed a little off, but perhaps that was because he was alone so much and uncomfortable around people. After all, he did not have any family and lived out in the woods all by himself. Most of all, Phoebe liked the way Nathan upset Harold.

Nathan stopped just a few yards into the shadows cast by the trees. The hour was late, but not that late, and the moon had drifted above the thunderclouds on the horizon. He watched Phoebe close the door, let his eyes bounce from window to window until he found what he was looking for.

The hours went by slowly, but Nathan was in no hurry. He had nowhere to go. He sat in the shadows until the lights of the house started to blink out, one by one, and then there were only two left. The light in the upstairs bedroom where he had seen Harold and one lamp downstairs where he had last seen Phoebe were still burning brightly. The world was quiet, lit silver-white by the waning moon. It was always quiet like this after midnight, a special time, and a special silence.

Then Nathan heard the music. "No," he moaned out low. "No music. It'll destroy everything." For Nathan, music was the sound of the Devil pissing, a direct expression of a hideous wound, sharp, torn, and ragged, flushed with pain. "Stop it!" No one listened, no one took notice, and the melody released an assault against him. It was like fire licking his face.

Nathan watched. He liked to watch, shoving the palms of his hands to his ears, and attempting to block out the music. He could see Phoebe by the window on the first floor, and she was dancing alone—he saw her dancing in the air. The vision, the pain, the memory of her, no, not of her, it cannot be her! She was dancing, but there was not much time left to dance. The music was screeching, like dull-edged screams drawn across frayed wires. There was no crescendo, no peak, however, just a continuous noise, and he simply had to make it stop.

Nathan spun out of control, blacked out, and then found himself on his back, blinking up into the bone-white face of the moon. The silence was breathing softly against his warm skin. He was dazed and cold. The dew had settled all around him. The Thornton house was dark. Everyone was sleeping, and Nathan decided to be neighborly, to go a callin'.

"Something borrowed, something blue, something old, and something new," he sighed.

Early the next morning, Phoebe was up before anyone in the house. There was nothing unusual, but she was singing, the sun was above the trees, and the temperature was pleasant. She took a bath like always and made her way downstairs to make breakfast for the family. It was the first time in over a month that she had felt like cooking a real breakfast, the kind they used to have, and she looked forward to the surprised faces.

Phoebe was halfway down the stairs when a strange feeling sent a chill up her spine. She stopped, noticed a few papers on the floor and the back door standing wide open. She looked frantically around the house, but she found nothing out of place, and her fears slowly passed.

Across town, Deputy Jimmy Kennedy was filling out a report of a burglary, and a strange one at that. The deputy was working on his second cup of coffee when Sheriff Chandler pulled into the driveway. The deputy didn't see the sheriff come through the door, and he jumped at the sound of the big man's voice booming from the living room. He collected all the papers from the kitchen table and was heading toward the back door when he heard Buddy call his name.

"I'm in here, Sheriff, just finishin' up the report," he answered and walked toward the door just as Buddy stepped inside the kitchen.

"Anything reported missing, son?" he asked and noticed the coffee cup on the table.

"No, Sheriff, can't figure it out. Not a thing was taken that Mrs. Metallo can tell. It looks like the drawers in her daughter's room was gone through, but nothing is missin'," the deputy said and then leaned closer to the sheriff. "Sir, Mrs. Metallo said she found something in her daughter's room, though. I put it in a plastic bag and took it out to the car. Really weird, Sheriff."

"Well, boy, tell me what is it," the sheriff said, a hint of impatience in his tone.

"Come on and I'll show you." The deputy took the big man out to the squad car and pulled out a bag containing what looked like a dog's paw. It was decaying, but they could still make out what it was.

"This was left in the house?" the sheriff asked, seeming confused.

"Yes, sir. What should I do with it?"

"Just take it back to the station and dump it, but make sure you take pictures and make a complete report." The sheriff was dumbfounded. What was happening to his quiet little town?

What the sheriff didn't know was that something had been taken from the house where the paw was found, something wrapped in a pair of white lacy panties. Nathan had found them in the dirty clothes hamper and inhaled deeply with the crotch pressed hard against his nose. He had run the panties over his face and thought of Sarah. The silky lace had danced around his hard cock as he had searched for a place to deposit his essence. Laughing to himself, Nathan had unscrewed the lid to the mayonnaise jar in the refrigerator, stuck his hard dick inside, and squirted the white liquid into the mouth of little Sarah, or so his mind let him believe.

The sheriff drove around for a little while, thinking and trying to remember why this dog incident kept coming back to him. He knew that it was important. He knew that the mind is a funny thing and sometimes operates on remote control when the rest of you fails to make the grade. He knew there was a connection here somewhere, about something that he had to bring to the surface, something buried under years of memory. But what?

The good sheriff also knew that the Thornton home and the burglary of the Metallo home were connected. He simply did not have time right now to deal with all that was happening, and the murder investigation took precedence. He decided he would just keep it to himself that Champion's paw had turned up at someone else's house and he'd look into it later when things calmed down.

CHAPTER

SIX

SEVERAL WEEKS HAD gone by, and Nathan had not been back to the Thorntons. He had wanted to go see Phoebe and Sarah badly, but he had been occupied with other matters. He had seen their van parked on a street in town a couple of times, but he had not waited around.

Harold had grown still more distant from the family, and Phoebe was still afraid to go out of the house. She would not allow the children to wander in the yard, and Harold Jr. demanded that they go back home. He had quickly grown tired of the fresh air and the country, and he'd had enough of this imprisonment and his mother acting so weird.

Junior had tried to talk with her, but Phoebe could not explain everything to her son. She could not tell him that she was afraid of a bogeyman and of demons in the dark. Phoebe had always been the strong one in the family, the one who made the hurt go away, the one the children called when bad dreams interrupted their sleep. She was the only one who told them everything would be all right. She could not tell them that now, so she decided to tell them nothing at all.

Harold spent his days riding his bicycle farther and farther from the house through the back roads of southwest Georgia. His endurance had improved, and he was seriously thinking about entering a cross-country marathon the next spring. His nights were filled with sporadic episodes of writing filled with unorganized thoughts and waning confidence, which of course he blamed on Phoebe. Harold knew that he would never finish his book. The university expected a complete project on his return, and Harold knew the dean would not tolerate wasted time and wasted money spent on a good try.

He could not believe what had happened to his wife. The woman had just fallen apart over a few odd events. She had always been the rock of the family, and he needed her to be again. Harold was hurt and angry with his wife. He could not fathom her needing him to lean on. He was not capable of that kind of responsibility, and she knew that.

The police had still not found whoever had broken into the house. Harold figured that the country bumpkins could not find their own names in the telephone directory, so how could they ever find a bad guy? Harold had a strong mistrust of police in general and figured all they did was waste tax dollars hanging around the local donut shop.

The other thing that Harold could not understand was what the burglars had been looking for, maybe money, or maybe they had even thought he and his wife had dope. Harold concluded that the burglars must have tried to get in before but good ol' protective Champion had stopped them. Maybe the dog had even chewed on one, and they had come back and killed him for his efforts.

With Champion gone and the recent events at the lake, Phoebe had demanded that a burglary system be installed immediately or she would leave with the children. She had wanted one with a panic button and a second control panel upstairs. She had gone off the deep end for sure, Harold thought as he made the last turn of the thirty-mile course. He checked his watch and was pleased with the time. Yep, he would give them a run for their money at the marathon this year.

Harold had not thought very much about Nathan since the night the strange man had had dinner with the family. He had seen Nathan a couple of times over the past few weeks, but he figured that Nathan had a good idea that he was not well received, at least by Harold. The guy was a strange one, always alone and always staring at his feet. Harold wanted Nathan to stay away from the house and his family. He wondered why Phoebe was so friendly with the man.

He had passed Nathan on the road the previous day, and Nathan had stared that queer, cold glare of his with those crazy eyes. The man never waved, never yelled hello, and merely looked at Harold like a startled animal. Harold zipped past Nathan at over forty miles an hour, and when he had turned to look back over his shoulder, the man had already disappeared, just vanished into the woods like a ghost in the fog. They had been in the middle of nowhere and without a house within ten miles, and Harold had wondered what Nathan was doing out there.

Nathan had stepped off the road and crouched down by a tree when Harold passed on his fancy red bicycle. Nathan thought about just running a snare wire across the road. Harold always took the same road and passed at about the same time, just like clockwork, and all Nathan would have to do was wait.

"Naw, too easy, and not personal enough," he told himself.

Nathan liked things to be up close and personal. He wanted to smell the fear and watch Harold's eyes roll back into their sockets just before death stole the show. He had seen a hound catch his neck on a wire strung across a deer-run once. Damn near took the dog's head clean off as it came charging down the path after a rabbit. The rabbit passed under the wire but the dog never slowed. There had been a yip and a splash of red across the ground, and a hunter had lost one of his best hounds.

Nathan had been following Harold for ten days, and he had the man's pattern down to the minute. Harold was predictable and boring. He did the same thing everyday—left at the same moment and came back to the house within fifteen minutes of the same time each day. Boring, boring, boring, Nathan yelled, but Harold was already more than a mile away. Harold was an obstacle, and Nathan needed a plan. He had to be careful, however, because good old Buddy was becoming suspicious. Nathan laughed because it was taking the sheriff so long to put all the pieces together.

Nathan told himself that he was working too hard, and all work and no play made him as boring as Harold. Besides, he deserved a reward. He had denied himself too long, he thought, and he started walking toward the old Joseph place. Nathan looked up at the sun, determined it was a little past four o'clock, and decided to take the long way to the house. He wanted to get there before Harold, but not that much ahead of him. Nathan needed Harold. He needed Harold to slow him down, to keep him from rushing and spoiling the long-awaited fun.

Two hours later, Nathan stopped at the lake for a drink of cool water and to watch the activities of the house. He knew that Harold would be back in about twenty minutes, give or take a couple. Nathan could not waste time cooling down, and he hoped that Phoebe would offer him a nice glass of lemonade. He knocked on the door with fifteen minutes to spare, perfect—not too long but just long enough to get his dick good and hard.

"Who is it?" Phoebe asked from behind the closed door, her voice filled with fear.

"It's just me, ma'am, Nathan. Just come to say hey."

"Nathan?"

"Yes, ma'am. I was passin' by and hadn't seen y'all in a while, so I figured I'd stop."

The door creaked open, and Phoebe peered through the narrow opening. Nathan noticed the security chain and the small gray strip of plastic for the alarm contact at the top of the door. He smiled, tried hard to look innocent, and waited. Phoebe hesitated. Nathan was about to explode. He looked down at the welcome mat and shuffled his feet. Phoebe smiled back and unlatched the chain just seconds before Nathan was going to kick in the door. *What a stupid bitch*, Nathan thought as the door swung open wide. He watched Phoebe punch in a series of buttons on the alarm pad by the door, but he was unable to follow the sequence.

"Hi, Nathan, I'm just a little nervous with all the things going on around here. Would you like something to drink? It sure is a hot day."

Bingo! Good ol' cow. "What's that thing by the door that you were a-pokin' at?"

"Oh, that. That is the new burglar alarm. We had a break-in a little while back. So I thought it was a good idea, you know, to keep the bad guys out."

"Yes, ma'am, I think that there is a real fine idea," Nathan said with a silent giggle.

Nathan was perched on the edge of the couch in the living room when Harold came through the door carrying his fancy red bicycle. Harold stopped dead in his tracks at the sight of Nathan and then glared at Phoebe. She immediately got up and went into the kitchen.

"Sarah, Deirdre, get to your rooms." Harold was very angry, and Nathan slid his hand down the side of his pants. His fingers found the sheath running along the outside of his leg. The leather strap was tied around his waist, and Nathan never tucked in his shirt. This was not the way he wanted things to happen, but he would be ready if Harold went crazy. Harold did not go crazy, however, and Nathan snickered to himself as he watched Harold stomp away toward the back of the house. "Pussy," Nathan whispered under his breath.

Nathan could hear Harold hanging up the bike and Phoebe in the kitchen fixing him something to drink. Harold was talking to Phoebe a moment later, but Nathan could not make out the words. Harold's voice was muffled, but Nathan could tell that it was filled with hostility. He heard Phoebe telling Harold to calm down, that Nathan had just come by for a short visit.

"Hi," the sudden sound of another voice caused Nathan to jump. He jerked around and found Harold Jr. near the front door.

"Hi yerself."

Junior plopped down next to Nathan and began to ask him how he liked living all alone in the woods. The boy was persistent and direct in his questions. Nathan felt uncomfortable and was irritated that he could no longer keep track of the conversation in the kitchen. Junior had one question after another, and Nathan could no longer stand the inquisitive child.

"Get the fuck away from me or I'll cut your balls off," Nathan hissed and pulled his shirt up to expose the top of his knife. *Stupid move*, he told himself. *Calm down, just calm down.*

The boy stared at the knife and slowly came to his feet. He started to walk toward the kitchen but stopped short of the door. Junior turned back toward Nathan and said, "Go fuck yourself, asshole," before running up the stairs.

Nice kid. It was going to be a pleasure taking him for a ride in the country. Yes, siree, too much like his dad.

Phoebe was the first one to walk from the kitchen. She was carrying a small plastic tray with sugar cookies in the shape of stars. "Sorry it took me so long. Harold is a little upset, but I just can't understand why."

"That's awright, ma'am. I just rub folks the wrong way. Do not ever do nothin' but be nice, but folks just don't take to me much. Do you want me to go? I don't want to cause no problem between you and the mister."

"No, Nathan, you sit for a while and have some cookies."

Harold never did come into the living room, but Nathan heard the back screen door and figured Harold had gone for a walk. He continued to talk with Phoebe and brought up the subject of the new alarm system. Nathan explained in his innocent way that he had heard about such things but had never seen one. Phoebe was quick to take him on a tour.

Nathan stayed until after dark and waited alone on the front porch while Phoebe fed her children. He heard the sounds of dishes being set on the table, and he recognized the aroma of fresh ham and slid to the window to watch the mama taking care of her babies. His thoughts ricocheted between lust and panic when Sarah turned her eyes toward the window. He wanted her now, right there on the table, and then he pictured her naked body pinned beneath him in torment. He could hear her screams, and when he closed his eyes, he could see the headless bodies of the rest of the family sitting in chairs around the room, watching him take her.

He envisioned himself spreading Sarah's butt cheeks wide, ripping the tender skin around the anus, licking the trickle of blood, and finally ramming himself hard into the small opening. The imaginary screams were a melody of delight, and his blood exploded. He had to run, to leave now, or else risk everything. He turned back at the edge of the trees lining the yard and could stand the intensity of his feelings no longer. Nathan masturbated until he rubbed the skin raw, and then he settled to his knees, leaning against a thin pine tree. He was exhausted and fell fast asleep beneath a black velvet sky filled with stars.

Shouts and slamming doors jarred Nathan awake. He was disoriented and squinted in the bright morning sun. Harold was standing on the front porch of the house, yelling at the door. Nathan worked the stiffness out of his back, stretched, and lay down on his stomach to watch Harold.

"Go ahead, be nuts the rest of your life, but I hope you understand that I don't need some loony tune dragging me down."

Loony tune? Nathan had no idea what that was, but he would remember the expression. Maybe it was a song or a pet name or something, but whatever it was, he would remind Harold about it. Harold approached the driver's side of the van and jerked open the door. He stood and stared into the cockpit, shook his head, and slammed the door. Nathan watched him pat his pockets and heard him yell, "Shit," before storming back into the house.

"He's fixin' to leave," Nathan whispered and started trotting toward the van. He made it to the driver's door, opened it, and disappeared inside just before Harold came back to the front. Harold was still yelling, and now Nathan could hear other voices. He recognized Phoebe's voice, and there were the children's voices as well. The voices were crying out for daddy not to leave.

Nathan heard Harold yell again, and the sound of footsteps advancing toward the van. The door was jerked open, and light spilled across the carpet. Nathan slid further back in the cargo space behind the passenger seat. He had to bite down hard on his tongue to keep from laughing as sweat soaked through his clothes. Yes, siree, it was show time.

The engine of the van growled to life, and with a spin of gravel, Harold raced down the driveway toward the road. He was cursing and talking to himself. Nathan held on to the bottom of the bench seat and bounced with every turn. *This is going to be great*, he told himself. *Yep, the fucking bastard is going to shit himself!* Nathan suddenly thought of Phoebe, and for a brief moment felt sorrow crawl up his throat. He swallowed, and the feeling passed. A quick look out the window, and he determined that Harold was heading toward the interstate. Nathan patted the side of his leg and smiled.

Harold roared through the back roads toward the only road in the area that connected with the interstate. He had not thought this action out very well, and with every passing mile, his interest waned. The faces of little Sarah and Deirdre standing at the door with tears streaking down their faces began to take their toll on his determination. Nathan sensed that the van was slowing down, and he chanced another peek out the window. He was right, the van was indeed slowing, and this was a good thing, because Nathan was a little concerned about how he was going to get ol' Harold to stop. He did not want to take a chance of Harold crashing the van. He listened to the slow crunch of the tires as Harold pulled to the side of the road. Perfect. Nathan waited until Harold shoved the selector into park. He heard Harold crying and started slipping toward the driver's seat.

Nathan had his skinning knife already in hand when he crouched behind Harold. The sweat was running down his face, and he could hear the pounding of his heart. He tried to calm himself. Harold must have sensed something, because he jerked his head around. Nathan smiled, blew Harold a little kiss, and brought the blade across his face. There were screams, confusion, and blood. Nathan was able to reach around and hold Harold to the seat as he stabbed him repeatedly in the chest while whispering, "Who's the loony tune now?" in his ear. Harold stopped moving, and his body fell against the door.

Blood had splashed across the windshield and dashboard. Nathan collapsed against the back of the seat and wiped the blade of his knife on the soft fabric. He reached over and shoved Harold to the passenger side. Then he opened the door and dumped the body to the side of the road.

"Motherfucking loony tune." He giggled and entertained himself with Harold for a while.

CHAPTER

SEVEN

A FEW WEEKS had passed since Harold had been killed when Nathan knocked hard on the Thortons' front door. He could hardly contain himself. He was excited, visibly vibrating with delight and about to explode with emotion. Phoebe answered the door quickly. He could see that she was annoyed at the persistent banging. Phoebe had flung the door open, but she stopped abruptly when she saw Nathan. She was surprised and hesitant. She smiled and wondered what he was holding behind his back. Phoebe had not expected to see Nathan, praying that news of Harold had brought someone to her door. Nathan did not smile back at Phoebe. He only stared, glaring with his bright eyes shining, and there was an immediate red flash of warning in her mind. Her mouth hung partially open, and Nathan could smell the wonderful scent of raw fear flowing from her body like a fragrance from a rose. There was a moment of hesitation, panic consuming her slowly, and before Phoebe could turn to run, Nathan tossed the gasoline in her face.

"Uh, uh," he told her. "Don't touch that panel."

Phoebe gasped and felt the overpowering burning in her eyes as the smell filled her lungs with every gasp of air. She staggered backward, unable to run, and flung her hands madly in front of her. She was blind and in pain. She did not know where Nathan was and never heard the metallic sound of the lighter. She only heard a soft giggle and heard him say, "Flick your Bic, bitch," before her head burst into flames.

The fire was pretty. Fire was good. It cleansed the soul and burned away all the shit. Nathan pursued Phoebe farther into the house, prodding her through the living room with the tip of his knife, and each time he stabbed her, a fresh trickle of blood flowed down the skin from the puncture. She screamed, stumbled, and slapped at the flames. The pain was intense, to the point that she was about to black out. Nathan extended the blade and, with ease, sliced off her right ear.

"Dance with the Devil and pay the price," he whispered before bringing the razor-sharp edge of the knife across the back of her right knee. He cut the tendons, and the woman collapsed to the floor. She thrashed about screaming, and Nathan kicked her toward the center of the room. Her hair had burned away, and blood oozed from between the cracks in the charred flesh. Blisters filled the inside of her mouth, and she had bitten through her tongue. Phoebe could do nothing more than shake and groan.

He brought the knife down again across the back of her left knee and laughed hysterically when he felt the dull thud of bone. She dug at the carpet with her fingers in desperation and felt her fingernails rip away. He slowly followed her painful excursion, prodding her along with short jabs from the glistening blade turned crimson along the edge.

"Where are the children, my lovely? Where are the spores from your filthy cunt?" Nathan screamed. His words seemed to give Phoebe a sudden strength. She rolled to her back and abruptly tried to spit into his face. Nathan was surprised and impressed. He smiled as he punched her hard in the stomach. Phoebe sprawled across the floor.

He found a pair of pruning shears on the table above her head. He seized them in a second and carefully snipped the woman's tendons at the back of each heel. He dropped a heavy knee with practiced precision to her chest, pinning his captive to the floor with slow deliberation. He drew the blade across the delicate skin under each armpit and watched the blood flow. Nathan stood back and admired his work. He smiled with satisfaction and was about to walk away to let the poor woman suffer a bit more while she bled to death on the pretty carpet, but then he heard *her* voice. It was his sweet Sarah along with her brother and sister coming up the steps and into the house. "Oh what fun."

Sheriff Buddy Chandler was ashen faced when the deputy opened the office door. The sheriff was weak in the knees and going to fall down if he did not sit down. The deputy made two steps into the room before the big man collapsed to the floor.

The sheriff had been on the telephone, talking with Lieutenant Peterson of the Georgia Highway Patrol. The lieutenant had advised that one of his road units had come across a green Dodge Caravan with Boston plates. The vehicle matched the description of the one the Caulking police department had placed in the locate-and-notify data entry file in the computer. Lieutenant Peterson further advised that there was a lot of dried blood inside the vehicle and that a search of the area had revealed the torso of what he believed to be a white male. The vehicle was registered to Harold Thornton.

"Sheriff Chandler, we think the body is about a week, maybe two weeks, old, and we can't find most of it. We are going to start searching the woods as soon as we get enough men together. I was hoping you could spare a few," the lieutenant stated, but the sheriff never heard the lieutenant. The shock of hearing about Harold had overwhelmed the sheriff.

"I'm, uh, I'm going for help," the deputy said, and then he was out the door looking for someone, anyone, to help the sheriff. Five minutes later and with the assistance of four deputies, the sheriff was off the floor and sprawled across the couch. He came around slowly. The room was spinning when his eyes snapped open.

"Oh my God," he managed to mumble. The men standing around him stared as if he had just sprouted a second head.

"Sheriff, Ed's called the fire department, and there's going to be a doc or somethin' here in just a minute, so you sit back and rest," offered the deputy nearest the door. The man looked down the hall and said, "Yep, here they come now, Sheriff." He stepped aside and let the fire rescue team into the room.

The sheriff was connected to wires, probed, poked, and questioned until he was ready to explode.

A heavyset man in his late fifties placed a hand on the sheriff's arm when the sheriff started to object to all the attention. "Buddy, now I've known you since kindergarten. You sit down and let us finish," the man said in an even, stern voice that caused the sheriff to settle back down on the couch.

"Roy, I ain't complaining about your concern, but I've got to get over to the old Joseph place right now." The sheriff groaned and made it to his feet.

"Buddy, take it easy," Roy cautioned and braced himself for the big man to take a second nosedive.

"I'm all right, Roy," Buddy stated. "I need all available deputies to go in service and get your butts over to the Joseph place right now, on a code three."

"What's goin' on, Sheriff?" someone asked.

"The Thornton man has been found, or what's left of him, and I got a real bad feeling. Get your butts over there now, and be careful."

The three men ran from the room, and Buddy yelled for Ed to start calling the Thorntons' and let the phone ring until someone answered. He told Ed to just stay on the line until one of the deputies answered if no one else did.

"Roy, I think you better get over there too. It may be too late already," Buddy, said in a gravelly voice filled with pain.

Buddy's mind was a blank. Everything was soft focused and fuzzy-gray around the edges. He wasn't going to faint again. At least now, he had that under control, but it seemed that everything else was going out of control. How stupid could he have been, he screamed in his mind. That Pomeroy boy, that strange ranger, he had to be involved in this.

He had just seen him with Phoebe Thornton a couple of days before, helping her load a box of groceries into an old pickup truck. Buddy had never seen the truck before and figured it was something Phoebe had rented until Harold returned. It was odd how friendly Phoebe and Nathan were acting, like old friends. Buddy had never known Nathan to be friendly with anyone.

Ed was yelling at the top of his lungs for the sheriff to come quick, that Pete was on the phone and he had a real mess over at the Joseph place. Buddy dropped his chin to his chest and sighed heavily. He had never wanted to be wrong so much in all his life, and suddenly, he remembered the children. The Thornton's had what, two—no, three—kids.

"Ed, you still got Pete on the line? Ask him about the kids. Please, God; let the kids be all right."

Nathan was stretched out in the warm sunshine miles away and watching the arrival of the police cars at the old Joseph house. He liked coming here, to this spot in the grass, and for several days, he had waited for someone to find her. He was sad for a second, thinking how lonely it must be for Phoebe.

"Just waiting, all dressed up, and no one to tell you how pretty you are. I feel your pain, my darling," Nathan announced to the clouds drifting above, but the moment passed and he howled with laughter. He giggled and laughed until his sides hurt. He stopped suddenly, held his breath, and watched intensely as two men emerged from the house on a run. One man fell to the ground and vomited. The other made it to his squad car and shouted into the microphone.

"Well, beautiful, I guess you better think about changin' brands of mouthwash," Nathan whispered and then laughed hysterically.

One of the local television stations had been monitoring the police scanner, and a camera crew was arriving the same time as Sheriff Chandler. Nathan had moved much closer and now stood with a small crowd of people watching all the action from across the street. He followed everything with keen interest. Never before had he stayed around to watch the police. Nathan had always been certain to be far away before anyone found one of his little surprises.

The sheriff was doing his best to avoid being interviewed. Nathan was laughing as he watched the big man run away from the petite brunette wielding a microphone. The odor from the house kept most people, including the deputies, from standing too close. The fire department had delivered a large fan to help with the ventilation, which caused the crowd to move farther back from the house.

The body of Phoebe Thornton had been removed after the forensic photographer recorded everything in the room. Everyone was careful not to disturb the room, and when the detective finally began his investigation, all personnel in the room respectfully stepped over the dark red stain on the floor. The detective had borrowed a gas mask to avoid the stench of decaying flesh.

Phoebe had been dead for more than forty-eight hours, and the temperature inside the house had reached close to ninety degrees. The higher the temperature, the more quickly a body will start to rot away. Most people thought that the black flesh around her arms, shoulders, and head were simply evidence of advanced lividity, the settling of blood beneath the skin, and did not realize they were seeing severe burns. The medical examiner arrived and explained the error to Buddy. Nathan watched with empathy as the shoulders of the big sheriff began to sag as he listened to the coroner. The sheriff told the doctor that this was no way for anyone to die, that the pain and suffering that poor woman had to endure was beyond human understanding.

The doctor was explaining in exact detail the extent of the injuries Phoebe' received before she died, the cause of death, and how much of the damage to her body was caused after her death. Sheriff Chandler finally held up his hand to stop the onslaught of words. He could listen no more and rubbed a bear-paw–sized hand across his face. The doctor looked at the big man for a second, shook his head in understanding, and walked back into the house. The sheriff walked slowly to his car and ignored the reporter. He barely missed the woman as he opened and closed the door of the car.

"Ed, this here is Buddy. Get those assholes over at Albany on the phone. Tell them we have another murder over here that's going to need their attention."

Nathan watched the activity intently, fascinated with all the people and their reactions. *This is better than TV*, he told himself, and he waited eagerly for the sheriff to pull his giant frame from the car. All around him, something was happening, something exciting and new. This was a totally new experience for him, and he was anxious to take full advantage of the situation.

The dome light in the sheriff's car suddenly shone, and Nathan waited expectantly. He knew that the sheriff was the man in charge, the one to watch, and the man who would act.

Buddy stepped out into the last of the sunlight and ignored the rush of the press. He searched the crowd briefly, and Nathan wondered who the sheriff was searching for in the group of onlookers. The sheriff turned toward the house and yelled a name, but Nathan could not make out what the big man had hollered; Nathan complained to a woman standing near him at the edge of the crowd. She looked at him out of the corner of her eye but did not respond. A tall, lanky deputy trotted over to Buddy, and Nathan strained to hear the conversation.

The sheriff and deputy were only a few yards away from Nathan, but they didn't notice him. He could hear the anxiety in the big man's voice, the anxiety bleeding through the frustration. There was a sad quality to the way Buddy pronounced the names of Phoebe and Harold. The words were strained through teeth held tightly together by a clenched jaw. Nathan held his breath—this was getting better and better.

"I want that little bastard Nathan Pomeroy found. Search his house and get the damn dogs out if you have to—just find him. I want everybody on it **NOW!**" Then Buddy wiped the spit from his chin with the back of hand.

Nathan was in a state of delirium. The sheriff had mentioned him by name! The big man himself, the man in charge, wanted to find him! Nathan was giggling and stomping his feet while dancing in a circle; he did a little two-step shuffle before slipping away toward the shadow of a fire rescue vehicle. The woman who had been standing next to him watched suspiciously and called to a passing deputy.

CHAPTER
EIGHT

THE BODIES OF Phoebe and Harold Thornton were on slabs next to each other in the coroner's office in Albany. The doctor had finished his autopsy on the remains of Harold and was quietly dictating his notes into a micro-recorder. The notes would later be transcribed, typed, and placed in the permanent record. Doctor Peeples had attended the examination and noted every characteristic similar to those in the case of the actors. He had requested careful inspection of the joints and samples of the severed ligaments. The doctor performing the autopsy of both Phoebe and Harold noted that the appendages had not been removed by the breaking or sawing of bones but by the careful cutting of the skin and tendons. This had exposed the muscles, and further cuts had revealed the joints. The doctors speculated on whether some of the dismemberment had been done prior to death.

A thorough search of several square miles of woods around where the van had been found revealed only a section of the right leg. The piece recovered was from the hip to the knee. The blood type matched Harold's. Doctor Peeples was satisfied with the identification. The head and other body parts were never found. The official reports prepared by the highway patrol questioned the identity of the torso, but the HP had to yield to the findings of the medical examiner.

Fingerprints and dental records identified Phoebe immediately. The damage to her body was extensive, and it was evident that the killer had taken time to inflict maximum pain. Doctor Peeples did not have to speculate that the cuts and puncture wounds were administered before the poor woman had finally died.

The skin and tissue on the neck, face, and scalp extending from the back of the skull to the forehead had burned away, exposing a large section of bone. The eyes had exploded or boiled away, and an internal inspection of the throat and lungs indicated additional burns caused when Phoebe had been gasping for her last breath.

Her attacker had slowly immobilized her by cutting the tendons in her legs, arms, hands, and feet. The bruising and bleeding into the skin and tissue revealed that Phoebe Thornton was still alive during this phase of the assault. The opening in the abdomen was identical to that in the woman found by the lake, and it was stitched closed in the same fashion as well.

Doctor Peeples completed another profiling report, carefully listing all the wounds and the suspected sequence of events. He included duplicate sets of photographs taken at the scene and of the autopsy. The evidence was packaged and mailed to the FBI serial-murder experts in Quantico, Virginia.

Peeples had been the chief medical examiner at this facility for twenty-six years, and he had never seen this type of systematic torture in any other case. He wanted this man caught and the torture to stop. Little did the doctor know that the one thing he wanted most had already been accomplished. The killer was in jail, and in the Caulking jail at that, and had been in custody for almost twenty-four hours.

A deputy had arrested Nathan at the scene of Phoebe Thornton's murder. The deputy had been on temporary assignment to help the Caulking police department. Nathan had been caught trying to steal a rescue van and charged with auto theft. Nathan had used the alias of Jim Winston, a name he liked for no particular reason. Nathan did not have an arrest history, and his fingerprints had never been on file. The report sent to Atlanta and the FBI came back with a negative match, and Jim Winston remained in jail until someone posted bail. There was no one to post bail, of course, so Nathan spent his time eating three good meals a day with snacks in between, watching TV, and dreaming. Yes, siree, what a life.

Buddy had initiated a massive manhunt across the state of Georgia. Bulletins were posted, and because no photographs existed of Nathan Pomeroy, a sketch had to be completed by a police artist. The quality and completeness of the sketch were lacking because it seemed that no one had ever really looked at Nathan, including the sheriff. Dozens of deputies carried a copy of the bulletin with them as they walked past the gaunt man sitting quietly in cell D. No one recognized the face, and, in fact, no one gave Nathan a second look. When no one was looking, Nathan danced with glee.

The search team had reached over a hundred strong, but for all the manpower, not a single clue was uncovered to lead them to the children. Harold Jr., Deirdre, and little Sarah had vanished without a trace. Divers from five jurisdictions, two of them from as far away as Tallahassee, Florida had helped explore the lake and local canals. Scores of K-9 tracking dogs accompanied by a pack of bloodhounds from Savannah scoured the countryside. Several times, the dog teams would report a finding, a trail through the brush, but it would lead nowhere, and soon, the dogs were whining in failure.

The manpower for the search slowly started to dwindle as departments and responsibilities demanded the return of the men on loan. There were several injuries, including one officer who broke his leg in a fall. The attention of the press disappeared, and because there were no family members to push, the search for Nathan was abandoned by the second week.

The sheriff confiscated photographs of the Thornton's and tacked them to a bulletin board in his office. He tortured himself by looking at them daily. He would stare into the face of Phoebe, apologizing to her and crying for her lost family. The children were assumed dead, and Buddy's mind played with the torment they had most likely suffered. He often prayed that their deaths were quick and painless, but he knew better.

Buddy, the big smiling sheriff, was no longer smiling. He was a driven man with only one purpose, and that was to find Nathan and prove that he was the sick animal who had done this. The sheriff had consulted with the district attorney's office a dozen times, and each time, he had come back empty-handed. He demanded a warrant for Nathan's arrest and received a lecture on probable cause. He demanded repeatedly, and each time, he came back to his office with more colorful adjectives.

"I can't believe this shit," Buddy shouted as soon as he slammed the door. Ed found a reason to escape, and the sheriff complained to the emptiness of his office. He had been turned down yet again; lacking probable cause was still the reason.

Buddy collapsed into his leather chair and fell silent. He played with things on the desk and restacked files scattered across the top. He had neglected most of his responsibilities since the Thornton murders. Nothing else existed for him. Nothing was more important than tracking down Nathan, the person he was certain was the killer, but the man had disappeared.

The sheriff tried hard to focus on other matters. He was growing tired of the arguments with the DA, and he knew everyone was questioning his ruthless pursuit of the Pomeroy boy because there was no real evidence linking him to the killings, only his gut feelings. But that was good enough for the tired sheriff.

"That miserable piece of dog shit," he told himself. "He can't get away with doing that to poor Phoebe and her kids."

Buddy thought of Phoebe lying on the floor in the living room against the wall, her face burned away and empty sockets where once those bright eyes had watched her children, her body cut to pieces, and all that blood. Tears ran down the big man's face, and he felt his age. He felt the effects of being responsible for their safety and failing them horribly.

Ed came back when he thought the coast was clear and felt the sting of regret when he saw the big man crying, totally exhausted, and spent, a perfect picture of defeat. "Hey, you want a cup of coffee, Buddy?" Ed asked, offering him a steaming cup of black liquid.

Buddy looked up and accepted the cup. There was a slight hint of thanks in his sorrowful expression, but the look immediately changed and the coffee fell to the floor. The sheriff grabbed a file and stared at the cover. He slammed a fist into the black-and-white photograph stapled to the corner of the rap sheet.

"Jim Winston my ass," he shouted and exploded from the office.

The sheriff pushed Ed to the side and raced toward the door, yelling, "Call the jail and make sure that nobody is down there but Mr. Jim Winston when I get there!"

"Just wait a damn minute, Sheriff," Ed screamed, and the sheriff came to a halt just outside the door to his office.

Ed took a deep breath and glared at the determined expression on Buddy's face. Now that he had the sheriff's attention, the deputy took his time and adjusted his uniform. Ed was in no hurry and took a moment before saying, "Jim Winston was scheduled to go before a magistrate at ten o'clock, and the time is now ten forty-five. So before you go a-runnin' down the hallway like a mad man, let me call the courthouse and find out the status of this guy. That okay with you?"

Buddy looked at Ed, smiled to himself, and shook his head slowly from side to side. He had been waiting for Ed to grow a set of balls, and the wait was over. "Yeah, Ed, why don't you give them a call and tell the correction people that I want Mr. Jim Winston to remain in custody. He is the main suspect in the Thornton murders, or, as the DA puts it, wanted for questioning only."

Ed picked up the telephone and made the call. He spoke directly with the bailiff after verifying the courtroom where the bond hearings were being held.

Buddy headed toward the stairs. He was too impatient to wait for an elevator, and his mind was forming the conversation he was about to have with Nathan. He wanted to look at the man's face and listen to the excuses, the lies, and the bullshit. Buddy wanted to watch him stutter, fall, and admit to the horrible things he had done to Phoebe and her family.

The bell sounded, indicating that the elevator on the left was about to open, so he forgot about the stairs. There was a few seconds' delay before the polished metal doors slid open. Suddenly, the sheriff was standing face to face with Nathan Pomeroy. A deputy was on either side of him, and Nathan was just chatting away, having himself a good ol' time. He wore a bright orange jumpsuit like those given to all the inmates while they awaited their court appearances. The bond hearing had been delayed until the following week because the court system could not handle the overload of human crap passing through and adjustments had to be made. *My lucky day,* Buddy thought.

"Well, hey there, Buddy, ol' boy. I was 'bout to give up on you comin' to see me. What took ya so long?" Nathan asked with a smile.

Buddy ignored Nathan's words and spoke directly to the deputies. "Why don't you boys get on back to court? I'll take care of Mr. Winston here," the sheriff said, never taking his eyes off Nathan.

The deputies exchanged puzzled looks as one of them handed the sheriff a manila envelope containing all the items removed from Nathan at the time he was booked into the jail. The deputies stepped back into the elevator without saying a word. Nathan watched the doors close and giggled softly to himself. Buddy stared at the metal and breathed heavily through his nose, trying to maintain his composure.

"What's the matter, Buddy, ol' friend? Got yerself one of them there summer colds? They be the nasty ones, ain't they?"

The sheriff never answered but motioned for the prisoner to follow him over to the holding cells. Nathan obeyed happily and shuffled across the floor to the bars of the first cell. The handcuffs cut into his skin around his wrist, but he didn't complain, for he could no longer feel pain—that part of him had died a long time ago. He waited without looking anywhere but through the bars.

"Ain't ya gonna let me in, JC?" Nathan asked. The words were brittle, issued in expectation of the worst, but in a laughing tone. He watched the sheriff look down at the floor, chewing words and ideas in his head, working a plan over, and finally looking up again to bore a hole through the back of Nathan's head.

"Yeah, I'm going to let you in," Buddy said and let out a low growl. The hate was thick and visible, floating like a toxic cloud between the two men. Nathan loved every minute of it.

Nathan giggled that insane sound and taunted the sheriff. "I met a friend starin' down with cat eyes a-gleamin', glassy eyed, watchin' the reflection of his own humiliation flow across the floor like a spreadin' pool of piss."

Nathan stiffened when Buddy poured the contents of his envelope across the countertop. The sheriff ran his fingers through the collection, shoving items with a careless index finger across the gray Formica, all the time staring at Nathan.

Nathan's mind was racing, on the brink of panic and anger. How dare this fat piece of shit touch his precious treasures? He wanted to move, to fly across the room, and gnaw the offending fingers from that stinking mound of flesh. His mind danced with pleasures, filled with delight and pain, and he slowly turned his head to watch more clearly from the corner of his eye. Nathan felt his crotch straining against the fabric of the orange suit.

Buddy was watching Nathan, watching him grow anxious, and he turned to see him better. What Buddy saw disgusted him. The man's erection was tenting the loose orange material, and Nathan was moving his hips as if fucking the air.

"You sick fuck," Buddy told him.

Nathan answered with a simple grin—words were not necessary. Yes, he was a sick fuck. So what? He needed to get the sheriff away from the counter, to get the sheriff's hands off his treasures, or he was going to lose control. There was a way, a way to divert the sheriff's attention. It would be risky, but he had to risk all to save his treasures.

"Hey, Buddy, you know what I'm thinkin' 'bout?" Nathan asked in a quivering voice, taunting the interest of the big man.

"I can't imagine shit that sick, boy."

"Well, maybe you should try. Reckon how old little Becky-Ann would be today? Somewhere in her twenties, don't ya think? Maybe even with kids of her own? She probably be a real sweet fuck 'bout now, with some stretched-out pussy from so many dicks pushin' in. You ever try out yer little girl, sheriff, put yer dick deep up her little-girl cunt? I can just see her now, squirmin' and groaning with your big sheriff dick up her ass."

The response was immediate, blindingly fast, and filled with venom and crushing pain. Buddy hit him hard in the right kidney, and Nathan's entire body was smashed against the bars. With everyone else in court, no one was there to see the blood flow down Nathan's face as he fell to the floor. The sheriff was not finished, and soon Nathan had received massive injuries that demanded immediate medical attention.

"SHIT, SHIT, SHIT," Buddy screamed at himself. The very mention of his daughter, the rose of his life, was more than he could stand. His Becky-Ann, seven years old, full of life and wonder, head covered with auburn hair hanging past her waist, and her eyes like polished emeralds. He closed his eyes hard against the memory, pictures that filled his mind with anguish, when he remembered her crumpled body. The little girl had been found on the side of the road. She had been beaten, raped repeatedly, and tortured until her death. She had been dumped on the side of the road like garbage thrown from a window. It had taken more than a week to discover her remains. He had failed his daughter, just as he had failed the Thornton children. The case of Becky-Ann was still open, and on the anniversary of her death, Buddy would touch the file filled with reams of dead-end leads and gruesome pictures. Buddy never opened the file. It simply sat on his desk and haunted him, and then he would drink himself blind.

The sheriff had to think fast. He knew that beating this puke was a mistake, but Nathan had pushed him to do it. "Why?" the sheriff kept asking himself. He had to understand why Nathan wanted him to beat him like that. The first thought was that a defense attorney would have a field day with civil-rights–violation issues and a multitude of other charges. Nathan's court-appointed attorneys would have Buddy dead to rights. However, that was not it; there was something he was missing. Think, what could it be?

He looked over at the bloody mess on the floor and shook his head. He looked around the room and thanked God that his budget did not allow for security cameras. He looked back at the counter. It had to be there, something in all that crap that Nathan carried around with him.

The sheriff ran to the counter, scattered all the items, and looked hard for something, but what? There it was. It had to be, but why did it mean so much to him? Buddy carefully picked up the playing card, a queen of spades, and looked at the layers of black tape across the back. He could tell that something was under the tape, and sick thoughts ran through his mind. He ran his finger over the area and felt a shape, something hard.

"You fucked up, Sheriff!" Nathan squealed through his pain and his swollen lips. He tasted the blood in his mouth, spit out a couple of broken teeth, and gave Buddy a crooked, grotesque smile. Buddy looked at the man on the floor, held up the card, and showed it to him. It was Buddy's turn to smile, and he wondered what could be so important. Slowly, he peeled back the layers of tape; after he removed the seventh piece, a small gold chain dangled from the card.

"Just put that down Buddy," Nathan screamed. He coughed up blood for the effort. "You ain't got no right to touch that. That's mine!"

"This is going to burn your ass in Hell, boy—and with all you've done, you are going to burn twice."

The cell was quiet. The two men stared at each other, and Nathan tried desperately to regain control. He had to finish this fight his way. The clock on the wall ticked, the air hung silent in anticipation, and Buddy started to pick up the telephone.

"Make that call, asshole, and you'll never find those fuckin' little Thornton maggots."

Buddy froze, listened, afraid to look because that might make Nathan stop talking. He thought about those things he had read about killers like Nathan, how they liked to have their egos stroked, how they were proud of their work. He had to let Nathan think he had the upper hand. *Shit*, he thought, *he does have the upper hand.*

"Yeah, you're probably right, Nathan. Whatever you did, you did real good. You sure fooled me for a long time. Yep, you are one of best I've ever seen." Buddy immediately thought that Nathan could see right through his efforts.

"Damn straight, I am. Yes, siree. And you ain't never gonna find them maggots or my folks or any of them other shit-birds. They be goner than gone, gator bait, turned back to the shit they came from," Nathan told the sheriff, and the pride filled his strained voice.

The sheriff thought of what he could say to keep Nathan going, to piss him off so he would ramble on without thinking. "You know, Nathan, I knew your mama, and as a matter of fact, I fucked her real good a couple of times. She would suck a donkey dick for five dollars."

Nathan blinked the blood from his right eye and was still smiling. "You fucked my mama, sheriff?"

"That's right, gave it to her up the ass a few times, even."

Nathan howled with laugher. "Hell, you and everybody else in this fuckin' town. Even me. I fucked her every time my ol' man shoved his big dick up my ass." Nathan was enjoying this.

Well, that didn't work, the sheriff told himself, but at least the boy was still talking to him.

"Between you and me, Nathan, why on earth did you kill Harold Thornton?" Buddy asked, trying to sound nonchalant but wanting desperately to know as many facts as possible.

"Cuz he was a piece of dog shit. He didn't treat Miss Phoebe too good at all. He didn't like me none, neither, called me names like faggot and weirdo. I heard him myself, I did. So I just did my time, waitin', pissin' him off just by hanging around. Finally, he up and left, and I figured he didn't need to come back, if you know what I mean."

"What did you cut him with? Must be pretty damn sharp. Why didn't you just shoot him?" Buddy asked. He hated himself for being impatient. He had to take his time.

"Cuz, Sheriff, when you stick someone, there ain't no noise. It lets you smell 'em when they piss all over themselves, and you can hear the screams loud and clear. You gettin' all this, Sheriff? I don't want you to miss anythin'. Maybe you should be writin' this stuff down." Nathan smiled as his body started to give in to the pain.

Buddy and Nathan stared at each other. Nathan continued to smile, and Buddy was amazed. The lights overhead were buzzing, and a set of bulbs above the cell were flickering, producing a sudden burst of bright light every few minutes. There was no one else in the room, and the clock faithfully kept track of the passing minutes.

"You be one real dumb fucker there, Sheriff," Nathan announced. "Why don't you take a good long look at that there chain?"

Buddy was still holding the card in his hand, and he turned it over to look at the back. The chain links were small and delicate. Buddy shrugged his shoulders. "Who does this belong to, Nathan? It looks like a child's necklace. Is it Sarah's?"

"Don't go saying her name, asshole. But you need to look a little harder, and think."

Buddy stopped talking and pulled the chain completely free from the tape. It dangled down about eight inches from the sheriff's hand. A small gold medallion swung back and forth from the chain, an angel. He looked at it closer, saw the emeralds glowing where the eyes were, and he felt the blood slam to the front of his heart and then turn to ice. The pain in his chest was beyond anything he had ever felt before in his life.

"Becky-Ann..." the sheriff whispered, and tears filled his eyes. "You bastard, all these years, you fucking bastard." The sheriff took a step toward Nathan and stopped. His chest was hurting bad, and he knew that if he touched this sick animal again, he would kill him. Buddy took a deep breath and held on tightly to Becky-Ann's chain. His mind flew back in time and remembered when he had given it to her, on her sixth birthday. Becky-Ann's mother had died the year before, and Buddy had given his little girl this angel and told her that her mother was watching from above and to never take it off. Buddy had searched the area where his daughter's body had been found, looking for the angel, but after several long days with no results, he had figured it was lost forever.

Nathan giggled in his sick way, enjoying the pain running across the big man's face. "So, Sheriff, ol' boy, do ya want to know what happened to your little girl, or what?"

Buddy held his breath; frozen where he stood. His memories held him captive as this sick perverted soul spoke about his Becky-Ann.

With his mind and body on overload, Buddy snapped. He picked Nathan up by the throat and shoved him hard against the concrete wall. Nathan never stopped talking, telling Buddy of all the things he had done to Becky-Ann. Buddy slammed his fist into Nathan's face until the flow of words was so distorted that he could not understand what this madman was saying.

Just before the sheriff was about to land a fatal blow, Henry walked into the holding cell area. "What the hell," he shouted, then pulled the big man off the bloody body lying on the floor. Henry called for the paramedics and waited for a couple of deputies to arrive before escorting Buddy back to his office. As the sheriff was leaving, Nathan moaned, "You sure did fuck up, ol' boy, violatin' my civil rights, and all. Maybe next time I'll be a-visitin' you in jail."

Buddy looked hard back at Nathan and wished Henry had been just a few minutes later in coming. "I did this for Becky, you asshole," he whispered to himself.

The bell from the elevator sounded, and the room became a flurry of motion. Three more deputies rushed in to help the sheriff, took one look at Nathan, and froze. One deputy let out a low whistle and gave Buddy a worried nod.

"This don't look so good, Buddy," Henry said and stepped aside as a team of paramedics rushed in and took charge of Nathan Pomeroy.

"What happened?" one of the paramedics asked.

Nathan was happy to respond. "The goddamn sheriff beat the piss out of me, fer no reason at all. He just don't like me none." Nathan then gave the paramedic a little smile.

The paramedics negotiated Nathan onto a stainless steel gurney, the blood and spit dripping from his chin down the front of his jump-suit. His face was swollen and turning purple, one eye already shut. A vertical rip in the skin extended from his hairline to his brow, caused by the bars on the cell. Nathan was also bleeding internally, and his blood pressure was dropping fast. One of the paramedics was on the telephone with the hospital, giving a nurse the vital statistics. Buddy shook his head in regret, not from beating Nathan but from not finishing the job, and headed to his office with Harold.

CHAPTER

NINE

"ARE YOU CRAZY, Buddy? What evidence do you have? Where is the probable cause? We will be damn lucky to keep your ass out of jail much less keep his in there," District Attorney Thomas Henderson shouted with a smirk. "You do realize, Sheriff Chandler, that you violated Nathan Pomeroy's civil rights and you could be very easily brought up on charges yourself—not that I would mind, but some people like you around here."

Buddy glared at the little man with the black bifocals sliding off the tip of his nose. The man was arrogant, a by-the-book damn Yankee from one of those fancy colleges up north, and he was enjoying having Buddy scrambling for answers.

"The man's a killer, a sick piece of shit who butchered at least two people, kidnapped their three children, and has done God only knows what to them, while I sit here and play footsy with you," returned the sheriff, slapping the top of the DA's desk with his hand.

Henderson came to his feet and stated, "Prove it, Sheriff. Where is the evidence? Give me the evidence, and I'll go after Mr. Pomeroy with every resource at my disposal. But without it, you don't have diddly-squat, and you know it."

Buddy rubbed both hands across his face, groaned like a bear with a stomachache, and let out a blast of air. He looked at the DA and then toward one of the DA's assistants, who had slipped through the door. The woman's name was Roberta Austin. She was new to the office, fresh out of the University of Georgia School of Law and assigned just this morning to prosecute Nathan on the auto-theft case. She gave Buddy a tight smile and sat on the edge of the desk.

"The man confessed, Thomas. He told me things that only the killer would know. Hell, he told me right out that he killed the Thornton's and a lot of other people we don't even know about. What else do you want?" he explained for the third time, and a sudden weariness clouded his mind.

"I heard you, Sheriff, but you know what the defense is going to say. Even those jackass public defenders are going to scream police brutality, and as far as the so-called confession, maybe he was just tired of you beating him up. He could easily say that you made up the whole story in your desperation to get the press off your ass. Mr. Pomeroy has proof of you beating him, Sheriff. What do you have?"

The DA watched Buddy collapse into a chair. The sheriff was tired, worried, and damn upset about the DA's position. Thomas looked at him and then looked down to his left hand. He studied the hand hard, thinking, playing with his gold wedding band. He looked back up at the sheriff in a few minutes and smirked at the face of a defeated man.

Ms. Austin watched her boss and felt sorry for the sheriff. The man was doing the best he could, and she wanted to help. She had read the arrest affidavit, looked through the medical examiner's report, studied the photographs of the crime scene until she could stomach no more, and had slowly developed a burning hatred for Nathan Pomeroy. She believed the sheriff, with or without proof, and she wanted to burn Nathan's ass.

"Thomas, let's hit him hard for the grand theft auto, go for the maximum, and that should give the sheriff time to further investigate the murders. We have a few weeks left in the speedy trial requirements, and my bet is that Pomeroy, alias Winston, won't fight us a bit. The man is playing with us and having a damn good time with it. So I think we should play with him a little."

Hearing this, Buddy knew he had at least one friend in his corner.

The district attorney looked back down at his hand, noted the lines of puffiness, and gave a quick, almost imperceptible, nod of agreement. Chandler came to his feet, smiled at Ms. Austin, and disappeared out the door. He had work to do and no more time to waste with tight-ass Henderson.

Buddy was formulating a plan as he skipped the elevator and took the stairs two at a time to the ground floor. Ed tried to get his attention, but Buddy waved him away and closed the door. He wanted every file, report, and parking ticket that had Nathan Pomeroy's name on it.

Nathan had never been arrested, that was fact, but the man had been mentioned in a couple of juvenile reports. There was nothing important, just nuisance calls and something about cruelty to animals. Damn, that was it! The animal-cruelty call almost twenty-two years ago. *Funny how the mind works*, Buddy thought. *Pukes up a memory covered with layers of time and other things.*

Ed returned to his desk a few minutes later and heard the big man yelling. "Ed, get Doris from records in here on the double. I got some overtime headin' her way!"

Six weeks after Nathan had been officially charged by Deputy District Attorney Austin for grand theft auto, a trial date was set. The public defender presented over twenty motions to stop the trial and to have it dismissed for various reasons. Nathan was declared competent to stand trial, and the public defender's office was outraged. The judge, Jeremy P. Stone, advised the public defender that a formal protest could always be filed with the district court if he did not like the decision, but as it stood, Nathan was considered competent for trial.

"Mr. Henry," the judge said in a loud voice, "I do appreciate your enthusiasm to defend Mr. Pomeroy's rights, your sense of justice, and, most of all, your outstanding silk suit," he announced with flair and good humor. Michael Lee Henry sat straight-faced and listened intently to the judge. He was fuming inside and refused to play the fool or to be played as the fool. He waited for the judge to finish his little charade. Stone continued to make a mockery of the public defender's office in its attempt to have the case dismissed prior to a trial.

"Your Honor, the public defender's office appreciates a sense of humor as well as the next man, but we do not find humor in a civil-rights violation by Sheriff Jefferson Charles Chandler. Mr. Pomeroy is a first-time offender and has already spent many weeks behind bars, and a couple in the hospital, thanks to the sheriff. The DA's office is stalling, and again, my client's rights are being violated in the process. This is an outrage!"

"Save it for the jury, Mike. We ain't tryin' your boy yet." The judge slammed the gavel down and announced that the trial would begin in the first week of December, right after the Thanksgiving holiday. He stepped away from his desk, and everyone in the courtroom stood. The bailiff announced that this part of the calendar was concluded and that anyone else with business before the court should be back in thirty minutes.

Pomeroy, prisoner 97654, was held in jail without bond, and he giggled when his attorney went through the morning's events with mock indignation. "I'm truly sorry, Mr. Pomeroy," the public defender said, "but the judge just wouldn't listen. Unless you can come up with the bond amount, you are going to have to wait for the trial date."

Nathan stared at the far wall of the jail cell and let his mind dance a little jig. He heard the screams, the unanswered cries for help, the gasping, and the giggles. He watched vivid memories claw holes in the back of his eyes and listened to the sweet sounds with ears that burned with pleasure. He watched with his mind's eye as Junior, Deirdre, and, finally, little Sarah came through the front door. The talking stopped, the laughter drifted through the air filled with the smell of charred flesh. The children could not understand what was wrong, why their mama was on the floor, why Mr. Nathan was sitting in their daddy's chair, smiling at them. What was that smell? Was there something burning? Nathan motioned for them to come into the room and told them that Mama was not feeling well. Junior was suspicious and ran toward Phoebe, but Nathan stopped him with an arm around the neck. The break was clean, and the effect was immediate—Harold Thornton Jr. died by his mother's side.

The girls were terrified of Nathan as he stood before them, wild-eyed and grinning. They watched Junior fall hard to the floor, his head bouncing against their mother's leg, and their innocent minds could not understand what was happening. They obeyed every command, not believing Nathan when he told them that Mama and Junior were only sleeping. The little girls did not protest or question Nathan; they did not want to make him angry.

"We won't disturb your mama. She ain't feelin' all that good, kinda' burnin' up with fever. We are goin' on a little trip 'til she's feelin' better. I'll just carry Junior here so he won't be a-wakin' her up. Come along, now. You don't want to get me mad now, do ya?"

The trip to Nathan's house was long, and about every mile, he would double back. Nathan spent a lot of time creating dead ends for the search party that he knew would be coming soon. He figured a day, two at the most, and his little piece of heaven would be crawling with police. But it was worth it. He laughed when he pictured Buddy yelling and cussin' like a fool. The sheriff would be shouting orders, all pissed off and red in the face. No smiles now, no, siree! Deirdre complained, and Nathan slapped her to the ground. Sarah squealed and tried to escape, but Nathan ran her down.

"Where ya goin', princess? You're the guest of honor at my little party."

The girls could not be taken to the main house—that would be the first place searched. He had a special house, really nothing more than a large shed, built about a mile to the west. Nathan had constructed a high ceiling with exposed rafters and dug a basement, but actually, the shed covered nothing more than a very deep pit. The house was sitting on four wooden beams suspended across the pit. This was his fun house, and he had filled it with all his wonderful toys.

Junior's body was dropped between the beams, and Nathan smiled when he heard the dull thud. *No more Mr. Nice Guy*, he thought. "You go fuck yerself," he said to the dead boy.

Deirdre was shoved into a corner with a burlap sack tied around her head. Her arms and legs were bound with rope so tightly that the circulation was stopped, and soon she had no feeling in her limbs. Sarah was favored with a special treat, something Nathan had been dreaming of using for months, and he pulled the little girl off the ground. The leather harness suspended her about two feet from the floor. "She is dancin' in the air, yes, siree."

Her little dress was crumpled on a table that contained a dozen knives, a small saw, plastic bags, and a short piece of rubber hose. Nathan was on fire with excitement and could no longer contain himself. He quickly pulled off his pants, removed the burlap sack from Deirdre's head, and masturbated, forcing her to open her mouth and taste his essence. When he was done, he danced around the room and around Sarah. He apologized to little Sarah for letting Deirdre taste him first, but he was saving the best of everything for her. Nathan continued to dance and kicked Deirdre occasionally to be sure she was still alive. The little girl could only moan.

Nathan's blood was racing. The room was breathing, and dust swirled through the sunlight shining in from the holes in the roof. He picked up the knife, and the muscles of his heart gasped. This was his special knife, and Nathan dropped to his knees, holding the blade up in the air. The moment felt comfortable, absurd, and Nathan wept. There was a powerful magic working here. Things had to be handled with care, and no slicing or dicing until all prayers were said. He prayed the Rosary in a singsong voice. It was Sunday morning, and the body of Christ was hanging high on the cross, waiting by the side of the road, waiting for his journey to Hell.

A glint of light struck Nathan in the face and shattered the moment. What was that? He saw a gold necklace dangling from Sarah's neck, a crucifix suspended beneath her throat, and Nathan carefully lifted the necklace with the blade of his knife. His mind soared back in time, and he remembered another girl, another necklace. The eyes of the girl grew wide with panic, and with a flick of Nathan's wrist, the chain grew taut and the cross fell free. The gold charm spun in the air toward the floor. How weird, he thought. The body of Christ was dancing in the air with his beloved Sarah. Nathan watched it bounce, and the glint of sunlight reflected from the edge of polished gold. He heard the dirge of another funeral march and chased after the melody. There was mold and mildew along the notes, something borrowed, something blue, but nothing new. He saw another face from another time, but he pushed the memory out—there was no room in his mind right now for past pleasures. There was work to be done here and now, and so he must let the past pick the bones of what had been. He would deal with what was here and now. Yes, siree!

A smirk commanded Nathan's face as he picked up the hose and shoved one end between little Sarah's legs. She screamed from the sudden pain, and urine flowed out of the other end of the tube. Nathan washed his hands in the warm, yellow fluid and took a drink for good measure. He took a bite from Sarah's buttock and spit the bloody piece of meat from his mouth after he chewed on it for a while. He decided abruptly to slow down the pleasure with his Sarah and turned his attention to her sister. He dragged the girl to the table and staked her down with ten-penny nails through her thin arms. Deirdre could see Sarah hanging above her with the blood and hose running out of her body. Deirdre went into shock and did little more than whimper when the blood flowed from her own wounds. It was playtime, and Nathan was enjoying himself, saving the most fun for his prize, his little Sarah.

"Nathan, are you hearing me? Unless you can come up with the bond, you are stuck here. Do you understand?" When Nathan did not respond to the public defender, Mike Henry realized that his client had gone off daydreaming again. He wondered what the man was thinking about so intensely and started to ask, but he stopped. The wicked grin on Nathan's face said it all, and Michael decided he did not need to know.

CHAPTER
TEN

THE SHERIFF HAD found little in the old files about an animal-cruelty incident. Apparently, no one had bothered to write a report. Buddy remembered it had something to do with a hunting dog and an old woman who lived somewhere near the old Bethel Road. Odd how the mind remembered little pieces of useless information, but this wasn't useless now, and he probed his mind for more memories to come to the surface. The incident had occurred perhaps fifteen—no, maybe seventeen—years before. Maybe he remembered because there had been a dog involved. He sure wished he had remembered earlier.

"Doris, when did the department start the daily-offense report list?"

"Hell, Sheriff, I may be old, a dinosaur compared to some of these youngsters around here, but that don't mean that I got a memory like an elephant. Let me check, okay?"

Good old, Doris, he thought, the cornerstone of the department. Buddy depended on her, as Sheriff Tate and Sheriff Lowry had before him. Hell, she could be sheriff if she had a mind to apply for the job, but Doris liked being a backseat driver. She was the best secretary in the county, and, in fact, she did have a memory like an elephant, no matter what she said to the contrary.

Buddy picked up the phone and punched in a series of numbers. He tapped his fingers along the edge of the desk while waiting for Doctor Peeples to answer. Buddy knew very little about how the mind of a serial killer worked. He knew very little about the mind of any killer. The last time there had been a homicide in Caulking, old man Riddle had been blasted with both barrels from an old Remington shotgun. His wife had got tired of him coming home drunk and using her for a punching bag. A jury had found her not guilty, and she still lived in the same house over by the Methodist church on Old Bethel Road.

"That's it, old lady Riddle," Buddy yelled at the same time Doctor Peeples said hello.

"Stop your yelling in my ear, goddamn it!"

"Sorry, Doc. Buddy Chandler here. I think I just got a break on this murder case. Guess I'm a little excited."

"Hello, Buddy, I sure hope so. What can I do for you today?" The doctor was jovial and more than willing to assist.

Buddy asked for a rough profile of what made a man become a serial murderer. He wanted childhood characteristics, a list of things that warped the mind of a child and produced a brutal, sadistic adult. Buddy remembered a few details from the Bundy trial in Tallahassee, but 'they weren't much help. Peeples recommended a few books and gave Sheriff Chandler a thumbnail sketch of the twisted minds that hunted humans for sport.

Doris was back in the office with a worn box containing a list of calls spanning a time frame of fifteen to twenty years. He took the box from her arms, dropped it on the desk, and gave her a hug. Doris was beaming with pride and knew that once again, she had saved the day. The sheriff thanked the good doctor from Albany for the information and settled back into the embrace of the leather chair.

"Damn, that's a lot of paper in that box," he said out loud to an empty office.

Three hours and thirty-six minutes later, Buddy was staring at a faded photocopy listing eight calls for a three-man shift. The top line read "Caulking Sheriff's Department, June 18, 1970," going back to when Buddy had been just a deputy with two years on the force. A third of the way down the page, he located a nuisance call at 1530 hours—the complainant was Mrs. William S. Riddle. "Yes," he yelled. This was the call that kept haunting him, and he knew that the widow Riddle was still alive even after all these years.

Ed called the old woman and asked if she would mind if he stopped by for a short visit. She told him that she had nothing to do and would welcome the company. At the same time Buddy was pulling out of the parking lot, Nathan's mind was pulling out for another short trip back in time. He could hear the blood running down the inside of his head. "Yes, sweet Jesus," he whispered as sounds and odors tapped him gently on the arm. He could smell shit and fear in the air. He could hear Deirdre's moans of pain when the fingers on her right hand disappeared in a mist of blood and shattered bone.

Nathan was watching the shadow of the bars in the window along the wall above his bunk. The bandages were being removed tomorrow, and the scars would fade in time, the doctor told him. He was a lucky man, the nurse explained. Some people die from this type of injury. "Yes, siree, I am a lucky man, Miss Nurse," Nathan giggled and wiggled his tongue. The expression of the nurse changed to one of disgust, and she left the room.

In Nathan's memories, he watched Deirdre slip into a coma and never regain consciousness. Nathan slapped Sarah on the butt and giggled. The little girl was limp but aware of everything, and the pain was keeping her from passing out. She had been in the harness for hours and survived all the abuse Nathan had given her. The girl had felt every pinch, slap, and probe. The bite on her cheek had finally stopped bleeding but was painful and swollen. Nathan licked the blood that ran down the back of her legs, and he chewed at her tender flesh.

He danced with his dreams and savored the special moment as Buddy parked in front of the Riddle home. The sheriff saw a woman standing in front by the door; she waved as the sheriff closed the door of the car. Buddy determined that the woman had to be around seventy, maybe sixty-five, and it appeared that the years had been good to her.

"Mrs. Riddle, it was good of you to see me on such short notice."

"Ruth, call me Ruth. I remember you, Sheriff. You are Roger Chandler's boy, ain't ya? It's been a long time. Seeing you so grown up makes me feel my age."

He held the front door open and followed Mrs. Riddle into a small but elegant room. She offered him coffee from a porcelain cup and asked if he minded sitting on the couch by the window. The sunlight was bright through the glass and warmed the room. Buddy tried to balance the little saucer on his leg and felt awkward perched on the edge of the cushion.

"Here, Sheriff. Set that down on the table and get comfortable."

He was grateful for the rescue and slid back into the overstuffed couch. Mrs. Riddle talked about the town, about the changes taking place, and about the recent murders. This gave Buddy the opportunity to state his business. The sheriff was anxious to get to the point, and it seemed that the widow had a good memory. He brought up the subject of the nuisance call and was surprised by the response.

"Nuisance, my ass! That little bastard killed my dog and then gutted him like a deer."

The big man's jaw fell open, and he stared at the face of a still-angry woman. She let out a loud snort and asked in a more calm voice if he wanted a little more coffee.

"Yes, ma'am." He thanked her and continued. "I need your help, Mrs. Riddle," he started to explain as she handed him the coffee.

"I'll help all I can, son. Besides, I don't have a thing to do today anyway."

"Good, then I will get right to the point. I think that the Pomeroy boy, now a man, the one that killed your dog, is the same one that killed those people by the lake and the Thornton's, and he may kill a lot more."

The old woman sat back with a sigh. "Well, I'll be. Ain't that somethin'? But what can I do for ya, Sheriff?"

"Just tell me everything you can remember about Nathan Pomeroy."

Mrs. Riddle talked for a long time about Nathan. She knew the family and what type of people they were. Mrs. Riddle was a retired schoolteacher, and that was how she had first met the Pomeroy boy. He was strange, a loner filled with hate and anger. She explained that he could just explode with unprovoked violence and that he had come to school often with big bruises on his body or with a split lip. Nathan would never talk about how he got injured, and he fought a lot with the other students.

"He sure was a strange one, that boy. Found him once in the bathroom with a little girl. Nathan was around nine, I think. The poor little girl had to have been one of the kindergarten kids and couldn't have been any more than five. He had trapped the child and forced her to strip down so she was naked. Don't know what would have happened if I hadn't come in. I snatched that boy up and dragged him to the office. As young as he was, he still cursed me bad as a sailor. Said I would pay someday.

"The principal tried to get hold of his parents, but no one would come. They never came. If I recall, the mama was a dancer, and if you'll pardon the language, a bit of a whore. I'm not too sure about the daddy. I believe he farmed a little, but mostly, he just stayed out in the woods or in the bars. I guess the Pomeroys still own that old place out in the woods. I ain't ever heard of it being sold or anything."

The sheriff took notes and asked questions. He made notations and references to events that matched with the information from Doctor Peeples. The doctor had explained that most serial murders liked to torture animals when they were children, abused siblings, and played with fire. Nathan had been the suspect in several arson investigations, but nothing had ever been proven and he had just been labeled a misunderstood, mentally slow teenager.

The interview lasted more than two hours. Buddy drained the last of the cold coffee from the cup and thanked the widow Riddle for her time. She had an excellent memory for detail and loved to talk. Mrs. Riddle had never had children of her own, and so the sheriff promised he would come back soon for another visit. The woman was lonely and enjoyed the chance to talk.

The sheriff heard the door softly close behind him and made a mental note to contact the local senior citizen organization about this nice old woman. The organization held monthly meetings and often got together for a dance or a game of bridge. It helped the elders of the community to stay young and active. Mrs. Riddle would be running the show before long, he thought with a smile.

A note was taped to the lampshade where the sheriff would not miss it when he got back to his office. He tore it off and held it out so he could read the print. Buddy had been needing glasses for years but refused to admit it. "Call Ms. Roberta Austin, DA." There were two telephone numbers written on the bottom, one designated as a home number. The note said to call the home number if it was after six.

Buddy checked his watch, seven-fifteen, and dialed the number. The phone rang five times before an answering machine announced that Roberta was not available to take calls but to leave a name, number, and short message at the tone. The sheriff was about to hang up when he heard a real voice saying hello.

"Ms. Austin, I was just about to hang up. It's Buddy Chandler. You left a message for me to call."

"Yes, Sheriff. Thanks. We need to talk about the Pomeroy case. How about coffee at my place?"

"When?"

"As soon as you can get here. If you have a pen, I'll give you the address."

He thought about protesting, begging off because of all the work he wanted to be done, but maybe she had something important. Buddy wrote down the address and was impressed with its location.

"Well, Ms. Austin, a rookie DA gets paid a whole lot more than I thought."

"Call off the investigators, Sheriff. This is my parents' house. They were well off, but I'm just a poor girl."

The drive to the Austin residence was short, and Buddy was pulling up to the front drive in less than thirty minutes. The house was huge, two stories and built with the dark gray brick that was so popular in the area. The grass was emerald green and the gardens well kept. The house was set back from the road about a hundred feet, and he could see Roberta sitting on the front porch as he exited the car.

"Howdy, Sheriff. Thanks for coming over so soon. How about a cookie? Made them myself," Ms. Austin said just as Buddy took the first step into the house.

Roberta invited the sheriff to make himself at home and gave him a brief tour. Buddy sat down with a cup of coffee in one hand and a cookie in the other. Ms. Austin immediately launched into a tirade over pending problems with the state's case against Nathan. She agreed with Buddy that Nathan was guilty as sin and should be hung, shot, and fried like a slab of bacon. Buddy liked this woman and knew that his first instincts were right. She was a friend and definitely in his corner, but her comments about how weak the case was concerned him greatly.

"Well, Sheriff, those are the problems. The defense is going to have the confession dismissed, and everything else, which is not much, will be lost. He did it. I know it; you know it; and he damn sure knows it—but we can't prove it."

Buddy stared at the rug between his feet and absently played with the necklace he had taken from Nathan. He talked with Becky in his mind, cried with her, and told her how sorry he was. He could hear her crying; calling for her daddy and telling him that she loved him very much. Tears slowly ran down the big man's face. He could no longer hold back the flood of emotions, and as Roberta watched this giant man cry quietly, her heart broke.

"Buddy, I'm truly sorry. I knew you were passionate about this case, but I had no idea how this would affect you," she whispered, and then she noticed the delicate gold chain hanging from his hand like a rosary. "What is that, Sheriff?" she asked, and she reached out to touch the small angel dangling from his big trembling hand.

The sheriff pulled the hand to his chest, protecting the only link with his daughter, and let the tears flow. Roberta sat very still and let the man cry.

Miles away, Nathan was licking the last of the gravy from the dull metal food tray. "That sure was nice, Pete," he told the deputy. "You got anymore of that there cornbread?"

The deputy ignored the prisoner. He hated it when Nathan called him by his first name. Deputy Pete Simms never had determined how the prisoner had learned his name, but he refused to let the man know how much it bothered him. He ignored Nathan and continued watching the football game. Georgia was down by ten points against Florida with only four minutes remaining in the fourth quarter.

"Hey, Pete, what's that ya watchin'?" I ain't able to see the TV from where I am."

Silence. Pete turned up the volume and shifted further around in his chair. He wanted to get a soda and wash down the last of his popcorn, but the game was almost finished. Nathan giggled and lay back on the bunk. He drifted away with wild thoughts floating on wings of dull, faded hues of silver and black. He heard the cough of his daddy's old pickup truck and looked down the road to see Becky-Ann Chandler peddling along on her bicycle. Nathan loved to drive that old truck, and with his daddy gone, he could drive it any time he liked.

Nathan pulled alongside the girl on the bike to look closer at her. Yes, she was the one, so beautiful and so ripe.

"Hey, girl. Ain't you supposed to be home by now?" he heard himself call to Becky-Ann. He watched himself downshift and pull the truck to the side of the road. The words came out thick and coarse, coated with lust as perverse need squeezed through parted lips. Becky-Ann was nine years old and Nathan was in love. He watched her approach with skinny legs hanging down from a short shirt. The phantoms were laughing in his mind with their vacant eyes and insatiable demands. The hollow images saturated his thoughts and taunted his feelings.

"Hey yerself, Mr. Nathan."

The girl recognized him and grinned. Nathan was a local boy, about sixteen and rather cute. He could drive, work, and do just about anything he pleased. Becky was thrilled with the attention and blushed. She could not look Nathan in the eye and shyly kicked pebbles with the toes of her school shoes.

"How's school doin'?"

"It's awright. You know how it is. Whatcha doin' round these parts? I thought you lived on the other side of the lake."

"Oh, I ain't doin' much. How's yer daddy?"

"He's awright. He's probably wonderin' where I am." Becky smiled and looked up at the sky, embarrassed.

A storm was coming quickly from the north, and the wind was beginning to blow hard. She shivered with the unexpected blast of cold air and told Nathan she had to be going.

"Yeah, the storm is comin' fast. You best be runnin' along or your daddy will be hell-bent if you get wet."

"I know. I told him I'd be home by now. You know how my daddy is. See ya."

Nathan forced a smile. "Yeah, I be knowing how daddies is." He rubbed the swelling of his erection with one hand and tried to shift the truck into gear. He watched Becky-Ann push the bike and jump on the seat. She peddled hard to get the bike moving, and Nathan groaned. He watched her ass rise up and down with the pedals. Her skirt flew up in the wind, and Nathan drove slowly behind her. He had to have her, and in Nathan's sick mind, she wanted him just as badly. *This is torture*, he thought, and he decided to give her a ride, just to be neighborly.

Nathan was dancing with his memory and escaping beyond the confines of the jail cell. The metal plate slid from the bed to the floor, and the sudden crash caused the deputy to jump. "What the hell was that?"

Nathan never heard the man. His mind stayed within the sweet embrace of his private inner world. Deputy Simms walked over and stood in front of the cell. The light was out, but he could see Nathan on the bunk. The deputy spit on the floor and said, "That's disgustin', Pomeroy. You keep wackin' your dick like that and you're gonna pull that thing right off." Nathan ignored him and watched Becky-Ann close the passenger door behind her. The short skirt slid past her thin thighs, and Nathan stole a glance at her smooth white skin.

He had the girl now. She was in the truck, smiling shyly and saying it would be best if Nathan dropped her off down the road from her house. She explained that her daddy would bust her butt if he knew she was accepting rides from boys. Nathan smiled and told her that he would never tell a living soul. He put the bicycle in the back of the truck, and he could feel himself throb. Secret looks at white panties riding high into her young crotch and nipples on newly forming breasts pressing against the clinging material of her shirt were more than he could stand.

The memory danced and laughed as Nathan watched with black eyes shining. His bed sheets became wet as he heard the love of his life screaming rape in the middle of his mind. Nathan was weeping, laughing, and then a name crawled from a red-raw throat to dangle from the tip of his bloated tongue. "Mother." He slipped into slumber, and the moment passed.

Roberta waited for Buddy to get his emotions under control. She had gone into the kitchen and brought back a handful of napkins. She dumped the napkins on the coffee table in front of the sheriff and sat across from him. She knew the anguish the big man must be feeling, but not fully. The case had brought back painful memories for her also, but they were distant and hidden in the corners of her mind. "You okay, Buddy?" she asked. The earnestness of the question was not lost on the sheriff. He smiled and wiped the tears away with a handful of napkins.

"Yeah, I'm sorry. I can't believe I'm doing this. I don't even know you. It's just that everything is so out of control."

Roberta smiled and nodded. She understood and wanted to sit down next to him, hold him, and tell him he did not have to always play the tough guy. There was something about this big strapping man that had turned her head from the first time she had seen him, and she found him creeping into her mind in the middle of the night while she hugged her pillow tight.

"I mean it, Sheriff. It's okay. I really do understand."

Buddy told himself that she did not have a clue but it was kind of her to try to make him feel better. Damn good-looking woman, he had said before, and he told himself that again. He told himself that he was being an ass. The woman was fifteen or more years younger than he was, and she probably had every dick in the office chasing her around.

He looked thoughtfully at Roberta, looked into her pale brown eyes, and watched her grow uncomfortable under his stare. The memory of Becky-Ann chewed at the back of his mind, and he came to the decision that Roberta should know all the facts.

"Listen, there is a whole lot more workin' here," he began to explain and motioned with a wave of his hand that she should listen. Buddy told the story straightforwardly, holding nothing back, and Roberta sat with a hand over her mouth. She had tucked both legs under her and remained perfectly still while Buddy poured out his heart. His voice broke, and once he had to stop for a moment to get the rage under control. He told her how Nathan had taunted him at the jail when he had found Becky-Ann's necklace, and of all the things Nathan had said he had done to Buddy's little girl.

"Shit," was all Roberta was able to say for a while. She watched Buddy get up and walk over to the bar. He helped himself to a tall glass of bourbon and poured a little over ice for her. She downed the drink in one gulp.

Yeah, this is a southern girl, he thought. *No other woman could drink straight bourbon like it was water.* He smiled to himself. "That's the whole story, and why we have to get him. So, my beautiful DA, where do we go from here?"

Roberta untangled her legs and stepped away from the chair. She walked straight over to Buddy and took his drink from his hand. The woman looked into his eyes, and without saying a word, she kissed him hard and passionately. Buddy was stunned and froze, but seconds later, he returned the kiss and held her tightly. He started to talk, but Roberta silenced him with another kiss. Never had anyone been so open and honest with her, and he had shared such deep, painful feelings. He had made himself vulnerable with the truth, and he had trusted her completely in doing so.

Roberta pulled back from his embrace and whispered, "We'll get him. Somehow, we will get him, I promise."

CHAPTER
ELEVEN

THE SLAMMING OF the gavel three times demanding silence heralded the beginning of court. The good Judge Stone was a stickler about time, and the trial began precisely at ten o'clock. The bailiff repeated a call for silence, and after several seconds, the audience settled down. The trial had attracted a full house; most of the townspeople attended. Everyone was familiar with Nathan Pomeroy and the sheriff's suspicions. The Pomeroy family had been a topic of gossip for years, and the rumors of Nathan's possible involvement in the Thornton murders attracted even more attention to the simple grand theft charge he was facing. Sheriff Chandler sat in the first row behind the prosecutor's table and whispered with Roberta. "Now, Sheriff, you are going to have to be quiet," ordered a tall black man with a large bushy snow-white mustache. Chester T. Olson had been the bailiff for Judge Stone for more than thirty years and insisted on absolute silence in his courtroom.

"What?" asked a perplexed Sheriff Chandler. "Now, Chester, we have important business to discuss."

"Not right now, you don't. You hush up and listen to the judge."

The sheriff leaned back, and Roberta laughed. Chester returned his attention to the rest of the courtroom as the judge began to give the final instructions to the jury. Nathan was brought in by three deputies, and Buddy noted that most of the bruises had faded with time. Nathan gave Buddy a polite nod and a wide grin after sitting in the chair next to the public defender. Chandler stared back at the insolent face and envisioned the back of Nathan's head exploding after a bullet passing through his forehead. The thought pleased him greatly, and for a moment, he forgot the pain of remembering Becky and what that man had done to her.

The first hours dragged while both lawyers offered their versions of justice to the jury. The jury was a good mix, and Roberta explained to Buddy that she felt they had an edge. The jury consisted of more men than women, and the majority was black. Roberta explained briefly that white females would have identified themselves with the defendant in a motherly way, sympathized with his pathetic life, and ultimately found him not guilty of any charge in the world. Buddy was listening to every word as he scanned the faces of the jury, and he took note of which ones were actually paying attention. He estimated that less than half were interested and that the rest were daydreaming.

Buddy forced himself to stay focused and tried hard to remember that this was just a stolen-car case that the real case, the only one that mattered, sat in the clerk's office pending filing. With Roberta's insistence, District Attorney Henderson had bought him a little time to complete the investigation, to try to find the evidence that the DA's office would consider probable cause, something called proof. The sheriff had all the proof he needed, however, and he reached a cautious hand to his throat. He gently touched the delicate gold angel that now hung around his neck, and he promised Becky-Ann that Nathan Pomeroy would die for what he had done to her. Buddy remembered her last day, and a flood of guilt engulfed his heart. There had been an argument, something silly about riding her bike so far away from the house, and he saw himself looking at the clock on the mantel in the foyer, wondering where she was. The memory of finding her bike hidden in the bushes by the side of the road brought tears to his eyes, and his mind screamed of sorrow and regret so loudly that he didn't hear Roberta.

"Sheriff...Buddy," she called out low, trying not to draw the attorney's attention. "Pay attention, damn it."

The sheriff was lost in the past and was listening to the laughter of a little girl long ago silenced. He was watching her wave good-bye from the bright yellow bus. How could they have known it would be her very last day of school?

"Damn it, Buddy, if you don't move your ass, we're going to lose this case before we even start!"

"What..." The sheriff blinked, trying to remember what Becky-Ann was saying to him and then realizing that he was in court. Chester was glaring down at him, and Roberta was telling him to leave. Judge Stone looked irritated and loudly tapped his fingers across the polished surface of his desk. Buddy was bewildered, embarrassed, and he walked toward the exit, not knowing exactly what was going on.

The judge had ordered the room cleared of any persons having knowledge of the case. The arresting officers, witnesses, and victims of crimes could not be present in the court when evidence was being presented or when other officers, witnesses, and victims were testifying. While the sheriff sat wrestling with the past, the court proceedings had carried on without him. Buddy heard the whispers and the laughter following him into the hallway. Judge Stone rapped the gavel, and the seriousness of the courtroom returned.

"Let's have quiet in the court," demanded Chester as he stared down a group near the aisle.

The judge rambled on for another thirty minutes, and Michael Henry, the public defender appointed to represent Nathan, checked his watch. The entire defense was built upon an educated guess that everyone would be happy with a plea bargain, and he had full intentions of working a deal. The plan was simple. Nathan did not have a criminal record and did not fit the profile of a career criminal. He was no threat to society and had lived in Caulking all his life. Michael would enter a plea of guilty for the grand theft auto charge in exchange for credit for time served, a little probation, and a clean record at the end of the probation. Yes, this strategy was a win for everyone.

Stone was coming to the end of the lecture on his version of the American justice system, and Michael glanced openly at his watch one more time. It was almost noon; he had hoped to stop by his office before meeting his wife for a late lunch.

The judge noted the public defender's impatience. "Are we keeping you from something important, Mr. Henry?"

"No. No, sir. Sorry, I was just rehearsing my opening remarks."

"Do you keep notes written on the face of your watch, Michael? Sorry if I've been long-winded, but you do want a fair trial for your client, don't you?"

This last remark brought another round of laughs, and old Chester was once again demanding quiet. The public defender felt the blood rush to his face and gave a quick glance at his client. Nathan was laughing good-naturedly, enjoying his day in court, and he even winked at his red-faced attorney.

"It sure is a lot of fun in court, ain't it, Mr. Michael?"

Michael Henry stared at Nathan with a perplexed expression and kept his eyes on the man until he stood to announce that the defense was entertaining the idea of a plea. Michael further explained that, in the interest of his client, he would like to discuss the matter with Deputy District Attorney Austin. The judge looked toward Roberta and received a curt nod of acceptance. She looked over to the defense table and watched Nathan laugh. The man was incorrigible, playing the idiot, Peter Pan's dark side, but his eyes betrayed him. They never changed. The man did not even blink as childish laughter poured from his disarming smile. His eyes glared with a certain animal intensity like pools of boiling oil ready to peel the skin from the naive and unsuspecting. She knew that this man was never to be taken for granted. A shiver commanded her body, and she knew in her heart that there was something cold and deadly lurking in the midst of those eyes. The personification of Death was sitting at the other table, ostensibly sharing the experience of spontaneous humor, pointing a long, bony finger at them all and announcing in its quiet, inconsequential way that none of these petty proceedings were of any importance in the grand scheme of things. Evil was in their company, the very essence of debauchery and vileness—if she only had a gun.

Roberta felt a rough hand run a callused palm along her face, and she involuntarily shivered from the invisible caress. What was that? Her head spun in frantic search, but she found no one near. Had it really happened? She turned to look toward Michael, who was saying something to Nathan. The man was ignoring the attorney and sat smiling, staring completely through her. His lips were moist and trembling, moving silently. Sounds not readily recognizable as words were issuing from him in flat, errant tones. Roberta could not hear Nathan's voice, but the words echoed inside her head. There were two voices, urgently arguing, demanding her attention. *No, this cannot be!* Her sanity was being wrestled to the ground. The voices intertwined, flowed apart, and slammed together like abrupt thunder on a clear hot summer day.

He was calling to her in a thin voice filled with loneliness, masking a painful wail dripping with vicious warnings. Each voice held her name for ransom, delivered an invitation to let go, to soar to the depths of perdition—the voice was calling for her to come home. A chill ravished her body as she stared at Nathan. He was a creature that lived in the shadow and walked the earth only when night filled the sky. Winter's glare lived in his bones, and those things that defined mankind's gentle side were a travesty to him. Flowers died on the vine beneath his sneer. There was no room in him for love or care. The man was nothing more than a desert sucking up all life around him, seething with hate, and repelling everything bright and warm. He was a tundra, frozen and forbidding, decimated by howling winds of madness twisting and tearing all hope. He was Death itself.

Roberta felt a sharp twist as she realized that the depths of her isolation and loneliness erupted to the surface of all that was solid and safe in her mind. She felt assaulted by thoughts that sever the mind from its natural foundation and cut loose the moorings of understanding. She was adrift in uncharted waters, but there was something familiar in the landscape. She watched a light on the horizon visible only for abrupt moments during the rise and fall of the waves, a black and solitary light burning in Nathan's eyes.

Buddy paced back and forth in the hallway like an expectant father. He hated this part of any trial, the waiting, depending on someone else to make the right decision. The case was simple, straightforward, and the facts were irrefutable. Roberta called his name as he headed toward the bathroom.

"Sheriff, wait up."

She explained that the judge had called a thirty-minute recess, largely to let both sides discuss the elements of a plea bargain, which would hamper their plans of hammering Nathan with the maximum allowed sentence. The defense would never agree to jail time, and the judge would never consider a harsh penalty for a first-time offender. Furthermore, Roberta explained that she was certain that the judge would order credit for time served and a short conditional probation term.

"So he's a free man after today. Is that what you are saying?"

Nathan sat in the courtroom under guard and smiled serenely as the jury took advantage of the break. He oscillated between shrill laughter and vacant stares after the courtroom emptied. The three guards watched the show and shook their heads. The man was crazy, it was plain to see. One of the guards asked Nathan if he needed to go to the bathroom and explained that now was the time to do it because everything would be starting back up soon.

"Nah, if I gotta go I'll tell ya, but I would like somethin' to drink. How 'bout one of them there soda pops. I like them orange ones. Can I have one of them, please? I seen a machine down the hall."

The guard, a man named Jenkins, nominated to buy the defendant a soda, grudgingly headed toward the exit. The other two guards laughed about seniority having its privileges. Jenkins stepped aside in the hallway to let Roberta and the sheriff pass.

"Where the hell are you going, Jenkins? Aren't you supposed to be guarding someone?" growled Buddy.

The guard tired to explain. "Well, Sheriff, I was fixin' to get Nathan, the defendant, a soda."

"I know who the damned defendant is, son, and fuck him! He can piss in his hand if he's thirsty! You got that!"

"Ah, yes, sir."

Nathan heard the sheriff, and his shrill laughter filled the courtroom. He roared and fell from his chair. The public defender heard the commotion and burst through the doors. "What the hell is going on here? Leave Mr. Pomeroy alone. Haven't you hurt him enough?" declared the outraged lawyer.

"Hurt him enough? Why, you bleedin'-heart piece of shit!" boomed Buddy as Roberta stepped in front of him. She placed both hands on his chest and gently pleaded.

"Not here and not now, Buddy. Calm down."

The sheriff all but lifted her off the ground and set her aside. Jenkins pulled her out of the way, expecting fists to fly. Buddy towered over

Michael Henry and tried not to look at Nathan. The public defender felt somewhat safe in the embrace of the courtroom, for surely the sheriff wouldn't do anything stupid, not here. At least he was praying that he would not.

The sheriff's voice was deep and grinding. "Let me tell you about the grinning piece of dog shit you call Mister Pomeroy. This ain't about stealing, and this ain't about plea bargains! This is about killing, about treating people like leftovers from a bad meal. This is about the butchering of children and mothers. This is about..." Buddy let his eyes look toward Nathan, felt his voice fade and his anger rip away all control.

"Becky-Ann." Nathan mouthed the name in a whisper and licked his lips.

The guards managed to grab the sheriff just before he reached the defendant. Michael Henry leaped over the railing by the jury box and, in the process of getting away from the big, angry man, knocked Roberta to the floor. The public defender's glasses flew from his face as he cowered behind Judge Stone's bench.

"I'll kill you, you fucking puke!" Buddy's booming baritone voice exploded through the courtroom and into the hallway. People stopped and listened throughout the courthouse. Bailiff Olson heard the threat, recognized the voice, and raced from the judge's chambers.

Nathan sat quietly, unmoving in the wooden, straight-backed chair, with his hands folded in his lap like a choirboy as he watched the three men straining to hold the sheriff back. Buddy was foaming at the mouth, and spittle ran down his chin. Roberta stayed on the floor, unable to move as she watched. The sheriff's voice faded as he clenched his basketball-sized fist and his eyes sideswiped the dull shine covering Nathan's smiling face.

"What in God's name is going on in here!" demanded Chester. "This is a place of justice, and a sacred place, and I'll have none of that in here, Jefferson Charles Chandler!"

Moments later, Judge Stone entered the courtroom with a flurry of black streaking across the worn tile floor. "You best calm down right now, Sheriff, or I swear to God you'll be looking at the world from the wrong side of your own jail," Stone demanded.

Buddy relaxed a little. He let the men push him back, and he sat on the corner of the table. Nathan giggled softly and chewed his lower lip. "You in trouble now, Sheriff."

"It's okay," Buddy told the guards. "I'm okay. Where's Roberta?"

The men parted and revealed the prosecutor still sitting on the floor. Jenkins helped her up, and she adjusted her skirt and brushed the hair from her face. Walking over to her table, she glared at Buddy and said, "That was stupid, Chandler, really stupid."

The big man felt like an ass. Nathan had played him like a fiddle, and he was angry with himself for allowing it.

"Ms. Austin, Mr. Henry, I want to see you in my chambers, NOW!" announced Judge Stone. "Chester, you have the jury wait in the lounge, and Sheriff, you can come to my chambers as well. Guards, take Mr. Pomeroy to the holding cell for a moment."

The judge led the way to his private chamber and then perched on the edge of his desk with his arms crossed as he waited for everyone else to find a seat. He took a deep breath and glanced at each face sitting before him. The silence was intense.

"Your behavior was reprehensible and without excuse, Sheriff Chandler. Shall I remind you why we labor here? Shall I give you the reason?"

Buddy had yet to look at the face of Judge Stone. He sat like a crumpled bag in the middle of the leather couch, and for the first time, he questioned his own ability to perform the duties of a sheriff. Any reasonable man would have eliminated all personal participation in the case, and he would have demanded that from someone else. These circumstances were too close, the case too personal. He should have stepped aside and let others handle the investigation. He should have let Roberta handle the prosecution in a professional manner. She would not have let emotions dictate her actions. He felt like a big out-of-control fool, and once again, he had failed Becky-Ann.

Nathan sat alone in the metal cage and listened to the voices in his head. They demanded to know what he was intending to do. Was he just going to sit and giggle like some dimwit, or was he going play his games? The voices demanded action. They demanded blood and revenge. Nathan was smiling in agreement until one voice leaked through the whispers loud and clear.

"Let Mama see the baby. Time for us to play."

"No! No! No!"

The world went berserk in a flash, and Nathan fell to his knees, holding his hands to the sides of his head. He thrashed back and forth against the bars and screamed for the guards. No one came to help drive out the memories. The guards had abandoned their watch and were off having coffee. Nathan was left to visit with his mother all alone.

Judge Stone had demanded an explanation from Sheriff Chandler. Buddy just sat there, trying to get the rage under control and failing miserably. He refused to offer any excuses, any reasons for his outburst, and so Roberta came to his rescue. She knew the case was all but over even before the courtroom scene had occurred. The moment of truth was now before her, and she decided to explain Buddy's actions by giving a brief outline of the murder investigation. She knew what she was risking, giving the defense so much information before charges had been officially filed, but she had to help Buddy. She had to save the big man whom she had grown to love. Buddy never interrupted, but his eyes spoke volumes. She felt like a traitor handing over secrets to the enemy, and she prayed that once he had time to think, he would understand what she was trying to do.

The defense attorney was dumbfounded. He found the story preposterous and the deputy district attorney's actions incorrigible. Michael was fuming at this charade. He demanded a mistrial immediately and advised the judge that he would be issuing a request for a full investigation about this entire incident. He offered a lengthy lamentation over the treatment of his client from the beginning, and he charged Ms. Austin with the responsibility of considering criminal charges against Sheriff Chandler.

"Kiss my rosy-red ass," the sheriff snorted as he stood up.

"Sheriff, I find your attitude inexcusable and your actions reprehensible. You should be ashamed," responded Stone.

"Oh yeah, I'm the bad guy," Buddy said in a sarcastic tone. "Did you hear anything Ms. Austin just told you? That little bastard out there is linked to as many as a dozen murders, four or five of them children, and that is just what we know about so far. How can you sit here like some cock-of-the-walk preacher telling me that I ought to be ashamed?"

The moment was charged with burning emotion, and Roberta watched Buddy shake with visible anger that lifted from his skin like oily smoke. She was waiting for him to explode and knew that no one in this room would be able to stop him.

"Now see here, Chandler—" the judge started to say, but Buddy stopped him with a look that would have stopped the Devil himself.

"No, Judge, I don't want to see any more. That piece of shit killed my little girl, and he did God only knows what to her before the good Lord let her die. He did things to Phoebe Thornton that I had never heard of before, much less seen. We still have not found hide or hair of her children, and I can't imagine the hell they went through. My God, man, we still haven't found all of the pieces of her husband, and what about the two actors found over by the lake?" The sheriff abruptly stopped talking. He could tell that his words were falling on deaf ears, and he headed out the door with nothing more than a mere glance back.

Michael Henry jumped up and shook a finger in the air. "What about proof, Sheriff? Evidence? Probable cause? And a little thing called constitutional rights. You ever heard of innocent until proven guilty?"

Buddy stopped and turned. The attorney immediately regretted saying anything at all and reprimanded himself for not just letting the big angry man leave.

"Yeah, Michael, I have heard of all those things. I have even dedicated my life to supporting and protecting all those things. But there is nothing innocent about Nathan Pomeroy. He is the Devil's own child, and he had my daugh—"

Roberta jumped to her feet and almost screamed, stopping Buddy from continuing. "That's enough, Jefferson Charles. We have given Mr. Henry here enough information. I'd like to have a chance to file the official charges before we give him everything that we have. Okay?" Roberta smiled a crooked smile, and her eyes danced as they met his. The look caused Buddy to pause, but then he realized what she had said. She was actually going to charge Nathan with murder.

Everyone in the room turned to face Roberta. No one had expected her office to entertain the thought of filing such a weak case. Public Defender Michael Henry was the first to speak. "You have got to be kidding." His voice was practically inaudible, but the surprise came across loud and clear.

"As serious as a heart attack, sport. You'll receive a copy of the probable cause and the warrant by the end of the month. I assume you know that you will have to request discovery before you receive any more information about our case against your client."

Judge Stone closed his eyes, inhaled deeply, and stretched his back as he tapped an index finger against the side of his nose. The sheriff involuntarily blinked his eyes and waited for someone else to say something. The moment was broken when the door on the other side of the office opened and Chester peered in from the crack in the door.

"Ya'll plan on gettin' back to work today?"

The defendant was returned to the courtroom, and the jury was reseated. The case continued without further interruption, and Buddy decided he would better serve the prosecution by staying out of the way. He went to his office and busied himself on preparing the reports that would help indict Nathan for the murders of Phoebe and Harold Thornton. The vast majority of the evidence was conjectural and held together by a confession that only Buddy had heard, one received from bruised and bloody lips just prior to Nathan going to the hospital in critical condition.

The sheriff pursued every possible lead, reread all the reports, and started sifting through the staggering amounts of information supplied by ViCAP, the Violent Criminal Apprehensive Program report, courtesy of the FBI. The best-case scenario amounted to a rudimentary circumstantial connection between Nathan and the Thornton's. He could hardly accuse a man of murder because of a similar animal-abuse investigation. Besides, there was no proof that

Nathan had anything to do with the break-in and the killing of the Rottweiler, let alone of Phoebe and her family.

The judge conceded that someone, anyone who might be the killer, could have easily disposed of the Thornton children's bodies on Pomeroy land because of the close proximity to the Joseph house. He also made it clear to Buddy that even if evidence was found on the property, it did not imply culpable negligence on Nathan's part, nor did it require his knowledge or participation. Judge Stone signed the search warrant for the property only. Buddy had everyone available search the Pomeroy property, but the judge would still not grant a search warrant for Nathan's home. The nasty requirement of probable cause reared an ugly head once again when it came to the defendant's residence.

Buddy doubted seriously if Nathan would have taken the children to his home anyway, and if by some miracle they were still alive, they were secreted away in some hellhole far away. The best tracking dogs in the state failed to find a scent that did not lead the handlers back to the starting point. The kids had just vanished into thin air, gone like a puff of smoke. The monster had come rushing unchallenged through the translucent membrane that separates the real world from nightmares, snatched them from their mother's bosom, and carried them off into a deep, endless chasm of terror. The escape was complete, made good by the ignorance of the pursuers, by this demon mocking the light and saying, "Catch me if you can." The sheriff could do nothing more than stumble and weave through his guilt as an appalling howl clawed the dark air, swallowing his pride.

The trial of Nathan Pomeroy for charges of grand theft auto and resisting arrest without violence lasted two more days. Roberta dragged out the proceeding as long as she could. Eventually, Nathan was found guilty on both counts. The maximum sentence allowed for each crime was three years in the state prison, but Nathan, as expected, received credit for time served and probation for two years. Judge Stone commended everyone for a fine professional job and thanked the jury for its patience and understanding. The case was closed, and Roberta was glad just to have it finished. She immediately left the courtroom and called Sheriff Chandler from the pay phone.

"Hey, Jefferson, this is your favorite deputy DA."

"Hey yerself, pretty lady, and never again call me by my given name. It's Buddy, got it?"

"But I like Jefferson. It's so, I don't know, provincial. I think it's cute."

"Cute, now that's a word I have never associated with myself. Give it to me, pretty lady. How bad is it?"

"Just like we thought: guilty, credit for time served, two years reporting probation. Not what we wanted, but at least he has to stick around until we can put him away for good."

"Are you really going to file the murder charges against him? I didn't think we had enough and what about your boss, Mr. Henderson? He's not going to like this."

"You never mind. Let's give it a shot. First thing I'm going to do is ask for a change of venue. We'll hit him with three counts of first-degree murder, aggravated child abuse, kidnapping, and three counts of suspicion of murder."

Roberta was curious what type of case Chandler had constructed against Nathan and if it would be enough to secure a warrant. Details of the evidence along with his rendition of the famous jail-cell confession were in bad need of refinement to be developed into something the defense could not have thrown out.

Chandler had reached up and touched Becky's angel, removed it from his neck, and wound the chain around his finger. He listened while Roberta painted a bleak picture of impending failure and doom. He worked the chain through his fingers like worry beads. Chandler felt the lump in his throat and hesitated before asking, "What's it gonna take to nail this bastard, Roberta?"

"Something we don't have right now—concrete evidence that puts him at the crime scene. A motive would help, as would showing the ability and means to have killed Phoebe or Harold or somebody else on the list."

"You said you wanted a change of venue. Why? What court do you prefer?"

"Any place that Judge Stone does not have jurisdiction."

"Yeah, I hear that. How 'bout some supper?"

"I'd love to," she said in a soft voice filled with excitement.

"It's a date then. I'll pick you up 'round seven and we'll paint the town red."

"Sounds wonderful. See ya then."

Roberta and Buddy worked diligently on preparing the case over the next couple of weeks, but the harder they worked, the more evident it became that the chances for success were nominal. The sheriff sank into a deep depression bordering on manic manifestation. He was watching any hope of ever avenging the death of Becky-Ann dissolve. Roberta was having a difficult time maintaining a professional approach to the case; she loved Buddy, and it hurt her deeply to watch him suffer. Every new setback pushed Buddy further into a black cloud of guilt, and Roberta was spinning out of control, desperately trying to salvage the situation.

Deep in her heart, she wanted to save the case, to deliver vengeance in big economy-sized helpings. The faces of little Becky-Anne and the Thornton kids loomed in her mind, holding a not-so-silent vigil with her own ghost. She had just three hours before meeting Buddy for dinner, plenty of time to work out the details of a scheme wrapped in guilt and tied with a bow of wayward love. It would be a deed of desperation, a secret pact with herself to seek salvation and retribution. Her thoughts crystallized into chunks of disjointed intentions that demanded the truth, which demanded that justice be served in the tradition of a long piece of rope and a sturdy oak limb. When losing one's mind, undeniable peace comes from excluding rational thinking, and that, in turn, stuffs the soul with a wonderful confidence.

Sheriff Chandler arrived early at the Austin home. The nose of the truck cleared the hedge just as he noticed movement in the rearview mirror. Someone had walked behind the truck close to the shoulder of the road. Whoever it was walked with a long stride, a masculine gait, almost a swagger. Buddy killed the engine and watched the figure advance toward the driveway. The body was lean, athletic, and the figure's weight shifted comfortably from the heel to the toes. A baseball cap was pulled low over the brow, and whoever it was kept looking down. The person's hands were shoved into the pockets of a rough-cut suede jacket to guard against the cold.

Buddy watched the shadow draw closer, still without looking up, and he felt an itch crawl from the nape of his neck. The hairs stood up, and warning bells clanged loudly in his head. He was certain it was a man, and the man was less than ten feet behind the truck. The sheriff counted slowly, told himself that on five, he would roll out the door and take the asshole down. As the figure came closer, Buddy could see a square cut to the jaw and that the hair was short, mousy brown—or was it red—and the skin was smooth, almost feminine. He felt an inkling of recognition, and an unsolicited fear ripped through his mind. One, two, three, four, and the door flew open. Buddy tackled him just as he advanced to the truck cab.

"Got you," Chandler yelled, and the man landed hard on the frozen ground with a resounding grunt.

The cap flew across the yard, and shoulder-length hair fell around Roberta's face.

"What the hell is wrong with you, Buddy? Have you gone mad!?"

"Roberta?" He couldn't believe it was her. He shook his head and cursed himself for seeing ghosts on every corner.

"Yeah, now get off me. You weigh a ton!"

The big man rolled off and pulled Roberta to her feet. He helped clean the pieces of grass and dirt from her clothes. "Shit, I'm sorry. I thought you were someone else. What were you doing on the road, and why were you sneaking up on me like that?"

Roberta pushed Buddy to the side and picked a sprig of weed from her hair. She wanted to be mad but found the situation funny instead. Buddy looked embarrassed and angry at the same time. She burst out laughing, and soon he joined in.

"I'm really sorry, honey, but for a second you looked like..." His voice stopped, and the big shoulders shrugged in resignation.

"Looked like who?" Roberta was still laughing, but her eyes took on a more serious expression. The laughter lingered, and before Buddy could tell her, a giggle bubbled from moist, full lips. The sound was childish and innocent, but the sheriff stood there, nonpulsed, with his mind racing in absolute confusion.

"Why did you do that?" he asked.

"Do what?" She let her eyes drift away from his, turning slowly, heading toward the house without saying another word. Buddy followed, trying to shake the feeling that he had just awakened from a bad dream. The image turned in his mind like a leaf taking flight on a sudden gust of wind.

Roberta made coffee to fight off the chill of rolling around on the ground, and soon the idea of going out was replaced with a nice cozy night at home, a good movie, and a wonderful man to hold her. Roberta had found her paradise. With a long day ahead of them, she suggested that Buddy spend the night. He accepted with a smile and kissed her hard.

The next morning, Roberta gathered all the criminal files, forensic reports, photographs, serology reports, and the few pieces of physical evidence recovered at the various scenes and piled it all on top of her desk. The case was pathetic, barely meeting the criteria to charge Nathan, and she had seriously considered throwing in the towel. The facts pointed toward a serial killer operating with impunity over several years in the area. The causes of death and the profiles of many of the victims were similar, and the systematic torture and mutilation were the same. The sheriff had gone to great lengths to accumulate missing person's reports for people linked to the Caulking area over the past five years. Even though the Caulking police had not taken most of the reports, he found the names of thirty-three people who had passed through or in some way encountered the Caulking area and then never been seen again. Most of the missing persons found murdered were female between the ages of five and forty, and the few males were in their early forties. Buddy had made a side note—Nathan's father had been in his forties when he had allegedly abandoned Nathan.

Chandler gave serious thought to trying to have a search warrant issued to dig up the Pomeroy property. He had no doubts that the copse of woods behind Nathan's house would resemble a graveyard, but he knew that Judge Stone would never consider the idea. *Good ol' Nathan has rights, you know,* he thought as the words spat into his mind.

Buddy decided that it was high time to pay Nathan a visit. Because he was the sheriff, he had a civic duty to make sure that everyone adhered to probation restrictions. He shared his brilliant idea with Roberta and asked if she cared to go along for the ride.

She agreed, but she also questioned the logic from a legal point of view. She pointed out that there was still a possibility that Buddy would be charged for civil rights violations, and then there was the general lack of control he displayed whenever he was around Nathan. Not to mention, there was the possibility of a harassment charge that the public defender's office would tack on if they learned about the little visit.

"Just doin' my job, ma'am," he said with a grin. "I only want to ensure that Mr. Pomeroy knows that we are still hot on his trail, and just maybe he will get nervous and mess up. Besides, it ain't illegal for the sheriff to ask a resident of this fair town if we can have a little look around. It will be interesting what he says to that, don't you think?"

Roberta had a look of defeat, but she lifted herself up on her toes and gave the big man a kiss on the cheek. "This will be an unofficial escort, okay? And I will swear that you never told me anything. But you will have to promise that if I say we need to leave, we will get out of there right then. Deal?"

Nathan sat for a long time, playing tag with dark thoughts, letting them spread across the fields of wildflowers and scraggly elderberry bushes. His thoughts were an advancing army, invincible, single-minded in purpose, much like him. His eyes touched those special places across the land, dead and silent like the rotting wood of the beetle-infested stumps dotting the landscape. The land behind his house extended for miles in all directions, and he rolled back time in his mind to help find a few old friends. He had reached a stage in life when his buried treasures could offer him a hand, a leg, or, better yet, a skull.

Nathan danced through the woods until he found a mark on the side of a sprawling oak tree. Thirty minutes later, a shovel-load of red clay contained a torn piece of shirt. After digging for a few minutes more, Nathan was wiping the dirt from a skull. He lovingly caressed the yellowing bone and recalled the face of the man not that much older than himself. *What fun he was*, Nathan thought, and his mind drifted. Carlos Godfry was a drifter whom Nathan had given a ride late one night. Carlos had found Nathan's boyish ways irresistible, and after a short conversation, he had reached out an eager hand and felt the bulge in Nathan's pants. Carlos had smiled with pleasure and suggested that Nathan pull over so they could have some fun. Nathan had driven them back to the house, and they had enjoyed a couple of beers before settling into each other's embrace. The night filled with angry, violent sex. Nathan had hated that he wanted to fuck this man and had punished him for the need. Carlos had screamed from the pain of Nathan ramming himself into the already bleeding hole, and Nathan had reached his climax at the same time that the knife slid across the throat of the unsuspecting Carlos. The memory passed, and Nathan continued his work. He carefully removed all the remaining teeth in the ghoulish grin before he collected the rest of the skeleton and laid out the bones on the ground with a smile.

He threw the skeletal remains of Carlos Godfry into a canvas sack. Nathan carried them back to the house, washed each bone with hot, soapy water, and licked the ends with an eager tongue. He held the bones up for inspection, and with a pleased, "Yep, those could be mine," he giggled and ran his hands over the bones. He had to be sure that all dirt and other signs of having been buried for the past few years were washed away. He then dumped the sack in the corner of the dilapidated porch.

The last five miles to the Pomeroy house were over a dirt road filled with potholes and weeds. Nathan never bothered to clear the road. He liked the property to be overgrown and inaccessible. Roberta and Buddy bounced around in the front seat of the sheriff's marked Crown Victoria. Roberta was actually grateful when the ramshackle house came into view.

The original house had been built a decade before the Civil War by Jonathon T. Pomeroy, the only son of a Virginia land speculator. The house enlarged as the family had grown over the years. The old slaves' quarter still stood behind the main house but had been used to raise chickens until the roof collapsed. Today, the house barely stood, weathered, and unpainted, in the middle of the forest. The sideboards were warped, crosshatch repairs helped to stop the leaks in the roof, and one side of the front porch had given way to wood rot years ago. There was a cold brutal sense to it that sent shivers across the skin.

"Does anyone live here besides Nathan?"

"Nope, he's been on his own for as long as I can remember. Besides, who the hell would want to live in this dump and with that wacko?"

Buddy walked around the old pickup truck parked in the front and knocked on the house's torn screen door, but there was no response. He waited a while before knocking hard on the wood-framed edge of the door. Rotted wood crumbled under the pressure. Again, no response. He noticed an odd smell about the place mixed with the stench of decaying tree stumps and the sharp odor of mildew.

Roberta struggled to keep a mounting fear from overwhelming any semblance of control. The place was hard and indifferent to their presence. Deadness surrounded them, issued from the very fibers of all things that lay within the boundaries of the house. The house was devoid of life, as a cemetery would be, and the absence of life was more threatening than the imagined monsters lurking in the crumbling ruins.

"Well, guess I better check 'round back and make sure everything is okay," announced the sheriff, and Roberta followed close behind him.

"You're not leaving me here. I'll go with you."

Black eyes followed the two from the window. Nathan smiled to himself as he moved cautiously through the maze of garbage and ran from the back door before they rounded the corner. He stood inside the tool shed and walked up behind Roberta. He was only a foot away and had to bite his tongue to keep from giggling out loud. Buddy had taken a step beyond the threshold and called out, "Is anyone home?"

"Sure as shootin'. I'm right here, Sheriff," announced Nathan. Roberta screamed at the unexpected closeness of the voice. Emotions played across the taut skin of her face with the clarity and speed of a wildfire consuming everything in its path.

Nathan could no longer contain himself, and a loud laugh erupted from the pit of his stomach. Sheriff Chandler spun around, drawing his revolver.

"Goddamn you, Nathan!"

Roberta choked after the scream and was in the middle of a coughing fit. Nathan thought the whole thing was hilarious until he suddenly remembered the sack of bones sitting on the porch. He stopped laughing and gave the sheriff a sullen and dangerous look. Buddy recognized the dull expression from having to stare down other desperate men. He moved quickly to step in front of Roberta. A black dissonant thrumming issued a warning from his pounding heart. The further the big man got away from the porch, the more relaxed Nathan seemed to become, but Buddy still held the revolver tightly in his hand. The tension was liquid in the air, and before too long, the moment would reach an impasse.

Roberta felt the fear enclose her in an invisible cloak—she had to do something to stop this Old West-style showdown. "I'm all right, Sheriff," Roberta told him, trying to break the moment, but the anxious expression on Buddy's face gave her pause. She did not understand the full extent of the threat and took several steps backward.

"Now, don't go gettin' yer feathers ruffled, Sheriff. I ain't the one pokin' round inside yer house," offered Nathan with a faraway look to his eyes. Roberta noticed that Nathan never looked Chandler straight in the face but instead he kept glancing toward the house. *Maybe someone is in there*, Roberta said to herself, *and maybe we should go inside and look.*

Sheriff Chandler hesitated before re-holstering the weapon, but he did not relax even as the weapon slid into the leather. He caught the sudden glance Nathan gave to something over his shoulder. He could not remember seeing anything but a dusty old canvas sack along with tons of other garbage on the porch. He thought, as Roberta did, that maybe someone was inside the house, perhaps a guest, or the next victim.

"Who's in the house, Nathan?"

Nathan laughed that insane sound. "Ain't nobody home but us ghosts and other such critters."

Buddy thought about this for a second and ventured a quick look back to the porch. Nothing in particular tickled his concern, but when he looked at Nathan, the uneasy expression returned to Nathan's face. What was he missing? Nathan suddenly laughed, and the tension broke into small, manageable pieces—it was close, but those things feared most would not happen today. The sheriff would never know just how close he was to the real evidence, and sweet Carlos would have to wait a little longer before Sheriff Chandler found his bones.

"I don't suppose you'd let me and the lady look around a bit, would ya, Nathan?" the sheriff asked, but he knew what the man would say.

"No, I don't think so, Sheriff. You ain't my kind of people. I don't think I want you snoopin' 'round, doin' things, maybe leavin' things, if ya know what I mean," Nathan said with deliberation. "I got me rights, Sheriff, the judge done said so. So don't be a-thinkin' 'bout runnin' no more games on me. I ain't stupid, and I ain't scared of death, Sheriff," Nathan said flatly, with no emotion and expecting no response.

The sheriff sucked wind through his teeth and snickered a little. He looked back at Roberta and saw the fear in her eyes. She was waiting for Buddy to lose his temper, but instead, he just smiled. He would let Nathan win this one—the trick was to let Nathan think he was running the show.

"I would be much obliged, Sheriff, if you and the girly here just be leavin' me alone," continued Nathan, and again the tone of his voice caused Roberta much concern. She did not hear the childish giggles or see the flash of humor to smooth the sharp angles of his face. This man was dangerous and easily provoked to violence. She wanted to leave, and she wanted to do it now. The goose flesh rippled across her skin, and a cold, nervous sweat soaked into her blouse.

"Come on, Buddy, let's get going. Please," she begged, but she felt something trying to get her attention. Something else was happening here, and she stared at Nathan. She watched the corners of his mouth curl into a tight smile, the eyes locked onto hers, and there was a brief contact like the sudden slap of a leathery palm on her face.

Roberta felt the odd sensation dance along the edge of her sanity, a queer feeling, but what was it? It was as if she was hearing a dull echo demanding attention from a faraway distance, a call of some kind that was not readily recognized, and yet there was an unrelenting gnawing of something important just beneath the level of her understanding. There it was again! It was like a desperate, wounded screaming, a fore-warning from a soul divided and yearning for unification, a call for kins-manship in this circus of depravity! *Don't be stupid,* Roberta chastised herself. *You're frightened, scared to death of this psycho! Just grab Buddy and get the hell out of here!*

Buddy chuckled out low and gave Nathan one last glance before giving in to Roberta's demand to leave. She grabbed his arm and hur-ried him along, afraid to look back, but she listened intently for the sound of following footsteps. The sheriff stopped, and Roberta grew rigid. She wanted to run, run hard and fast, because she was terrified.

"Don't suppose you have a telephone I could use, Nathan?"

"Nope. Don't be needin' no phone. Who'd I call? And you ain't gettin' in my house to have a look-see, Mr. Tricky-Dicky."

As they drove back to Roberta's house, Buddy became very quiet. To be close enough to reach out and touch Nathan Pomeroy and yet deny himself the pleasure of feeling the man go limp, of feeling the life slowly drain from his body, was more than he could stand. His body quivered at the thought of wrapping his giant hands around that shitty little neck and squeezing until Nathan was no more. The mem-ories of Becky-Ann invaded his dreams of revenge, her sweet smile, and innocent face. The silence was interrupted only by a heavy sigh escaping from his lungs and forcing him to breathe again. The tears found their way to the sides of his eyes and made trails down his cheeks. Roberta watched this bear of a man fight to control his grief. He didn't have to say a word; she knew that the visit had thrown the memories to the front of his brain and that he was once again hearing Nathan's voice tell him all the foul things he had done to Buddy's lit-tle girl.

Roberta reached a gentle hand out and wiped away the tears. She slid over beside Buddy and whispered, "It will be okay, sweetheart. I promise. He won't get away with it." Buddy put his arm around her shoulder and pulled her closer.

The night was filled with passion and long talks. The sorrow and pain made the lovemaking intense. Roberta woke to the wonderful feeling of a warm body molded to her side. She searched his face while he slept and knew that she had to find a way to end this man's sorrow. She wanted to be the one to save the day and put that bastard Pomeroy away forever and, in doing so, make her sheriff love her that much more. She kissed him awake and hurried into the kitchen to make breakfast. There was a lot to get done, and she had no time to waste.

CHAPTER
TWELVE

ROBERTA DROVE FOR five hours before she finally saw the "Welcome to Alabama" sign posted on the side of the road. She knew that what she was about to do was taking a big chance, but it was worth it. She would do anything for Buddy and anything for love. She drove through small towns with well-shaded streets from the large trees that formed a canopy lining the roads. The homes were beautiful, with a historic quality that was mesmerizing, taking her back to a time when life was simpler. She had written the directions to the home she was looking for in haste, and she was having difficulties reading her own writing. A two-story blue home with white pillars had been described on the phone. You can't miss it, the man had told her, and he was right. Roberta pulled into the drive and took a deep breath. She had to maintain her composure and not get over-anxious, just plant the seed and let him make the suggestion. She told herself this over and over.

The large white doors opened, and a tall man in his mid-sixties greeted her. "Ms. Austin, I presume?" The voice was firm yet soft.

"Yes, sir, and you must be Mr. Calhoun."

"Please come in and make yourself at home," he said with a smile and placed her coat in a closet by the door. He took her on a tour of the house, pride ringing through his voice as he explained that it had just been honored as a historical landmark.

Looking around, she noticed that the home was well furnished with antiques and family portraits. "Your home is beautiful, Mr. Calhoun," she said with a sincerity that came from the heart.

"Let's go in here so we can talk. I know you didn't come all this way just to take a look-see at some old house," he said as he showed her the way to a sitting room. "Would you like some tea, Ms. Austin?"

"Yes, that would be lovely," she heard herself say, but her mind was screaming for a shot of good old Jim Beam to help build up her courage.

Victor Calhoun sat on a chair facing Roberta. As she sipped her tea, she chatted politely, finding out little insignificant details about the man and his family. His wife and their son had gone to the cemetery to clean and place flowers on the grave of their daughter, Melissa. His voice cracked when he said the girl's name. Roberta recognized the look of sorrow in his eyes, for she had seen that look the night before in the eyes of the man she loved.

"Ms. Austin, on the phone you said that you needed information about Melissa's disappearance, and about later, when she was found. What exactly do you need? It has been over three years, and I'm sure you have access to all of the reports," the man said, taking a direct approach.

Taking a deep breath and swallowing hard, Roberta proceeded to tell the man her story. "Yes, sir, I do have all of the reports, but they don't tell me enough. I know how painful this is for you, and if you do not want to go into the details, I will leave. But I know who killed your daughter, along with a lot of other people, including the daughter of a good friend of mine. The problem we are having is obtaining enough probable cause to search his house and get the proof we need to prosecute him."

"You know who killed my Melissa?" the man said with excitement in his voice. "I have waited three long years for someone, anyone, to tell me anything about what really happened to my little girl. You tell me what you need, Ms. Austin, and if it's in my power, you'll have it."

Roberta knew she had to be cautious. She couldn't just come out and say, "Oh, Mr. Calhoun, I need for you to arrange for someone to make a call to me when I get back, to say that they read the paper and were in the woods where Nathan's house is and saw him with a little girl fitting the description of one of the Thornton kids reported missing, that he was seen taking the little girl into his home." She wanted to scream the words, to beg for the assistance in putting Nathan away, to not play word games and to just come right out and tell him what she needed. Her heart kept telling her to trust this grief-stricken man, but her head raged in protest and prevented her from revealing her true thoughts. *This is illegal,* she heard a little voice say in a low and dangerous whisper. *You cannot do this. You'll lose everything if you're caught.*

"Ms. Austin...Ms. Austin...I can see the wheels turning. You might as well go ahead and just come out with it. If you are trying to get the man that killed Melissa, or anyone else's child, I will do whatever it takes to help." The man's voice was as piercing as his eyes. She knew that he could see right through the charade but wanted confirmation. He opened the door when he added, "Legal or illegal makes no difference to me. No one should have to go through the suffering that my girl did, and the rest of the family. So you just quit biting your tongue and being afraid of what I might think or do, and tell me what you need." With that said, he settled back into the overstuffed chair and waited.

Roberta thought hard, and the same reasons for not doing this continued to pound in her head, but her heart won out. She knew there was no other way, and she had to do this for Buddy.

"Mr. Calhoun, I am taking a huge risk by coming here like this. I don't know if we will ever prove that Nathan Pomeroy killed Melissa, although I know he did, but we will prove that he killed all those other children, if we can just get into his house. What we're lacking is a little thing called probable cause to obtain a search warrant so that Nathan is directly linked to the missing children. To do that, we need someone who maybe saw Nathan with a little girl who looks like this." Roberta pulled out the picture of Sarah Thornton she had taken from Buddy's office and showed it to Victor.

He ran his fingers over the outline and said that she looked a lot like his girl when she was that age. "All that hair, and such big innocent eyes," he said in a sad, low voice.

"You see, Mr. Calhoun, if someone was, let's say theoretically, hunting out in the woods near the Pomeroy place late at night, perhaps that person accidentally wandered onto Nathan's property and saw him carrying a little girl who looked like the one you have in your hands. If someone, theoretically, came forward with this information and said...let's say...that he saw them go into the house but didn't think anything of it at the time, then this person could say that they saw the pictures of the missing kids in the paper but was afraid to come forward right away because they were hunting illegally and were afraid of being prosecuted. If someone came forward with something like that, I'm sure the district attorney's office would appreciate the information so much that the illegal hunting would be forgotten in exchange for convincing testimony. If someone saw something like that, I am sure I could take care of placing the final nail in Mr. Pomeroy's coffin."

Roberta held her breath and wondered if she would get a lecture on ethics and law. Victor handed the picture of Sarah back to Roberta. He sat silently for a moment, got up, took her empty teacup, and left the room. She hung her head in defeat. After going through all the files of missing people, all the reports, this was the only family that she thought she stood a chance with in using this approach. Melissa had been twenty-seven three years ago, looking forward to getting married and having lots of children. The young woman had agreed to meet her family at a hunting lodge north of Caulking and was driving there by herself, as she had done so many times before. The official report stated that her car had been found abandoned approximately fifty miles from the lodge with a broken radiator. She was nowhere to be found. Three weeks later, part of a woman's body had been located in a wooded area hundreds of miles from where the abandoned car was found. The torso and right arm were identified as Melissa's. The family had had to go through the horror of waiting for two more weeks until the rest of the body had been located. Melissa had been hacked to pieces, and Roberta knew the crime had Nathan written all over it. Roberta stood to leave and wondered if she should just get her coat and be gone by the time Victor Calhoun came back, but just as she was headed for the door, a relaxed, almost happy voice stopped her.

"Going somewhere, Ms. Austin?"

"I thought that maybe I should just leave now. I hope that I have not offended you in any way, and I am sorry for bothering you."

Victor looked surprised and confused. "Bothering me? Ms. Austin, you have given me the first sign of hope that I have had in years. Just knowing who killed Melissa and having the opportunity to help put him away is a godsend."

Now it was Roberta's turn to look confused. "But when you left the room, you didn't say anything. I thought that I had offended your sense of... Hell, I just thought that maybe I should get out of here."

Victor laughed and told her to sit down, that all he had done was put on another pot of tea. "I figured that we would need it since we have a lot of talking to do." Roberta relaxed, and the two settled into a quiet conspiracy.

The hours passed by quickly, and eventually, Victor's wife returned home. Their son had gone home with his wife, and Roberta was invited to stay for dinner. The night was filled with conversation about Melissa, and photo albums dusted off and each picture explained in detail. Martha, Victor's wife, was a kind, gentle, but very strong woman. She stood only five feet, two inches,'" with thick brown hair. When Victor excused himself from the table, the two women were left alone. Martha was very much like her own mother, Roberta thought, so loving. Martha spoke first, and in a low voice to make sure Victor did not hear.

"You are a godsend, you know," she said with tears forming. "Melissa's death was horrible for all of us, but Victor took it the hardest. He has this idea that he should have been able to protect her and has blamed himself ever since. She was a wonderful child, and I am grateful to have had the time we did with her." Martha picked up the last photo ever taken of Melissa while she was alive and held it to her heart. "I've missed her so much, but as much as it hurts, life must go on, and I have managed to enjoy her memory without it crippling my soul. Victor has not been so lucky. He is stuck in a dark place that won't give him peace until the killer is found. What you have done, Roberta, in your quest to save other children's lives, is save my husband's life as well. It has been years since he has acted so alive. I don't know all the details the two of you have discussed about this person who killed Melissa, but I do know that you have given that dear sweet man hope and maybe a chance to put all his irrational guilt to rest. For that, I will be forever indebted to you, and if you need my help in any way, please tell me. I am as eager as my husband to have the man who killed Melissa pay the price for his crime."

Roberta looked deep into the woman's eyes and understood the pain she had learned to live with since her daughter's death. "Melissa was very fortunate to have had such wonderful parents who love her as you do."

After a piece of homemade chocolate cake, Roberta told the Calhouns that she had to be going. Martha insisted that she spend the night, that they didn't want her falling asleep at the wheel. Roberta thought about it for a few seconds and accepted the invitation. The plans she had made with Victor still had a few loose ends, and it was best to get everything perfect before she left. They discussed a variety of things, and finally, Roberta got around to asking about the local shops in town, specifically if any had an extensive selection of knives. Without blinking an eye, Victor suggested Miller's Pawn and Knife Store. What a simple name, she thought, but then again, from what she had seen of the town, these people had no desire to dress things up. Plain and simple was what they enjoyed the most.

Roberta asked to use the phone and was left alone in what looked like an office. The only out-of-place object was a huge portrait of Melissa in a sundress with big yellow daisies. The girl was sitting on a white fence post and was smiling from ear to ear. Roberta looked closely at the painting—the date was just two months before Nathan had taken her life. The artistry was impeccable, right down to the small gold pin she wore on the right strap of the dress: #1 daughter. And she realized how unending the terror Nathan had caused would be even long after he was gone.

She dialed Buddy's number. He answered with a sleepy "hello."

"Hey, handsome, it's me. Are you asleep already?" she asked with a soft laugh.

"Yeah, I guess I must have fallen asleep watching the game. What time is it, and where are you?" he said with concern.

"It's only nine o'clock, sleepy head, and I am out and about following up on a few things. I am going to stay with some friends overnight, but I will be home tomorrow around four in the afternoon." Roberta danced around his questions, not wanting to hear the warnings and discouragement she would receive from him. He wanted Nathan put away worse than anyone did, but she knew that he would not stand for her scheme to obtain probable cause. Maybe someday she would tell him, but not now.

"I have to go, Buddy. I love you," she said and held her breath.

"Me too, sweetheart. Be careful and have fun with your friends. I'll see you tomorrow." After they hung up, Buddy sat for a moment, thinking of the three little words she had said and of his response. He smiled and told himself that this was a good thing, that he had been alone for way too long and was overdue for companionship and happiness.

Roberta's heart was pounding; he had said "me too." That's not quite the same as I love you, but it was close enough, and she knew once again that she was doing the right thing for everyone.

The pawn and knife store opened at nine in the morning, and Roberta was waiting by the door. She had reread all of the reports describing the type of blade that had been used to cut and dismember the victims. She even had a photograph of a possible replica, or at least what the investigators thought the knife should look like—a very simple hunting knife and really nothing special in appearance. The only problem she knew that she might have would be finding one with a double-thick blade. The reports stated that the knife had to be thicker than the average skinning knife to cut through the bone joints with ease. Victor had explained to her that if a knife like that existed, the Millers would have it, and they did. Roberta told old man Miller what she needed and explained that it was a gift for her father. She told the man that her father didn't like new knives and wanted one already broken in, and she explained that the blade needed to be extra strong because he hunted and he quartered the animals in the woods to make for easy transport. The man behind the counter smiled, and the first knife he showed her was perfect. The blade was double-sided and sturdier than any other in the store, explained the man. "You won't get any stronger than this, ma'am. Why, this will cut through anything you can think of," he told her with animated gestures.

She thanked the good man, paid him with cash, and drove back to the Calhoun's home. As he walked Roberta to the car, Victor assured her that he would take care of everything on his end. With a quick phone call, a short good-bye, and a Tupperware bowl full of cookies, Roberta headed to Albany to see Doctor Peeples. With all this set up, she had only one more thing to do to make the case unbreakable, but it was the most risky.

Roberta had called Doctor Peeples, the chief medical examiner in Albany who handled the forensic evidence of most of the homicides attributed to Nathan Pomeroy, prior to leaving the Calhoun home. She had told the man on the telephone that she wanted to review certain aspects of the evidence and have a chance to enforce major points she would want him to reveal during the trial. She had also told him that she wanted to see the physical evidence, to understand what exactly the doctor was going to present on the stand.

Once she arrived in Albany, Roberta wasted no time in reviewing the evidence. Doctor Peeples had created an impressive display on a table in one of the laboratories. Photographs had been enlarged and mounted on poster boards. There were several sets of pictures for each victim, and each set documented the investigation from the crime scene to the autopsy. The doctor was a perfectionist, and she had complete confidence in the presentation, but that was not her true objective. She waited patiently as the doctor explained the significance of each item, but finally, he was called away. Roberta was left alone in the room and quickly took advantage of the situation.

The knife she had purchased in Alabama had been hidden inside her purse, and within seconds, she produced the weapon. She carefully removed a vial from the refrigerator containing a sample of Phoebe Thornton's blood, pulled the stopper, and smeared a small sample on the blade. She inserted the knife in the sheath several times to ensure that the blood was spread well across everything. After completing the tainting of the knife, she replaced the glass vial of blood with time to spare.

When Doctor Peeples returned a few minutes later, she wondered if he could see that she was shaking. Roberta thanked him for his time and told him that she hoped to have the indictment filed by the end of the week, before the Christmas holidays, and to hope for the best.

Roberta walked into Buddy's office at four-thirty. She had made good time driving home from Albany. Buddy was going through the homicide files and making notes on all the cases. He knew that the case was weak, to say the least, and that even if Nathan was brought to trial for the murders, chances were that he would be found not guilty based on lack of concrete evidence. Everything he had in front of him was circumstantial, and nothing but speculation linked Nathan Pomeroy to the Thornton family. It all looked hopeless to him.

Roberta sat on the big man's lap and kissed his forehead. She wanted to tell him her plan but knew that she could not. She was committing a crime, and if she did get caught, she didn't want Buddy involved.

With little encouragement, she persuaded him to have dinner with her at the local mom-and-pop restaurant. Roberta's mind was racing. She had to figure out how to get the knife into Nathan's home, but at that moment, Buddy gave her an early Christmas present. Nathan had been stopped for speeding earlier in the day by one of Buddy's deputies. The deputy had checked Nathan's driver's license and it had come back expired, for more than a year, and that meant that the deputy had the pleasure of putting Nathan in jail on a simple misdemeanor. The public defender was already screaming harassment, and he had assured Nathan that he would be out of jail tomorrow and would not be considered in violation of his probation. Buddy laughed when he described how outraged the public defender was.

Roberta could not believe her luck. With Nathan in jail for the night, she would have the opportunity to place the evidence they needed.

CHAPTER

THIRTEEN

ROBERTA WAS HOLDING her breath as she dressed to take a drive into the woods. Her mind was screaming at her not to go into that house, to stay away, to run, but she did not listen.

The moon was bright and the night was clear. Roberta parked her car on the roadway and put a note in the window that said it had broken down. If anyone saw it, they would just assume that the owner had walked or hitched a ride to get help. The hike through the woods was difficult. The bushes seemed to reach out and grab her, trying to hold her back. The trees whistled in the wind, a memory flashed with lighting speed through her mind, and then it was gone, leaving only a taste of something strange but familiar in her mouth. The house was ahead about a hundred yards, and the smell of death was growing stronger. As she stepped onto the crumpled porch, she thought, "*The Devil's own den*," and then she slowly pushed open the door. The interior was as she had thought it would be, full of garbage and other foul-smelling things. The flashlight that she carried would illuminate only a small portion of the home at one time, and Roberta was rapidly growing grateful for that. Hearing all the little feet running around the floor protesting her intrusion caused a shiver to race up her spine. She had to find a place for this and get out of here. A loud creak under her foot made her pause, and she kicked at the board—it was loose. Roberta kneeled down and pulled the board until it sprang free from its hold on the rest of the floor. "Perfect," she said out loud to herself and placed the bloodstained knife in the hole. Roberta put the board back in place and walked over it several times to make sure that it still made a loud creaking sound when stepped on. She headed for the door, looking around one more time, but she stopped before leaving the house. She saw the mattress lying on the floor and walked to it. Her head was spinning, her eyes straining to see as she sat on its edge. Roberta cried softly for several minutes, not really knowing why but feeling the depth of sorrow and pain this house had seen. She could feel the black wings of a forsaken dream coming for her, and she shook her head and ran for the door. Roberta didn't stop running until she made it to her car.

Nathan was released the next day as promised, and Judge Stone gave Buddy a "Nice try" look when he tried a violation-of-probation charge. Nathan was a free man once again, and he giggled as he made his way out the door with a polite "thank you for the hospitality and fine cooking" expression on his face. Buddy just shook his head. What would it take to put that animal away forever? He asked himself the question repeatedly until he got back to his office.

Roberta was busy in her office when she received a frantic phone call from Ed, the dispatcher at the police department. He had just gotten off the phone with a man named Patrick Richardson. Ed was almost screaming into the phone, he was so excited, and then Roberta heard the equally excited voice of Buddy.

"Roberta, Ed just got a call from a man who said that he saw Nathan going into a house in the woods with Sarah Thornton a few days before we found Phoebe. I got his name and number and told him that you would call him back immediately. He said something about illegally shining deer at night and that he would only come forward if the DA's office agreed not to prosecute him. We have been waiting for this break. Please call me back and let me know if this is for real. God, I hope so, honey." Buddy gave Roberta the contact information, and she smiled to herself, looked up to heaven, and mouthed a thank-you to Victor. She didn't know who had called, but she did know the information he was about to give.

She ran to the office of her boss', District Attorney Thomas Henderson, and flew in without knocking. She had to maintain the same excitement level and surprise as everyone else, or someone might get suspicious. "Thomas, I need you to listen in on a phone conversation. Ed from the police department just called, and he gave me the name and number of someone who can put Nathan with Sarah Thornton right before she came up missing."

Thomas had a look of disbelief on his face, and he told Roberta not to get her hopes up, that it could be just mistaken identity. Roberta knew better. The phone rang several times before someone answered. Just as Roberta was about to hang up and recheck the number, she heard an out-of-breath "hello."

"Hi, this is Deputy District Attorney Austin. I was told to ask for Patrick Richardson. May I speak to him, please?"

"That would be me, ma'am."

With Thomas on the other line listening to the conversation, she prayed that the man would not give the slightest hint of recognition of her name or accidentally say something that would give the plan away.

"I was told, Mr. Richardson, that you have some information about a missing child that we are looking for. Would you tell me about it please?"

"Yes, ma'am, but first I want to make a deal, and then I will tell you what I know."

"What kind of deal, Mr. Richardson?"

"Well, you see, ma'am, I was doing something illegal when I saw what I saw, and I need a guarantee in writin' that you won't try and put me in jail if I talk."

"Could you hold on, Mr. Richardson? Let me consult with my boss. He's the one who makes the deals, not me."

Roberta punched the hold button, and Thomas placed his receiver down as well. "Well, what do you think?" she said, hoping that she wouldn't have to push Thomas into cooperating.

"Roberta, we don't even know what illegal activity he was engaged in when he claims to have seen what he saw."

"Yes, we do, Thomas. He told Ed that he was hunting at night— you know, shining deer—and it was on a reserve, so that makes it a felony, and he knows that. Come on, Thomas, we need this. This will get us in the Pomeroy house. Please make a deal with him. Please. You saw what Nathan did to Phoebe. Please, Thomas."

Thomas looked long and hard at the pleading eyes and agreed to make a deal of immunity for the man's testimony.

Roberta jumped from her chair and kissed him hard on the lips. "You won't regret this, Thomas."

"Mr. Richardson," Roberta said, knowing now that she had her search warrant and knowing what the search would turn up. "My boss, Mr. Henderson, is going to get on the other line and listen in, if that is all right with you."

"Yes, ma'am. I don't have a problem with that. Do I get my deal?"

Thomas reassured the man that, in exchange for the information he was about to give and for his testimony in a trial, no criminal charges would be filed against him. With that confirmation, Mr. Richardson told his story just as he had rehearsed.

When the phones were hung up, Victor shook the hand of the man who would have been his son-in-law. The two did not talk about it ever again. Patrick and Victor had both known what had to be done. It had been discussed in detail and then executed. Both were satisfied that justice could finally have a chance to prevail.

Thomas was happy for Roberta. With this information, the search warrant for Nathan's home was in the bag. He wanted to get that piece of shit off the streets as badly as anyone else did, but in his heart, he wanted the man to remain free also. He knew the torture that Sheriff Chandler put himself through every day over the Pomeroy case, and he enjoyed every minute of the suffering. To watch the big face turn and twist in pain gave him great satisfaction.

Roberta called Buddy, told him the good news, and planned to celebrate with him. She asked if he wanted to spend the night. He agreed eagerly and wanted to hear all the details. Roberta told him to hold his horses, that she could not divulge any more information than he already had because it could jeopardize case. He agreed just to be happy that the search warrant for Nathan's house was being signed as they spoke.

"It can be served tomorrow, honey. But do me a favor and don't go yourself. Send your men, but you stay away from that house. We don't need the defense saying that you planted evidence because of the possible case of rights violation against you. Do you promise?"

"Yes, damn it. I promise," he said reluctantly, but he knew that she was right. If he stepped one big foot in that hellhole, the defense attorney would be all over anything they might find.

Nathan could hear the roaring engines coming and knew that something bad was about to happen. His animal instinct was to stay and fight, but the survival instinct is always stronger. He gathered up the canvas bag that contained his friend Carlos and slipped out the back door to hide in the woods. He could see several deputies and the lovely Ms. Austin standing in front of the house. He wondered what they wanted, and he remembered the strange feeling he'd had when he'd come home from the jail. Someone had been inside his house. He had recognized the smell and had run dirty hands over the mattress where she had sat. "That bitch," he wanted to yell out to her, understanding now why she had been there.

Roberta Austin had gone along with the sheriff's department to ensure that the efforts of the Caulking deputies did not extend beyond the restrictions of the affidavit. She also wanted to be sure that a certain loose floorboard was not overlooked. A young deputy, naive and anxious to prove himself, unwittingly became the co-conspirator.

"What was that?"

"What was what, Ms. Austin?"

"I don't know. My heel got caught in a loose board or something on the floor."

The rest was, as they say, history, and the young deputy was soon pulling out an old leather sheath with a ten-inch razor-sharp blade inside. The leather of the sheath was stained, cracked, and appeared very authentic. The knife was intimidating, dangerous to look down upon as it rested partially concealed inside the soiled case, and if one had the imagination, they could actually hear the screams of victims dying.

Perfect. The ball was not only rolling, it had shifted into high gear and was heading directly toward Nathan Pomeroy. The deputy bagged the knife and walked outside with Roberta. He held the bag up to the sun and noted the dried blood stains on it. Roberta was a happy woman. This was working out great, she thought, when a chill came over her. She felt him watching her, could hear his giggle in her mind, and suddenly, she needed to sit down. She knew he was close by and that he knew what she had done. Nathan was screaming "foul" inside her head, screaming that he had never seen that knife before in his life, but she pushed out the sounds.

The knife was immediately forwarded to the forensic labs in Atlanta to be examined against the wounds of the murder victims, to detect any markings left on bones or cartilage of victims that could match defects or patterns on the edge of the blade. She had also requested that a serology test be performed to determine if any of the victim's' blood was on the blade.

With all the evidence they now had against Nathan, the trial would be the easy part. She called Buddy from the car phone and went back to the office to inform Thomas of the wonderful discovery. Thomas had left for the day, so she started preparing the arrest affidavit for Nathan. It would take two days for the serology report to confirm that the blood on the knife was Phoebe's, and she wanted to be ready.

Thomas had decided that this eyewitness coming forward at just the right time was all a little too convenient, and he had the phone call traced to a small town in Alabama. He was now taking a drive. His first objective was to prove that Buddy Chandler had set up the whole thing and then to watch him try to weasel his way out of felony charges.

Thomas found the town he was looking for and decided to hang around for a few days just to see what he could find out about his eyewitness. Patrick Richardson was in the phone book and worked on a farm when he wasn't selling insurance. Everything seemed legitimate, but the DA continued to have a gnawing feeling in the pit of his stomach that the whole thing was a setup to nail Nathan Pomeroy, and the one who would benefit most if Nathan went to jail was Buddy Chandler. Thomas had a hard time thinking of Buddy without getting lost in anger. In his opinion, Buddy was no better than Nathan. He phoned his office late in the day, and Roberta told him the good news.

"You could be a little happy, Thomas. Nathan will finally go to jail for good, thanks to this," she said with enthusiasm.

Thomas just grunted and ended the conversation with a polite "I have to go now." After checking into a motel, Thomas walked around the town and admired the small-town friendly atmosphere. Courtney would have loved this place, he said to himself while looking into an antique shop full of furniture.

The next day, Thomas made his way to a few of the stores. He was determined to link Buddy Chandler to the witness. He had a picture of Buddy in hand, with Roberta sitting next to him and staring at him in a strange way. *"The look of love,"* Thomas thought. He knew that look, and his mind wandered to a different time in his life, a happy time full of hope and dreams."

"Can I help you, sir?" the man behind the counter said with a southern drawl.

"Yes, I am wondering if you have seen this man around town any-time within the past few weeks." Thomas showed him the picture of Buddy.

"Nope, can't say I have, but I don't usually work here. This here is my daddy's shop, and he went to Mary's diner to grab some donuts. He should be back pretty soon, if you want to wait."

Thomas agreed and passed the time looking at the collection of knives in the case. He noticed the stack of business cards on the counter and picked one up. "Miller's Pawn and Knife Store," he read to himself. *"Not bad stuff for such a hole-in-the-wall town,"* he thought as the time ticked on.

Roberta had put a rush request with the knife but knew that it would still take at least two days. She and Buddy waited with big smiles and bursts of laughter, knowing that Nathan would be caged for life if not sentenced to the electric chair. They went over the previous reports and thanked God that Nathan had been found competent to stand trial for the grand theft auto, which meant that he could not plead insanity just a few weeks later.

Buddy called Doctor Peeples to tell him the good news and to ask a favor. Neither Buddy nor Roberta knew anyone in the lab department in Albany to have them speed things up, but Doctor Peeples did. Buddy asked if the good doctor would call in a favor and get the knife tested immediately. The doctor agreed and said that he would call them back by the end of the day with the results. He also mentioned to Buddy that Roberta had visited him two days prior and told Buddy that he was a very lucky man. Brains and beauty were a rare combination, and he told the sheriff that Roberta had that and much more. Buddy hung up with Doctor Peeples and asked Roberta about the visit and why she had not mentioned it to him. She let the question float around the room, answering without really answering, and then the topic was dropped.

Thomas waited for more than thirty minutes, and old man Miller never returned. The young man behind the counter said that it was just like his pa, and he had probably gotten to talking to someone and lost track of time. Thomas left the shop and said he would come back later.

Nathan could feel the walls closing in around him. His house now held the stench of many trespassers, and he got sick with anger. He pulled the skull from the canvas sack and had a lengthy conversation with Carlos. He told Carlos all his problems and how the bitch had wronged him by planting that knife. He knew they were coming for him, that it was just a matter of time, and he whispered to Carlos what he planned to do.

Doctor Peeples phoned the sheriff, and with a loud, happy voice sang, "Congratulations, you are the proud father of one matching blood test." He went on to explain that the blood was an undisputable match with Phoebe Thornton's but that no one else's blood could be found on the knife, only hers.

"I could kiss ya, Doc," Buddy said, and he gave thumbs up to Roberta.

"In that case, I'm glad we're on the phone," the doctor said with a laugh. He wished them luck and told them that he would be seeing them at the trial.

Roberta hugged Buddy and kissed him hard. "See, honey, I told you everything would work out."

The arrest warrant was signed, and the next day, Nathan would become the subject of an intense manhunt. He had not been seen since he had been released from jail, and Buddy worried that he had sensed what was coming and skipped town. Roberta again told Buddy to stay clear of Nathan for the same reasons that she 'hadn't wanted him to go on the search. He played the hurt little boy and mockingly pleaded with her to let him go outside and play with the other kids.

"No, young man, you are grounded," she said in a teasing tone. "And for your punishment, you have to...let me see..." She let the words linger in the air, and then she leaned over and whispered in his ear, "Let me lick you all over."

He laughed out loud. "Wow, some punishment. I'll have to be bad more often." And they made their way to the bedroom.

Nathan sat on a stump in the shade and held a bloody towel to his swollen face—the pain was beginning to lessen. He'd had a hard time choosing the teeth he did not really need and had pulled only five before passing out cold. A jar of corn whiskey helped with the pain. He noticed that there were only two jars left, but that would be enough.

Nathan wrapped the teeth in a dirty gray cloth and shoved under the mattress. He would need those later, but not right now. He went out to the old tool shed and found the can of gasoline. He touched the rotting wood and spoke to the rats and bugs in loving tones. He sure would miss this place. He carried the can up the steps to his house.

Thomas waited until just before he left the small Alabama town to return to the knife shop. He would give it one more try and then concede if nothing came up. He had been all over town asking questions, and so far, no one had ever laid eyes on the Caulking sheriff. The young man was once again behind the counter, and he smiled politely as Thomas walked through the door. "Damn," Thomas murmured to himself; the old man was out again. Oh well, he thought, and he decided to make a few purchases to complete the presents he needed for his Christmas list. He hated shopping; he hated Christmas. Presents were always Courtney's job, and she had made Christmas fun and exciting. Now it was just another day, made worse by all the jolly people around him. Throwing three small pocketknives on the counter, he pulled out his wallet and was waiting for the final calculation. He just wanted to pay and get back to Caulking. He had been gone for two days, and for what, a stupid idea that there was no such thing as luck—not the luck that Buddy was having, anyway. He bit at the name and spat at the words until the sound of the little bell hanging above the door broke his train of thought.

The old man nodded his head and walked behind the counter. He patted the young man on the back. "You best be gettin' home, son. Your mama is madder than a wet hen. You were supposed to clean the barn, you know."

The young man got a worried look on his face and rushed out the door. The old man laughed. "He's a good kid, just forgetful sometimes. Guess he's like most younguns'."

Thomas smiled and watched the father's pride follow the young man out the door. "Okay, now what have we got here?" the old man asked as Thomas was pulling the necessary $62.24 out of his wallet.

"Are you Mr. Miller?" Thomas asked, counting out the correct change to pay for the knives.

"That would be me."

"Would you look at a photograph and tell me if you have ever seen the man in it? I am trying to follow up on some information and need to know if he has been into any of the stores around here."

"Yeah, I reckon," the old man said, giving Thomas a suspicious look. Thomas pulled out the picture of Buddy. The man looked at Buddy and confirmed that he had never been in the shop. The comments that followed caused Thomas's heart to jump to his throat. "Nope, I ain't never seen him. But the young lady sittin' beside him was in just a few days ago. She bought one of my old knifes, said it was for her dad and he didn't like to have to break in a new one."

"Wait a minute; you're saying that you have never seen the man in this picture but the woman bought a knife from you?"

"Yep."

"Are you sure it was her, this woman?" Thomas said, shaking the picture in front of the man and not liking what he was saying.

"That's the woman, mister. Why? She in some kind of trouble?"

"I don't know yet," he told the man and thanked him for the information.

The drive back to Caulking was filled with mixed emotions. Thomas could not wait to see the look on Buddy's face when he realized that Nathan would never be prosecuted, that the reason was because Roberta had screwed everything up. He cursed himself and hated the idea that Roberta would risk her career for the asshole sheriff. If anyone deserved a loving, devoted woman, it was Thomas. As he thought this, another plan formed in his mind.

Nathan licked the empty eye sockets of the skull he was holding. He laid it down on the mattress and fired one shot through the forehead, which exited from the left side. He assembled the rest of the bones in the appropriate order and pulled a dirty blanket over the remains. Everything was almost ready. He rubbed his jaw as the throbbing started to return, and he took a large gulp of the whiskey to chase it away again. Someone would pay for this pain, he thought, and a name danced through the dark corners of his mind, someone who had betrayed him long ago and left him to become the animal he was.

With the arrest affidavit ready to go, Buddy was glowing. He had waited for this moment for what seemed like his whole life. Nathan Pomeroy, the man who had murdered his little girl, would be in jail forever. Buddy looked at Roberta. He could see how much the woman loved him, and he knew that she would always be honest and faithful. His own love for her would come with time, he told himself.

Buddy decided that this was as good a time as any to ask Roberta to marry him. She was a good, honest woman and he needed to have someone in his life now. She had shown him that.

"Roberta, you know that I have been sheriff here for a long time, right?"

She listened with concern at the tone and wondered where this conversation was going. "Yeah, Buddy. I know."

"I have been thinkin' of retiring after this Pomeroy trial is over. I think I need a change. It's been a long time since I just sat around doing nothing, you know, just feeling the sand between your toes and a warm breeze off the ocean."

"What sand and what ocean, Buddy?" Roberta said with a scared look on her face. She heard the beginnings of a breakup and was not prepared for this, not after all she had done for him, all she had risked.

"I was thinking Miami Beach, and I would like for you to come with me," he said and waited for her response.

"I can't believe you, Buddy. After all I have..." She stopped herself just before a full confession and realized what he had just said. "You want me to do what?"

"Come with me. I want to get as far away from all this as we can. Miami is great. It's always warm, and I think we'd love it there."

Roberta sat with her mouth open. She had been prepared for a letdown, but this was unexpected. This was a dream come true. She ran to him and wrapped her arms around his neck, kissing him with fast, furious, wet lips. "Yes, yes, yes. I'll go anywhere with you."

The rest of the day was filled with making plans. After the trial, Buddy would go to Miami and find them a place to live. She would give a two-week notice, finish her job with the district attorney's office, and join him later. She was happier than she had ever been in her life.

The following morning, Roberta was in the office early. She managed to clear her desk and update all her current cases in the computer before a second cup of coffee. She was still flying high when she saw Henderson coming through the door. "Good morning, stranger. Good to have you back."

"Thanks. Come see me when you're done. We need to talk."

Roberta's heart immediately went to her throat. The tone in his voice warned her that something bad was about to happen. "What seems to be the problem, Thomas?"

"How's the case coming along against Nathan Pomeroy?" he asked, ignoring her question.

"It's fine. I had to re-file the arrest affidavit and include a few more charges, and we are waiting for the judge to sign it and then it's good to go."

"So, Roberta, is your boyfriend happy about all the new developments?"

Roberta did not like the way this was going. Thomas was playing with her, dragging this out, trying to make her uncomfortable. "Yes, of course. He's very pleased."

"Does he know how much effort you put into making all of this happen for him, or is he in on it himself?"

"I don't know what you're talking about, Thomas."

Thomas didn't say another word. He reached in his pocket and pulled out a card. Roberta caught it as it flew across the desk. The blood slowly drained from her face as she read the words: Miller's Pawn and Knife Store.

"Did Buddy have anything to do with this, or did you do it all for him?"

"Thomas."

"Stop, Roberta. I know everything. I figured it all out. What on earth were you thinking?"

"I was thinking that a killer would be put away for life, that deaths would be vindicated and countless other children would be saved. I was thinking about Buddy and how much he needed this to happen, how much we need Nathan to be convicted. What are you going to do, Thomas?"

"I don't know, Roberta. I don't know. I was hoping that Chandler had set all this up. That would have been easy." Silence fell across the room like a black fog coming to swallow up all the efforts of righteous people in the world.

The knock on the door was a welcomed interruption. One of the other DAs had accepted the signed arrest warrant and rushed to get it to Roberta. When the door was closed, Roberta threw the warrant on the desk. Thomas held all of the cards now. It was up to him what they would do about Nathan Pomeroy.

Roberta waited with her hands folded neatly in her lap. She knew that Thomas hated Buddy, but she had never explored the reasons, and now she wished she had. It could have been useful in her argument to save the case. Thomas took several deep breaths and shook his head. Roberta was a good person, he thought, and a good attorney. He had entertained the idea of pursuing a relationship with her when she had first come to the office, which would have been his first since Courtney. He looked hard at Roberta and thought of all the ways he could use this to make her do anything he wanted, and he smiled at the thought. This was Buddy Chandler's woman, and he was going to enjoy watching the big man crumble when he found out all she had done to ensure that

Nathan went to jail and, worse, when he discovered what Roberta would do to keep Thomas quiet. He went over everything with lighting speed in his mind. Roberta couldn't complain because of what she had done. Buddy wouldn't complain because of what she had done to help him, and Roberta could not refuse or Thomas would go to the authorities. It was a win-win situation for him. He thought about how long it had been for him, how long he had been satisfying himself when the need hit, but not anymore. He rationalized his actions by telling himself that he deserved to have what Buddy Chandler was getting, what Buddy had taken away from him so many years ago.

"Okay, Roberta, I won't blow this case. But you are going to have to do a few things for me to keep quiet."

"Like what, Thomas?"

Thomas walked from around his desk, locked the door to his office, and stood in front of her. She looked up into his twisted face, and it slowly came to her mind what he intended for her to do. His smile was sickening as he unzipped his trousers.

"I will not, you sick bastard."

Thomas could feel his dick growing hard. Just the thought of her lips touching him was enough to get him going. He had thought of her many nights and pleasured himself while doing so. Now, he would have the real thing. She could see the bulge in his pants growing and got up to leave.

"If you refuse, Roberta, the first phone call will be to your boyfriend. I'll bet he won't be so thrilled that you planted evidence and screwed up any chance to put Nathan Pomeroy away. Of course, the next phone call will be to internal investigation, and your career, your relationship, your life will be over. I suggest you sit that tight little ass down and convince me to stay away from the phones. The smile was still on his face. With the door locked, he felt at ease enough to pull his pants down and stand fully exposed in front of her. The rush that the power was giving him made him worry that he may just squirt all over her face the second her tongue touched him.

Roberta felt like she could vomit. She had always respected this man, and now he was blackmailing her for sex. She could not refuse under the circumstances, and he knew it.

"Thomas, please, you really don't want this to happen this way."

"Fine, Roberta," he said as he rubbed the taut skin and reached for the phone. "It's up to you." He stroked himself as he hit the intercom button on his telephone. "Angie, get Sheriff Chandler on the phone right away, and I don't want to be disturbed for the next two hours."

Roberta's eyes swelled up with tears at the realization that he was really going to do it. "No, Thomas. Please."

"I'll cancel the call, Roberta. It's totally up to you."

"If I agree to this, you won't tell Buddy and you won't tell anyone about the evidence?"

"It will be our little secret, just like this will be. But understand one thing: I have a healthy appetite and it has been a long dry spell for me, so you better be an eager participant, and any time I say, or we will have to renegotiate our agreement."

The phone buzzed, and Angie told Thomas that Sheriff Chandler was on line one. He looked at Roberta and felt like exploding in his hand just from the expression of helplessness on her face. His dick was growing harder in his hands, and he reveled at the intense pleasure he was getting from total power.

"Well, Roberta, what will it be?"

Roberta sat in the chair facing him, removed his hand, and took the hard cock into her mouth. She felt his body shiver and stopped. "I'll live up to my end of this arrangement. Now you live up to yours."

Thomas told Angie to tell Sheriff Chandler that he had found the information he was looking for and that he no longer needed to speak with him. He then reminded the secretary that he was not to be disturbed, that he was working on something that had to get done immediately. With that, he was free to instruct Roberta on all of her newly acquired duties.

"You can continue now, Roberta. But first take off your blouse. I want to see those tits that you jiggle in front of me all the time." Roberta inhaled deeply, trying to focus on the reason for this, trying to think only of Buddy and how much she loved him. Thomas traced the lace bra with his fingers as the blouse fell to the floor. Then he cupped the full breast and squeezed hard. "Get on your knees. I want my dick in your mouth now, and you better suck me good."

Roberta kneeled in front of the man, and she slowly took him into her mouth again. She could tell that he was ready to lose control and wanted to hurry. She sucked him hard, taking the full length of him into her mouth and down her throat. She ran her hands over his balls and let her tongue tease his hole as his hard-on rubbed across her face. She could feel the wetness increasing between her legs and hated herself for enjoying the forced submission.

Thomas could tell she was getting excited. He grabbed her hair and forced himself down her throat again. "Suck me, bitch," he demanded and filled her mouth with his essence.

CHAPTER

FOURTEEN

BEFORE THE ARREST warrant could be served, the sheriff's department got a call that there was a fire out at the Pomeroy house. When Buddy arrived, the house was fully engulfed, and the fire marshall instructed his men to build firebreaks around the property and to wet down all the surrounding trees and bushes. The last thing Caulking needed was a forest fire along with all the other bad publicity it had been getting lately. Within minutes, the house had burned to the foundation; the heat had been so intense that the porcelain sinks and toilets had exploded.

The fire marshall explained to Buddy that it would take at least two days for the embers to be completely out and to ensure that the forest was safe from burning. Sifting through the rubble, one of the firefighters came across the remains of a person lying on what had once been a mattress. A large portion of the skeleton had burned down to ash and crumbled, but most of the upper body, including the skull, was still intact. The coroner responded and collected the remains. He made meticulous notes of every piece of evidence he collected. When the skull was lifted to be placed into the plastic body bag, several teeth fell to the floor; the coroner retrieved them and noted that the skull had what appeared to be a gunshot wound to the head. The arson experts concluded that several gallons of gasoline had been used to soak the floors. A search was conducted of the remains of the house but did not produce a bullet, nor did the investigators expect to find one. They did estimate that the victim, alleged to be Nathan Pomeroy, had died before the fire, but the extensive damage to the skeletal remains made an accurate determination difficult.

There was not a lot of concern about exactness, and further investigative efforts were stopped. Everyone seemed satisfied that Nathan had been shot and his house burned, that the skeleton was his. No one cared to know the truth beyond that, and no one even wanted to find the perpetrator after the first body was discovered under the front porch.

Sheriff Chandler was granted an amendment to the original search warrant to include a complete excavation of the Pomeroy property, and eight bodies were unearthed under the foundation. The area being examined was enlarged each day, and by the end of the week, they had discovered twenty-four graves. The small bodies of children were carefully examined, but none were the Thornton children. The town was paralyzed with fear, and once again, Caulking was big news.

Buddy kept Roberta informed about the progress of the investigation and said he would have to see her in a few days, that he would be tied up for quite some time. Roberta said she understood and cringed when she heard Thomas's voice on the intercom.

"Roberta, could you come in here, please. We need to talk."

Roberta prayed that, with Nathan dead, Thomas would stop playing this little control game. She would talk to him about it and hope for the best. She knew that he still had her ass over a barrel, however, even with Nathan gone. He could still go to internal investigation and, worse yet, he could still tell Buddy what she had done and what she was doing now to keep him quiet. She would appeal to Thomas's sense of decency, she thought as she walked into his office.

"Lock the door and take your clothes off." The statement was made without emotion, barked out as if ordering a dog to sit.

Roberta did as she was told. She watched his face change as she stood in front of him. She saw the effect this newfound power was having on him and realized how much he enjoyed it.

"I want to make one thing perfectly clear," he said in a matter-of-fact tone. "Just because old Nathan is dead and gone does not mean our deal has changed in any way. You will continue to do as I command, or your dear, sweet, big dumbass sheriff will be told everything, including the details of our little arrangement. You wouldn't want that, would you, beautiful?"

"No, Thomas, you know that I will do anything to keep Buddy from finding out any of this. So, what do you want today?"

Thomas laughed out loud and told her to come and sit on the desk in front of him. She did as she was ordered.

"Now, spread your legs and make yourself cum, and don't fake it, Roberta." Thomas sat inches from her and licked his lips as she reached down between her legs. He watched her fingers disappear into the wet folds, and every few minutes, he would pull them out and lick them clean. He watched as her excitement built, and then he rammed himself hard inside her just as she reached her peak. She spread her legs to take more of him while his body shook out of control, denoting the end of yet another humiliating session.

"You can go now," he said, and he laughed as she pulled up her skirt and tucked in her blouse.

"I hate you, Thomas," she said just before she opened the door and went back to work.

The news of what was being unearthed was received with gasps of horror, but no one could have gauged the magnitude of revulsion when it was reported that Nathan had his particular serial-killer province in the removal and maintenance of the viscera. Scores of airtight jars were being removed from the ground, containing unusual souvenirs stored in a compound of herbs and spices that delayed decomposition so he could take them out and play with them from time to time.

"Sheriff, this here is Ed. Are ya on the radio?"

"You go ahead, Ed."

"I got some people from the FBI here askin' lotsa questions. Can you get back over here and help me out a bit?"

"I'll be there as soon as I can, Ed. Just hold tight."

Three agents and a supervisor were sitting in Buddy's office when he walked through the door. Their immediate concern, they told him, was trying to identify the remains in Nathan's extensive graveyard. There were scores of missing persons reports being attributed to Caulking's most celebrated, and recently departed, citizen. The newfound popularity was unwelcome by the townsfolk, and many of the inhabitants of the small, retiring town were talking of leaving for a less egregious neighborhood.

"You see, Sheriff Chandler, some time back, we received a VICAP package from a medical examiner in Albany, a Doctor Peeples. This program was designed to identify and help track offenders with violent predatory appetites, known more commonly as serial murderers. The initial report and supplemental investigations have developed a disturbing pattern. Your Mr. Pomeroy has been a very busy fellow," announced the special agent unceremoniously, a tall, dapper man, a bit of a dandy. Buddy flinched when he called Nathan "your Mr. Pomeroy."

Buddy listened to thirty minutes of redundant case information, jurisdictional mandates, and a lot of federal double-talk. Buddy stopped paying attention twenty-nine minutes in and finally held up his hand.

"Cut to the chase, boys. What the hell do you want?"

They wanted to control the investigation, to lead the charge to solving perhaps as many as eighty open homicides across three states. They wanted the glory and the publicity, and Buddy wanted nothing more than to give them that distinction.

"We have just one more question, Sheriff, and that is, who killed Mr. Pomeroy?"

"Interesting question. No one around here really gives a goddamn, and as far as I am concerned, it was probably suicide." He told the four men in their clean white shirts and colorful power ties that contrasted with their very conservative grey pinstripe suits his suicide theory. The delivery was met with silent, conspiratorial glances and disbelief.

"If that is what happened, Sheriff, where is the weapon?"

"Couldn't tell ya. I suppose it burnt up. That was fire from Hell itself. It melted the pipes in the walls and made crackling out of the sinks."

"Crackling?"

"Well yes, you'll have to forgive a good ol' country boy, but I'll translate. The sinks and toilet exploded into itty-bitty pieces. Nothing survived that fire, absolutely nothing."

"Well, Sheriff, understand that we consider this investigation open and ongoing, and we will be conducting our own examination of the evidence," continued the dapper agent. "You need to arrange for a driver to take us out to the scene, and make sure it's a big car, not some pickup truck used for hauling hay."

"I don't think so," Buddy said as his tolerance level bottomed out.

The agents looked at each other and back at the bear of a man who was getting more than aggravated with their holier-than-thou attitude. The sheriff calmly stared down each and grinned. "If y'all want to do your investigatin', go on and do it. The place ain't hard to find, but you see, we've done ours, and it's just that—DONE. Nathan, or what is left of him, is in Albany. The house is gone, and all the bodies we found are jammed in a refrigerated trailer awaitin' the next of kin," Buddy explained. "The Georgia State Police are the ones that handled the real work. You see, we are just a town full of poor country rednecks who happen to be asshole-deep in big-city investigatin', and we look at things a little different. All the investigatin' in the world can't bring those good folks back from the dead, and it can't take away all the pain from their families. Nathan is a burned-up piece of shit. He's gone back to Hell, where he came from." The grin on the sheriff's face broke into a complete, down-home type of smile. "Y'all have a nice stay here in Caulking. It has recently become a much safer place to visit, and by all means, let us here at the sheriff's department know if we can assist you in any way, okay?"

The agents stuffed their papers back inside their leather briefcases before storming out the door. The agent in charge turned back and said, "Don't you ever get tired of living in the dark ages, Sheriff?"

"No. Don't you ever get tired of making mountains out of molehills?"

"This is not over, Sheriff Chandler. We will be back."

"Yeah, thanks for the warnin'. We'll be here."

Buddy fell back against the chair and wondered what made some federal agents such pompous assholes. The next thing he did was call Roberta with an invitation to lunch.

"Technically speaking, Buddy, the FBI does have jurisdictional authority due to the interstate aspects of the investigation. If the murders happened in one state and the subject crossed state lines, that gives them the authority. That is the whole theory behind the VICAP operation, where all agencies share information. All other agencies must work with and through the FBI."

"Yeah, yeah. Well, whoop-de-do. They can interstate this thing right up their jurisdictional...authority. Our tax dollars at work," said Buddy.

"Who cares? Let's just enjoy the day without talking of work, Nathan Pomeroy, or the Federal Bureau of Assholes. Let's talk about Miami."

"That sounds like a great idea," the sheriff agreed, and he gave Roberta a long, hard kiss.

The FBI did assert their authority and take control of the case. Ten agents were assigned by the end of the week, and the cooperation of the GBI was requested. A special investigator from the Office of the Attorney General in Atlanta was appointed, but after a few weeks, life in Caulking returned almost too normal. Nathan was becoming a memory, a new bogeyman to scare children at Halloween parties, and weeds were starting to cover the charred landscape, hiding all the scars. Sheriff Chandler thought about a vacation, something he had not done in five years, and he wondered if Roberta could get away for a few days. Maybe they would even go to Miami and look around together.

Roberta loved the idea, and she loved Buddy Chandler. He made her think thoughts she had avoided while carving out an existence for herself in a world designed by men. There had been law school and apprenticeship with the district attorney, but when accurately translated, the apprenticeship meant servitude. She hoped for a private practice sometime down the road. She thought of Thomas and wanted to puke. Yeah, she would gladly leave this place with Buddy. Life for her had always been viewed in the singular. She was straightforward and ambitious, without time for romance or family or other complications. She had not anticipated Jefferson Charles Chandler, but she was not running. He was older and settled and not the type she had dreamed about when late-night desires forced her heart to confront her loneliness. He was sweet and romantic in a rugged, tough-guy way. She felt good with him. She felt safe and looked forward to spending her life loving him.

Their conversation led to talks of the distant future, the type of home she wanted, the color of carpet. Their lips parted, and the passion overtook the moment. The kiss grew into a hungry search of tongues darting, devouring with growing intensity. They made love and explored each other with a frenzy that surprised them both. They needed each other. The wanting was all-consuming and left them exhausted.

Roberta slept late and found a pot of coffee waiting for her in the kitchen. Buddy had already gone to the office. She sat with her thoughts, sipped the warm black liquid, and prayed that Thomas would leave her alone today.

"Good morning, Roberta. You look especially appealing today, almost glowing. Did you have a good night?" Thomas almost spat the words at her. "Come see me at noon," he demanded, and she nodded her head in agreement.

The minutes dragged. The waiting was the worst part. She wished she could just get it over with, then push the horrible act to the back of her mind and pretend it had never happened. She was good at that, a learned practice, a survival technique.

The clock in his office said 11:58 when she arrived. "Very punctual of you, Ms. Austin. I guess you enjoy your new duties more than I thought."

"What do you want today, Thomas?"

"I want to talk about your sweetheart, Sheriff Chandler," he said flatly and watched her face for a reaction.

She refused to show any emotion and wondered what he was up to now. "Okay, what about him?"

Thomas walked to where she was sitting and reached up her skirt. He felt the silk panties and ran his fingers along the edges. Then he pushed them to one side and shoved two eager fingers deep inside her. "Did he do this to you last night, Roberta? Does he fuck you as good as I do?" Roberta remained perfectly still as he removed his hand. He held the two wet fingers to her lips and gently opened her mouth. He moved his fingers over her tongue and then walked back behind his desk.

Good girl, Henderson thought before he decided to drop the bomb. "The feds are thinking about charging our good sheriff with the murder of Nathan Pomeroy."

"They can't be serious, Thomas. On what grounds?"

"Well, for starters, let's talk about the episode in the jail, and after we have established a motive with regards to the death of his daughter, shall we proceed to the incident in the courtroom? You were even a witness to this last infraction. And to conclude our prima facie case, let's add the field trip to the Pomeroy house, which you again witnessed. We have motive and opportunity. We have a distraught father out of control and using his official position to cover up the act."

"That's bullshit, Thomas, and you know it."

"Do I? Let's not jump to conclusions, Roberta. There is a consideration for sympathy—I mean, looking at it from a father's point of view. I would be capable of almost anything if someone took a loved one from me, especially a child. I think maybe your sheriff did kill Nathan Pomeroy."

"That's just great, Thomas. You have jumped from innocent until proven guilty to guilty with no chance of being innocent."

"Think objectively, not emotionally. This is going to be rough, and I wonder if you will be able to approach this situation professionally."

"You aren't seriously considering that I work on this investigation, Thomas?" Roberta was shocked, unable to fathom the possibility that she could earnestly pursue an attempt to prove the man she was in love with, had made love with just hours ago, guilty of first-degree murder.

Special Agents Bell and Rodriguez accompanied Rita Moore to Judge Stone's private office. Rita Moore was a special prosecutor from the attorney general's office and specialized in corruption investigations. She brought a ninety-seven–page brief detailing the allegations against Jefferson Charles Chandler with her. Lieutenant Dancer from the Georgia State Police Department was listed as the lead investigator but was unable to attend this meeting. The affidavit accompanying the original complaint requested a search warrant for the Chandler residence and the sheriff's office, which was located on the bottom floor in the same building.

Judge Stone carefully read the documents and made several remarks regarding the language and content. The judge was not a fan of Sheriff Chandler, but he refused to allow personal opinion to influence his decision. He found the request for the search warrant lacking in probable cause, and he refused to sign the affidavit. Special Agent Bell expressed his disappointment and advised that he would deliver the request to Judge Bradley, a federal judge in Atlanta.

"I'll have the order in less than a day, Judge Stone. There is nothing unconstitutional in the request, nor is there anything lacking in establishing the facts that would lead a prudent man to concur with your judgment. What is lacking is your desire to accept that Sheriff Chandler is capable of committing murder. Understand, Your Honor, we are trying equally hard to prove him innocent. This is a search warrant, not an arrest warrant."

"Listen here, son. Don't you ever lecture me again, and if you try to ramrod this bullshit by making this a federal case, need I remind you that your agency does not investigate local murders? You do not have the jurisdiction, the authority, or the balls to make good on your threat. Now get your ass out of my office."

Stone picked up the phone when the door closed and called Thomas Henderson. "Tommy, we need to talk now. How about your office in fifteen minutes?"

Judge Stone was entering the elevator at the same time Deputy District Attorney Austin was leaving Sheriff Chandler's office on the first floor. She would not proceed with the investigation without informing Buddy—she was already keeping so much from him and did not want to add to the secrets. She told herself that she would find out everything she could and then take herself off the case for personal reasons. She told Buddy about the investigation reluctantly, however, guilt holding her heart in a tight grip. She was the one guilty of so many things, and yet he was being investigated for murder.

Buddy laughed when she told him about the murder investigation. "Can't say that I didn't see that one coming, sweetheart. The last time those fed boys were here, well, we did not part on real good terms. I had a gut feeling that they were here for more than just a routine howdy-do. What are you going to do?"

"Hold you real close," she whispered, and the tears began to drip from the corners of her eyes.

"Now, baby, it ain't all that bad. The facts will not support an arrest. You can't go after a guy because he had a few run-ins with a local killer."

"I've read the affidavit Judge Stone turned down, Buddy. Rita Moore and I went to law school together. She broke the rules, but she wanted me to know what they have. It's not perfect and Judge Stone won't sign it, but they'll make it perfect."

Judge Stone was a hard man to work with. He had a reputation with both defense attorneys and prosecutors alike, and no one felt comfortable when he called demanding a meeting. Thomas Henderson went to the bathroom twice in ten minutes, and he jumped when his secretary announced Judge Stone had arrived.

The judge walked past the woman without as much as a grunt and shook the district attorney's hand. "The FBI is trying to nail the sheriff," he stated and walked toward the window.

"You read the file, Judge. Is there a case, or did he just piss someone off? He's real good at that, you know. Hell, he could piss off Mother Teresa."

"Yes, that's true, but could he have killed Nathan Pomeroy?"

Thomas Henderson joined the judge at the window, and together, they watched the medley of people parade down Main Street. The time passed while Thomas thought deeply about the question of whether Chandler was capable of committing murder. He thought about the earlier conversation with Roberta, and finally, he said, "Yes, I think he could have blown the man's brains all over the walls."

Judge Stone studied Thomas's face reflected in the window and remembered the day eight years ago when Deputy Chandler had rushed into a roaring house fire. The house had belonged to Thomas and his young bride, Courtney. The fire had started somewhere in the living room, faulty lights on the Christmas tree or something, if the judge recalled correctly. Chandler had found Thomas slumped over the couch and dragged him to safety. He had gone back in a second time but could not find anyone else and had barely made it out himself. Courtney had been in the bathroom. She had been terrified and could not move or even scream when she heard the Chandler calling for her. The flames had grown hotter and the roof had started to come down. Deputy Chandler had not had a choice but to leave the structure. The flames were too intense and the house was completely engulfed. Courtney Henderson, twenty-one years old and eight months pregnant with her first child, had perished in the fire. Thomas had blamed her death on Buddy and swore he would never forgive the man, that some day he would even the score.

Eight years later, Stone prayed to God that Thomas was able to see beyond that day of hurt and beyond the hate, but he also doubted that Chandler would get a fair deal from the DA's office. The judge wanted to find out if he was the only official in Caulking thinking that the sheriff was innocent. He really could not blame Henderson for his feelings of rage, just as he could not condemn Buddy for his hatred of Nathan Pomeroy—both men had lost something precious. But neither of these men was capable of committing murder. Of this, he was sure.

Stone looked at the DA as he stood in front of the window looking down on the world outside and told him, "Well, you're wrong, Thomas. Sheriff Chandler did not kill Nathan Pomeroy, just as he did not kill your wife and unborn child in that fire. Get it straight in your head, Thomas. The man saved your life, and he almost lost his trying to save Courtney's. If you don't let this go, the malice will destroy you."

Henderson did not look away from the window and did not wipe the tears away from his face. He was blind with the memory of Courtney, of the baby he would never know, and of the horrible things he was doing to get his revenge.

CHAPTER

FIFTEEN

THE WEATHER WAS cold, and the sky held the promise of another snow. The world was hiding behind a thick cloud shrouding the sun in a mute sphere of glaring white. The wind brought an extra chill to the gloom, and the sun was occupied with thoughts of hibernation. Caulking was under a blanket of white, and the sky was filled with the pungent aroma of wood fires. Everyone was thinking about Christmas, which was just two days away. The little town looked good all dressed up in its winter finery.

Roberta had the week off from work and decided to fix Buddy an old-fashioned dinner with all the trimmings. Her home was decorated in cheerful colors, and life was good. Thomas had left her alone for several days. Although she wondered why, she didn't dare ask for fear of renewing his interest.

The volunteer fire department was battling the wind, trying to get a twenty-foot fir Christmas tree balanced in the park again after the wind had knocked it down, and Sheriff Chandler was working his way through a turkey sandwich. He had been trying to finish lunch all day, but something or someone seemed continually determined to prevent him from eating. Ed was on vacation with his family in Arizona, and Buddy was left to answer the telephones.

"Hello, Sheriff's Department. Sheriff Chandler speaking," he managed to say without choking.

"Well hello yerself, big guy. Where the hell is Ed?"

If Buddy had a quarter for every time someone asked where Ed was, he could have bought a new truck. "Ed's off for the holidays. What's on your mind?"

"Hey, Sheriff, and Merry Christmas to ya. This here is Clarence Jones out on Route 66, by the Pomeroy place."

"How ya been, Clarence? What's got you calling today?"

"Well, Sheriff, there's somethin' funny goin' on at the Pomeroy place."

"Get on with it, Clarence. What are ya talking about?"

"There's been somebody just a diggin' through the dirt all mornin', some guy in a suit."

The sheriff shook his head sadly. He was tired of people diggin' up his bad dreams searching for souvenirs. He picked up his coat on the way out the door and silently cursed Clarence for being such a busy-body. Damn fool. Doesn't have anything better to do than drive around the back roads in the cold. He complained to himself about Clarence all the way to the Pomeroy farm, but he stopped when he recognized the blue Chrysler parked on the side of the road.

Buddy pulled the gloves from the pocket of his coat and stepped out of the warm embrace of his car. The sounds of a shovel digging in hard, frozen clay carried through the cold, crisp air, and the sheriff followed the noise. He soon found Thomas Henderson on a small ridge overlooking the remains of the foundation, and he walked directly toward the man. The clatter of the shovel biting into the cold, wet clay masked the sheriff's approach until he stopped within feet of the DA.

"What the hell are you doin', Thomas?" The unexpected sound of the deep and resonant voice scared the DA. He dropped the shovel and spun around toward the sound.

"Buddy! I didn't expect anyone to be out here."

"No, I suppose not. You lookin' for something? It must be pretty damned important to bring a body out in this weather."

Thomas watched Buddy grab the handle of the shovel from the ground and felt the dam break that held back the years of his pent-up hate. Thomas drew back his right fist and struck the Sheriff one time in the mouth. The attack was swift, unexpected, but not very effective. Buddy was a man accustomed to using his hands in defense of his ideas and had spent his life fighting someone or something. He stood back, wiping the blood from his mouth, and sneered at the DA.

"Is that all you got, Thomas? You could have picked a warmer day for this, don't you think?" The DA looked like he was about to run, and the sheriff threw down the shovel.

"What's this all about? You ain't out here digging for treasure, ol' son, and I don't think you collect bones. You damn sure ain't out here for your health, or mine, you dumbass. So come clean. What brings you here on a day like this with such an attitude? Speak up, Thomas, or so help me, I'll take this handle and shove it up your puny ass!"

Henderson broke and ran. He tried to make it to the car, but Buddy was quicker and hit him one time hard in the stomach. Fried eggs, grits, and coffee never taste good the second time; the DA crumpled to the ground in his own vomit. He managed to stand after a while and faced the sheriff, but he was still trying to catch his breath.

Chandler was ready to tag him again if Henderson tried to do anything stupid. The sheriff was finished playing games and wanted some answers. "Have you gone nuts, Henderson! Just what in God's name are you doin'?"

"Okay, this is not going very good," Henderson said and held up his hands in a sign of surrender before continuing. "I got a call, anonymously of course, from a guy who said he saw someone burying a box out here last night."

"Yeah, so what, and why didn't you call me?"

"Why? Because the guy said it was you."

"Bullshit! Nice try, asshole." Buddy was going to hit him again just for good measure when the DA fell to his knees.

""No, it's true. What the hell was I to do?"

"Exactly what you are doing. I guess the temptation to catch me doing something bad was just too hard to pass by, huh, Tommy?"

"Fuck you, Buddy."

"No thanks, Tommy. You ain't my type."

"You're right. I guess fucking one DA is enough, huh, Buddy? Well, I hope you don't think you're the only one she's turning tricks for."

"Stupid thing to say in your position, Tommy. I ain't on my knees suckin' up puke with my suit pants," Sheriff Chandler snarled as he leaned back against the Chrysler. He watched the vaporous columns of their breath float in the air between them and thought about what was really going on here.

"Listen, Tommy, I am not responsible for the death of your wife. Shit, boy, I pulled you out and went back in, and I damn sure didn't see you running into a burning house to get her. I couldn't find her before the roof collapsed. Tommy, I did my best. Stop hating me because you got out and she didn't."

The tears ran down Henderson's face, and he sat back on the ground. The suit was ruined, and his shoes were filled with red mud. The man was a disaster, broken and out of control. Chandler had never felt pity for the man, but he did understand the sorrow. He allowed the DA to drag himself from the ground and gave him one more chance to run. Henderson collapsed completely. The fight was over; he was in no condition to run. The sheriff relaxed, waiting for the man to talk.

"The caller on the phone also said that he watched you drop a pistol in the box before you buried it."

"Oh, how convenient, and you figured it was the pistol I shot old Nathan with, right, Sherlock?"

"Fuck you, Buddy."

"Thomas, do you really think I'd go burying a pistol out here, of all places?" He watched Henderson giving up. The DA was falling apart all over the place. He slid off the fender and crashed to the ground.

"Just stay down before you hurt your fool self. I didn't kill Nathan, although I thought about it long and hard and probably would have if I hadn't thought about it," the sheriff said. "You find that box yet?"

"Buddy, I think you are guilty as hell of killing Nathan Pomeroy, as well as Courtney and our baby. You can stand here and play games and be real cute about it, but I'm going to nail your ass someday, just wait and see."

Buddy knew he was up against something he could never defeat. Henderson would never be his pal and would never listen to reason. Buddy spit in the slush and said, "Let's go find your box."

"What? You're going to help me find the box? I don't understand."

"No? Now that's a big surprise. Listen, someone went to a lot of trouble getting you out here. If there is a box with a gun, and if it has something to do with this Nathan business, then I want to find it too."

Henderson and Buddy searched for hours without any luck. The box was not discovered until after the sheriff made a phone call. A dozen men armed with metal detectors, sifting screens, and shovels explored three acres before a wood cigar box was located. The box contained a thirty-two–caliber revolver with a dirty barrel.

The sheriff told everyone to leave the box alone and asked one of his men to take photographs. He contacted the Georgia State Police and requested a detective assigned to the Pomeroy case to respond.

"Tommy," Buddy called.

"Yeah?"

"You take charge of the evidence, if it is evidence, and I'll be heading back to the barn. Roberta has a nice hot meal waiting on me, and I'm already late."

"I can't take the evidence. That is your job," Thomas protested.

"Bullshit, Tommy. This quit being my job months ago. You started this shit. Now you finish it, ol' boy."

Chandler tried to rub the cold from his stiff joints as he walked back to the squad car. A light snow was beginning to fall, and the entire world was gray. He felt tired and beat. This was no way to live, and he thought again about retiring to Miami. He made a decision to call it quits and submit the paperwork as soon as he got back to the department. Enough was enough, and Roberta had already agreed to go with him anyway. She shouldn't mind if it was moved up a few months. He stopped at the car door and yelled back, "Hey, Joe, give that roll of film to the DA, will ya?"

"You sure, Sheriff? Ain't there somethin' 'bout the chain of evidence and all that we should be following?"

"Don't worry. Ol' Tommy ain't going to bitch. Just give him the film, and you guys get back home to your families."

The indictment against the sheriff never materialized, and the case was placed in the inactive status with the GBI. The revolver was found to be of no value to the investigation, and the allegation that Buddy was seen burying the box was dismissed as a hoax. The agents of the FBI collected their files and computers and went back to

Atlanta. The federal case was never closed, but the agents were reassigned and the investigation eventually abandoned.

Buddy pulled up to Roberta's house and knocked on the door. He decided he definitely wanted to speed up the retirement. He had already informed the city council days ago, and now it was just a matter of paperwork, but he wanted to talk it over with Roberta. She told him that she had a lot to do and that she would start working on downsizing her cases immediately after the holidays. He told her what had happened with her boss, the DA, and it worried her that Thomas was acting so strangely. If he told Buddy about their little arrangement, it would destroy everything that she had worked so hard for.

Buddy went to the office the next day and worked on completing all the paperwork for retirement. He knew that it would take a couple of days in Albany to arrange for the final transfer of his retirement funds to a new account in Miami Beach. There would be dozens of forms to fill out, letters of intent, meetings with accountants and clerks to start the process. He only wished he could do it now, today, but with it being the holiday season, all the businesses were closed. He would have to wait. The sheriff was a little nervous about having enough money to survive on for the next thirty years, but he decided that he could always find a part-time job doing security if he needed to. Besides, Roberta would probably want to look into working for the DA's office down there. He had already contacted a real-estate agent, and she was sending information daily about condos on the beach. He had everything set, ready to go.

The department would operate by itself while the city council conducted a sham search for a replacement. The salary offered was insulting, and they had already handpicked Steven Ward, the deputy chief from a small town just outside of Caulking.

Ward had been to Caulking a dozen times in the past week, and some of the men were already calling him sheriff when Buddy wasn't around. Chandler was a short-timer. They all knew it, and there was no use pretending otherwise. The deputies pooled their money and bought him a retirement present. Doris had been sniffling all week and gave him a big hug every time they passed in the hall. She had outlasted the previous three sheriffs, but she claimed this one was the last and that was going to retire next year—nobody believed her.

Late that night, just around the time Roberta was feeling warm and cozy under a thick blanket, the telephone rang. A glance at the clock told her that it was going on eleven. Late-night calls usually brought bad news.

"Hello, who is this?"

Buddy detected the anxious tone in her voice and felt foolish for waiting so late to call. "It's me, honey. Did I wake you?"

"Where are you, baby? I thought I was going to have to fill out a missing-sheriff report."

Buddy laughed. It had been a long time since someone had worried about him, and he liked the feeling.

"Are you coming back over here, or are you going home?"

"Well, if you don't mind, and I know it is late, I'd like to come see you."

"Get your behind over here, boy. I'll get some hot chocolate going."

"Be there in fifteen minutes."

Buddy slammed the door against the cold and blew warm air into cupped hands. The temperature was dropping fast, and more snow was forecasted for dawn. He slipped the truck into a low gear and edged slowly toward the center of the road. The warmer afternoon temperatures had helped melt away some of the snow, but ice had formed as soon as the sun went down. The back tires spun and then finally grabbed as he shifted into second gear. The stillness of the night was broken by nothing but the soft crunch of tires on freshly fallen snow.

Buddy never looked back and did not notice the light shining through the district attorney's office as he headed toward the highway. Thomas Henderson was sitting at his desk, staring at a picture of Courtney. She would have been twenty-nine tomorrow, and they would have been celebrating their ninth Christmas together as a family. He had stopped crying some time ago. An empty bottle of scotch hit the floor when he yanked open the desk drawer. He picked up the envelope containing a detailed account of Roberta's evidence planting.

He laughed to himself when he slid the videotape of them together inside and sealed it.

Thomas went to the sheriff's office and placed the envelope with a nice red bow on it and "Merry Christmas" written across the front on Buddy's desk. He went back to his office and pulled out a small wood cigar box from the bottom of the otherwise empty drawer. It contained only one item, the revolver he had so very much wanted to prove was used by Sheriff Chandler, killer of his beloved wife and unborn child, to shoot Nathan Pomeroy.

The weight was threatening in his hand, and he removed it without looking at the gun. He felt the cold steel in the palm of his hand and smelled the rust. There had been three rounds in the cylinder when Buddy had tossed him the box that day at the Pomeroy' place. "Fuck you, Buddy Chandler" were the man's last words as he shoved the barrel into his mouth just before pulling the trigger.

Ten minutes after the dull explosion ended the tortured life of Thomas Henderson, Sheriff Chandler rolled the Ford pickup truck to a slow stop in front of the Austin home. Roberta could be seen standing by the window as he ran to the porch, and she opened the door before he could knock.

"Damn, it's cold. I can't remember a colder winter in all my many Decembers." They laughed and kissed.

"Hello to you, too. Give me your coat and close the door."

He followed her to the living room, shedding clothes as he went, and the blast of hot air from the furnace felt great. Roberta had the hot chocolate waiting for him and told him to sit down so she could rub his back.

Roberta and Buddy stayed locked in each other's arms throughout the night. They talked of all their big plans and fine-tuned the timeframe. Everything was wonderful as they made love for hours, laughing and giggling, and then growing serious and letting the passion take them to higher heights.

They fell asleep with dreams of a warmer place dancing inside their heads. It was a quarter past four o'clock in the morning when the phone rang and Roberta said hello.

"Ms. Austin?"

"Yeah, this is she," Roberta answered, and she thought again about bad news coming so late at night. The voice on the telephone told her that Thomas Henderson had blown his brains all over the wall in his office. The caller told her that they needed her to come down and help. She gave the phone to Buddy and walked toward the stairs. She smiled when her back was turned, and she would have jumped for joy but knew that Buddy would want an explanation, so she played the sad-coworker routine while her heart sang with glee.

The body was being wheeled out the door on a gurney from the local funeral home when Buddy and Roberta arrived. Two squad cars, an ambulance, and a plain white van were blocking the entrance to the parking lot. Buddy left the truck in the street and helped Roberta step down.

"You okay with coming here? You didn't have to, no matter what that jerk on the phone said."

"No, I'm okay, really." And she meant it. She wanted to see proof of this stroke of luck for herself.

They walked in the front door, and a deputy took Buddy to the side. "Sheriff, we bagged his hands and haven't touched the gun. We had everyone stay out of the room. Ain't no note, and the cleaning lady, Mrs. Kirkland—you know her—found him hanging off the side of the chair," he told Buddy in one breath.

"Okay, take a break. Breathe. Did anyone photograph Henderson before he was moved?"

"Yeah, thirty-five millimeter and Polaroid. Here's the Polaroids."

Sheriff Chandler flipped through the graphic record of the DA's last official act. The sheriff harbored no doubt that the man had taken his own life, and he handed the deputy back the photographs. He was finished here and headed toward the stairs and down to his office. Roberta was standing with a small group of people as Buddy approached. He took her to the side.

"He did a good job, the poor bastard. I didn't like the guy, but that's a hell of a way to celebrate Christmas. What are you going to do?"

"I don't know. I guess just wait for you guys to finish and start getting things back on track. I'll call the governor's office before they hear about this on the news."

"All right. I'm going to my office to get a few things. Then I'll come back up."

With a quick kiss, they went their separate ways. Buddy gathered the things he needed from his office, along with the two gifts that had been left on his desk, and headed back to the scene. The entire hallway was cordoned off with yards of bright yellow plastic tape. A deputy was standing guard at the door to ensure that no one entered the room. The deputy gave Buddy a nod as he lifted the tape and walked inside the plush office. The first thing the sheriff noted was the mess on the wall. A spatter pattern of blood and crusted brain matter covered a three-foot section behind the desk. It was easy to determine that Henderson had been sitting in the chair when he'd pulled the trigger. The next thing he noted was the picture of Courtney on the desk. There was not much else to see, and the sheriff instructed the deputy to let the cleaning lady into the office.

The sheriff found it ironic that the revolver the district attorney had used to end his life was the same one he had tried to enter as evidence to put Buddy in jail for murder. Buddy carried the small blue-steel gun in a brown paper bag, tagged it, and threw it into the property room safe. He thought to himself how suicide was a pathetic, cowardly act, and he still held no pity in his heart for Tommy Henderson.

"I saved that boy's butt from a burning house, he hates me for it, and then he blows his stupid brains all over the office anyway," the sheriff said out loud to himself as he made his way to the office where Roberta was waiting.

They walked out of the building, into the parking lot and as they reached his car, Roberta noticed the two packages he had taken from his office. "What's that?" she said.

"Oh, I don't know. Doris probably wants me to believe Santa has been here delivering his goodies."

"Well, are you going to open them?"

"Yeah, when we get to your place. I have got a little something for you to open yourself." Buddy had purchased a solitaire diamond ring for Roberta for Christmas, and he was excited about giving it to her.

When they got home, they sat at the foot of the Christmas tree and held each other for a long time. Roberta excused herself and went to the bedroom to put on the little surprise outfit she had bought just for the holidays. While she was changing, Buddy opened the package that Thomas had left on his desk. He quickly read through the papers and was in shock at what he saw. Roberta had planted the evidence on the Pomeroy property and set up the witness to get probable cause. She had lied to him. He then pulled out the video cassette and shoved it into the VCR in the living room.

Buddy sat on the couch with his mouth open. The date on the tape was just last week, and he didn't want to believe what he was seeing. Roberta and Thomas were together, and she was doing things that caused the big man to start crying instantly. He pulled the tape from the box and sat there in silence, looking at the ring he had planned to give to her that night.

He didn't wait for her to come out of the bedroom. He wrote a note on a piece of paper, put the video on top along with the information about the evidence, and left Roberta's life.

Roberta came out of the bedroom and found an empty house. She saw the papers on the table, and with trembling hands, she pushed in the tape. She cried to the heavens and cursed Thomas Henderson to Hell. He had gotten his revenge on her and on Buddy. She slowly picked up the note as the floodgate of tears washed through her broken heart.

"Roberta, how could you betray me like this? I thought you loved me and wanted the same things I did, at least you said you did. Guess I'm the fool. I would have understood about the evidence if you had trusted me. I would have told you not to do it. I can never forgive you for the relationship with Thomas. Goodbye, Roberta."

Roberta raced to her car and drove fast to Buddy's house, where she found him already throwing things into the covered truck bed. She knew Buddy would never accept her story, and even the truth was beginning to sound like a lie. Heartache and guilt wore down her pride, however, and she decided to tell him the truth anyway. Roberta tore out her heart as the big man sat, pale-faced, on his sofa. This was what he had been trying to avoid.

"Buddy, baby, I did what I thought was right. I tried to help with the case. Thomas found out and was going to turn me in unless I did what he said. Please, Buddy. God, please forgive me for loving you so much. I risked my career, my dignity, and my freedom for you. Please understand that I had no choice with Thomas. I couldn't risk losing you," she told him between the sobs.

Buddy listened, shifted his weight, and chewed on his lower lip as Roberta cried, pleaded, and mostly just pissed him off. Ten minutes into the rehearsed speech delivered with the maximum amount of emotion, he stood and looked down at the woman he had wanted to spend the rest of his life with. He said, "You could have told me about the evidence, given me a clue, and I would have said no, don't do it, that we could go with what we had. You lied to me over and over again. I have no doubt that Thomas would take full advantage of a situation like this, especially knowing that I intended to spend my life with you, but you didn't have to go along with it. How could you, damn it?" He walked out of the house. He already had everything set up to move to Miami. Now he would be going without Roberta. Anything else he would need that he could not carry with him now, he could just make arrangements for long distance.

Roberta eventually assumed the role of District Attorney, appropriately taking Henderson's place. She took the oath of office a few weeks after the suicide and her horrible breakup with Buddy. She still cried every night, thinking of all that she had lost, but she was a survivor and she would live through this. On several occasions, she attempted to call Buddy in the hope that time would have softened the hurt and they might have another chance, but he would never return her calls. She threw herself into her work, and the nightmares continued.

CHAPTER

SIXTEEN

MIAMI BEACH, FLORIDA

The night waited for him to emerge, the quiet man who rented the room down the street. It waited for him to walk through the back door, to usher in the night with a thin arm wrapped around night's cold shoulder, footsteps kicking against the solid wood walls as he passed by. Each step would sound on the stairs with a voice whispering stale jokes beneath the weight, and he would pause at each door until he found the right one. He fumbled with the lock, giggling softly, and the door cracked open. The sound of leather-soled shoes scratching the face of the scarred floor accompanied him into the room, and then the door closed behind him with an impatient click. He patted the sheath and smiled as he touched the cold metal it carried. He smiled again as he watched the women sleeping with slow, rhythmic breathing. The intruder was still smiling as he stroked the knife's razor-sharp edge, saying, "And like a woman, cold and hard, waiting to dance, sharp of tongue. Yes, siree."

The bedsprings spoke a soft complaint as he pressed his face into the pillow, but he spoke to no one. Their scent was everywhere. There were stains holding the essence of womanhood to the fibers of the cloth. The calm that had settled in this darkness inhaled ragged sobs of air from the room, and nausea rammed a hard fist into his gut. Hundreds of scenarios of doom spoke to his imagination, while words of contempt relieved their swollen bladders with a warning and a desperate plea to be brutal, with a promise of eternal suffering if he failed, enlisting Nathan's fear as an accomplice.

Tired eyes, red and raw, screamed as swollen lids slid over the dry sheen of eyes which had become strained from staring into dark dreams, a stirring of things forgotten and left festering like spoiling fruit, seeds overripe. Dream eyes do not burn. They do not grow tired or weak, but they do scream and twist the truth, distort light and seek false visions bright and clear. The metamorphosis of night and day, that nameless second, that derelict riding the wind in search of nightfall, came strolling under the door. It shouted to his imagination, "The black horse is loose." It was a forewarning to take hold, to brace himself and hide the child in his mind behind all that he considered to be sacred and righteous, and yet nothing happened, and the warning slipped by when the man blinked. He had missed it while reflecting on other things, and the dream eyes had seen it, but they would never tell.

He lay motionless on the floor next to the bed and dreamed of many things before easing into the lair of sleep, death's cousin. He remarked knowingly about the wallpaper, said polite things about the new chair in the corner, and strolled back out in time to hear the hooves of the black horse dig at the floor in the background. The hot breath, the pungent breath, licked his face as he kneeled to listen by the bottom of the door. The gentle laughter of the winds came rushing, climbing over each other's backs. He noticed how quiet it was in the room and how the air hung still and thick like a spider's web. The night had feasted upon wasted dreams, stuffed itself until sated, and sat napping by the window. The wind was picking at a crack running across the wall, bored, waiting for something to beg attention before passing on with a sneer.

The man reached over to the nightstand and quickly pulled the chain for the lamp. He removed a notepad from a back pocket and found a red pen on the floor. The lamp light fought with the shadows in the darkness, trying to shove them back to the far corners of the room as the light filled the void. He opened the round door to the past as a tear slid, wet side down, along his cheek. Memories filled his mind with dust and fear as the hourglass fell to one side. A door closed on the world, and imagination escaped into a secret world of illusion, a world with black velvet drapes stretched tightly across cracked glass to stop the sun and protect the cold colors of the room.

He wrote in his pad that he disliked the thought of suicide so intensely that he would not discuss it with himself. He had decided to force the issue and let death deal with the issue alone. Death was the master of the game. The man was only a pawn. He wrote, "I don't want to end my life. There'll be other chances to let the river run red, to let the dreams come dancin' across that river red." He described the room, the sleeping women, and he gave those names, secret names that he only told himself but gave to all of them.

"No one took notice of the disappearances. There were the rumors, lots of stories, and some were downright unpleasant, but only I knew the truth. All the rest of them told lies," he reminded himself, and he smiled when the older woman slowly tuned her head.

The whining voice had disturbed her from a sound sleep. The eyes of the man watched her move and finally come alive, and he smiled at her confusion. He tossed the pad toward the foot of the bed, and it slipped into the night's share of the bedroom. There was something unpleasant in the room. It had imparted unrequited yearning into her unconscious, and in the distance, screams called from the cold light of day. They spoke to his soul, revealing weakness and strength. The tremors of vulnerability were intolerable as torment wallowed up from the summoned memory.

"Somethin' like this has to be handled with care and treated with deserved dignity. We have to avoid confusion. Don't want to be givin' folks the wrong impression." He grinned at her terror and thereafter ceased revealing the true nature of his visit.

"The eyes are the only good parts left," he whispered, and he reached for her hand. "Eyeballs rollin' 'round. They let all the light into your brain! Damn pretty eyes. Never blinkin' or twitchin'. Full of fire and action! Forced to see so many things. Can't look the other way and pretend not to see. How cruel!"

The woman tried to scream, but the cool night air had dried the tender skin of her throat to coarse leather. She could only choke and cough. He balled a hand into a fist and sang, "Jeepers, creepers, where did ya get them peepers," before he shoved the index finger through her right eye. The scream exploded from her lungs and filled the once soft and silent bedroom air with a savage and shattering noise. The man grabbed the old woman by the hair, yanking her from the bed. She hit the floor hard and bounced. The top plate of her dentures shot under a chair. He moved with practiced precision and quickly wound yards of thick silver tape around her head to cover her face.

The younger woman was awake and screaming. All this noise caused such a pounding in his head, and he had to stop the noise. He slapped the girl once, twice, and then again until she too fell to the floor. He wrapped her mouth swiftly and pulled her whimpering body to the other side of the bed. He yanked the old woman and heard a bone snap in her arm as he tied her to the frame of the bed. The experience exploded a rush of adrenaline in him. He was lost in the delirium of the moment, and the dream and the past shot with a jolt between the divide in his brain. The eyes of the younger girl grew wild with panic as the sobbing of a small boy sounded from the door. She was staring at her little brother over the man's shoulder. He saw her eyes and turned to follow the lead of their direction.

"Oh, what a night this would be, what a sweet and special night," he whispered. "You have given me an angel, an angel of my very own," he growled with lust, and the tiny boy standing just inside the room fled in terror. The grandmother tried desperately to stand, to move, to scream for help, but she could not. The women were forced to listen for hours to the pleas and screams and cries of the little boy until there was silence.

The man returned to the bedroom, exhausted. His face and hands were covered in red blotches, blood splatters. Dark wet stains appeared on his shirt and pants. "Damn, that was mighty tasty," he told them, wiping his mouth with the back of his hand, but the grandmother never heard him. She had died a while ago. The horror existed for her no longer. He pulled the knife from the old leather sheath and kissed the edge of the blade. "Fuckin' whores, breeders that leak piss and cum into the waters of my world and foul the air I breathe!"

Hours later, he could have been seen sitting on the windowsill with skinny ankles hanging down from baggy pants. He sat facing the night with his fish eyes wet, watching the moon. The work was finished, the cutting was done, and he set down a bloody bag full of presents for himself. He was not selfish, though. He also left presents for those who would come to scream and vomit, those who would have to live with the nightmares forever. He did so like to share, and their lives would go on, but perhaps not quite the same as before.

"I'm awaitin' for it to fly away," he said to the moon, "waitin' for the engines to fire up, for them to brush away the barnacles, the rust, and say damn!" He laughed, and small, yellow teeth flashed in the moonlight. "God will say, 'Hot damn! Why didn't I think of that?'" He laughed harder, holding his feet and rocking back in the windowsill. His shoes fell and spun silently to the ground.

"It'll upset the cheese lovers, and there'll be no more werewolves or high tides. Hot damn!" he shouted. Then he whispered to himself, "It'll be fuckin' great."

The man fell quiet for a while, and very still, lost in confusion. He did not write any more. He thought of new friends and looked to see if the shoes were still there. Dark brown leaves and green-black grass returned his look. The moon did not shoot across the night sky. He mumbled and tried to cry, to force the feelings of isolation and anguish, but he could not feel the overwhelming sense of emotion he wanted to feel. He only felt the loss of a decent pair of shoes.

Everything that had been building melted away, and the man sat alone in the window for a long time. Now, for the first time, he wondered why this was the way it had to be for him. He strained to force tears to his eyes, and he listened to the slow beating of his heart. The tears would not fall, and his heart did not warm the cold recesses of his soul.

The wind hissed and whispered strange words in his ear.

"Some fight time…" he whispered back to the wind in a voice that told of the years of defeat, a voice that hid in the corner of the room and glared back at the rest of the world. "But I, I wage war and *face the sun*. I watch it abandonin' scared skies and return with a rush each new day. Return when I am done and gone."

He continued to talk about thunderstorms, whispering softly to the lonely night. The man talked to himself and cried, and no one called out for him to stop. No one saw him, but he saw everyone who had once been something to him a long time ago, stuck in time like insects in amber.

A large strangler fig grew outside the window, and he stretched to take hold of the nearest limb. They seemed to move swiftly about the soft gray trunk, and climbing down proved more difficult than he had thought. The chill from the dew sent shivers up his spine, and the ground was cold to the touch of his bare feet. Nothing looked the same at night as it did when the sun was bright, and the shadows laughed behind his back.

"Have y'all noticed what quiet sounds like?" he jotted down in his pad. "How it really sounds?" he asked. When no one answered, he continued, "The noiseless hum that taunts and echoes and breathes, that emptiness filled with nothin' special, and yet, the quiet screams."

The man seemed about to explode, and the pad quivered in his hand. "It is truly strange to hear nothingness..." he whispered in a low voice. "But that's what I am."

A memory howled a name, "Sarah," and he saw her dancing in the air for him. He felt like a junkie who had just taken another hit, the drug racing through worn-out veins, saying everything was okay. So this was love, this was the magic, fucking moment. This was great. Yeah, he could live with this, yes, siree. Everything was going to be all right.

Nine hours later, a cough interrupted a troubled sleep and eyes shifted under the weight of eyelids bleeding tears. Someone whimpered, wrestling with issues long ago dead and settled, dancing with spent effort shot between wet sheets. Little time was left, and the clock was ticking like hot metal cooling, clicking, winding down, and the dreamer was delivered into the hands of daybreak. The air vibrated as the sleeper snapped open haunted eyes that stared that dead-fish stare that had seen it all before, seen those things that scared people for the rest of their lives.

The memories had taken him here before. They all had been disgusted before, sick from too much and from not enough. The eyes, empty voids of black ice straining to focus, narrowed to slits. A tired face smiled from the edge of its mouth, and the Devil held his hand through the moment. The man watched as they continued along the street, stepping over trash and shadows. Dry mouths let a whisper sail, "Wait...let me come too..," and a voice, sounding like broken glass, groaned. The voice competed with the sounds of the day's beginning and loss. Laughter ricocheted between bits of unfinished conversations slithering through cellophane-thin lips. The laughter was booming, full of energy, and ended between the fragments of lost, disconnected words hanging in the air.

The gray image of a man lingered around a lamppost, a figure crawling from the shadows and listening to a thin, one-sided voice licking nonsense into the middle of his mind. Layers of fog swallowed the streetlamps, and the moon hid behind a pale yellow light. He could detect the lingering hint of perfume and closed his eyes. His right hand slowly, mindlessly, stroked the blade in his pocket. He could feel the cold hardness, hear those thoughts brought to life by the touch, and the memory excited him.

The man from the shadows relived his memories, and the experience intensified to a scream in his mind as he approached the outer limits of glee. The emotions were hard to resist, and he unzipped his tan work pants. He slowly masturbated with his left hand and continued to stroke the razor with his right. His breathing settled into shallow gasps, and he could no longer stop himself. The moans and screams and pleas echoed inside his mind. His muscles ached from the cold, and his mind tripped over the remains of unfinished conversations. He saw black eyes dancing on the outer edge of insanity. There had been no reaction, and all that vomiting of blood could make a body sick.

"Don't! No, no, no," the scream played over and over in loud replay. There was that scream, and he remembered lying against his shadow on the cold concrete and weeping. He could not remember how he had gotten outside. He thought of words that had slid across the surface of that part of his mind, unattached to what had been and still allowed to keep track of what was, but now, now that all that was had settled like dried blood between cracks, there was nothing more to it. The moment had passed in the wink of an eye.

The man decided to sleep in the alley, although the weather had turned cold, damp, and miserable. He was nothing more than a refugee from the solitude he sought, craving sanctuary from the disorder and wanting nothing more than to be allowed to stand alone, shivering in the dampness. He saw the world from a distance, but as he drew closer, it recoiled from his touch. The silence echoed around him like thunder in a canyon, and he failed to follow the ricochet of reports as he studied the thick white scars on the backs of his hands and the dirt trapped beneath his fingernails. The scars were left there from the wire used by his father to tie him down on the bed. He traced the lines with deliberate interest, something to do while time wandered aimlessly through the streets, and he slowly rubbed the skin raw, longing for what had been but could never be again. He saw himself hiding in small dark places, and he heard his own voice screaming in terror.

The darkness had faded, and as he looked back toward where he had spent a few hours sleeping, he saw other men slowly staggering into the street from the alley—drunks, perverts, and thieves, brothers of the night, all quietly surrendering to the promise of day and giving up their place of nighttime hiding. One by one, they disappeared around corners and became nothing more than ghosts exposed to bright light. The streetlight above the man's head blinked out, and he watched an old woman wander through the rooms of her apartment. The slow parade of human rubbish continued escaping from the alley, but the shadow man had lost all interest. He leaned against the lamppost and saw the open window, the missing screen, and heard the sweetness of her voice singing to the morning.

The world was awakening around him. It yawned and emitted small gurgling sounds as it too stirred from slumber. A small grin, and then a big smile, exposed cracked yellow teeth for but a brief second. He stood for a moment longer and absorbed the moment in silent concentration as his swollen tongue scraped across a yellow sore on the inside of his lip. Then he said, "Damn pretty eyes, never blinking and full of fire. Round glossy balls of emotion, forced to see many things and pretending not to see."

The words were floating, spat into the air, and followed by a laugh that ended the smile on his face. He felt for the wet spot in the pocket of his jacket and pulled out a pair of silent blue eyes. "Look, isn't it a beautiful day in the neighborhood?" he giggled. "Jeepers, creepers, where did ya get them peepers?"

He had set off without direction, stopped and pissed against the wall, adding to the stench that burned his throat. He heard the sound of the ocean. It beckoned and tugged at his feet to drift in that direction. The walk to the beach was short, and he sat on the white metal beach chairs to watch seabirds bobbing on the waves, their necks bloated from eating the small silvery-green fish. The air remained cool and damp as the sun wandered effortlessly from cloud to cloud, stealing the stars from the sky.

Four days later, Buddy Chandler, retired for about two years now, clicked the lock open on a sliding glass door and stepped out on the balcony. It was as hot as he could ever remember, and the plastic thermometer on the wall showed signs of melting. But there was always a breeze off the ocean, and he had an incredible view of the Atlantic Ocean from the twenty-third floor. His shirt stuck to the sweat on his back, and Buddy wondered if he would ever get accustomed to the Florida heat. The ocean was a solid sheet of emerald-green glass. White sails were drifting like ghosts, and a cargo ship from South America was just appearing on the horizon. Yeah, it sure was hard work doing nothing.

Chandler had bought a condominium with the proceeds from the sale of his house in Caulking. He now lived with six hundred strangers in a glass-and-steel tower perched on the edge of a private beach. The temperature had reached close to eighty-nine last Christmas, and the only snow he'd seen since leaving Georgia had been on the television. He had never been back home. There was nothing back there but bad debts and bad memories. Buddy spent every day swimming and drinking beer in the shade of palm trees. He played handball sometimes with a group from the building, and on the weekends, he went to malls to kill time.

Buddy read the *Miami Herald* cover to cover every morning. He liked a couple of the regular writers and tried to stay current on what was happening around the world. It was easy to let his brain go numb and vegetate, like most of the people who lived on his floor. He especially liked reading about the crimes—old habits were hard to break. He desperately missed police work. He had never regretted leaving Caulking and turning in his badge, but he did miss the mystique, the pride of feeling the weight of the service revolver pulling at his side. Buddy had been a damn good sheriff.

It had been his job to enforce the peace, to stop speeders and drunk drivers, take strangers by the elbow, and see that the public places closed on time. He liked to stand in front of his own jail cell and look into the eyes of the one inside. They seldom would return the look. Buddy would stand before the judge after serving a warrant on a neighbor, stand there with teeth grinding and a jaw not seeming to set well. It was his job. No one else would do it, and no one else could do it as well.

The headlines jump-started the sheriff's old heart as he read the article about a grandmother and her two grandchildren brutally murdered in their Miami Beach apartment. Hell, the address was only a few miles away from the condominium that Buddy had called home for the past couple of years. The story was graphic, the brutal torture explained with black-and-white detail. He read the story twice, and each time, the sweat ran cold across his skin. It could not be, he told himself, but who else would have sewn the old lady shut with waxed blue thread?

The receptionist was polite when Buddy called, polite to the point of being obnoxious, and she was damn good at saying nothing while using so many words. She avoided direct questions and asked a score of her own before transferring his call. The phone rang a couple of times, and then another receptionist answered. He endured several more minutes of questioning before a new voice answered the line and said, "Homicide, Detective May."

Buddy introduced himself and told the detective that he was a retired sheriff from Caulking, Georgia. Detective May asked just where in hell Caulking, Georgia, was, and Buddy felt a little sorry that he had bothered to make the call. He felt even more foolish when he tried to explain the reason he had called. He was preparing to hang up when the detective softened.

"Listen, Sheriff Chandler, today's been a bitch. How about coming by the station around ten o'clock tomorrow and we'll discuss your theory."

Buddy felt stupid and like he was being treated with less than the respect he deserved. He may be small town, but damn it, he had been the sheriff of that small town, not some wet-behind-the-ears, smartass, big-city, rookie detective! Chandler slammed down the telephone and kicked a chair over. There, that felt better. He also considered not going. "Fuck 'em," he told himself. Let the big shot handle his own damn homicide. Then Buddy thought hard about what was written in the paper. "Nathan Pomeroy," he whispered to the walls around him. "It has to be you, sent back from Hell by the Devil himself, and you're in my neighborhood again."

A few minutes later, Buddy was checking his closet for something to wear to the meeting. Most of his clothes were either too down-home or too formal. He did not feel like wearing a three-piece suit to a two-minute meeting. He decided that he would worry about his wardrobe some other time and grabbed a towel before heading out the door for the pool.

The next day, Buddy was early for his meeting with Detective May, forty-five minutes early, and he wasted time in a cafe across the street from the Miami Beach Police Department. He could see the four-story structure from the table and wondered if the architect had been drunk or stoned when he had designed it. This was Florida, land of sunshine, and the building did not have a window in the place. The most beautiful beaches in the state, and the poor slobs who worked here had to stare at plasterboard and cheap art. The art-deco clock on the café wall told him it was time to go to keep his meeting with Detective May.

The inside of the building was not as bland and unadorned as Buddy had expected, but windows would have made a welcome addition to the atmosphere. The detective bureau was on the fourth floor, and he waited for the elevator in a lobby that was bigger than the entire Caulking Sheriff's Department. The officer at the desk told him that their department was over four hundred strong, with another fifty officers in a reserve program. A two-year veteran could make more money in one year than could three deputies combined back home. A bell sounded, and the stainless steel door in front of Buddy slid open with a slight hiss.

A second lobby greeted Buddy, along with a pretty, dark-haired woman behind a glass partition. She smiled, and the retired Caulking sheriff smiled in return. He asked for Detective May and gave her one of his old business cards.

"Please have a seat, Sheriff Chandler, and I'll see if Detective May is here."

He waited ten minutes, occupying his time reading a year-old edition of *Sports Illustrated* and growing angrier by the minute. The moment Buddy started to leave, a tall, heavyset man opened the door.

"Sheriff Chandler, good of you to come. I'm Stan May," announced the man as he extended his hand.

"Buddy Chandler," the sheriff said and returned the handshake. He gave the detective his last business card.

"What's the J and the C stand for, Sheriff?"

"Just that, Detective, a J and a C."

"I'm good with that. Why don't we grab a cup of coffee and discuss whatever it is that you want to tell me?" the detective asked. He noticed the two thick files Chandler had brought with him. "What's that?"

Buddy answered the detective while following him through a maze of desks and bodies to a small conference room. "These are copies of the original case files on our investigation involving who I think is responsible for the murder of that grandmother and her two grandchildren the other day," Buddy responded, and he added, "I'll have mine regular, with real milk if ya got it."

Chandler sipped at his coffee while Detective May examined the case file on Nathan Pomeroy. He had laid out the crime scene photographs of Phoebe and Harold next to the ones of the two actors. He read the profiling reports prepared for the FBI and the background reports on Nathan.

"Well, I have to admit that I owe you an apology, Sheriff Chandler."

"Why is that, Detective?"

"Seems like I have misjudged the ability of a small town to handle a case of this magnitude, but you have already handled several, and I think we could learn a thing or two from you guys."

"I'll take that as a real compliment, Stan. We aren't as backwards as you big-city cops think."

"Let me ask you something. You are retired, right? Sold the farm and moved to our beautiful city?"

"Yep, about two years ago. Why?"

"I don't know. It just seems like you still have this Pomeroy business in your gut. Why leave it all before it was finished?"

"It was finished, or so we all thought. He was dead and gone, but then I read about your homicide. He's not dead anymore. He came back, and he's found his way to my backyard again. It is Nathan Pomeroy, Detective. I don't know how, but it is him, and that means you have a big problem."

The detective laughed a nervous laugh and then asked questions about the various investigations. He paid special attention to the facts concerning the Thornton children. The three children had never been found and were still officially listed on police records as missing but presumed dead. Scores of bodies had been exhumed in the acres surrounding the Pomeroy property, but the children had never been found.

"What do you think happened to the Thornton kids?"

"I think we just missed them. There's a lot of rough land up there, some of it swamp and all of it hard to get through. It is a shame that we couldn't bury them with Phoebe and Harold."

"Well, Sheriff, I don't know if your boy Nathan is responsible for the death of Mrs. Helen Sutton—that's the grandmother—or Pamela and Billy Cecil, but there are definite similarities. Hell, the blue waxed thread alone is good enough for me, but I'll have to run it by the captain. Let me fill out a VICAP sheet, and I'm sure the FBI will immediately match my case with the cases in Caulking. I'll need that to help convince my boss, okay?"

"That's good enough for me."

"One more thing, Sheriff. You sure he didn't die in that fire? Hell, you had a skeleton of a white male, same age, same height, and the teeth matched. You had the forensic dentist in Albany verify the match. Maybe you're chasing a ghost."

"There were only five teeth. I never really considered the question before, but what happened to the rest?"

Detective May thought about the question and grimaced. "You think your boy pulled out his own teeth? Now that is sick."

"Nathan is the Devil himself, Detective. Nothing he could do would surprise me anymore."

Stan May was an experienced homicide detective, and he could smell a good case a mile away—this one smelled like a week-old corpse. He also knew how to present the evidence to the bureau captain in the proper format. First thing on his list was to contact the Caulking Sheriff's Department and a close second was contacting the Federal Bureau of Investigation. May's secretary had prepared the ViCAP report from the preliminary notes taken from the original homicide investigation of Helen Sutton and her grandchildren. The report was faxed to save time, and May expected to hear from the feds by the end of the day. There were just too many similar facts to be ignored, like how many weirdos used blue waxed thread to stitch the incision closed after all the guts had been torn from the body?

Detective May spent the rest of the morning listing the facts in the computer, ate lunch at his desk, and finally hit the print button just before five. He calculated that he had roughly forty minutes to spare before the captain headed home. He would have just enough time to give an introductory speech and leave the case file.

"Hey, May, there is something in your mailbox marked urgent. Looks like the Bureau is interested in the Sutton homicide," the duty sergeant informed him.

Stan read the first couple of lines and dialed the number Chandler had left. The phone rang once, and May recognized the growl that answered.

"Chandler here."

"How fast can you get your big butt back over here? I've got an inquiry from the FBI that will interest you."

The meeting with the captain would have to wait. Besides, once the captain had read the report from the Bureau, he would not have to sell the case. May had just enough time to drink a soda and visit the bathroom before Chandler was beating on the door.

"I don't know when the fax arrived, but I do know that you are going to want to read it," advised May. Chandler took the three-page letter and read the fist line. The official advisory from Special Agent Chuck Garabona in Charleston, North Carolina concerned Nathan Pomeroy:

> Please be advised that the skeletal remains submitted by Special Agent Thomas, Albany, Georgia, and received from the Albany Medical Examiner that were believed to have been those of homicide suspect Nathan Pomeroy were not in fact his. Previously, forensic dentist Dr. Charles W. Remington, after examining several molars, stated that the teeth compared against known dental records of the suspect. However, recently, the bones were examined by two independent laboratories with the following results: The bones exhibited evidence of having been exposed to minerals, chemicals, and other foreign particles associated with the soil composition in the immediate area of Caulking, Georgia, for a period exceeding one year. It is believed that the person died approximately one to two years prior to the fire and was buried in the immediate area until exhumed by unknown persons and left in the residence prior to being mostly consumed by said fire. The teeth submitted do not match the cavities available in the upper and lower jaws of the examined skull, and it is not known how or why said teeth were found or left at the scene. The gunshot

wound to the skull was post mortem and believed to have been received just prior to the burning.

The notice continued for an additional two pages, and included excessive carbon-dating evidence and an involved explanation as to why the gunshot wound to the skull was believed to have occurred two years after the victim had died. There was also a reference to other tool marks, specifically evidence of a sharp cutting instrument like a knife, found on two ribs and a vertebra. The cause of death was listed as possible stabbing. Buddy read the fax twice and was dumbfounded. He knew Nathan was alive, that son of a bitch, and that he was here in Miami. Buddy put the fax down on the desk and smiled. It was strange to feel happy about a killer still being alive and slaughtering innocent people, but Buddy was pleased because now he could kill the maniac himself.

"Well, Sheriff Chandler, you were right all along. Your boy is alive and partying here in the Magic City. Where do we go from here?"

"To Hell, Detective May. We have to go to Hell and piss on the Devil."

Chandler called Caulking immediately when he got back home and spoke briefly with a friend who was now second in command. He did not want to talk with the new sheriff, and in fact, he believed that Sheriff Ward had withheld information from the reports Detective May had been receiving. Buddy was also under the impression that attempts by the FBI and people with the Georgia State Police to contact him had been waylaid, for what reasons he could not imagine.

"Listen, Henry, I don't want to sound bitter or pissed, but what the fuck is Ward up to? How come none of your guys ever told me about Nathan and the forensic pathology reports from the FBI?"

"What the hell you jawin' 'bout, Buddy? Sheriff Ward said he explained all of that to you last year and that you told him it was all old news and not to go botherin' you in your retirement with such bullshit."

"Henry, does that sound like me to you? You think I would say or think or do something like that, huh? Would I? Ward never said a word to me. Hell, the last time I talked to the man was when I left Georgia."

"It did sound a little strange, but hell, Buddy, you're retired, and we figured just maybe you were done with all this shit. I know that when it's my time to get gone, the door won't be hittin' me in the ass on the way out, you know? What do you think Ward is trying to pull? This don't smell right, Buddy."

"Don't go makin' a big deal out of nothing, okay? Just do me a favor." Buddy asked his friend to copy the entire Thornton file and to include everything new since he had moved to Florida. He wanted all the reports from the FBI and GBI, and everything from Albany. Chandler would deal with Ward some other time. Right now, he was going after bigger fish.

"And just where do I send all this shit, Buddy?"

Chandler started to give him the address of the Miami Beach Police Department, and then he thought better of it. He wanted an opportunity to study the file before anyone else, and if anything was important, he could make a copy for Detective May. Right now, a steak cooked medium with a couple of glasses of beer sounded good, and the retired Caulking Sheriff headed for his favorite spot for Dinner.

Buddy had developed a fondness for Latin cooking since the move to Miami, and it wasn't very hard to find a good Cuban or Puerto Rican café, or one specializing in another variety of great-tasting Caribbean dishes. The Palomilla steak smothered in thin, crispy French fries over a mound of black beans with white rice was a local favorite. He had taken to running every morning just to keep the rice and beans from pushing his weight to a ton.

The next morning, with dawn hardly a consideration on the horizon, Buddy woke from a fitful dream that fled his mind as he woke. Just shreds and pieces remained like smoke after a fire. He jerked awake, and the sheet stuck to his skin. He listened to muffled screams echoing inside his head. He could not remember the last time he'd had a nightmare, and it took a moment for his heart to stop racing. It was half past five o'clock, and the sky outside was still black, haunting in the predawn stillness. The rustling noise from the hall told him the morning paper had been delivered.

A cup of coffee later, and Buddy was awake and reading the paper on the balcony. He looked at the date and noticed it would be a new year in a few days. Thoughts took him back to Georgia to another holiday eve, and he remembered a beautiful lady, a promise, and a broken heart. Thinking old thoughts and wallowing in old hurts never did anyone any good.

Buddy brought his attention back to the present and noticed the coffee had grown cold. He went to refill the cup and tossed the paper on the countertop. A long, deep sigh escaped from between his lips as he remembered the letter he had written to Roberta after his first month in Miami. The letter had been very long but not long enough, because it had not contained the words "I miss you" or "I forgive you." It had said things like "I still don't understand what you were thinking," "where was your head," and "were you out of your mind?" He cried again from the pain he had felt while writing the letter, and guilt shot through his heart. The sun was turning the sky over the ocean crimson, a promise of a beautiful day painted across the morning, but Chandler never noticed it.

He still missed Roberta greatly, and a deep state of depression overtook him for the moment. He remembered her smile and how she had made him feel. Buddy needed more than just coffee to help with his mood, and he headed toward the bar to find some brandy.

CHAPTER

SEVENTEEN

NATHAN HAD ARRIVED in Miami with enough money to have room and board for a short time, but soon he was broke and hungry, without friends or the slightest idea where he would live or how he would eat. He survived the first few months on the courtesy of strangers, begged rides from truckers and lonely travelers wanting a few hours of talk, and slept most nights under the stars. Once in Miami, he met a horde of homeless people on the street, and they found his southern drawl amusing for a while. The homeless knew a different life, created their own city, their own language, and lived apart from the rest of society.

A ten-dollar street whore named Candy took Nathan to a shelter run by nuns in a Catholic outreach program. Candy was a transvestite, and Nathan found this oddity amusing for a while. The whore wanted to tell him more about life on the street than Nathan cared to know.

"Don't be shy, country boy," she whispered to Nathan one night between their bunks at the shelter. The building was big, designed like a military barracks, and it held three hundred beds. The nuns issued cards to the men and women who accepted their hospitality and endured mass after breakfast. The card had to be stamped each time Nathan stayed at the shelter, and he could only stay three days in a row, but the soup line was available to him every day. He would never go hungry, and with a little help from the good sisters, his soul was always full, too.

"Just let me be," Nathan growled darkly and turned away from his newfound friend. The whore was persistent, and he soon reached the limits of his patience with this person touching him. Nathan stroked the edge of his knife as he masturbated in the bunk. The whore could hear his efforts, grew excited with each stroke, and pleaded with

Nathan to let him help. The conversation he was having with old friends in his mind was being interrupted, and the memories were dissolving into a blend of yesterday.

"Please, country boy, just let me suck you off. It don't make you a fag or anything. I take care of a lot of guys, and they are as straight as they come, with wives and everything."

The hate seethed inside Nathan. He would not find peace if this queer in a woman's dress would not leave him alone. He told the transvestite he was shy and did not want to do it in the barracks where everyone could watch. The whore smiled brightly, blew Nathan a kiss, and told him to follow. He led Nathan outside, holding his hand, and Nathan heard someone say, "Looks like Candy has a new boyfriend."

"Where you takin' me?"

"Just out back to the alley. There won't be anyone watching us in the alley. I use it all the time with my tricks. The sisters never come back here, unless they're the black kind of sister and work on their knees." The whore laughed at his own joke. Candy stepped out the back door with Nathan in tow and carefully assessed their privacy. Yes, siree, there was no one watching, no one playing tricks and spitting cum between the gap of missing teeth.

Nathan watched Candy walk with exaggerated femininity, his steps dainty and his wrist limp. Nathan thought of the pretty boys he had seen back home and tasted the disgust in his dry mouth. The whore existed on animated lust and on the mind-numbing effects of the drugs each act of fellatio purchased.

"You sure there ain't no one back here? I thought I heard somthin' over yonder by that garbage dumpster," Nathan said, trying to get the whore further away from the door.

"There ain't no one here, unless some crackhead is gettin' high. You ever get high, sugar?" the whore asked as Nathan counted their steps.

He would want three more, and he counted quietly to himself. "One, two, three." He smiled. "Yeah, whore, I get high." Nathan cut the transvestite's throat. The whore spurted and gurgled and fell backward. He sprawled onto the ground and tried to scream, but his voice was only a squeak.

Nathan dropped to one knee beside the dying man and kissed him like a lover, slowly and ever so intimately. The whore's eyes went wide with confusion before the dull touch of death half-closed the lids. Nathan reached under the dress and pulled down the black lace panties. He shoved the dress to the man's waist and was puzzled when he could not find a penis. He rolled the dead man onto his stomach and found something that baffled him more. The head of the whore's cock was pulled between the cheeks of his ass, with a thin cord wrapped around his waist. This was an old trick of the trade for transvestites and gave the appearance of a vagina. Nathan laughed before cutting the cord and doing what the dead whore had wanted all along—he cut off the cock before disposing of the body in a trash pile down the street.

The death of a male prostitute brought little attention from anyone other than the other transvestites concerned with safety in the streets. Nathan went on living in the shelter and learning how to survive in such a strange and alien world. He learned a little street Spanish and was starting to understand Creole from a group of Haitians. Miami was a smorgasbord of cultures and lifestyles, a little of something for everyone, a town that could satisfy all tastes and desires. Nathan was a survivor, a loner who stayed away from what passed for the mainstream of street life, and he quickly developed the trust of the nuns at the outreach program.

One sister in particular, Sister Delores, took a personal concern for his welfare, and when a full-time position opened in the maintenance department, Nathan was hired. The job required little beyond a handyman's understanding of construction, and, having lived on his own for so long, Nathan could handle just about anything. The position paid little but gave him a permanent bunk and three meals a day, even on Saturday and Sunday. And it required him to attend daily services at Parish Hall behind the outreach building.

"Nathan," Sister Delores called to him from the kitchen.

"Yes, ma'am, I mean, sister?"

"Delores is fine; we don't have to be so formal. Could you help me move the refrigerator? I think something dropped down the back."

This ploy was becoming commonplace, and Nathan gladly attended to the continuation of the deception. She would find an excuse to touch him, to rub against him, and Nathan could feel the desire racing through her body. The reasons for contact were becoming more frequent, and the attraction was mutual. Nathan was experiencing strange and uncommon emotions for the first time in his life. He wanted to prolong the intimate, private moments they were sharing, and the longing to hold her, to kiss her lips, were creating havoc with his feelings. He wondered where all this would lead. What did this all mean with regard to his continued relations with the sister? He was astonished by the absence of shame or revulsion when he kissed the soft nape of her neck one day.

The conditioned and expected Catholic response to pleasure of any variety, absolute disdain and abhorrence to the carnal, did not prevent Sister Delores from turning gracefully in his arms and returning the kiss longingly on his lips. Her mouth was hungry for his, and she shoved her pelvis tightly against him, rubbing and moaning. The act was not immaculate, and conception was highly likely in the fever of the desire that commanded the young lovers in the church kitchen. Delores deftly took both of his hands in hers and shoved them inside the pockets of her habit. The pockets were unfinished, the lining inside the robe not sewn, and he felt the smooth silkiness of her exposed skin. A heavy sigh and groan announced her pleasure. As Nathan ran his hands higher and found the flesh demanding attention, her groans grew louder. He squeezed Delores's breast and twisted the swollen nipples until she cried out from the pleasure she found in the pain.

Voices from the dining room interrupted the mood, and the sister immediately shoved Nathan away, turning and running out the back door. He was left panting, electrified, and demanding more than three minutes and a good-bye.

"Sister. Sister Delores!" A medley of noise resembling that of irate geese filled with urgency came from a group of other sisters as they suddenly appeared at the entrance to the kitchen. They found Nathan breathing heavily, red faced and trying to hide his obvious arousal behind the counter.

"She ain't here, ladies. Seen her headin' towards the office a spell back," he managed to say and busied himself cleaning the stove. Curious looks were exchanged between the pious faces, a snicker escaped from someone, and a disapproving grunt was immediately issued collectively from the other women.

"Well, young man, you spend your time concentrating on less corporeal concerns and remember you are now in the service of Him, our Lord," the more matronly of the group admonished.

"Yes, ma'am."

The group departed with a rustle of fabric filled with stolid purpose and scorn. Nathan let out a loud sigh after they left and shook his head to clear the cobwebs. He checked in the alley behind the kitchen, the very same alley where Candy had brought Nathan a few weeks earlier, and found the young sister hiding behind the door.

"What's with you?"

"Oh, Nathan, this is terrible. I am so uncertain. This has been a terrible, terrible sin against my sacred oath to the Church!"

"Ain't gonna be nobody knowin'. Don't ya like me?"

Nathan, I adore you, and I want you in a way that I have never felt before, but please understand the situation this puts me in, please." Delores's face contorted into pain and shame as she begged for him to understand.

Nathan didn't have a clue. Oaths and promises, sacred vows, and the concerns for the Church were foreign concepts for him. He only knew the overwhelming demand of instant gratification and was preoccupied with his desire to the point of obliviousness to all other things. Delores pulled back and cowered against the wall as he approached. She tried to look away, to not touch him, but the erection in his pants defeated all her efforts. Perhaps this one time, this one exception. It was what she had wanted for some time now, and what Nathan wanted as well. The Lord does work in mysterious ways, does He not?

The dam holding back that craving, the greed to satisfy basic human needs denied, exploded with a force that surprised them both.

Delores gave in to the passion, surrendered to the need of the body, and abandoned her vow of chastity with no more than a fleeting moment of regret. Nathan had told her a joke. He had told her that once he had a friend who was a nun, but she had decided to leave the calling. Sister Delores had asked why, and he'd responded, "Because she discovered what none meant." Her laughter had been genuine, knowing, and in return, she had told Nathan a story of two spinsters and a cat.

Clever actions and prudent restraints helped camouflage the runaway affair. The vigilant persistence of the sisters to treat Nathan like a disease assisted in maintaining the masquerade that he was nothing more than a servant to the Lord and an unskilled street rat. Sister Delores oversaw the day-to-day routines of the shelter, supervised the day labors, the cooking, the medical staff, and Nathan. His responsibilities grew alongside the increasing demands of attention from his lover.

He was under a spell cast by the dark side of human nature, craving that which most appears illicit and illusive, a demand to risk all by seeking out a moment's seclusion with the forbidden. "This will be just our little secret," he told Delores, but he was actually speaking to the beast within that snarled and howled from the pain of being denied, granted no longer the place of honor, the direct countenance of hunger feeding upon itself. His feelings took wing and soared, but not toward the familiar cacophonous callings of night. Rather, his feelings were now seeking the sweet leitmotif of dawn's early murmur, that resounding beckoning, that lucidity in colors of wine and roses and filled with the scent of lilacs, the essence of a woman brought to the edge of emancipation.

During an early morning stroll several days later, Nathan yawned luxuriously as he stepped to the street from the side door of the shelter. He scratched and stretched, trying to chase the sleep away, and then he heard the unexpected crackle of a police radio. He peeked slyly around the corner and found an unmarked, dull gray car noticeably lacking trim but adorned with numerous radio antennas parked by the front entrance. The occasional presence of a regular squad car was not unusual, considering the class of customers visiting the shelter, but a detective's car was an exception. Nathan decided that a closer inspection of the car and the detectives would be in his best interests.

A casual stroll down the litter-strewn sidewalk brought him within feet of the car. There was nothing special inside, just a police radio, a flashlight, and a bench seat in the back containing two large boxes of files. He wanted to get a look at those files, and he started to check if the doors were locked when a very familiar voice boomed from inside the door.

"Well, ma'am, we just need y'all to look at a photograph of a man, a really bad man that we've been told by a reliable source has been sleepin' in your place."

There was no mistake about that voice. Sheriff Chandler had come to town. Nathan concluded that Chandler was talking with one of the sisters inside the office. The office was less than fifteen feet to the right of the door, which would allow for him to slip by unseen and make his way to the back window.

"We try to cooperate with the police, as I am sure Detective May could verify, but we do have to try and remain neutral, Sheriff Chandler. Understand that we are not an extension of the police department. Our mission is to help, and sometimes in the efforts to do the Lord's work, we have small conflicts with secular law enforcement," Sister Delores told the men sharply and asked if she could see the photograph. A serene expression failed to reveal the shattering effects to her mental composure once she looked into the eyes of her beloved Nathan. There was no mistaking that it was him, and there was no doubt that she would fail to help these officers of the law. Nathan had carefully peered through the lower windowpane and saw his mug sneering back from the eight-by-ten black-and-white glossy Delores held in her hands. Rage and panic shook his confidence that the good sister would not spill the beans. He had to get away quickly and pound his head against the wall in an attempt to remember what there was inside the shelter that could hurt him.

"Damn that pig-headed sheriff! Damn him to mother-fuckin' hell on a broomstick, and that piss-ant Dick he gots workin' for him!" Nathan was screaming to himself, and the words ricocheted back and forth inside his head. He had some money, less than a hundred dollars, hidden in a coffee tin in the kitchen. His knife, a change of clothes, and a few other personal items were inside the mattress in the storage closet. His mind was occupied with a plan to get everything and run, so Nathan did not hear his lovely Delores tell Chandler and May that she had never seen the man here at the shelter.

"Your—what do you call it, a snitch?—he told you that this person was here?" She asked the question straightforwardly, with a sweet, angelic smile. "I do get around a little, Detective," she told Detective May, as if she needed to explain how she had come by the terminology.

"Yes, I guess you do, considering the company you keep," he answered, and the detective looked around at the men sitting on the bunks behind them.

"Like I was saying, your snitch is mistaken, gentlemen. There are a precious few other shelters. Have you checked them?"

Chandler thanked Sister Delores for her time and took back Nathan's photograph with an impolite grunt. The detective handed her a card and asked if she could call if the man in the picture should ever appear. Sister Delores walked them out to the car and stood at the doorway with her professional smile. The sheriff hesitated before climbing into the car. He wanted to search the shelter because there was something not quite right with the sister.

Delores sensed something about the sheriff and thought fast. "Just why do you want to find this man, Nathan?"

"Bingo," Chandler whispered to May, and Stan smiled knowingly.

"What did you say, Sister?" May asked, still smiling.

"I was just curious. What did he do?"

"You called him Nathan. How did you know his name?" Chandler was gearing up for a blitz. He could smell blood in the air.

"I'm sorry, what?"

"Don't play games, sister. You know this bastard, don't you?!"

The face of Sister Delores exploded in color, and fire shot long fingers from her pale blue eyes. "This is the Lord's house, gentlemen. I refuse to allow such language here!"

"Impressive, lady, but I don't care. Where is Nathan?"

Chandler slammed the car door and towered over the small but defiant nun. She did not cower from this massive bulk of a man and firmly held her ground, blocking the entrance to the shelter. May was apprehensive and waited by the car.

"Listen, you big bully, someone wrote the name Nathan Pomeroy and a date, a birth date I assume, on the back of the photograph," she said in an even, angry voice just before shoving the shocked Sheriff Chandler backward from the door.

"Is that right, Stan?" Chandler asked without turning to look at the detective. Silence. The sheriff figured it was time to leave, but he would be back.

There were no more words exchanged, and Chandler crawled into the passenger side of the car. May desperately tried not to laugh and avoided looking at the burning expression of the retired Georgia sheriff. He watched Sister Delores disappear inside the shelter and slam the door. "Shit, this is gonna be a problem," he told himself and started to snicker.

"What's so damn funny, May? That broad knows something!"

"Yeah, she knows how you boys operate back home, and she sure as shit knows the phone number to internal affairs."

Nathan heard the spin of tires and let go a heavy sigh of relief. He had the money in his pocket and was pulling the clothes from the mattress when Delores called his name.

"I'm out back, just cleanin' up the storage room a little."

The sister appeared at the door, and a mournful look saddened her regularly bright and cheerful eyes. Nathan smiled weakly and shrugged. "What's the matter with you?"

"We had visitors, Nathan. The police were here looking for you. Why?"

"The police? How should I know. Did you tell them I was here?"

"No, we don't always cooperate with law enforcement. We want this shelter to be a sanctuary, not a jail. The Lord often hid from the oppressors, was considered an outlaw, a common criminal by many."

"I ain't Christ, sister, and I ain't runnin' from the law."

"Okay, that's fine. Do you know a Sheriff Chandler?"

Nathan hesitated, wondering how far he should push this charade. The lady was not stupid and already knew the answers to most questions before she asked. He decided on a different tack, one Delores would most probably accept.

"Okay, don't go worryin' your pretty head. I know Buddy. He was the sheriff from back home. Yeah, I lied. He's lookin' for me, but I thought he'd retired or somethin'."

"Why?"

"Why what?"

Delores smiled, the tears dancing at the corner of her eyes. She reached out and took Nathan by the hand, pulling him into her arms and saying, "Look, I am not judging you. That is for the Lord to do, but please don't play me for a fool. I don't care what happened before in your life. The Lord forgives you, and I forgive you. Let's just start fresh, okay?"

Nathan was astonished. *It is as easy as that, huh? This lady is as dumb as a mule. Hell,* he thought, *get her pussy wet and the brain shuts down. Yes, siree!*

How painfully eager he was to share his past with her, but black thoughts crept up on him, and he saw Buddy bearing down on him from a tunnel of bright white light. He was not going to be safe here. He was not going to be safe anywhere as long as that damn sheriff was roaming the city. Nathan told himself that he would have to do something about Buddy Chandler, and he returned the kiss to Delores's lips.

The old ways were working their magic on Nathan again, and he found himself waking in the middle of the night with the sounds of the past screaming in his ears. The palms of his hands were moist, and there was a tickle starting in the pit of his stomach. The urge was irresistible, and to ignore the demand was painful. Nathan stroked the blade of his knife. He wondered out loud how Chandler had tracked him to Miami, to this shelter. Someone across the room yelled for him to shut up, and Nathan hissed, "Try to stop me, asshole." A walk in the cool night air would calm him, and Nathan strapped the sheath tightly to his waist, adjusted the handle of the blade to the small of his back. He smiled when he stood and felt the rigid resistance between the cheeks of his ass. Memories. It was time to go a-visitin', to be neighborly.

It had been six weeks since he had visited the grandma and those bratty kids. He knew the urge was coming, "like a bitch waiting on her period," he would tease himself. The time had come, triggered by forces only Nathan understood, and he set off in search of satisfaction. Pangs of hunger shot through his stomach. The voices were calling again, and again the itch that could not be scratched tingled irritably across his skin. The problem was that he did not have a plan, only a terrible hunger, and the shelter was built in the middle of an industrial neighborhood. There were a few derelicts and old bag ladies who liked to sleep in the open with the rats. He followed the drifting smell of a cigarette, and before too, long he heard a hoarse cough.

Nathan found the old woman straddling a plastic trash can, relieving herself with intense concentration. She never heard him step through the piles of garbage she called Treasure Island, her home in the street. He punched her hard in the back of the head and sent the woman sprawling to the ground. A stream of yellow piss continued to flow from between her legs as Nathan grabbed the woman away from the light and into the cover of shadows. Her wrists and ankles were bound with tape, spreading her apart, and he shoved a wad of paper between her jaws.

The old woman came around as Nathan finished cutting the filthy rags from her fat, grimy body. Her eyes were not focusing, but her brain knew she was in a world of trouble. The scream caught in her throat, and the force bulged her cheeks. Life on the street had always been hard on this Russian woman, and a score of times, she had been raped, but never before had anyone gone to such extremes. Nathan giggled, danced, and beat her until she had stopped struggling against the bonds. The old fat woman did not really exist for him, and her appearance and smell did nothing to excite or repulse his unnatural passions. The helplessness fueled the yearning, and the terror he knew she was experiencing ignited his lust. Soon, Nathan was soaring in exhilaration. She was being raped again, an act of violence the old woman recognized, anticipated, and she almost felt relieved that it was happening because the humiliation would be over soon.

She fought hard against the attack, but the tape held her tightly to the fence. Finally, the man stopped, exhausted and, she hoped, satisfied. She wondered how she would get free and hoped the bastard would cut the bindings. The twinkling of light from the edge of the blade gave her false hope, and an unbearable pain soon followed. Nathan rammed the knife to the hilt up her vagina, giggled, and slid the blade in and out, slicing the tender flesh. He took time collecting souvenirs, wondered if he should send one to Chandler in a passing moment of lucidity before rolling the fat woman to her side. The contents of her stomach were dumped on the street.

A city worker would find the remains of the naked Russian woman the following day, and because of the proximity of the shelter, Chandler and May came back to visit Sister Delores. They brought her photographs of the crime scene, hoping the shock would bring out the truth, but the nun stared at the harsh reality of death before. She remained stoic, unruffled by the blood and guts, and tossed the folder containing the color blowups into the sheriff's lap.

"Poor woman. I will pray for her soul," she told the policeman.

"You may have been able to save her life. Nathan has her soul," shot back Chandler.

"Sheriff, I respect your work, your determination, and your somewhat off-center sincerity, but don't waste your time with your tough-guy routine. I've seen a lot worse. Man can be terribly cruel, to the point that I have often questioned God's wisdom, but why do you think I know anything that could have helped that poor woman?"

"You are protecting the animal that did that. You are harboring Nathan Pomeroy in the Lord's house, and because of this, you are not only committing a terrible crime but a sin."

The face of the woman remained impassive, and neither of the men could detect whether they were getting close to forcing her to talk. Sister Delores smiled slightly, fingered the silver crucifix hanging from around her neck, and stared at the door.

"Who is going to pray for your soul, sister?" Sheriff Chandler asked with disdain.

"Why do you think this Nathan Pomeroy killed this woman?" the sister asked, running the tips of her fingers across the frozen display in the photograph.

Chandler had a glimmer of hope and looked sideways at May, wondering if he should let the detective take the lead. May hesitated, and the sheriff took the opportunity to further press Delores.

"Because there is something called an MO. Are you familiar with the term, sister?"

"Yes, I watch the television, Sheriff. Please continue."

"Nathan has killed at least three dozen men, women, and children. He has a preference for little girls, a practiced ritual, and he likes to use a knife. He cuts his victims open, as you can see from this photograph, rips out everything through the hole, dumps his own feces inside, and sews the opening shut with a rough blue thread."

The pause extended for several minutes. The sister looked hard at Sheriff Chandler and the rest of the photographs he dropped on top of the desk. Delores licked her lips nervously, her composure beginning to crack as the horror began to splinter her hard cover of control. She questioned her feelings, sought guidance from her beliefs, and felt like fleeing from the room. Could this possibly be true? *Dear God, have I made a terrible mistake? Sweet Jesus, forgive me,* she said to herself and stood suddenly, surprising Chandler. She told them, "You'll have to excuse me. I don't feel well."

Sister Delores was struggling hard with all the things she was feeling inside. She could not breathe in the closeness of the room. She had to escape, to run and hide. She had to find Nathan and confront him with her fears, to beg him to tell her it was not true.

"Sister, we have to stop him. You cannot protect this man any longer," Detective May told her, and Delores could not look at his face.

"I know," she whispered, and collapsed to the floor.

Nathan had not come back to the shelter. He had collected all his belongings and slept in an alley behind a closed building. The sirens had attracted the attention of everyone within blocks. A handful of bored uniform cops took turns chasing away the curious, and the body of the fat Russian woman remained under a yellow plastic sheet while her murder was documented for the record as another statistic.

Homicide detectives matched notes from the Sutton and Cecil killings with the most recent. A third report was tossed into the investigation as possibly connected, a transvestite named Jorge Diaz, known as Candy on the street. Diaz had been killed with a knife, and there was evidence of sexual assault—the penis had been severed and was missing from the crime scene. The victim's throat had been cut and the stomach cavity had been sliced open, but nothing had been removed or added as in these other cases. It was not uncommon for an unsuspecting customer to become so repulsed that extreme acts of violence soon followed the discovery that the prostitute was a man. Initially, the homicide had been thrown into the pot of unsolvable murders involving victim's no one cared about or would miss.

The Russian vagrant, Nina Solowoski, would have been forgotten the moment her body left the morgue had she not been tragically connected forever with the late Helen Sutton, a rich and powerful woman. No one would give a second thought about a dead street dweller; she was just road kill. But this time it was different. The deaths were identical, and the only common factor in their lives was Nathan. Because of him, the poor vagrant would be front-page news right along with the rich and famous.

"What a combination," one detective remarked. "A blue blood, a bag lady, and a fag whore!"

"Yeah, guess that proves one thing—death does not discriminate," added another.

"Ain't you the philosophical one."

"Yeah, bet you can't spell that."

Nathan had sat across the street and watched the arrival of Sheriff Chandler from a vantage point on the fifth floor of an abandoned office building. Detective May had been driving, and he'd pulled the same dull gray police vehicle to the curb by the front entrance. A collection of men and women lingering around the door waiting for lunch parted to allow the men to pass. Nathan was furious because Chandler was spoiling all his fun, interfering with his life, and ruining his chances with Delores. He had wanted to make a go at real life. Delores had been his only chance at salvation. She was the road to the future and the destruction of the past. He wondered if the good sister would break this time. She must know that he had left the shelter, that all his things were gone. Nathan would have been missed at breakfast.

"Oh well, it was fun, but all good things gotta end," he whispered to the memories floating through the dust around the sill of the broken window.

Sister Delores fainted gracefully to the floor at the feet of Detective May. Chandler snorted impatiently and glared down at the woman. Buddy had little time for histrionics. He could smell Nathan on this woman, the odor of evil reeking from her womb. Delores moaned and opened her eyes only to see Stan May and Buddy Chandler. They did not look concerned for her welfare, and she prayed that divine intervention was not too much to ask.

"Sister, get off the floor and let's talk about your friend," the sheriff told her with a harsh chortle.

She explained everything straightforwardly, embarrassing May and producing only a sneer from Chandler. The only fact that disturbed the sheriff was that they were too late. Nathan had fled two days ago, and he had been within their grasp. Sister Delores would have to live with herself, with the sin not of the flesh, which was guilt for mere human weakness, but with the knowledge that she could have prevented the death of another person. Nina Solowoski would still be wandering the alleys of downtown Miami, ignorant, blissful, and very much alive had Delores confessed just a few days earlier.

Buddy wanted to arrest the nun for harboring a fugitive, interfering with a police investigation, and culpable negligence for being an accessory to the Russian woman's murder. May calmed him down, however, explaining that Sister Delores was not going anywhere and that he would present the facts to the state attorney for consideration of any further action against her. They could always come back with an arrest warrant. Tears streaked Delores' face, and the sister wondered how she could reclaim her immortal soul.

Across the street, another lost soul was thinking how wonderful it would be to kill Sheriff Chandler. "Think I'll take his fat monkey boy, too! Yes, siree!"

Detective May used the telephone in the office of the shelter to report that Nathan Pomeroy was at large and that he may still be in the area. Thousands of fliers were distributed to local agencies with the suspect's picture and vital statistics. He was listed as armed, extremely dangerous, and psychotic. Officers were cautioned not to try to apprehend Nathan by themselves. This was a second massive manhunt for the benefit of one man, and Chandler had his doubts that just the use of more manpower was going to be the solution to finally flushing the toilet on this piece of shit. Little did Buddy know that the reason for all the concern was less than a hundred yards away, that if he had only looked up, he would have seen the face of Nathan looking down at him.

"If he's still in Miami, we'll have his ass by daybreak," bragged a confident Stan May as he opened the driver's door of the car.

"I doubt it, May, and I ain't knockin' you big-city boys. It's just that this ain't no ordinary man," corrected Chandler.

"He's just one man, one sick puppy, and I'll see that he burns in the chair."

"You can't burn the Devil, Stanley—you can only lock him away. The boy is gonna plead insanity, spend some time in a nice little hospital for a while, and that's 'bout it."

"Maybe. I guess you can't burn the Devil, that was pretty good, but he ain't bulletproof," answered the detective with a wide grin.

Buddy invited the detective to dinner, and May accepted without hesitation. They drove to one of the largest and oldest Latin restaurants on the Beach. The owners were from San Juan, Puerto Rico, and it was strictly a family-run business. They served a variety of main courses, all authentic and delicious. Buddy had been coming to La Puerta Sague for more than a year and had never had a bad meal.

"You ever eat here before, Stan? If not, you're in for a treat, ol' son." Buddy smiled and enjoyed introducing the detective to his favorite restaurant. He greeted one of the owners by name, received an emotional hello, and was seated at the only table in the house that afforded some privacy.

"I guess you eat here often, or else you leave one hell of a tip," jested May, and Buddy just grinned.

This social side of the sheriff surprised the detective, and he enjoyed watching Buddy laugh and exchange jokes with the waiter. Most of the other customers seemed to know Chandler. May knew he could relax here. The atmosphere of the place was almost like being at home among friends and family.

"You know, I often wondered if you had a life. You always seem so serious and absorbed. It's good to know there is another side of you, Buddy."

"You would be shocked to know that I have always gone out of my way to separate my professional life from my private one. It's real important not to take bein' a cop too serious, Stan. Remember that. Just don't take yourself too serious, okay?"

May had to laugh at this bit of sage advice, especially coming from this man, someone who always reminded him of John Wayne or a gun-slinging marshal in a bad Old West movie. He guessed he would never be too old to learn something new or too proud to admit he had been wrong. "So, what else have I misjudged about you, Sheriff?"

Buddy studied the face of Stan May for a moment and slowly smiled. "What would you like to know detective? That I wear ladies' underwear or live a secret life making obscene phone calls to lonely old ladies?"

"The old-ladies part maybe." He laughed. "But seriously, you have me intrigued. Do you have a special lady hiding somewhere?"

Buddy stopped smiling, and May figured he had made a mistake. "Yes, I do, as a matter of fact, a very special lady that I met the first day I came down to this God-forsaken part of the world. Y'all have really gone out of your way to fuck up a good thing, you know that? This could be a really great city, perfect weather and beautiful beaches, but the place is filled with the most arrogant, stuck-up bunch of assholes in the world."

It was May's turn to smile. He took no offense, and, in fact, he agreed with the big man and told him so. They were interrupted with plates filled with aromatic specialties, and both men spent the next hour shoving food in their faces. The conversation was light, humorous, and their professional relationship took a swinging turn toward friendship.

"You never told me about your lady," May said when the plates were cleared away and a fat woman, introduced by Buddy as the wife of one of the brothers who owned La Puerto Sague, brought two little cups of steaming coffee and a plate of sweet meat pies for dessert.

"Nicole Hughes, the real estate broker that helped me buy my place. She and her daughter, Sharon, live just over the bay in Miami. She is very pretty, bright, and a tough woman making it in a tough business," Buddy bragged, and May could tell that the poor boy was in love.

"How does that country song go, sounds like love's got a hold of you."

"Oh yeah, I just hope she will accept a fat old has-been like me," Buddy said with a look of concern.

"She'd be a fool not to. Don't be so hard on yourself, Sheriff. The lady should consider herself lucky."

Buddy looked shocked, and Stan May laughed. They spent the rest of the night into the early-morning hours talking, drinking Mexican beer, and telling lies. It was a great evening filled with good times, the type of evening that made good memories and good friends.

Nathan had spent the rest of his day making plans. He waited until after the meal was served at the shelter before trying to sneak back inside the office. He had wanted to use the phone, make a few inquiries about one Sheriff Buddy Chandler, and he would try to talk with Delores. Good-byes were so hard on the telephone, and he would much rather have things up close and personal. The good sister had almost saved his soul, or at least had given it a nice vacation, and she deserved something much better for being so good to him. Nathan smiled as he slipped the lock on the window by the alley.

It did not take him long to call the Miami Beach Police Department and find the answer to a couple of pressing questions. He had asked the duty officer who was working the bag-lady homicide, advising that he had important information and would talk only with the person in charge. The officer was very helpful and gave Nathan the name of three detectives who would be interested in speaking with him. Next, Nathan wanted to know the names of the two officers who had been to the shelter asking questions. The officer looked at a message taped on the bullet-resistant glass in front of him. The message advised that anyone with information on a subject named Nathan Pomeroy should contact Detective Stanley May. The officer was quick to transfer the call to Homicide and, in the event that Detective May was not available, gave Nathan two beeper numbers. The second beeper belonged to Buddy Chandler, and it did not take Nathan long to determine which number he should call.

Nathan was about to leave the shelter without confronting Delores, but he could not resist the urge to say good-bye. A few minutes later, he walked inside the rectory, a converted house purchased by the arch-diocese and utilized by the priest. The Sisters of Mercy had the use of an office, little more than a storage room, near the front entrance. He did not bother to knock on the door and found no one in the building after conducting a room-by-room search. He decided to leave a note and pissed all over the desk.

No more than an hour later, Nathan found a strung-out whore, nicknamed Bullets for obvious reasons, who beeped Chandler for him. He paid the woman twenty bucks to tell the sheriff that she had information about the killing of the Russian vagrant. Buddy told her that he would meet her by a convenience store only a few blocks away in ten minutes. Nathan giggled, gave the prostitute the money, and quickly shoved the knife under the left side of her ribs. He pushed the blade upward and cleaved her heart in one quick motion. Nathan plucked the money from the dying woman's hand and hurried to keep the meeting with Sheriff Chandler.

A peculiar thing followed as Nathan jogged down the street. The world slid askew, and the sounds of the city collided with the voices of colors whispering quietly in this decaying section of the metropolis. Vertigo grabbed him by the back of the head and slammed the concrete sidewalk into his face. The taste of blood filled his mouth, and the world went black. The memories were laughing at the sport of it all, running free and wild through the last bits of awareness as they flowed into the violent embrace of a seizure. He had never before experienced a collapse like this, and although his faculties had raced out of control, Nathan still maintained some measure of understanding. Paralysis gripped his limbs, his body was numb, and his eyes reacted to light with burning torment. His skin tingled with an odd sensation, and his brutal headache felt like a dull file was being dragged across the inside of his skull. He could hear odors, smell the roar of noise, and taste the colors ripping through the center of his eyes.

Buddy Chandler arrived at the corner and barely took notice of the drunk sprawled across the sidewalk next to the car.

The world was slowing down, returning to normal, and feeling slowly bled back into Nathan's body.

Buddy waited ten minutes before chastising himself for chasing desperation down a blind alley.

The man Buddy had thought was a drunk propped himself up on one elbow and turned in time to see the sheriff drive away. Nathan screamed and dragged himself from the street, but the opportunity had been missed. The quarry had flown.

Chandler returned to the police station and wasted thirty minutes waiting for May to return. The detective had driven to the shelter to acquire a formal taped statement from Sister Delores. Once the statement was transcribed and an official report documented the evidence, May would present everything to the state attorney. He knew he faced nearly impossible odds of convincing a very politically motivated chief prosecutor to issue an arrest warrant for a nun, but he would try.

Buddy had decided to call it a day and headed for the elevators when his beeper sounded. The number was unfamiliar, and Buddy hesitated, then started to walk out the door but changed his mind.

The phone rang a dozen times before a voice announced, "Three-forty four and all is well," and a giggle sounded.

The laughter was interrupted when Buddy managed to say, "Hello, who the hell is this?"

This was luck. Nathan recognized the booming baritone voice, and if everything was as it should be, the owner of the voice would most certainly recognize his as well. Hesitation, fear to approach the end of the road, of this road at least, crept into the center of his mind. The moment of destiny had arrived like a child on the first day of school. Yes, summer was over and it was now the beginning of autumn. The Indians believed a man's soul started dying in the fall, readying itself for a final departure when winter's glare turned to face the sun with a silent, frozen indifference.

"Hello yourself, Sheriff Chandler. How are they hangin'?"

It could not be. There was no way it could be. The bastard couldn't have the balls to call him directly. Thick black blood oozed from the edges of old wounds when he recognized the voice, and Buddy found himself breathless. He wanted to throw the telephone away like it was some dangerous, sinister thing. His mind snatched at incoherent thoughts, attempting to apply meaning to the confusion, while cold fingers squeezed the life from his panicked heart.

"Nathan?"

"Ain't nothin' to be fearin'. Death ain't real. Nothin's real, Buddy. I've been meanin' to see ya. Wouldn't wantcha to get bored."

"Where are you, Nathan?" Chandler asked, and he listened to the deranged laughter screeching above the rushing noise of his mind as he tried to get everything under control.

"Oh, I'm close, Buddy, real close. Just take a look out them big ol' windows and see me wavin' at ya."

Chandler threw the phone down and raced to the other side of the room. He searched the street below and found Nathan. The man was waving like a fool, laughing and jumping around. He motioned for Buddy to come down and settled on the curb by the side of the road to wait. There was no hesitation as the sheriff raced from the room like flames were licking at his heels. The three other detectives in the room were absorbed in a heated discussion and took no notice of him.

By the time the sheriff made it to the street, Nathan was gone, and a search of the side streets proved futile. Buddy was angry, and he screamed in frustration amidst the sounds of the city. Maybe he was crazy, he thought. Just maybe the events of the past ten minutes had never occurred; he was not going to tell a soul. The beeper sounded again, the same number the informant had used the first time. The sheriff raced to the pay phone and punched in the number. When the line was engaged, he snarled Nathan's name.

"Yeah, boss, it's me. You be knowin' where I'll be. Catch me if you can, you dumb son of a bitch!"

"Where, Nathan! Where are you goin' to be?"

"You really are dumb, ain'cha? Think I'll be vistin' my girly friend. Got to admit, she ain't as pretty as Becky-Ann, but the bitch gives better head." And then the phone was dropped with an open line.

Buddy listened to the silence and could have sworn he heard something faint in the background above the ethereal hiss. There it was again, and he heard it plain the second time, along with another giggle.

There was no time for a second telephone call. Besides, he did not need help killing a rabid dog like Nathan. He thought about Nicole and shook his head in sorrow that Nathan would probably ruin this relationship also. Racing back to the garage, he thought, "*May said it right the other day. The boy ain't bulletproof,*" and yanked open the car door with keys already in hand. A squeal of tires and the smell of burning rubber filled the air. This time, there was to be no doubt. The world would contain one less piece of shit.

May had already rewound the cassette tapes, snapped that little piece of plastic on the side to avoid accidental erasure, and written the case number on the first side before Buddy had talked with Nathan. The detective had said good-bye to Sister Delores, a shattered and humbled woman, and was accelerating down the avenue as Nathan entered the building across from the shelter.

Nathan barely had time to climb the stairs to the fifth floor and look down the street as a car jumped the curb below the window. Nathan waited until the driver disengaged himself from the seatbelt and kicked the door open. "Hey, Buddy boy, up here," he yelled down.

Disoriented and unable to determine the location of the voice for a second, the sheriff drew a dark revolver from the small of his back. His head whipped back and forth as he tried hard to find Nathan and slipped further out of control.

"Up here, you dumb shit. Look straight up," Nathan taunted. "Hell, I could piss on ya."

Chandler's head snapped up, and he stared into the dead eyes of a dead man. There was no need for words. The bitter end was racing hell-bent for the finish line, and Buddy disappeared into the building. Nathan laughed softly and felt saddened by the moment. Thoughts of something that almost resembled regret dragged through the quagmire of his soul. It caused him to realize that this was truly the end of a long and beautiful relationship. The sound of footsteps crashing up a floor below announced the arrival of the sheriff, and Nathan told himself it was time to finish the game.

Buddy exploded through the door. There was no time to rest. His heart was straining to pump blood fast enough through his huge body, his lungs burning, starving for air. It was like looking down a tunnel; the world was round, black along the edges, and stretching far away into a kaleidoscope of colors. He was losing it. Despite recent efforts to get in shape, genetics and a lifetime of eating southern fried food had decided what was healthy and what was a waste of time. Everything was turning soft and gray. His heart was a sledgehammer slamming in his chest, and he never felt the sharp edge drag across his throat. Sheriff Chandler was dead before the skin was cut. A massive heart attack stole

Nathan's glory, and only a slow trickle of blood stained the top of the sheriff's shirt collar.

Buddy had escaped this world of pain and misery, cheating Nathan from enjoying the final victory of the game, and quietly stepped into the lair of eternal slumber. A serene expression was his death mask, and long before the weight of his earthbound body pinned Nathan to the floor, the sheriff felt the loving squeeze of a small hand in his. His eyes grew bright with emotion, and for the first time in a long time, he held Becky-Ann in a smothering embrace. Father and daughter were united forever, and neither of them looked back as they headed for eternity.

Nathan cussed and struggled under the weight. He knew he had been cheated and everything had gone wrong. He pulled himself from under the dead sheriff and crawled to the far side of the room.

"You fucking bastard!" The words echoed through the deserted offices. "You ain't got no right dyin' on me. I had ya! I had ya good!"

Across the street, Sister Delores' eyes drifted toward the front door. She searched up the front of the building on the other side. What was it she had heard? Something had distracted her—a voice, maybe, a cry for help. She did not know, and after a few moments, she returned her attention to prayer. It was time to talk with Father Menendez. It was time for her to offer a complete confession to Christ and Church. The walk to the rectory was short in distance, but to Delores, it seemed a long and arduous path.

Nathan's astonishment abated. After all, it was not important who or what had killed Chandler—the deed was done and he was free. He pushed himself up the wall and staggered drunkenly to the body. The spit bubbled around Nathan's lips as drool dripped from the corner of his mouth, his eyes bright but unfocused, his giggling uncontrollable. He screamed again at the body, "You ain't gonna be fuckin' with me no mo', Sheriff! No mo,' no mo'!"

Three hours later, Nathan had finished dragging the remains of Sheriff Chandler down the stairs and had stored the body in an empty grease pit in the alley. The bin was to have been removed when the restaurant that had occupied the first floor of the building closed, but the Department of Building and Zoning had made a mistake and the records reflected that the bin was not there. Nathan had no way of knowing the plans of the Department of Building and Zoning, he was just lucky that way. He laughed as the lid was resealed and no one from the road crew had bothered to check what might be hidden inside the old grease pit. There was very little blood because the heart had stopped beating before Nathan had sliced open the neck. A fire on the fifth floor would nicely conceal any evidence of the murder, and Nathan was blocks away before the emergency call was received.

Activists demanding that city authorities do something to stimulate the growth of the downtown area took full advantage of the story in the paper detailing how careless vagrants cooking dinner had gutted one of a dozen closed buildings. The fire had swept through the top three floors, and trash in the stairwell had prevented fire fighters from reaching the blaze until the roof had collapsed. No one noticed the blood smears, the drag marks, and all the other evidence that could have brought the attention of the police to the building. It all disappeared in a matter of minutes. The fire department dumped hundreds of gallons of water through open windows, and dozens of men ran up and down the stairs. Ash, smoke, and mud erased any traces of the killing.

Father Menendez bowed his head on the other side of the confessional screen. He recognized the voice and knew who was pouring her heart out just inches away with sobs of anguish. The distress of the father mounted with each word of the confession. He had sat through thousands of stories of personal tragedy, real or imagined, listened with professional patience, but his years of experience failed to comfort him in his own moment of deep sorrow. Who would listen to his confession, he thought. Who would be able to comfort him as he was expected to comfort the young nun questioning her beliefs at this moment? He wondered if Christ Himself would be able to sit here as he was expected to do and not question the wisdom of the Father.

Nathan lounged in the comfort of a discarded couch left on the sidewalk. He felt the king of all he surveyed. He had met the enemy and triumphed. Victory was his to savor. The sun would be setting soon, and darkness would come with a special invitation not to rest but to invigorate the soul. This was the time to hunt, to prowl the far corners of the city and feed the hunger spreading from the pit of his stomach. The voices were calling, the past beckoning, and old friends looking for new company, and Nathan would not disappoint them. He watched the last fire engine turn the corner and the police officer placing barricades on the street. He decided it was time for him to find something else for the civil-servant assholes to do—obviously, the work here was done.

CHAPTER

EIGHTEEN

ROBERTA AUSTIN STARED blurry-eyed at the computer screen, dreaming of a short soak in a hot tub before a long night of peaceful dreams. She knew the bath and long night were definite, but the peaceful dreams were something not easily managed. The recurring nightmare was brutal, relentless, and guaranteed to make every attempt to sleep a futile endeavor. Hitting the off switch with the tip of a polished nail, she decided to call it a night, but as the office went dark before the door closed, the telephone rang.

"Hello, Austin here, and this had better be important," she announced, too tired to even be polite.

"Ms. Austin, this is Detective May from the Miami Beach Police Department. Sorry to be calling so late, but I have some important information and some questions. I need your help."

"Go ahead, Detective. With an opening line like that, you have my undivided attention. What can I do for the Miami Beach Police Department?"

"I believe you know Sheriff Buddy Chandler. He retired from Caulking about two years ago and moved to Miami?" He stated this as a question. Stan was not certain what the relationship was between the sheriff and Roberta Austin, but he understood that Caulking was rather small and most everyone knew everyone else.

"Of course I know Buddy Chandler, but we really have not spoken in a while. I'm sure he told you that we parted on bad terms," Roberta offered.

"No, Buddy and I kept most of our conversations geared towards professional discussions," May lied, getting the feeling that he had stepped into deep waters.

"I think you're lying, and I hope it's for a good reason. What's this all about?"

"Buddy is missing, and I think something is terribly wrong. Have you heard from him, or do you know any family members that he would stay in touch with?" Detective May explained that Buddy had not been seen for several days, that there had been no answer at the condo and no message at the department. Chandler was not returning any of the beeps either. This was unusual, May explained. Buddy had been spending so much time at the Homicide Bureau that the duty sergeant had assigned the sheriff a desk.

The more the Miami detective explained, the more worried Roberta was becoming. It was not like Buddy to disappear. May went on to explain about the new developments on the Nathan Pomeroy case. Roberta knew more about the case than she realized, but she explained it away in her mind, realizing that she must have heard it on the news. Her concern for Buddy was genuine, and she knew that Buddy took the business of law enforcement very seriously, especially Nathan Pomeroy. "Yeah, Detective, I agree that this is unusual. For Buddy to stop looking for Nathan, he would have to be dead and gone..." Roberta stopped talking in the middle of her sentence and wondered to herself, "*Why did I say he had to be dead and gone?*" A terrible pang of guilt and dread coursed through her heart. She heard May talking far away, the voice barely registering in her mind. He was asking a question.

"What did you say, Detective?" I'm sorry."

"I was asking if Buddy had any family. Perhaps he needed a vacation and went to visit someone."

Roberta had to check the records, but just maybe this was the time of year when Becky-Ann had been murdered. People most often went to visit the gravesite of a loved one on the anniversary of the loved one's death. She had never known that much about Becky-Ann's mother— Buddy had never really talked about her. There was so much that Roberta did not know about her beloved sheriff, but she did know that she still loved him and always would. Tears burned her eyes as the thought arose that she might never have a second chance with him.

Roberta had nothing of importance to offer the Miami detective, and she felt like apologizing for not being of much help. She and Buddy had not talked in two years, not since the misunderstanding with the trial and Henderson. Roberta had honored Buddy's wishes to not open old wounds and had let time pass without contact. Now with him missing, however, she regretted that decision. She informed Detective May that she would check out a few possible contacts that Buddy might still have in Caulking and would get back to him. She also told May to call her night or day with any news, told him that Buddy was still very important to her. With polite good-byes, the two hung up the telephone.

Roberta went home and thought of Buddy and the lost relationship that she so desperately wanted to recapture. She thought of Nathan Pomeroy and how he had brought Buddy and her together and then ultimately ripped them apart. Her mind played with thoughts of love and revenge. Nathan was still alive. She had heard the rumors but never thought to look into the gossip to see how much truth was in the stories.

Roberta's phone rang and she answered on the second ring, and said hello. A silent gulf filled with tension answered her, and the air drained from the room, leaving Roberta in a vacuum and gasping for a breath. She could not slam down the phone. She could not move and knew that he was on the other end of the line. She pleaded with her mind to let her wake from this recurring nightmare, to allow it to end and fade like all the others, only this nightmare was real, and she was awake and holding the phone to her ear.

"We are of the same blood, you and I." The words cleaved the distance between them in two, and suddenly, she was suffocating as if he were inches away. She felt the outer edges of her soul stretching, feeling, connecting, and emerging with something foul. A burning sensation dripped along her bare skin, and Roberta felt more than just naked. Nakedness was merely exposed skin, but what she felt was the very center of her being stripped bare.

"What are you saying? How did you get my number?"

"Think about it, Ricky-Lou, gettin' yerself clean of all that stuff messin' "round in your head. Get it clear. We ain't no different, and that's your problem, 'cause you know it's true. You've felt those little black feet crawlin' round, got all tingly and wet when the voices start whisperin' late at night. Tell me I ain't wrong—"

The world went black and the telephone disconnected. Roberta slipped into unconsciousness and slumped to the floor, but not before a torrent of memories flooded her mind. Hundreds of miles away, the giggling was uncontrollable.

Nathan had called her Ricky-Lou. Why did that sound so familiar, and why did the sound chafe against her like sandpaper? Dark images flowed in and out of focus, and voices screamed from the past. And why did she remember the clicky-clack of a train? A ride to where? Who were those people chasing the train, some able to keep the pace and others still who ran faster, jumping in front and being crushed by the wheels? Names were being called from the mouths of the dying, but she could not understand the language.

Roberta slept until dawn, and as the hint of a new day's arrival stained the horizon in shades of pale yellow, she dragged her stiff and cold body from the floor. Minutes passed, and the effect of a fitful sleep left her confused. The phone was lying next to her, unhooked, and she looked at it with puzzlement. Then the conversation came back with a roar. The remembered sound of Nathan's voice cut her like a knife, and she wept, surrendering to hopelessness. A dull pain pulsed in her head, and the world around her was as silent as peeling paint. Voices started to whisper like the tittering insects hiding in the corners of the room. They called out to Ricky-Lou, and Roberta asked aloud, "Who the hell is this Ricky-Lou?" Why couldn't she remember anything? Obviously, she had blacked out for a while and then sleep had given her time to forget.

She knew she had to pull herself together, and she ran to the shower, leaving a trail of rumpled clothes down the hall. The cold water stung her skin but revitalized the senses, and after a brisk rub with the towel, Roberta felt ready for a second chance to tackle Nathan. A direct course of action had slammed all efforts against a brick wall.

Detective May had not been helpful. The man was full of pretentious bullshit, and she could not understand how Buddy could have befriended the man. A short two hours and a dozen telephone calls later, Roberta had a pile of luggage at the door and was ready for a trip to the Magic City—Miami, Florida.

The flight down was uneventful, even though Roberta was more than a little nervous about flying over the ocean, and the Boeing 737 touched down on time. She had never been to Miami before, and the first impression left Roberta feeling that she had left the United States. The first police officer she asked if she had to have a passport to enter Miami found small humor in the joke. The thin smile and vacant eyes explained that it was an often-heard quip, but Roberta heard only a few people speaking English, and those who did were too busy to give complete answers to her questions.

The headlines on the newsstand stated in bold letters that the City of Miami was bankrupt. The gateway to South and Central America was heading down the lane of extinction. The reasons offered in the paper were ineptness, corruption, and sloppy government, which explained a lot to Roberta, and she wondered how a town with so much potential could wind up on the chopping block in only one hundred years. She checked the plane ticket to be sure there was a departure date. Her travel agent had made all the necessary arrangements, and she resorted to merely showing baggage handlers and cab drivers the written name of a hotel. Two hours later, she opened the door to her suite on the eighteenth floor of the Colony Arms Hotel overlooking an endless stretch of azure-blue water.

The view was breathtaking, and the collection of rooms was beautiful. Roberta took little time unpacking. She was anxious to get on with the business at hand. She called Detective May. He answered the phone on the third ring, and if he was surprised to hear that the district attorney from Caulking, Georgia, was in town, he did not say it.

"Ms. Austin, how may I help you?"

"For starters, how about if we compare case files on Nathan Pomeroy, and then we can conclude with officially reporting Buddy as a missing person, with foul play suspected?"

Silence. Stan May was not prepared for Roberta's aggression, and the last thing he needed was another partner who sounded like Aunt Bea from Mayberry. He already had Sheriff Andy. *Caulking must be a great place to live after retirement,* he thought. *No one seems to have anything to do but mind my business.* He wrote a note on the calendar to check on land prices in the area. He and Roberta set a tentative appointment to meet the following day, and both parties ended the conversation on a note of skepticism. May started wondering just what made this case so damn important to everyone. He understood about the personal involvement with Sheriff Chandler. After all, this Nathan character had allegedly killed his daughter.

The most hardened of police officers could handle anything a man was capable of doing to his fellow man, except the violent death of a child. Death dogged homicide detectives down every path they traveled. It was expected, part of the job, but all police officers grew uneasy in the face of the slaughter of children. May had seen the horrible things people could do to each other, husband to wife, stranger to stranger, desperate and frightened men lashing out in panic and anger. All those things he could accept. He was able to go home every night, forget the faces, and ignore the stab wounds, the bullet holes, and the shattered bodies. He could close the door on the reality of the human condition and explain to his sanity the reasons for the things people did to each other. His mind had accepted the attempts to justify the job, just to document the violence and establish a course to pursue the one responsible. This was business, police business, and May preformed his duties without hesitation.

The business of dealing with the death of a child was never handled with haste, as it was not considered a routine part of the job. The men assigned to document the facts for the record approached it with trepidation, and they dragged along more than a small amount of prejudice and hate. This reaction had nothing to do with the cold understanding that the true nature of man was violent, but rather, it spoke to the soft underbelly of man's frailty and proved beyond doubt that we are different than the beasts of the jungle. Detective May had fallen in league with Sheriff Chandler, without hesitation, and he believed Nathan

Pomeroy should be put down like a mad dog. He had spent a career filled with long hours looking into the shredded souls of men like Nathan, men who lived in a cesspool filled with cruel, repulsive memories. Such men hated all things, and for them, precious little existed beyond the pain and chasing after the humiliation. These were men who pursued love ruefully, yearning for the sweet touch of kindness only to destroy it fully and to triumph in the vindication that the lack of conscience supplied. These were dead, hollow men begot from twisted lust and capable only of exploitation and violence.

Roberta spent the remainder of the afternoon and well into the early evening wrestling with strange dreams. The train whistle announced the departure of the present, and the blurry past wandered the tracks with hypnotic motion. She heard sharp cries, witnessed bright lights skipping across the surface of dark, liquid pools pulsing with an assortment of emotions. The name Ricky-Lou drifted across the babble of children's voices rising and falling to a beat and rhythm only they understand. The sound coaxed a tingling sensation along the edge of her teeth, teasing a memory from hiding, failing to bring it to a level of recognition before it was jerked back to the safe embrace of distraction. She could not make out the image, or were there two? It was difficult to tell.

The fog filling her mind lifted slowly, and Roberta was eventually left with emptiness, left talking softly to a deep, painful loneliness settling between the ravaged spaces of her consciousness. The passion and tenderness she had desperately sought with Buddy had disappeared in a matter of hours. The hollowness in the center of her heart reminded her about the trial. She knew that the misery would stalk her for all eternity, or at least as long as Nathan still lived. She had known this the second her eyes had touched his cold stare.

The grand theft trial and subsequent events had been a total disaster, and she took full credit for the failure. Henderson's tracking down the truth could have been an incredibly bad career move, but she could have lived with that. What she couldn't forgive herself for was the loss of the only man she had ever loved, and that had dealt the lethal blow. Roberta had had her reasons, even though she shook her head in bewilderment and with regret today. She had loved Buddy that much then and still did today. She curled into a fetal position in the middle of a strange bed, in a strange hotel, in a strange city, and failed to put away the hurt. The plan had been to allow Buddy time to forget the past, to find closure on the death of Becky-Ann, and to get on with the business of living. She had wanted so much to burn Nathan, to nail the son of a bitch to the wall with a case so perfect no one could defend the animal's actions. All she had gotten was a broken heart and the humiliation that Henderson had put her through, and then in the end, she had lost Buddy anyway. Roberta felt the night closing around her as sleep beckoned for her to come. She fought the darkness for fear of the dreams, and then finally, the slumber overtook her.

CHAPTER

NINETEEN

DETECTIVE STAN MAY prided himself on several things, and the most recent was being patient with down-home, redneck attitudes, like Roberta Austin, the tenacious prosecutor from the great state of Georgia. He sat quietly reading the morning paper in a favorite restaurant that specialized in freshly baked muffins and sipped his coffee. The feelings of regret and compassion were entertaining his subconscious mind when a brown-haired woman with auburn highlights walked through the door. She glanced around at the few patrons before heading directly toward May.

"Detective May, good morning. I'm Roberta Austin," she said, extending her hand.

"Gotta be from Georgia, but not quite as down-home as Sheriff Chandler," May responded as he accepted her hand. "Sit down, Miss Austin."

They discussed many things in several minutes, and both decided that they liked each other and allowed the conversation to drift toward topics that were more sensitive. They talked about the case, cursory points of view, finding detail and exactness as trust was built, and then they left the safe zones of guidelines and procedure for hunches and opinions. The question of what, exactly, may or may not have happened to Buddy gradually dominated the conversation, and their collective sentiment was that Nathan Pomeroy had taken his revenge. Roberta expressed her feelings in a vernacular not accepted in polite society, and at that point, Stan May decided, he really liked this lady.

"I wouldn't piss on the boy if he was on fire," Roberta ended her emotional and uninhibited comment.

May shook his head slowly and smiled. He could see what had brought that sparkle to Chandler's eye when he had mentioned

Roberta. Her name had also brought the big man a sadness that Stan had never explored. The lady was spirited and outspoken and did not give a damn about holding back.

"Well, I guess we both agree. Your friend Nathan needs about thirty minutes in the electric chair with artificial sponges."

The conversation lasted for another hour. Three cups of coffee and a muffin later, May announced that he had to be in court in twenty minutes. They agreed to meet for dinner after work, and Roberta told him to call her hotel around six. She left the restaurant first and decided to walk along the boardwalk before stopping by Buddy's condominium. The morning was beautiful, bright, and warm with the promise of a hot afternoon. A brilliant orange ball hung over the ocean. It was a perfect tropical morning, and all around, the intensity of the sun radiated from the transparent nothingness between things, as if it were a bleached but almost tangible fluid, undetectable by any sense, kept under control only by the perpetual motion of a city that refused to sleep. Roberta made a note to buy a pair of sunglasses.

She stood by the railing and listened to the sound of the waves throwing themselves across the sand, dragging tiny bits of the beach back to the embrace of the endless ocean with their every try. Someone passed close by, and Roberta was startled for a moment. She turned quickly and watched a man dressed in near rags stumble down the steps leading to the beach. Nathan giggled, not looking back, and smiled to himself.

The Miami Beach Police Department officially listed Jefferson Charles Chandler, retired sheriff of Caulking, Georgia, as a missing person. The computer entry alerted every police agency and sheriff's department in Florida that foul play was suspected. May emphasized in the remarks section that Sheriff Chandler had been assisting a murder investigation and once again repeated a complete description of Nathan.

Roberta was mesmerized by the subtle motion of the beach, the gently sway of the palm trees, the white foam dancing on the waves, the warm breeze caressing her face, and she lost track of time. Voices and the sounds of running feet brought her attention back. Groups of bathers were making their way down the boardwalk carrying chairs, umbrellas, and coolers filled with cold drinks and snacks. The camaraderie and laughter from private jokes, sharing the close intimacy of having known each other well, cut a small notch in her heart. She remembered with rude clarity what had brought her to this beach. She missed Buddy greatly and suddenly bolted down the boardwalk like a terrified child.

Detective May had given her directions on how to find the condominium and told her it was the tallest building on the beach, north on the boardwalk. She had almost run past the towering glass structure and was impressed by the exterior opulence, although security was lacking and no one challenged her right to enter from the pool area. Roberta strolled across the expanse of the foyer and found the manager's office next to the stairs. A tall, painfully thin man politely listened and studied her identification.

"I would like to have someone go with me to Mr. Chandler's apartment. There is an official police investigation involving the Georgia District Attorney's office jointly with the Miami Beach Police Department. Mr. Chandler is a critical witness in a very important matter. May I anticipate your cooperation, sir?"

The eyes of the thin man went wide for a moment, and Roberta felt uncomfortable under the scrutiny. His eyes blinked slowly, and she decided to try a less formal, friendlier approach.

"You know, Buddy Chandler and I were going to be married. This makes everything so hard." Roberta sniffled and rubbed her eyes before continuing. "Me being the official having to investigate his disappearance, I mean. I don't know what will happen if I find..." Her voice trailed off right on cue, and the effect was perfect. The face of the thin man collapsed into itself, and tears formed at the corners of his eyes.

"I'm so sorry to hear that. Here, honey, you stop that crying, and I'll go with you to Mr. Chandler's apartment. What was the number, again?"

The man's name was Edgar White, a retired New York City police captain who did some part-time security work in the building to help stretch the limited funds of his pension. He lived on the fifteenth floor with a view of the city on the west side. Roberta heard the story of the man's life as the elevator soundlessly raced upward. A female-sounding mechanical voice announced their arrival, and Roberta followed the long strides of Edgar down the carpeted hall. The mixed aromas of disinfectant, fresh paint and bacon swirled around them shortly before being sucked away by the air-conditioner vent.

"Here we are, miss. Let me get the door."

One side of a set of double wood doors, which were painted dark green with gold metal numbers, opened, and Roberta stepped across the threshold into the apartment. The rooms were elegantly adorned. The assistance of a professional decorator was evident, and she knew there had to be at least one room where Buddy actually lived. The kitchen was clean, unopened mail was on the counter, spoiling food sat in the refrigerator, and an odor of rotting garbage rose from a paper sack by the second door leading from a utility room into the hall. The bedroom door was ajar, and there she found Chandler's inner sanctum. The bed had been left unmade, clothes were scattered, and the lights were left on in the bathroom, with towels on the floor. The distinctive smell of him saturated everything in the room. Tears fell from her eyes, and a deep ragged sigh escaped her mouth. Edgar placed a consoling hand on her shoulder with warm intentions, but she shook it off without looking at him and then immediately regretted the rudeness.

"I'll be on the balcony if you need me, miss," he said, and he left.

Roberta let her eyes drift around the room, kissing all that remained of her Buddy, lingering on familiar items, sliding across dead dreams. The rapid pulse of a red light on the answering machine grabbed her attention, and she raced over to the flat, black box on the nightstand. With a quick scan of the buttons, she found the rewind switch. The counter indicated that the memory was full and twenty messages were waiting for someone to hear.

The first three were from Stan May, and each new message documented his growing concern and revealed more to her than the meeting at breakfast had. The fourth call caught Roberta by surprise, and she listened to a female voice asking if Buddy would make dinner tonight.

The words breathed familiarity and intimacy and ignited a vast array of new fears for Roberta. There was another woman in the sheriff's life, but of course, the man was not dead. He had needs, feelings. The next ten messages were from the woman and were filled with anxiety, confusion, and pleas for Buddy to call her. Her name was Nicole, and she was obviously deeply in love with the retired sheriff from Caulking, Georgia.

Roberta searched the bedroom frantically until she found a red leather telephone directory. There was only one Nicole listed, Nicole Hughes with four telephone numbers, a beeper, and an address in Miami. Roberta hesitated, lifted the telephone, and punched in the first number. The phone rang for what seemed forever, and then a voice said hello, followed by a whimsical message advising to leave a message after the tone. Roberta was numb, and she felt like a fool, having rushed down to Miami to save a man who had forgotten her, who had found a new love and had gotten on with his life. What the hell was she thinking, for God's sake!

She tore out the page and shoved it in her purse. A second search of the room revealed files, notes, and photographs of the original investigation in Georgia, along with the ones in Miami. Roberta collected everything and satisfied herself that whatever had happened to Buddy had not happened in this apartment. She tried to call Stan May, but the secretary advised her that the detective was still out. No, Roberta told her, she did not want to leave a message.

The bum staggered down the gray wooden steps and slipped under the boardwalk. He watched Roberta open the metal gate as if she lived there and steadily make her way toward the back of the building. It sure was a big pretty building, thought the rag man, filled with glass and fancy people. He wondered who lived in such a place. They had to have a lot of money to be so tight-assed special. He wondered why that bitch from back home had come to bother with everything, but of course, he should have known that she would come. He had called her, after all. He bet she was real happy to hear his voice on the telephone. The thought occurred to him, as he dreamed of stripping her ravished body, that she may be leaving by the front door. Nathan raced around the building and damn near missed Roberta crossing the street.

Stan May finished the deposition later than he had expected and decided to eat lunch at the courthouse. The food was acceptable, but because there was only one restaurant, the prices were outrageous, and the conversation was always the same. Everyone in the place was a lawyer, a defendant, or a cop. The topics were limited, were expressed loudly, and did little to add to the culinary experience of eating greasy fried food. May ordered a tuna on rye and wondered how long the short-order cook behind the counter had been out of jail. He always expected a little something extra in the sauce when he ate here and tried to order something that either came sealed in a bottle or could not camouflage that little extra touch ex-cons loved to give to the customers carrying a badge.

He thought about Roberta again for the hundredth time as he watched the clock. The woman must really care about Buddy, leaving her home and job in the middle of the night, catching the first plane heading to Miami, and hitting the bricks, trying to track him down. The funny thing was that Buddy had hardly ever mentioned her, and if he did, it was like talking about just another person helping on the case. May thought about how little he really knew the big sheriff. The guy was a great cop, not some dumb redneck-riding herd on a town full of relatives. Stan liked Buddy, and he had mixed feelings about what may have happened. The hospitals had been checked, and he had already conducted an illegal search of the oceanfront condo and was praying a little more than usual that Roberta might be able to help solve this mystery. Mostly, he hoped that Buddy was still alive.

Stan felt he had failed Buddy in some way that he had not been there when Buddy needed him, which he had missed something, screwed up in some way he could not understand. And what about Nathan? The man had dropped off the face of the earth, which was not hard in a city like Miami, where everyone is a stranger. May had been back to see Delores a dozen times, held all-night vigils, watching the shelter without success, and never received a single phone call from anyone with news. Buddy must have found something and, like the bullheaded lone ranger he was, got himself killed being a hero. May knew in his heart that the sheriff was dead. He was just marking time until the body was discovered and Nathan could take official credit for the sheriff's death.

Nathan watched from across the street as Roberta approached the house. He could feel the hesitation preventing her from immediately ringing the bell and could smell the jealousy floating thick on the breeze and see the hurt in her eyes. Roberta was about to confront her replacement, the woman Buddy had chosen to fill that empty space in his heart, and the emotions were churning in her stomach. The chimes of the doorbell startled her, and she recognized the beginning notes of Beethoven's Ninth. Footsteps alerted her to the approach of someone in the house, and soon the door clicked open, revealing a young woman of about sixteen years of age.

"Yes, may I help you?" the dark-haired woman-child asked in an unexpectedly husky voice.

"Hi, are you Miss Hughes?"

"Yes, Sharon Hughes. Do I know you?"

"No, but I believe your mother and I have a common friend. This is awkward, but very important. My name is Roberta Austin; I'm from Caulking, Georgia. I'm here to investigate the disappearance of a friend, a man your mother knows named Buddy Chandler."

Silence. Sharon Hughes watched Roberta with suspicion and curiosity. Her expression was blank, showing no sign of emotion, but her mind was racing. Buddy was more than just a friend to her mother, and everyone was terribly worried because he had not called or been to the house over the last week. He never missed Sunday brunch and called on the phone at least twice a day. They knew he had been busy working on something with the police department. Buddy would not tell her mother the details, but they all were very concerned.

"Yeah, we know Buddy. Where is he? Is he okay? I don't understand what all this is about. Maybe you should come back when my mom is home, or call. I'll give you the number."

"No, let me explain, please. May I come in? This is very important."

Nathan was fascinated as he watched the two women banter back
and forth at the door. The young one was a beauty—long hair, great
face, and look at those tits! He drooled and felt the hard pulse of the
blood racing through his mind. The voices were talking, some screaming, and he knew this was going to be a great day. He watched the girl
grow more uncomfortable as the conversation continued, and then she
reluctantly stepped aside, letting Roberta enter her home. A stroll
around the neighborhood would tell Nathan just how easy it would be
for him to come back for a nice friendly visit.

Roberta felt disoriented in this house. She had a hard time concentrating, and strange, uneasy feelings that oscillated between unexplained elation and dark depression fought for domination of her
emotions. The girl looked similar to Becky-Ann, and maybe this had
been some sick attempt to replace the family Buddy had lost. Sharon
Hughes was beautiful, which meant that Nicole was a good-looking
woman too. Roberta instantly hated both of them. The young woman
was tall, a perfect size six stretched between her dainty feet and long,
luxurious hair. Nice body. Great tits and ass. Roberta found herself
fantasizing, getting excited in a way that scared her. She had never been
with a woman, let alone wanted to rape a girl like this right here on the
floor. Perverted images slammed around in her mind. There were
naked bodies grinding, groaning on the floor, sweat and blood pouring
from the skin, screams and groans filling the air. She watched herself
devouring every inch of Sharon Hughes, licking and sucking, fucking
her like a man, and suddenly, a burst of red showered the walls with
blood everywhere in the room.

Nathan was panting hard in the bushes only a few feet from the
window. He was watching the women talk, watching the dark sweat
stains appear under the armpits of Roberta, and he noticed how each
woman was fidgeting with the strained awkwardness of the moment.
He could not tell what they were saying. The bitch Roberta was
doing most of the talking, and prematurely, Nathan exploded
between his fingers.

"Fuck! I need her now!" Nathan growled, and for a moment, he thought Roberta had somehow heard him. The woman turned her head slowly toward the window and smiled. Nathan froze, afraid to move, and knew this fucking whore from Georgia was reading his mind.

Roberta could not shake the images and knew that the young woman was becoming more frightened by the minute. Roberta's nipples were hurting. The skin had swelled so hard, and the wetness between her legs caused great pleasure every time she moved on the couch. She was constantly in motion, fidgeting, rubbing, igniting waves of desire and lust crashing through her body. She had to leave now and get out of the house before it was too late.

"I'm sorry, Miss Hughes. This is very hard," she stuttered. "I need to talk with your mother as soon as possible. I'm staying on the beach at the Colony. The number is on this card. I'll call her this afternoon, but if you should talk to her sooner, please have her call me." Roberta was rambling, talking like the insane, desperate fool she was at the moment.

Sharon Hughes accepted the card and immediately dropped it on the table. She did not want to touch the hand of this woman. What did she have to do with Buddy and her mother? She thought about calling the police, but what would she tell them? Sharon had not said very much for most of the conversation, and Roberta had talked incessantly about Georgia, Buddy, and someone named Nathan. She had rambled on about a murder investigation and mentioned the name Stan May, a detective with the Miami Beach Police Department. Sharon wanted this woman out of the house and feared that if the woman didn't leave soon, something terrible would happen. The woman looked crazy, wild-eyed, and Sharon knew that she could go berserk any moment, and then what would she do?

Nathan watched, amused as Roberta wiped the sweat from her face and unconsciously ran shaking hands across her breasts and down between her legs, her fingers searching across tingling flesh that demanded attention. Her eyes were eating this young woman alive, and the expression on Sharon's face was priceless. He was jealous. The fear was an absolute coagulant fluid in the air between the two women that kept from ripping the skin from the younger woman's face only by the extreme control from the oppressive force of her naiveté. Her mind could never begin to imagine what thoughts had pillaged Roberta's consciousness, the extent of the anguish and pleasure those thoughts caused Roberta, and how she should run from the house, from the danger.

Roberta left in a rush, literally running through the door and into the street. Nathan watched as the younger woman slammed the door and threw every lock into place. She collapsed on the floor and cried from a fear she did not understand. Nathan giggled, masturbated, and waited. Roberta had disappeared around the corner, looking for a sanctuary from herself, needing to find a cab and a way back to Caulking. In her heart, she knew some beast had been unleashed. The feelings were real. The need was real, and Roberta knew that insanity was knocking on her door.

Detective May arrived back at his office in the late afternoon, skimmed the pile of telephone messages, and felt a slight pang of regret that Roberta had not called. The pink slips of paper went in the garbage pail, and May flipped on the switch for the computer. He went through a series of security-coded entries before a logo announced that he had successfully accessed the National Crime Index database. The stack of papers on the Georgia investigation listed several case numbers, and he decided on running the FBI numbers first. A quick check of his own files revealed that the fax received a couple of weeks ago reporting that Nathan had not died in the fire was referenced with the same eight-digit case number. Several more security passwords, delays, and final admittance indicated that the file was still active, and that was good news. Resurrecting a closed federal file was harder than exhuming the body of a dead president.

A scan of the file did not reveal anything new. He had read most of the facts in Chandler's file, and he did not have time to go over all the information from Roberta. There had to be something he was missing, and he was hoping the FBI psychological profile report would offer some help in understanding where Nathan might be hiding. The report was full of facts, medical statistics, doctor's opinion, but was largely useless to a police investigation. No one was arguing against the opinion that this Pomeroy pervert was a nut, a serial murderer with an open mind toward the type of victim he would prefer. He liked knives, had had a really bad childhood, and was alleged to have killed his own parents, but that had never been proven.

May read most of the file and downloaded the rest until he could find time to finish it. He had to meet Roberta in a couple of hours, and that did not leave much time to close a few leftover tasks from the previous week. He had time for a quick phone call to the Colony Hotel, and then he had to spend some quality time with the computer, just him and the keyboard.

Time and space were closing in on Roberta before she could reach the curb in front of the hotel. The edges of the world were turning dark, and objects around her were drifting a few feet off the ground. The woman was having a crisis. The words mental breakdown predominated her consciousness, and people on the street began to stop and stare. She was unable to talk and unable to stop shaking as a paralysis stiffened the muscles in her body. Someone on the street helped her sit down, but she could not turn her face to see the Good Samaritan or find the words to say how grateful she was for the assistance. The world looked one dimensional, and a bright, blinding light stabbed her eyes just before everything disappeared. Strange how she could hear people talking but hear the words jumbled. Hands were laying her body flat on the sidewalk, and in the distance, a whistle sounded.

Meanwhile, Nathan was on the other side of town, losing himself in conversations with friends from the past. He listened to the voices, recognized a few, and screamed to one that he had rather not hear, "Mother! Leave me alone, bitch. Go fuck a devil or whatever it is that keeps ya satisfied!"

There were still other voices hounding his memory, Becky-Ann Chandler for one, delicious little Sarah Thornton for another, and he heard the thin, raspy scream of Phoebe. Other voices whispered and shouted, pleaded and cried in a chorus of misery, such sweet sounds to his ears, and such torment to Roberta's. He laughed and giggled, trying hard not to be loud as he rolled under the bushes in front of the house. He could see the young woman on occasion, wandering from room to room, hugging herself, still crying, sometimes talking on the telephone, and, like now, just sitting on the couch where Roberta had sat, staring at the walls.

Sharon Hughes was chronologically a woman, old enough to be married in most countries, starting her senior year at the local high school, and she had been seriously dating the same young man for several years, but in some other ways, she was still very much a child. Nicole, her mother, had raised Sharon alone. Sharon's father had died from cancer many years ago, and theirs had been a quiet, secluded life. Money had not been a problem. Nicole Hughes had invested the money from the generous insurance policy wisely, spent a few lean years saving, and eventually opened her own real estate company. Things were going smoothly. Buddy Chandler had brought a missing part to the two women's lives, a balance and a loving harmony that they both missed very deeply.

Buddy had first met Nicole while negotiating the purchase of the condominium on the beach. There was an immediate mutual attraction, a brief period of adolescent flirting, and the inevitable romance. He had told her about Georgia, about his past life, and about Becky-Ann. She had asked about the women in his life, about Becky's mother, about being a sheriff and walking away from it all. She was bright, intimate, and made him laugh at himself. Nicole let him cry too, let him be soft and gentle, allowed him to be tough and protective. Sharon had loved him at once, and Nicole had known that he was replacing the lost daughter he'd never had a chance to kiss good-bye. Buddy had rapidly become the father Sharon had never known, and the dream of being a whole family had danced on the horizon.

Nicole had told her gallant sheriff about her late husband, and surprisingly, Buddy had listened, squeezed her hand, and understood how very difficult it was to lose someone you love very much. Nicole had told him the story of her life, and by the time she had run out of words, Buddy Chandler had been deeply in love. He had waited until she stopped talking to kiss her. Nicole had been waiting to be kissed for a long time. He explained that he had lost his first wife to cancer also and commented on how ironic it seemed that they both had been left alone by the same disease only to find each other. She understood completely the description Buddy laid out of the slow painful death, the sorrow, the relief, and the exhaustion when it was over. Buddy told her about Becky-Ann and how her death had shut him down emotionally for most of his life. He decided to let Nathan Pomeroy dwell unrevealed in the private hate seething in the black recesses of his heart, and he felt that she did not need to hear all the sick details.

The stress of not knowing what had happened to Buddy overwhelmed Sharon and Nicole. Sharon was unable to function, and now the visit from that strange woman was almost too much. She was terrified, and somehow she knew that Buddy had disappeared from their lives forever. The house was so big and lonely when she was alone. She jumped at every noise, but something sounded like footsteps. The back door was ajar. Was that a shadow slowly dragging across the floor? God, where was her mother? Where was Buddy? There was that noise again, which had to be footsteps in the hall, and wasn't that the sound of the door to her bedroom closing?

Sharon was petrified with fright and still not looking up as she watched the shadow drawing near from the corner of her eye, and she felt an itch crawl from the nape of her neck. She wanted to scream, but she could do nothing more than wait. The hair on her arms stood up. The body was lean. She was certain it was a man, athletic in the way the weight shifted comfortably from the heel to the ball of the foot. The figure took long strides and had a masculine gait, almost a swagger, filled with confidence. She could see the skin along the jaw—it was smooth, womanish. The hair was short, mousy brown with red streaks, and an inkling of recognition registered before an unsolicited fear ripped through Sharon's mind. The attack was fast and furious, and there was not time to react even if she could have put up some type of resistance.

Detective May tried several times to ring Roberta's room at the Colony Hotel. He had left one message already, and a glance at his watch showed the time to be six thirty-five. They'd had a date for six, and he had made a reservation at the Star Dust Room at the famous Darlton Hotel. He had no more than dropped the phone into the cradle when it rang.

"May here, go ahead," he answered, the annoyance left by Roberta standing him up evident in his voice.

Silence. He asked who was on the line and started to slam the phone down when he heard a distant whimper.

"Okay, who the hell is this?'

The whimpering continued, grew stronger, and he heard someone call his name, "Stan..."

"Who is this?"

"Stan, I need help."

He recognized the voice. It was Roberta, and he could only get the address listed on the pay phone from her. She was in the middle of downtown Miami, miles from her hotel, and sounding completely disoriented. Roberta did not know how she had come to be in decorator's row, a low-rent district consisting of warehouses and showrooms. May told her to stay put, that he would be there as soon as he could, with consideration for traffic at this hour.

Roberta was sitting on the curb, hugging the base of the telephone. May did not recognize the woman at first and had to look a second time to be sure it was her. Her hair looked like she had slept with it wet, the clothes were dirty and torn, and one of her shoes was missing.

"Miss Austin, Roberta?" he asked with uncertainty. When she looked up, her eyes were filled with confusion. May thought that maybe Roberta had had a seizure or been mugged or worse. He immediately called for an ambulance and jumped out of the car to help the woman stand. She looked like someone who had lost the battle with a runaway train. She was bruised, bloodied, and barely dressed. The long tail of her shirt covered most of her body, but somehow and somewhere, Roberta had lost her pants.

"Don't call anyone else," she whispered in a hoarse voice filled with desperation. "I don't exactly know what has happened to me, but I know for certain that I am not hurt. Help me get in the car and drive me back to the hotel, please. I beg you."

On the other side of town, a woman had just walked into her house and out of her mind. There was blood everywhere, and a full-sized doll that seemed to be torn apart and reassembled with legs and arms askew and in the wrong places had been dumped in the middle of the Queen Anne chair in the corner of the room. The face of the doll was contorted, with a grimace that resembled a smile, and it looked like the mouth had been sewn shut with blue thread. Where were the clothes, and why did this grotesque thing remind her of Sharon? The questions were issued from that part of her brain functioning on autopilot to avoid total derangement, to keep from ripping her mind to pieces. She screamed without hearing herself, and when the police arrived, they found Nicole Hughes on the floor, rocking back and forth with what was left of her daughter held in her arms.

May and Roberta had arrived at the hotel about the same time the first police car arrived at Nicole's house. They would not know about the brutal murder and dismemberment until the next day when the *Miami Herald* ran the homicide as the lead news story. The detective had other things occupying his mind long before the county sheriff's deputy handling the case called for assistance. There were things he had to get straight with Roberta. He wanted to know just what the hell was going on here! He came to realize that the she could not account for anything, including where her pants were. No, she had never before blacked out, and amnesia and epilepsy were not family traits. The Austin family did not have a recent history of mental disorder, schizophrenia, or seizures.

Roberta sat on the edge of the bed, holding her head in her hands and crying. May did not know whether to run, shit, or go blind. Roberta was terrified, and professional help was a prominent option at this point. The blackout, her disheveled condition, and the missing pants were disturbing. The dreams and illusions, and those powerful sexual urges had tipped the scale when she was in that bar, the bar that she did not include in the story she told Detective May. Roberta had been about to scream something to the dancer, a word or a name, she could not remember, and then everything had exploded at the speed of light. Reality had slammed into her mind in real time, and for hours, everything had seemed to move in a slow, liquid-filled motion. Roberta was miles from the hotel with a fist full of dollar bills, standing at the edge of a raised platform where a nude, female dancer was grinding a pelvis in her face. The world had come alive. The music was blaring, the lights were bright, and everyone in the bar had been staring at her. There she had been, with no pants, trying desperately to reach the dancer with one hand and with the other between her own legs, rubbing the skin raw.

A voice from behind had been filled with mirth and perversion. "You would do anything for money, huh, Misty?"

"Where you goin', girl? This was just gettin' to be fun!"

The dancer had watched the men at the bar and turned to let her eyes touch Roberta's face. "Where you goin', honey? Don't mind those assholes. You're the only one making the money."

Roberta had watched the sweat on the dancer's skin glisten in a rainbow of colors. She'd heard giggles and snickers. Names were being called between beer belches, and the dancer had called, "Don't you want to play with Mama no more, baby?"

A man had stood on the top of a stool and screamed for attention, but no one had taken notice, no one but Roberta. He was an older man, and something was familiar about him, maybe the eyes or the cut of his jaw. She had stood in the door, confused, unable to move, but not held in place by fear, but something else. There was a demand for details, a demand to continue as the voices had explained countless times in dreams and nightmares. She heard something strange and unexpected in a place like this, the cry of a child. The child was pleading, and Roberta had seen images laid over the top of what she was seeing in the bar, like a double exposure, older and in black and white. A small boy was grabbed from behind and thrown across the dance floor. He landed at the feet of the dancer, and Roberta saw in the woman's eyes a pale flicker of recognition. Misty looked down at her feet, blinked, smiled slightly, started to extend a weary hand, but stopped and looked back at Roberta.

The man on the barstool was still yelling, and Roberta had strained to hear his words. She could see his lips moving, but the sound of his voice would fade, return in a strong, clear tone, and then fade again. He was talking to someone, and from the way he had looked at Roberta, she had known he was talking to the small boy still cowering at the dancer's feet.

"Go ahead, boy, fuck the bitch!" Those were the words the man was yelling. The older man was the one who had thrown the child. He had grabbed the boy by the collar of his jacket with one hand as the boy had tried to run past. The boy had come out of nowhere, and Roberta tried hard to remember the old man standing on the stool. She had looked back to the dancer and seen the woman crying, her makeup running down her face. The dancer was talking to the boy and suddenly looked up to see Roberta watching. Her eyes were sad. The face had been fading, and Roberta had fled to the street.

Nathan found himself across from the shelter, looking down from a lofty perch, waiting for some sign of Delores. It had been almost three weeks since he had last spoken to the good sister, and after a peaceful sleep, he felt like renewing old ways with the nun. He had enjoyed hours of uninterrupted sleep then. The dreams and voices had not spoken to him, and it was as if a great exhaustion had taken its toll. He watched everyone coming and going from the front door while cleaning the blood from under his fingernails with the side of a tooth. Nathan could not understand how he had lost his shirt or why he could not immediately remember the past five or six hours. He thought of Roberta and wondered where she was staying while visiting his new playground.

May let himself out of the door after Roberta fell asleep on the couch. She had refused any medical help, did not want to eat, and May concluded that his role was finished. He wrote a brief note telling her to call him at the office in the morning, or sometime tomorrow, if she felt better. Privately, the detective hoped the woman would pack her bags and catch the first plane to Georgia. He knew that he was drawn to her for some ungodly reason and that she was trouble with a capital T.

He drove the few blocks along the ocean, drifting in another world. He did not see the crowds of tourists walking along the boardwalk, enjoying the last dying moments of sunset. The sky in the west was a shade of brilliant orange and purple as the sun slowly disappeared on the horizon. The detective did not hear the laughter or the music blaring from one of the countless taverns offering escape to one and all. He was trying to refocus his effort and energy, to get himself back on track—there were murders to solve. Nathan Pomeroy was not sitting back, waiting for someone else to solve his problems. The deaths of at least six people went unsolved. One name on that least was that of a friend, because Stan counted Buddy Chandler amongst the few colleagues he both liked and respected. The sound of a beeper brought the detective's attention back to the present in time to avoid running over a roller-blader. The office was calling him, hopefully with good news, but May sincerely doubted if he would hear any good news for a long time to come.

Roberta ordered some dinner, ran a bath, and tried to forget. Scenes from the bar ricocheted from the sharp edges of a distorted memory. She thought of Sharon Hughes, and lust filled her mind. Roberta was panting, fingering herself in rapid, jerking motions, and when the moment came, she screamed in pleasure. The sensation passed all too quickly, and she slept. Erotic dreams drifted in the air with the steam and were met without resistance or fear. Voices cooed and whispered at a level just beneath hearing, but her mind still heard, and a smile curled the corners of her mouth.

Dinner had renewed her strength, and the bath and the nap had done wonders for her tired muscles. Roberta sat in the middle of the bed, reading the copies of the Miami Beach homicide case files. There was little doubt that the same person had killed the Russian woman, the grandmother, and the children, and it was the same person who had killed all those people back in Caulking. The descriptions of the scenes were the same, the facts were identical over and over again, and

Roberta was just reading aimlessly until she found a new twist. Roberta was intrigued with the emergence of Sister Delores and the very holy Catholic Church. She was truly pleased that Nathan had finally found someone to develop a regular relationship with, if you could call it that. It was just grand that this woman happened to be a nun.

Roberta beeped May and asked if he minded her visiting with Sister Delores at the shelter. She did not want to interfere with the open homicide investigation.

May was just glad that Roberta sounded like her old self again. "No. In fact, maybe you could relate to her, you know, woman to woman, and get more information from her than I did?"

"Sure, glad to help. I'll bet she has a lot more to say," Roberta told him, and she felt ashamed of her earlier behavior. Stan was a straightforward, no-nonsense kind of man, and he was gentleman enough not to bring up the past events. She felt obligated to apologize, all same. "Listen, about yesterday, I am very grateful—"

"Let's drop it. No harm, no foul, and we'll just attribute everything to all the stress you must be under. Stress can do really strange things to a body. Okay?"

"Yeah, okay. Thanks. I'll call you after I talk with the nun, okay?" With that, she started to end the conversation, but then she thought of something else. "May, don't hang up just yet. Tell me about Nicole Hughes."

"That's going to take some time. How about a deal?"

"Shoot. Don't forget I'm an attorney. We're always ready for a deal."

"Okay, you pump good old Delores for everything she's got, and I'll tell you the little bit I know about Nicole."

"Deal," snapped Roberta.

Stan thought about the conversation Roberta would have with Delores, and he hoped that Delores could tell a story half as good as the one he would be telling Roberta tomorrow. His would be a story of hurt for the prosecutor, a tale of love that would break her heart, but then again, he knew Miss Austin was already familiar with the ending.

He slid the car into a vacant space next to the entrance, locked the doors, and headed upstairs to the roof, where his personal car was parked. Stan had lost all desire to continue working tonight. He was desperately in need of a shower, a good meal, and two weeks of sleep.

Roberta woke early the next morning, skipped breakfast, and hailed a cab in front of the hotel. The driver was familiar with the shelter, and Roberta listened to thirty minutes of praise for the Sisters of Mercy. It seemed that the cab driver had spent time enjoying their hospitality not that long ago and attributed his present good fortune to their confidence in his ability.

"The sisters are like angels. They not only fill your stomach when it is empty, but they fill the spirit of a man with hope when he is desperate. They saved me from the streets, from a life of drugs and crime. I owe them my life—my life, lady. Do you understand?"

Roberta saw a strange passion burning in the cab driver's eyes. The man was possessed, and she nodded a quick agreement to his question.

"Here we are, lady. That will be twelve dollars and twenty cents, but just make it twelve even, okay?"

"Okay, thanks," Roberta answered and gave the man a twenty. "Keep the change. I enjoyed the ride."

"Thanks. You are an angel too. Say hello to everyone. Tell them Tommy says hey, okay?"

Roberta promised she would—she would have promised anything to get away from the man—and turned to study the front of the shelter. The walls were painted in graffiti praising the Lord. She found the front entrance and stood in the doorway, waiting for her eyes to adjust to the poor light.

"Come on in, red. This is the last chance to get your act together," a voice greeted her from somewhere inside the dark.

"Thanks. Do you know Sister Delores?" she asked, feeling awkward, as if she had just stepped into a dimension of the human condition that is normally ignored, shoved into a corner where people can pretend it does not exist. The air was thick with hopelessness and desperation; she could see hundreds of people just sitting and whispering to one another, staring at her with a mask of despondency, and immediately, Roberta felt the danger.

"Hi, I'm Sister Delores. How may I help you?"

Roberta screamed, and the poor nun jumped back. Everyone in the room fell silent. Roberta was the center of attention. Recovering and embarrassed, she said, "Please, forgive me. You just appeared out of nowhere."

"I'm sorry. Please follow me to the office, and we can talk."

Roberta stared at the back of Delores and found it hard to believe this young woman was a nun. She wore tight jeans, a stylish T-shirt, and no shoes. The sister had style, confidence in her walk, almost an air of arrogance about her. She stood at the entrance to a small office and closed the door behind Roberta.

"Please, sit down. Would you like something to drink? Maybe coffee or a diet soda?" she asked, playing the hostess. Her ingratiating manner was beginning to irritate Roberta.

"No, this is not really a social visit," Roberta said, a bit of harshness in her tone.

"Oh, then what kind of visit is this?"

"I'm from Caulking, a small town in—"

"Georgia, yes I have heard of it recently. We had a man from your city stay with us for a while. I can't remember his name," the sister interrupted, and Roberta could detect a break in her confidence.

"Let's cut the crap, sister. I'm here about your boyfriend, Nathan Pomeroy, and I don't have time to play games. Got it?"

Delores looked toward the window, and her thoughts were like feathers in the wind, blowing in all directions without control. She was tiring of this ritualistic harassment.

"Okay, let's cut the crap. I am damn tired of you people, of your perpetual judgment and your bullying natures. Nathan is gone, and he has been gone for a month. We had a relationship, but I am sure those policemen have told you everything. What more do you want from me?"

"I want you to tell me everything about Nathan. The man is an animal, a brutal, sadistic killer, and he killed one of those policemen that came to talk with you before, Sheriff Chandler—remember him, sister?"

Delores looked hard at Roberta, and when the prosecutor failed to look away, the nun did. Everyone was telling Delores that Nathan was a killer, a savage animal, but she could not believe them, not her Nathan. "I don't know anything about that. Nathan was a sweet and gentle man. I love him, but I'm sure you know that—"

This time, Roberta interrupted. "He fucked you, sister. That does not mean he loved you. The piece of shit is incapable of love. I think Detective May and Sheriff Chandler showed you pictures of how gently Nathan expresses his love."

"You're quite the bitch, aren't you?" Delores said, and Roberta was momentarily shocked. The sister was not finished. "What do they call you, the hard-baller, sent here to verbally beat me up, to get the real story? Sorry, there just ain't no more, whatever your name is, so get your ass out of my shelter." Delores stood.

Roberta snickered, and it was her turn to look out the window. She was beginning to like this sister. The nun had balls, and this was going to be harder than Roberta had originally thought. "Well, sister, shall we start over?" The sister gritted her teeth and nodded. "I'm Roberta Austin, District Attorney. I would like to ask you a few questions about Nathan Pomeroy. I am trying to find my friend, Sheriff Chandler."

"He is really missing? I did not know that. Detective May has been here a couple of times alone, but I thought the sheriff had gone back home."

"He is home. He is retired from Georgia and lives here in Miami now, for about two years, actually." Roberta smiled and relaxed.

Delores returned the smile and settled back into the chair with one leg tucked under her. She absently ran a hand through her long hair and looked back at Roberta. The world was beginning to switch gears, and bright colors were beginning to leak down the walls. Voices were calling from far away, and the train whistle was blowing. Loud, metallic-sounding music heavy on the bass drowned out Delores's last words.

"I'm sorry, what did you say?" Roberta asked, beginning to panic, and her eyes blinked rapidly. Sweat was running down her back.

Concern was registering in the sister's expression. "Is everything all right, Ms. Austin? You really don't look so well. I'll get you some water."

Roberta grabbed the nun's arm before she could open the office door. The act was not threatening, however, and Delores patted her hand, stopping at the door and looking down at the terrified face. The room was slowly spinning, bright lights blinking on and off in rhythm with music. The voices were louder, closer than before, but the words were still not understandable.

"Help me, sister. I'm going to faint," Roberta whispered before falling to the floor.

Delores fled from the room, rushing to the kitchen for a glass of water and a wet cloth. She ran back to her office and found Roberta sitting on the edge of the desk. A gleam had replaced the confusion in her eyes. Roberta licked her lips with a slow drag of the tongue across the wet skin.

"Hey, sister, glad you could get back so soon. I was getting lonesome," Roberta said in a husky voice.

Delores stopped abruptly, closed the door behind her, and dropped the glass to the floor. She stared at the woman, opened mouthed, and could think of nothing to say.

"Why don't you bring your sweet ass over to me and let's get to know each other a whole lot better, sweetheart?"

The voices were screaming, and the music was pounding. The air in the office was thick and wet. Roberta ran a hand across her forehead and wiped away the sweat. Delores continued to stare, trying to find a reasonable explanation for all of this, but she was unable to successfully deal with what was happening. Roberta stood up, unbuttoned her own blouse, and walked over to Delores. She pinned the nun to the door, rubbing her hands over the nun's body, kissing her face, her neck, and, finally, her mouth. Delores was not resisting, not doing anything, just standing still and letting Roberta touch her, assault her with an overpowering lust.

"Give it to me, baby. Give your mama a little lovin'," Roberta growled, pulling the shirt over Delores's head. She savagely sucked the nipples of the nun's breasts, biting the tender flesh, moving down the body and between her legs.

Delores began to fight back when Roberta undid the snap on her jeans. "No, stop it! You're out of your mind, on drugs or something! Stop it or I'll scream!"

"No you won't. You're hot, bitch, and you want it as much as I do."

Roberta stripped Delores completely, then herself, and did whatever the urges commanded. The sister sobbed during the violation but did not resist, and she prayed this was the last of the punishment that God intended for her. She felt Roberta lick the flesh between her legs, biting, hurting her, and turning her abruptly over, continuing the assault between the cheeks of her ass. Roberta shoved Delores's face between her own legs, demanding the woman lick her, and when Delores could not bring herself to obey, Roberta beat her savagely about the head. The pain was unendurable, and the shame was worse, but the nun complied with the demands, and Roberta was soon groaning with pleasure.

The voices had stopped, the music was ebbing away, and Roberta was lying on top of Delores, gasping for breath. The nun was crying and praying to Jesus to forgive her sins. Roberta could hear nothing, nor could she see anything, and a black liquid filled her eyes and dripped from her ears. Delores, the shelter, the world did not exist anymore for her. She was sated, the urges fed, and a wonderful feeling flowed like hot oil down her spine and between her legs, collecting in a pool flowing to the floor. She had pissed herself during the last climax, but she took no notice. "Damn, that was nice," she said and laughed.

Delores shoved her to the floor. The unexpected fall slapped Roberta back to the present, and once again, confusion screamed in response to her mind trying to comprehend what had taken place over the past hour. She heard the cry from Delores, looked into the shattered expression of the woman and down at her own nude body. "What happened?" she whispered, and that part of her mind keeping track whispered back. It told her what had happened between giggles, ran images across the back of her eyes, and in the memory, she found again a strange pleasure gushing through her blood.

"I've got to get out of here," Roberta told herself, and she hurriedly redressed before running from the room, leaving the door open and Delores sprawled across the desk. The nun stood and stared out into the shelter at the faces watching, not caring if they saw her, and then she slowly closed the door. She did not call out for help. She did not call the police. Mechanically, she went through the motions of redressing.

Across the street, a man stood in the window, and he saw Roberta emerge from the doorway. He laughed at her panic, smelled the overpowering aroma of fresh sex on the breeze, the pungent sweet smells of wetness soaking through the crotch of Roberta's slacks. He smiled at the images dancing in his mind and waited until Roberta had flagged down a cab before heading across the street toward the shelter. He slipped through the door unnoticed, blending with the crowd, and listened to them telling each other what had happened. He heard a black woman tell a skinny crack whore called Panama how Sister Delores was standing bare-assed naked for all to see, how she had heard the grunts and howls of those two women doing it. The black woman was shocked, and the whore just grinned.

The shelter became quiet when the door of the office opened and Sister Delores, clothed and stone faced, walked out and toward the kitchen. No one moved, no one spoke, but the man from across the street slowly followed the nun. The sister had passed through the back door and into the alley, leaving the door open and not looking back to see Nathan following her. He watched her walk in slow, measured steps, heading toward the church. He could hear the music of the organ sounding louder as they drew closer. Delores reached the front steps, ascended with a dignified grace, and then walked through the front entrance.

Voices from the choir strained, singing songs praising the Lord with the chords of the organ vibrating the stained-glass windows. Nathan entered cautiously behind Delores, who had transformed magically into a devout member of the church as she walked down the soft carpet of the aisle. The stride of her long legs shortened, and the seductive sway of her hips disappeared. She carried herself with a straight, dignified walk. A few parishioners in attendance were swaying in rhythm with the soothing, almost hypnotic effect of the music.

Nathan never felt comfortable inside a church, and always found it intimidating and disturbing. He resented having to attend for his food and bed, but there was an air of peace about this place. It was like being back in Georgia, back in the familiar smell and noise of his swamp. If he closed his eyes, he could again hear the sound of the air being heated by the summer sun and smell the pungent odor of the muddy water. For the moment, he lost track of what had brought him to the sacred hall. He had found an empty pew behind Sister Delores, who was kneeling and praying. Nathan could hear her soft voice repeating prayers, and for a second, he considered leaving, but his attention stolen by something more interesting, something he had avoided seeing the last time he was here.

High above the podium and the choir, over the huge organ and the pipes extending toward the vaulted ceiling, was a life-sized figure of Christ suspended from the cross. Nathan looked into the eyes of the face formed with careful cuts of the sculpture's chisel. A certain sadness was captured in the polished stone. Deep lines ran along the edges like rivers running through ancient canyons carrying the tears of all mankind. He could actually see the water glistening between the smoothed, weathered edges and could hear the sorrow flowing.

The organ music sounded again, and Nathan noticed that a priest, not a nun was standing behind the podium. The voice was full of enthusiasm as it mumbled inaudibly, and the small crowd mumbled back. The heat was stifling in the church, and it gave Nathan a pounding headache. The voice of the priest was only a droning hum, and waves of vertigo swirled Nathan's consciousness into a shimmering, dreamland reality. He noticed everyone else was sweating but took the discomfort in stride, with looks on their contented faces as if they were relieved of great burdens.

"What a bunch of assholes," he muttered, and he let his eyes drift upward with the heat. The nun still prayed, her delicate fingers manipulating the beads on her rosary.

Nathan concentrated all his attention on the center of the Christ figure hanging above the priest. He wanted suddenly to walk up and examine the spikes protruding from the white marble feet, but he decided it would disturb the priest. The sweat was running into Nathan's half-closed eyes, and the voices sounded far away. He was floating in a tranquil delirium as he admired the craftsmanship, but as he stared, a tiny drop of bright red blood dropped onto the sleeve of the priest's robe with a distinctive heavy splat. Nathan was dumbfounded, unable to focus on the face of the figure. His eyes refused to focus and rolled around in his head as a sense of vertigo caused him to feel like vomiting.

"This heat is killin' me," he moaned, but no one took notice. Nathan looked around the church with blurry vision and saw only blurry, black faces staring forward at the priest. Another drop fell, and another, and a steady stream of blood rained across the face and shoulders of the priest. Nathan followed the steady flow of red drops to the source. The carved wounds around the spikes driven through the feet of Christ were puckered and fresh. No one else in the church noticed the white cloth of the ornate robe turning crimson, and Nathan sat there with his mind swirling in confusion.

He could stand it no longer and yelled out to the priest, "You fool, can't ya feel that thing is bleedin' all over ya!"

His words were without body, and the heat was draining him of all strength. The back of the pew offered support, and Nathan staggered into the aisle. The nun did not move, and the priest continued his sermon without pause as he stepped up to the podium. The sleeve was red to the shoulder, and Nathan saw blood running down the arm and soaking through at the waistband.

"What is wrong with you man?" Nathan yelled as he took the priest by the shoulder and shook him wearily. Blood splattered onto the back of Nathan's hand, leaving warm, thick spots. Nathan stumbled to the floor at the foot of the priest. He crawled behind the podium, unable to stand without supporting his weight on a metal banister. There he stood, trying to focus on the people in the pews. Nathan felt sick. He wanted to vomit, and while breathing in short, ragged gulps, he called out to the blank faces, "Y'all can't be takin' this blood bath serious. It's disgustin'!" Darkness filled his mind, and the dizziness took his head for a spin.

A voice sounded from far away and shattered Nathan's illusion of isolation. "Of course they do. They take it very serious."

Nathan opened his eyes, but he was afraid to move his head. He was afraid to say a word and gently moved his eyes in search of the source of the voice. Everyone was staring at the priest, still mumbling and still not seeing Nathan. Delores was still bowing in prayer, and the rosary was slipping through her fingers bead by bead. No one had spoken, no one had moved, and Nathan turned to look up at the priest. The priest had not spoken to Nathan either, and finally, Nathan looked up further to the figure on the cross. He could not believe it—the right big toe was starting to wiggle.

Soon, both feet were fighting and straining against the spikes. Nathan fell down the stairs from the podium and gasped, "I don't believe this. It ain't real, and I'm just dreamin'." The rigid texture of the marble skin stretched, and the muscles flexed against the spikes as the arms and legs pumped with a growing strength. The metal creaked and began to pull away from the cross with every new surge of energy. The face no longer maintained a smooth, stone-like surface, nor did it hold that sorrowful expression any longer as the chest swelled with life. The muscles in the neck tightened, the throat swelled, and an explosion of breath roared through gritted teeth.

The spikes ripped away from the splintering wood, and the feet now dangled free. A moan escaped from the quivering lips as color flowed across the pale, chalky skin and just as a small metal spike ripped away from the bloody wound. The straining stopped and the figure spoke. "I could use some help up here." Nathan stared with an open mouth, but he could not move a muscle.

"You are so damn useless," the figure told Nathan and looked down on him with a disgusted glare. The chest heaved several more times, the jaw slammed shut with the strain, and the last of the nails gave way. The shining white figure fell to the floor with a loud crash, knocking the podium over and the priest across the platform. The figure sat

242

there, staring at Nathan, and carefully pulled another spike from a bloodied palm. "How do you do?" it said to him. Nathan did not move. He could not move. It said, "My name is Christ, Jesus Christ, but you can call me J.C. for short."

Nathan looked up at the abandoned and broken cross, back down at the figure in front of him, and out toward the silent crowd.

"I don't believe none of this bullshit!" Nathan stammered, and the figure broke into a deep-throated laugh.

"My name is Christ, and you, you miserable worm, are one of my children," it yelled.

"No, not me," Nathan yelled back. "I'm leavin'."

The figure ignored him and stared right through Nathan at Sister Delores sitting in the front row. It rose with a groan and held out a hand to Nathan, saying, "You are one of the murderers, praying for forgiveness, a petty fornicator, a sinner." And added, "You want my forgiveness, right?"

Nathan began to crawl backward, scrambling to his feet as the figure leaped from the priest's platform to block his escape. Looking down at him, it said, "Well, forget it, sport!"

"Bullshit." Nathan spoke in a small voice, and the white figure slapped him across the side of his head. The force knocked Nathan into the first pew, and blood splattered into his right eye. The people never looked at Nathan. They just shoved him to the floor and continued praying with the priest. The figure picked him up by the front of the shirt. The side of Nathan's face stung from the blow, and the blood in his eye made it hard to see. Blood from the wounds in the hands ran down the figure's arms.

"Thou shalt not speak to me in such tones!" said the figure, and it delivered a second blow. The figure lunged at Nathan but missed as he rolled away under another pew.

"I don't believe this! I've gone nuts. This ain't happenin'!" Nathan cried out.

"You're going to Hell with me, my son!"

Nathan heard the Christ figure laugh hysterically from the floor, and then he saw it trying to stand and hit it hard on the top of the head with a hymnbook. The figure fell back to the floor, laughing and weeping at the same time.

"I am the Christ. Why do you want to hurt me again?"

Nathan made a dash toward Sister Delores, grabbed her by the arm, and started toward the door. A brittle snap marked the breaking of her arm, and as he turned to look, her body slowly withered to the floor, turning to dust and smoke. He held her arm in his hand and watched the flesh crumbling. He could only scream, throwing her shriveling limb toward the priest. Nathan bolted toward the door, shoving to the floor several people who were in his path, but the world went black before he could reach the brass handles to make good his escape.

Days later, Nathan awakened and immediately looked down at his clothes. There were no bloodstains down the front of his shirt as he had expected, and in fact, he was not wearing a shirt. He was dumbstruck. The side of his face did not hurt, either, but he found that he couldn't move. The room he was in wasn't readily recognizable, the walls soft and the light bright. Nathan then realized that he was wearing a straightjacket that was tied at the back and secured by a hook protruding from the padded walls. He had no recollection of how he had come to be here. He could only remember the terrible hiss and sudden evaporation of his beloved Delores. He did not know where he was, but he could see the peephole in the door. He could see that something was blocking the light from the hall, and he smiled.

The memory now danced like fireflies caught in a web. He could see the church, hear the bells ringing and the voice yelling, and he watched himself collapse across the street from the church, turning in time to watch it shimmer and dance, fade slowly and swallow itself whole, leaving a vast, tattered hole in the ground. The movement was soundless, but dust and flying debris streaked across the darkening sky. He had fainted on the sidewalk, slowly collapsing into a heap of dirty clothes, and he had not felt the strong hands pulling him from the warm slumber offered by the hard kiss of the concrete. He had not heard the screams and calls for help, nor had he seen the accusatory fingers pointing at him, and he had not protested the disrespectful manner employed by those men in uniform as they had yanked him to his feet with actions filled with intolerance and outrage. Cold, biting steel had restricted the movement of his wrists, forcing his arms to bend inward and causing sharp, excruciating pain. The world had continued to recoil from his understanding as he was launched not so gently into the caged area of the police car. The area was expressly designed for persons needing a physical barrier separating them from the rest of the world, something to create distance in deed and thought. This space was reserved for those persons not expecting courtesy at the hands of their capturers, those confused and simple souls accused of murder or rape, or any others who relied upon violence to speak directly on their behalf.

Voices joined together to offer an onslaught of evidence depicting Nathan as a man not worthy of compassion, for there was not a doubt that he had strangled Sister Delores to death. Her murder had been committed in full view of all who had attended the morning mass. The father had tried to intervene, had been slapped hard across the face and vaulted backward by a savage punch to the head. The attack had lasted less than a few minutes, and the body of the poor woman had been left draped across the back of the pew, discarded like a broken toy and left to be collected by scavengers.

Nathan turned to face the door and told the eyes watching him, "I am insane, or so I am told by those that speak so brazen and bold, those with tongues that wag and chatter on until all words are dead and gone.

"What is he saying?" asked one of the attendants outside the door.

"Hell, I don't know. It's some sort of poem. The daft bastard has been singing it ever since the cops brought him in here."

Nathan smiled at the door and continued, "Bright eyes stare into my world, while my eyes find dark corners. But let them in and occupy their time. I will break the rhythm of their rhyme."

"How long has he been here?"

"I don't know. About a month, I guess."

"What did he do?"

"He strangled a nun in a church not far from here. Did it on a Sunday even, in front of a whole crowd of people. Folks say they had been gettin' it on—you know, the nun and this weirdo—but she couldn't handle it anymore and confessed to the priest. She was sittin' in mass when Mr. Poet here charged through the doors and killed her, just like that." The attendant snapped his fingers.

Nathan could be heard still quoting poetry in a singsong voice from inside the room. He sang about soft padded walls, robots, and eyes watching him from beyond the world of black and white. He never recovered, but he improved enough to be allowed to wander the asylum without an escort. Nathan had stopped biting people, and the attendants had stopped strapping him to the wall. He was getting better, much better, yes, siree.

CHAPTER

TWENTY

ROBERTA HAD FLOWN home immediately following the arrest of Nathan Pomeroy. The man had been charged with the death of Pamela Angela Flanders, whose name had been changed to Delores upon the acceptance of her vows. Roberta had been exiting a cab in front of the Colony Hotel the exact moment Sister Delores died, and a great pain, a sense of loss, had pierced Roberta's heart. She had been certain a massive heart attack was going to take her life, but the pain had passed quickly. Her intentions were to pack that very moment and run as fast as she could from Miami. Her rape of the nun had pushed her beyond the threshold of sanity, and her only hope of escape, of seeking some type of salvation, was to return home. Her plan was to confess to what had happened, commit herself to a local sanitarium, and let the investigation run its course. Before this could occur, however, Nathan had taken care of Roberta's problem unexpectedly. She was happy in a perverted, immoral manner, and with Delores dead, her problems were all but concluded.

Peace and tranquility had returned to her life, and she gladly received the slow pace she had so often associated with monotony like an old friend. Normalcy had returned. Mountains of paperwork regarding the mundane affairs of Caulking, Georgia, awaited the return of the district attorney, and she closed the door on the legacy of Nathan Pomeroy. Roberta spent several hours with Stan reviewing the totality of the investigation. Before they said good-bye, sadness settled over the atmosphere of the conversation. There was so much they had not had time to discuss, and Buddy was still missing. Stan promised to make all the necessary arrangements to close the condo, to stop the mail and the newspaper, and to continue looking for their mutual friend.

Stan started to shake her hand, but Roberta held him close after a lingering kiss on the cheek and just waved. She could not talk—too much had happened—and she choked back tears as the door of the elevator closed. Her life had changed forever because of a few weeks of absolute chaos. She had come to Miami to find Buddy, and she had considered this her last opportunity to salvage their relationship, only to lose herself, her sanity, and her understanding of life. Stan watched the elevator door close with mixed feelings of relief and regret.

The interior surface of the door caught Roberta's reflection. She stared at the face, and although she did not recognize it as belonging to a stranger, she did notice the changes, imperceptible differences that gave her a hard, weathered look that battered against the feminine lines along the jaw. Experience had all but replaced the innocence of a small-town girl.

Stan could never determine what had happened, nor did he really want to know. All he could think about was a stiff drink in the loud embrace of his favorite watering hole. He did not go back inside the office but punched the button requesting a car going down. This would be a short day and a long night followed by a longer day tomorrow. He still had not found the words to explain the past twenty-four hours, let alone the past couple of weeks. He planned on preparing a cursory outline for the file. After all, Nathan had offered a complete confession detailing the murders of Helen Sutton, her grandchildren, Candy, Nina Solowoski, and Bullets. May did not associate the homicides of the two whores, Candy and Bullets, with the rest of Nathan's gruesome work because they did not readily fit the profile, but if he could clear four cases with a single confession, he'd take it in a heartbeat. He could smell a letter of commendation in the making here, a shot at detective of the year, and a well-earned vacation.

The detective should be a contented man with a brutal killer behind bars, or at least off the street, and four homicides solved. The chief had called him personally with congratulations, and Roberta Austin was safely flying back to Georgia. But Stan was not contented at all. He had a nagging feeling in the pit of his stomach that just wouldn't go away. Sometimes when things were nice and neat, all wrapped up and delivered with a bow, it meant he was missing the point, missing something, but what? The circumstances surrounding Nathan's capture had been all a little too easy, he thought, and he shook his head, wondering why he would question fate. Nathan's time had just run out, he told himself.

Stan had made a promise to Roberta to keep looking for Buddy, but more importantly, he reminded himself that the case was far from being closed—too many loose ends had been left dangling about his friend and his friend's life. One of those loose ends was Roberta herself, and like any good detective, Stan had collected a vast amount of information on Roberta. Things involving Miss Austin were not as she would have everyone believe. Stan collected and devoured the information with more than just an investigative curiosity—he needed to know more about this woman on a personal level.

The Office of Vital Statistics in Atlanta advised that details of Roberta Austin started with her graduation from middle school, a small private school in north Georgia. Her birth certificate, hospital records, parental information, and other evidence that she had had a life before the age of nine were not available. Roberta was listed as an orphan, origin unknown, and it was documented that she had been discovered in poor health, suffering from severe shock and with evidence of intense physical and sexual abuse. The first several pages described a child suffering from malnutrition, venereal disease, and vitamin deficiency and who was poorly educated, socially maladjusted, and initially believed mentally handicapped and possibly retarded.

Roberta had evidently been raised in a series of state facilities and had responded well to treatment. Later tests revealed an intelligent, normal teenager looking forward to the future, to dating, to a driver's license, and to college. The psychological analysis indicated permanent memory loss promoted by extreme trauma of some nature, causing the mind to block out large segments of her previous life—large segments that included birth to age nine. Roberta had been discovered wondering along a dirt road in a remote section of southwest Georgia near the Alabama border. A trucker had found her in a near-comatose state near a seldom-used railroad track, sucking her thumb, her eyes dull, and refusing to acknowledge anyone or anything around her.

George and Fern Austin had adopted the young girl after the state had sent her to them through a foster-care program. George and Fern were an older, childless couple in a good financial position. Young Roberta had stayed with them for more than a year before they applied for permanent custody and, finally, adoption. It seemed to Stan that Roberta was one of the few success stories, and he had personally been exposed to more than his share of failures. He also better understood Roberta's obsession with Buddy Chandler, an older man, stable, with more than a passing resemblance to George Austin. He remembered from a psych course something about a father fixation; perhaps the sheriff had recognized the complex and that was why he distanced himself.

A copy of her personnel file from Caulking started with Roberta being hired as an intern while at law school and ending with her promotion to district attorney. Hers was a continuing success story of an all-American rag-to-riches melodrama, but it was apparently starting to unravel and she was maybe spiraling toward self-destruction. May was still digging into his college coursework on psychology and theorized that bits of Roberta's past might be breaking through the self-imposed amnesia, manifesting in unpredictable behavior. There were no mentions of any negative aspects in her file, only letters commending her dedication, hard work, and intelligence.

May gave a good deal of credit to first impressions, and he had liked Roberta Austin from the first day, but he could not dismiss a nagging suspicion dragging his high opinion of Roberta through the muck. Stan couldn't shake the feeling that she may have a dark side that she kept well hidden. The thick file he had developed on Roberta revealed that the woman was not the person she pretended to be, and the facts were well documented. Roberta's adopted family had provided a stable, loving environment, but her strange behavior could have been inherited from a warped family tree that was just now taking root in the woman's mind for some reason. The mere fact that psychologists had documented the memory block suggested a horrible life of perversion, depravity, and aberration that a little girl's mind needed to escape, a life that she had chosen to forget but had also somehow escaped—or maybe she had just been cast aside like a used or broken toy. May pondered over Roberta for hours every day, wondering about her life, about the dark secrets that her mind held, and he worried that when the dam broke, the rush of memories would destroy the strong survival instinct that she now possessed. Yes, May thought about Roberta, and he dreamed of things in his sleep that his conscious mind would not entertain.

Exactly six weeks after his arrest, Nathan Pomeroy made a formal request for Detective May to visit him at the South Florida Institute. The institute was a state-funded hospital for the mentally disturbed that treated those with the more violent disorders and served as the receiving facility for those prisoners found not guilty of violent crimes by reason of insanity. May received Nathan's request via a mutual friend, John Vazquez, the attorney appointed by the court to represent him. John Vazquez was nothing more than a vehicle to have the prisoner institutionalized, and there had never been an attempt to have the charges dismissed or mitigated to lesser offenses, or to have the case dragged out in a lengthy defense.

"Detective May," Stan said, answering the telephone. He recognized the familiar voice of the defense council.

"'Morning, Stanley. I have a message from your good friend and my famous client, the repugnant and forever crazy Nathaniel Pomeroy," Vazquez told the detective.

"How great. I was hoping that he had cut his own wrists by now, maybe save the taxpayers some money."

"What a bad attitude, Stanley. You need a vacation, or maybe a change of jobs, my friend."

"Or both. What does Pomeroy want? Let me guess. He wants to confess to something else, maybe the Lindbergh kidnapping?'

"That's real cute, but you're close. He mentioned something about your missing sheriff friend, the guy from that little place in Georgia."

"You mean Chandler, Buddy Chandler?" May's voice was filled with tension. "Nathan wants to tell me about Buddy?'

"I don't know what he wants to tell you, but he would like for you to visit him, and he did mention Buddy. You know he could just be having a little fun. You know how these nutcases think, Stan. I wouldn't get too excited about this," cautioned Vazquez.

"Yeah, thanks, but it would be great to finally find out if your boy killed Buddy."

"You think he did?"

"No doubt, and probably a lot more folks than he has told us about."

"Maybe I should be there when he talks with you," Vazquez wondered out loud.

Roberta was busy reviewing a case from the Georgia State Police regarding possible political corruption in connection with a cocaine trafficking ring operating in and around Caulking when the telephone rang. "Austin. Go ahead and ruin what's left of my day," she growled.

"Well, you haven't changed a bit, Roberta, and I don't think I'll ruin your day," said Stan May with a laugh.

There was silence on the other end of the telephone. Roberta was trying to match the voice with a face.

"I'm crushed, Roberta. You don't know who this is, after all we experienced together? How could you forget me already?"

A face jumped into her mind, and she remembered. "Stan? Stan May? How the hell are you, Detective?"

"Man, I was sort of hoping that we were long past the titles, Ms. District Attorney Austin."

"We are, Stanley. It is so good to hear your voice. I can't tell you how many times I have thought about just picking up the phone and calling you. How's the Magic City?" she asked and thought of Buddy. "I pray this is good news about Buddy."

"It is news, but I don't know yet if it's all that good or not. Our boy Nathan wants to talk. He mentioned Buddy specifically, and I was wondering if you would care to sit in on the interview?"

"Shit yeah!" Then she quickly added, "But I don't know if I have the time to spare. I have a sticky investigation going right now, and the city fathers ain't too happy with me over a few things."

"Give them hell, girl, but I thought maybe I would make it an official request, advising that Nathan may have information regarding open homicides in your jurisdiction, like maybe he wants to make a confession, come clean with nasty details, names, dates, places, things like that, and of course you have to be here. Would that create a better time-management scenario for you?"

"That would do it, but are you bullshitting or what?"

"Just parlaying for a little professional assistance and a chance to finally take you to dinner. How about this weekend? We'll make the interview with Nathan on Monday?"

"You got it all planned, huh, Stan? I'll make some phone calls and see you day after tomorrow. I'll call you back and give you the flight details. Do you think you could arrange a room at the same hotel I stayed in the last time? I think the name was the Colony. I liked that place. It had a great view."

May made all the necessary arrangements at both the institute and the Colony Hotel. He also called John Vazquez and advised him of the pending meeting with his client on Monday. John was busy but did not ask that the meeting be postponed. He did ask that if Nathan offered any new facts about any known or suspected case that May was working on, May would keep him informed. May agreed. As soon as he hung up with Vazquez, Roberta called back and advised him of her flight information.

"I'll see you Friday night around nine, nine-thirty," she told him with a voice filled with enthusiasm and expectation.

Stan copied down the flight number on the edge of the blotter and unconsciously drew a heart around the three digits. Everything he had told her on the phone was not quite the truth, but he wanted to see her again for many reasons and had been unable to forget the feeling of her soft lips against his face. He was not playing games with his own heart and did not expect a sudden romance blossoming in the middle of an already complex situation, but he would not reject one either. Right now, he just missed her, and he missed the way she had entered his life, changing it forever. After she had left, after he had discovered so much about her life, he missed her even more. She had spontaneously embraced him and cracked his hardcore shell offered to the world as a rough defense; her touch had broken through to the real Stanley May. He could list the lingering effects along with scant other expressions that crossed her face. He told himself not to be stupid, that the woman had a lot of problems that she herself didn't even know about, and that he should just take a cold shower with a dose of reality and get over it.

Miles away, buried in the heart of a neighborhood filled with sprawling ranch-style homes attached to swimming pools; four-car garages containing German imports, Italian sports cars, and the latest Baby Boomer fad, Harley-Davidsons leaking oil, a hospital resembling a country club stood behind a conspicuous fifteen-foot fence. The designers of the mental health facility had attempted to hide the security fence behind a thick, sprawling hedge, but it still drew attention and anger from the residents. The zoning board demanded that the wings be limited to three stories and the bars installed on the inside of the windows, and nowhere was there to be a sign or any other type of identification stating that it was a mental hospital. The land had been donated by one of Miami's original families, but they did not have to live in the neighborhood and they never worried about an escape or property value because of the institute.

Nathan sat in the middle of his bunk and stared out the window. He could see above and beyond the hedge to the roofs of several nearby homes. Dreams of walking through the manicured lawns, peeking in the windows, and watching the little rich girls playing little-rich-girl games in the privacy of their bedrooms excited him. The voices mocked his efforts, but they had no effect on the desire to spread his mind beyond the limits of the room. He could see himself flying high, clearing the hedge and landing silently upon the grass. He would go a-visitin', being neighborly, and lick the cum from the palm of his right hand. Nathan swallowed the dreams like razor blades slipping and sliding down the center of his brain. The pain of knowing he was locked inside the room was exquisite. He liked to taunt his lust, pay tribute to the inability to feed the hunger gnawing a hole in his stomach. He had called his attorney following an exceptionally busy night of courting torment and anguish. This was the day his tolerance would end, and it was time to start the game anew.

Nathan had learned to live by the rules of the keepers, and like a well-trained circus beast, he would perform on command, forever on watch for the trainer to commit an error. He was docile, hiding the terror deep within, coddling the want and the need. He had learned to avoid the others who refused to cooperate, those other prisoners who actually belonged here within this world of white and tranquility, who needed to be bullied, beat, and sedated regularly. Nathan was not one of them. He belonged in the world of bright colors and loud noise. The real world needed him to teach them how to scream. Who else would hold the hand of the child in their minds and scare them to death? Only he knew how to whisper sweet obscenities in the middle of the night and arouse their not-so-gentle response to the discovery that monsters really do live in their neighborhood.

"Rise and shine, Mr. Pomeroy. It's time to have some breakfast. This is a big day for you, Nathan. Did you forget that Detective May was coming for a visit?"

Nathan lay perfectly still in his bed and watched the shadow of Max, his personal keeper, travel along the wall and fade into the bright sunlight pouring around the bars on the window. He had wanted a curtain, but the request had been refused. How he missed the simple little things in life. He counted silently to himself, one, two, three, and then he jumped suddenly, catching the big, blond-haired guard by surprise. The tray of food flew across the room, spilling scrambled eggs, hard grits without salt or butter, and instant coffee without sugar. This was a ritual played only once a week and followed by Nathan cowering against the wall, playing the nervous fool afraid of all things loud and of sudden movements. He would feign fear, stutter and drool, and, if he could, piss all over the bed sheets.

"Goddamn it, Nathan! Why the fuck do you do that, man?!" Max would scream, and Nathan would go into this act, cowering, sputtering, and straining to pee. "Damn it to hell, Nathan, don't you piss like a scared cat! Oh, man, you're gonna clean that up!"

Nathan would start to protest, giggle in a high-pitched voice, and conclude with coughing out of control until he collapsed on the floor. His mind would start to divide, concentrating on that portion concerned with survival, capable of issuing those commands necessary to ensure that tomorrow would be his, with thoughts flowing horizontally and through the clouds of chaos where insanity breeds. His senses would stretch taut, near to breaking, the cold center of his eyes watching, ears hearing all sounds but concentrating on only those sounds that come whispering between the edges of the two worlds colliding. Nurses would be summoned, and the stinging injection of drugs designed to control behavior would follow, and then several more hours of sleep would be his.

The flight from Atlanta had arrived ten minutes early the previous night, and Roberta had smiled at Stan while coming down the gangway. They had found her luggage on the carousel, and minutes later she was heading back to Miami Beach. Conversation had been light, restricted to anything not related to Nathan or Buddy, to things not remotely connected to police work. Stan liked the easy way he could talk with her. Roberta liked the way he let her talk and did not interrupt halfway through as she espoused an opinion. The music on the radio had provided a pleasant ambiance, and if it had been a different time, perhaps those suggestions gliding on the edge of their thoughts could have had a chance.

"Just what do you people do in a town like Caulking for entertainment?" Stan had to ask.

"What kinda question is that? You think we live in log cabins in the middle of the woods, cook dinner over an open fire, and wait for the men folk to come home with a deer or something?" Roberta countered with indignation. "Caulking had over thirty thousand full-time residents, and during the tourist season—and we do have a tourist season, you know—it swells to over seventy-five thousand. We have four malls, a lot of great restaurants, a thriving electronics industry thanks to federal incentives, a community college, and even a Blockbuster video rental store on every corner, just like here in the great big city."

Stan was embarrassed and had to laugh at himself. He guessed he had made Caulking sound like a three-mule town with Main Street stretching a whole two blocks. He smiled at a Roberta and said, "I surrender. Any town with a Blockbuster means *y'all* have made it to the big leagues."

They drove to his favorite restaurant, a well-known Thai place called the Red Orchid, with at least an hour wait with reservation. Roberta confessed to never having had the pleasure of savoring Thai food, and that set off another round of small-town quips, their bantering lasting until Stan stopped in front of the valet parking sign.

"By the way, what happened to the police ride?"

"What, you don't like my car?"

"Yeah, I love it. You big-city boys must get paid a whole lot better than the average Joe," Roberta teased, running her hands across the brown leather seat and admiring the apple-red corvette.

The look she gave Stan stopped the instant return of sarcasm, and he teetered between taking her comment as a joke and taking it as an accusation of illegal activity. He decided on the first to avoid dampening the festive atmosphere with such a serious conversation. Roberta took note of the expression on his face and started to apologize after realizing that he had been offended by her words, but she stopped before the "I'm sorry" left her mouth. She liked this man and was enjoying the knowledge that what she said and thought had bothered him.

Inside the restaurant, the lighting was dim, the air full of exotic aromas, and there were wall-to-wall people. There was an instant attack of panic, and Roberta scanned the interior for the emergency exits while a petite young woman with thick, long, blue-black hair approached and asked in thickly accented English if they would prefer to wait in the bar. The young hostess looked no more than sixteen to Roberta, and she had a complexion that reminded her of a porcelain doll.

"I don't know." Stan hesitated, waiting for a clue from Roberta.

"Sure, I could use a nice glass of white wine with a bourbon chaser right about now," she answered, unable to look away from the woman.

"It'll be about thirty minutes tonight. Please follow me," the woman answered mechanically. Then she bowed silently and led them to another room filled beyond capacity with everyone else waiting thirty minutes for a table.

The dinner was fabulous, and Roberta was a convert to Thai cooking. The conversation returned to more pleasant topics, and they found it easy to relax. The tab was paid and compliments offered to the chef, and Stan asked Roberta if she cared to take a walk around the famous South Beach strip, nicknamed SoBe by the in-crowd, a four-block section of old Miami Beach consisting of trendy sidewalk cafes, piano bars, and expensive eateries. The area was restricted to cars after six-thirty, and the streets were filled with sightseers, locals, and mainly people who just wanted to be seen hitting the popular nightspots.

Roberta was feeling the effect of the flight and tried to stifle a yawn. Stan caught her and without saying a word, steered their brief walk back to the Red Orchid and retrieved his car. The drive up the strip to the Colony Hotel was quiet but pleasant, and both of them enjoyed the music from the radio. The trip was short, and before Roberta could fall asleep against the soft leather of the car seat, Stan slid the car to a stop.

"Here you go, Ms. Austin. How's this for special treatment, right to the front door."

"Thanks. Sorry I was such a bore at the end, but I am beat."

"Don't apologize. I should have realized sooner," Stan answered, checking his watch. "Try to get to bed soon. We only have seven hours before the interview.'

"Great. I guess we'll skip the part about asking if you want to have a nightcap, huh? I'll be waiting right here, Detective May. Thanks for a great meal." Roberta stepped out of the car.

Stan drove away slowly, sorry there was not even time to explore the possibilities if she had asked him up to her room. He thought about the next day and wondered if Roberta would still think the trip back down here to Miami was worth her time. There was the chance that Nathan was just playing with them—maybe he was growing bored and missed the attention. Stan entered the entrance ramp to the expressway and shoved the accelerator to the floor. The rush of wind through the windows helped dissipate the lingering effects of the drinks and wine.

Roberta fell into the white sheets. As sleep overtook her, the dreams invaded her mind. Sweat poured from her body, and she gasped for breath, running, running. Just up ahead, her mind was taunting her with memories as her fingers dug into the sheets. Roberta woke in a dark haze, knowing but not understanding, hearing the name called but not seeing the face of the caller. She spent the rest of the short night in restless slumber, tossing and turning until the scheduled wakeup call relieved her from the torment.

Roberta was waiting at the curb as promised and smiled brightly as Stan approached. "What happened to the Vette?"

"Official police business requires an official police car, Ms. Austin. You wouldn't want to buck the system, now would you?" he answered and handed Roberta a cup of coffee as she slid into the seat next to him.

"Thanks, you're an angel. I didn't have time to get anything from room service," she told him.

Nathan had been agitated all night, had refused to let sleep quiet the demons chasing nightmares through his mind. The voices had outdone themselves, and he had sat rocking on the floor for the past ten hours, alternating between screaming and singing. The on-duty doctor had tried several times to sedate him, but the nurses and guards were tired of being bitten and spat on. They let the man rave and fight his own battles against whatever was raging inside his head. The doctor tried to cancel the pending visit from the police department but was unable to contact Detective May or John Vazquez.

May and Roberta were greeted by grim expressions and listened to staff members complain about Nathan's behavior. Stan stopped to listen to an intern at the front desk, and Roberta wandered ahead through the entrance. She hated the way the facility smelled. There was an odor drifting in the air that reminded her of both a hospital and an animal shelter. The brilliant effect of everything being white caused temporary blindness and disorientation. Roberta had to lean against a glass window in the hall to keep from falling down. Seconds later, she turned abruptly to stare past the glass at the figure huddled on the floor.

Nathan Pomeroy recognized her the instant she turned to face him. He could feel her presence, smell her ever-growing confusion, and he smiled warmly at her puzzled expression. He looked so small and helpless, sitting there wrapped in a blanket, and for a moment, Roberta felt sorry for him. She wanted someone to come and open the door so she could hold him close, warm him with her own body. The moment passed and the feeling was replaced instantly with loathing, as if she had found a dead roach floating at the bottom of her glass of soda. The revulsion was tangible, occupying the space between the glass partition, and Nathan felt it too. He giggled and wiggled his tongue at Roberta.

"He is one of our favorite guests," a voice announced from behind her, and Roberta jumped. She turned to face a giant of a man, Maxwell Green, Nathan's Max.

"I'm sorry, you said he was a favorite?" she responded, and the look of disgust on her face caused Max to explode with a fit of laughter.

Nathan was laughing along with his keeper, and the sight of the man rocking with his mouth stretched wide without the compliment of sound gave Roberta gooseflesh. She had to turn away and was glad to see Stan walking in her direction.

"They tell me that Nathan is already waiting for us somewhere in a room," he announced when he drew closer. Roberta did not answer but merely pointed a thumb over her shoulder toward the window. Stan looked inside and turned his head to the side with a strange, almost comical expression. Roberta turned to look back down at Nathan.

"Oh my god, that is disgusting!"

Max peered over their heads and hit the glass with an open palm, yelling, "Now you stop that, you crazy fucker!"

Nathan had managed to pull down his pants, even though he was restrained by some type of tether holding him to the wall, and had deposited a brown lump on the floor. He had grabbed his own feces and was smearing it around his face. His eyes pierced Roberta the second she looked at him, and this time, she could not look away; neither did she have a return of the motherly instincts to save him from this hell.

"This has been a problem all week with Nathan," said the intern who had been talking with Stan at the door. "We were making great progress with him and managed to create a dialogue with him about events of his early childhood."

Roberta snapped her attention away from Nathan and stared at the intern. He had her undivided attention now. For some reason, the matter of Nathan's past was very important to her, and she listened with unexplained interest.

"Continue, please. What did Nathan say about his past?" she demanded. "It could tell us a lot about why he is the way he is and help to solve a few more murders."

"He spoke briefly about his family, about their way of life in his hometown. I believe it is pronounced Caulking. He did not like his mother and father very much. They died when he was very young—"

Roberta interrupted. "Thirteen, when he was thirteen," she said in a whisper.

Both the intern and Detective May turned to face her. Roberta looked away and back down at Nathan. He had stopped smearing his body with the feces and was looking back at her with a face filled with an expression of peace.

"How did you know that, Roberta?" Stan asked.

"I don't know. I just did. Must have read it in one of the files or something."

"The records indicate that they just disappeared, leaving him to fend for himself for a long time before anyone found him," resumed the intern, looking straight at Roberta.

"Yeah right, that's a bunch of bullshit, sport! The fucker killed them, not that they didn't deserve to die, even the way he did it. They got exactly what they deserved," Roberta added. She did not notice the way both men continued to stare at her.

Roberta was no longer with them mentally. Her mind had taken leave of the present and was racing out of control back in time. She could see a little girl, maybe nine or ten years old, too terrified to scream, too afraid to stop moving. The train whistle sounded again, this time a little closer, and the voices yelling at her grew louder. There were people, men, maybe eight or nine of them, chasing her. The thorns from the weeds were tearing at the exposed flesh of her legs and arms, but it did not matter. She could see the train. It was not that far ahead, but someone else was running with her. The others were running after her, after them, but she could not see who was with the little girl. Her lungs were burning, her skin tingling, and the rocks were slicing her feet to shreds. She could not stop. This was her last chance to escape, and the rest of the world was a gray fuzzy ball.

"Catch the little bitch. I ain't had my turn, goddamn it!" a voice was screaming not far behind the footsteps, the loud hammering of boots that thundered all around. She heard another voice, recognized the deep growl, and knew it was her daddy. She ran faster. She had to hurry. The train was moving faster, and it was only a matter of seconds now. The smaller hand in hers pulled away, and a little voice cried out in pain as they crashed to the ground. She was running alone now, but the others were closing the distance between them.

"There she is, the little cunt. She's gonna make the train!"

The loud clamor of the train wheels vibrated the ground beneath her bare feet, and the whistle ripped apart the very air above her head. She could see the open door of the last boxcar. She had to reach up and grab the ladder without falling, reaching, straining to stretch small arms to their maximum length.

"You ain't goin' nowhere, you fucking whore. I own you, just like your mama!" someone yelled right behind her, and with great effort, she reached and felt the cold metal bar on the tips of her fingers. With one final burst of desperation, her little hand wrapped around it. The train surged forward, pulling her along and off the ground. She had to hold on, to pull herself up and into the car.

"Fuck," she heard her daddy scream, and with the last of her strength, the little girl made it up the ladder. She did not feel the pain ravishing her frail, nude body or the blood oozing from the cuts. She leaned against the boxcar and took a deep breath. She was shaking uncontrollably, but now she was safe. Her thoughts screamed at what this night, like most others, had meant for her, but this night was different.

They had raped her repeatedly, the nine of them, and her daddy had been the first in line. She had watched him collect the money as they came knocking on the door. He had taken her to the old wood shack behind the house by the canal. Each man had taken his turn, and when the last one was done, the first had been ready to take her again. She could hear her father laughing as the men talked about his sweet little girl and all the fun they were having. Two of the men had dragged the girl's little brother in the shack and told him to have a go at his sister. The boy had refused and was slapped hard to the floor, kicked in the side, and left moaning while their attention went back to the girl. She had known that this night was different and that she would never make it through the horror alive. Each man had been more violent with every turn, and she had almost lost consciousness twice already. She had to escape. She had to survive long enough to try to run for the train. The sound of the whistle had told her it was getting near. There had not been much time, but before she could finish those thoughts, another man had pinned her to the wall. He was laughing. Whiskey breath had choked her lungs, and he had brutalized her again.

"Leave her be!" the young boy had screamed, hitting at the man on his sister.

"Shut the fuck up, you little piss-ant cocksucker, or I'll shove it up your ass. Makes no difference to me!"

This was her chance; the men had briefly turned their attention to the boy and were laughing at his gallant attempts to help. She could see the door in front by the light of a full moon. This was it, her only chance to live and see another day.

Roberta heard her name being called somewhere in the distance, but she did not have time to listen to Stan. She had to finish the memory. She could see the sleek black shape of the train racing from nowhere and heading to nowhere through the midnight rush of cold air. Her heart was pounding wildly in her chest, and she could not breathe, just like the little girl in the boxcar. The sounds of the metal wheels shrieking against the rails were drowned out by the cry of the whistle and then by the screams of men being crushed beneath those same wheels when they had tripped trying to grab hold. The little girl crawled across the rough wood floor to the far corner of the car. She did not cry. There were no words demanding to be heard, and no tears left in her heart or her eyes. This was the beginning of the end, and she did not have a plan, only a desperate need to get far away.

"Roberta!" Stan yelled.

She suddenly jerked around, staring at the man with a crazy, confused look. She could not focus on his face. Something demanded that she look again through the present, back to the past, and she saw the face of a small boy disappearing behind the train. The face was familiar, and when Roberta rocketed back to the present, she found herself looking down at Nathan. He was smiling knowingly, but the hate could not be masked, the commonality could not be denied, and Roberta felt the air around her crush her with tremendous weight.

"Roberta, what the hell is wrong with you?" May yelled.

The intern pulled her away from the glass, breaking the connection, and Nathan howled like a wounded animal.

"Oh my God..." was all she could manage.

Stan May had been right in his amateur analysis that bits of Roberta's past were emerging from those dark, distant places buried beneath carefully constructed layers of denial, that they were thrusting themselves upon her conscious mind with no consideration for the timing or the damage they might create.

Roberta's sight came back to her, and her dull eyes dragged around the room, taking notice of nothing except the face of the intern. He was trying to get her attention, talking slowly as if she were a deranged child awakened from sleepwalking. She smiled and giggled before launching into hysterical laughter.

Roberta was not capable of fully understanding the implications of her memory. She only realized that the little girl was her and remembered the horrible events that had preceded her midnight race through the woods. Life would not be the same for her again. Things were not as she had thought, and now she did grasp the meaning of why she had blocked out most of her childhood. The only thing she could not comprehend was what role Nathan played in all of this. How come he knew her by the name Ricky-Lou?

Nathan sat in his padded cell, thinking wicked thoughts and listening to the voices in his head. He knew what Roberta had been thinking. He had always been able to read her mind or influence her thoughts, especially when they were near to each other. He had been there that day when she had come to interview Delores, and those had been his desires she had felt. He also remembered the night so long ago, felt the pain she had felt, and the panic manifesting into a singleness of purpose—survival. He had been there fleeing with Ricky-Lou but had fallen at the very doorway of escape, only to be captured and punished with a relentlessness that caused his mind to twist and metamorphose into a creature of survival. Nathan had become a beast of instinct, no longer human. He could not feel the pain any longer and could know pleasure only when he himself caused pain for others more fortunate than himself.

He sat in his cell and let the waves of time recede to the point of origin. He watched the train rocking steadily along the tracks, merely black ribbons racing into the night and touched here and there with moonlight reflecting from the edge of polished steel. Strong hands closed around his arms like a vise, twisting and smashing the muscles. The air filled with angry words, and still other voices contained screams of agony as men died. Those who were merely angry disappeared into the black woods, dragging him along to the same woodshed, and they did those things to him that had been meant for his sister. Nathan would never forgive Ricky-Lou for abandoning him, for leaving him behind and letting him become the demented demon he was today. She was to be held accountable for the same atrocities inflicted upon his young and fragile mind, and with the same vengeance as those who had actually committed the hideous acts.

The crushed bodies of the other men had been left to rot between the tracks. They had already died from the wounds received from the relentless turning of the huge steel wheels. The train had never slowed, and the engineer had never realized what was happening. The roar of the engines and clacky-clack thunder of the wheels had been more than a match for mere screams of dying, hateful men. Young Nathan Pomeroy had watched the train until the brush had become thick and the distance too far. The last of his hopes had disappeared along with that train and the only person in this world he had ever truly loved.

Stan May was not able to believe everything as the intern explained the manifestation of stress as hallucinations or blackouts while explaining Roberta Austin's behavior. The woman was as crazy as that damn fool locked behind the glass. There was something genuinely wrong here, and he did not care what his feelings were toward Roberta; he determined that the hospital had better prepare another room.

Roberta was sitting in the employee lounge, sipping a can of Diet Pepsi while May and the intern talked in the hall. The intern was animated in his movements, going to extreme lengths to explain why Roberta was having fainting spells, hearing voices, and seeing visions. May looked as if he were trying hard to be patient just before slapping the crap out of the intern. Roberta glanced in their direction from time to time, not caring what the center of the conversation was, and trying hard to pull it all together. Buddy Chandler was the main reason she was here again in Miami, the reason she was facing the worst nightmares of her life by facing the most despicable human being on earth, and beyond that, she had not a clue. Her head was pounding, her heart racing, and she wanted nothing more than to get on with the reason they were here in this institution of torture.

"So you're telling me that this woman is fine and what she is experiencing is something along the lines of delayed stress syndrome because of her own questionable childhood," May said with blatant disbelief.

"Yes, Detective. She is experiencing periods of extreme anxiety, actually sympathizing with Nathan in order to cope with overwhelming emotion, almost like the same thing a kidnapped victim might feel for their captors after a period of time."

"You are saying that she's not actually remembering her own past but is recalling events and situations that she read in Nathan Pomeroy's file, and her mind is making it her own in order to keep from what? Having a nervous breakdown or something?"

"In a brief summation, yes."

"Nonsense. This is the biggest line of crap I've heard in a long, long time," May exclaim and headed toward Roberta.

Roberta looked up as May entered the room. The detective looked back once at the intern before closing the door. May sat down in the chair across from Roberta and merely studied the expression on her face. It was like he was trying to crawl inside her head and determine for himself what was wrong with her.

"What the fuck is going on here, Roberta? I really need to know now, with no bullshit and no psychological games, just the straight shit. Got it?"

Roberta shook her head slowly and tried to smile, but the attempt was weak, and she leaned her forehead against the cool surface of the table. "Okay, Stan, I don't know if I can explain this all to you. I don't even know if I think you deserve an explanation. This is really none of your fucking business, but for some ungodly reason, I trust you," she told him.

This time he did not say anything but simply waited for her to continue talking.

"I keep having these dreams of a little girl, a terribly frightened little girl, who has gone through hell, but I am not asleep. I think the little girl is me. I have never been able to remember my childhood. My parents, the couple who adopted me, spent a lot of money trying to help me, but nothing seemed to work. I had blocked out that part of my life, so I don't know if the dream is about me, or about what I may think is me, or if it is nothing more than stress as Mr. Sigmund Freud explains it.

"All I know is something weird is going on here, and I don't understand it. Stan, I'm scared. Nathan is really psyching me out, like he knows something that I don't and he's fucking with me. I look at him and he gives me that odd little look, like he's waiting for me to catch on to something, but I don't know what."

Stan's expression softened a little as he listened to Roberta. He knew that she was having a hard time talking about this. He told himself to quit being a prick. He wanted to reach out to hold her hand, and he did. Roberta stopped talking the moment he touched her, and the tears began to roll down her face. She cried silently, and May drew her close until her face was buried in his shoulder.

CHAPTER

TWENTY-ONE

THE INTERVIEW WAS long and difficult, filled with histrionics and dramatic pauses orchestrated by Nathan to delay, to taunt, and to wrap everything in shrouds of confusion. He could not say more than a few words without letting himself take leave of all perception, circling the point, going on tangents designed to lead the listeners away from the reason they were sitting in this room.

May and Roberta waited for any mention of Buddy, but it did not come, and when the detective attempted to ask directly if Nathan had any knowledge of the sheriff, Nathan changed the subject and baited Roberta by asking if she remembered a little girl named Sarah. He asked if she also remembered the older brother and sister, the children of Phoebe Thornton, and he giggled. Nathan licked his lips like he had just tasted something delicious, and the voices reached new frontiers in expressing pleasure.

"What about Sarah? Do you know where she is?" asked Roberta.

"I know where everyone is, Roberta Austin, District Attorney, big shot comin' all the way from Georgia just to bust my balls."

Stan was listening carefully, digesting every nuance, studying the way Nathan changed the subject and which subjects he avoided, and the detective began to understand the pattern where earlier a pattern had not been detected. Stan had become impatient and stopped Roberta from answering Nathan. Nathan scowled at May, his eyes smoldering with hate. Stan had stopped the game. This uppity monkey-boy was going to spoil the fun, Nathan thought to himself. Roberta fell silent, sensed that May was onto something, and let him take the lead.

"Tell me, Nathan, why are you wasting our time? I don't think you know shit, boy. I think you are just missing all the attention, right? We'll be leaving. Enjoy your strained peas and milk," May told him and stood.

Nathan was mute, watching the detective walk to the door and ring the buzzer for the guard. Roberta never indicated she was puzzled but merely followed Stan to the door without looking back. The guard responded, unlocked the door, and stood back for the two of them to pass.

"Wait," came the response from Nathan, the one May was desperately waiting for. The detective had been beginning to think he had misjudged.

"Excuse me, did you say something?"

"Yeah, Mr. Fancy Pants. I said wait. Don't ya wanta know where little Ms. Roberta could find them three kids? You know, the Thornton brats."

"Yes!" Stan screamed in his head. The ploy had actually worked. He should have paid more attention to the serial-murderer seminar he had attended last year. The instructor had told them that these killers feed on huge dosages of ego and cannot stand to be ignored or believed to be simple braggarts. Roberta gave Stan's hand a squeeze of thanks and stepped back into the room. She took her time opening her briefcase and taking out a pad.

"Ya'll gonna take all fucking day?" demanded Nathan, and Stan smiled. Yes, they had him now. It was just a matter of playing the ego game, and then he would spill his guts.

Nathan described in excruciatingly fine detail the last few hours of the lives of the three children. Roberta bit her lip to avoid showing her disgust, and even the hardened detective was affected by the obvious show of pleasure and pride demonstrated by this monster. Nathan recalled the torture step by step for their listening enjoyment, itemizing every punch, slap, and cut. Roberta filled page after page with notes and made sure the tape recorder was getting every sick word. This would bury Nathan in this hole for the rest of his miserable life. She waited for him to pause before asking, "Where are the bodies, Nathan? Where did you leave them?"

Nathan smiled, looked slyly from Stan to Roberta, and slowly shook his head. He said, "Nope, it don't work that way, Roberta. No, siree, smarty pants. You ain't gonna be gettin' it all and leave me here holdin' my big hard dick in my hand."

May was not surprised and expected Nathan to play his last card. Roberta reacted well and merely folded her steno pad, delaying, waiting for Nathan to say more without her having to ask. The wait was not long. "Ain't gonna ask me what I want?"

"Why, I already got everything I need. Nobody is missing those little kids. Their mom and dad are dead. Nobody needs the bodies anymore, anyway. You keep your little secret," Roberta sneered. May was shouting with joy in his head. She had played Nathan just right. May was so proud of Roberta that he wanted to kiss her. She now had the bastard by the throat.

Nathan was stunned. The voices inside Nathans's head were screaming, "*Foul!*" and he wanted to rip the expression from Roberta's face, she was so smug and so damned pleased with herself. He sat in the chair and strained against the chain holding the harness to the wall; if only he could get to the bitch, he would make sure she would never smile again. "I ain't done with you yet, Ricky-Lou," he whispered.

The words crushed the protective coating she had wrapped around what was left of her sanity. Roberta sat up straight in her chair as if some invisible hand had jerked her backward. Stan missed what Nathan had said and waited for Roberta to say something. The silence hung in the air. Nathan had regained the upper hand, and the game was far from over.

"This is going nowhere. I'm outta here," stated Roberta. She grabbed the tape recorder from the table as she headed for the door.

Stan was perplexed, tried to stop her from leaving, and followed her out the door. He told the guard they were taking a ten-minute break and would be in the lounge having coffee. Roberta pulled away from him, but he caught her before she could open the bathroom door.

"What the fuck was that all about? Things were going great. You were doing a fantastic job of manipulating him. What did he say to change all that, Roberta?"

Roberta tossed Stan the recorder. "Play it back, and you tell me if I'm going crazy or not."

Roberta washed her hands and face, staring at herself in the mirror while Stan rewound the tape. He listened to the last two or three minutes and realized that she was right; something was going on between Nathan and her. Something weird. He handed her back the recorder as she stepped through the door. "So who is Ricky-Lou? Someone you knew back in Georgia? Who, Roberta?"

Her face was pale and her eyes were glazed as she searched for the answer that screamed in her mind.

"Roberta, who is Ricky-Lou?"

"She's the little girl from my dreams. You tell me how the hell that sick bastard knows the name of someone I dream about? This is not the first time he called me that, Stan. I think I'm going crazy."

Nathan was trying with his foot to open the briefcase that Stan had left behind in the room when the door clicked open.

"You stay away from that, you crazy fuck," warned the guard as he sat down in the chair across from Nathan.

Moments later, Roberta came back alone and asked the guard to leave them.

"You sure about this? He is one weird dude, lady."

"Yeah, I'm sure. You just stay close to the other side of the door."

She waited to speak until the man had left, and she felt the fierce anger oozing from Nathan filling the space between them.

"Whatcha want, Ricky-Lou? You and that asshole yer fuckin? " Nathan taunted.

"Who is Ricky-Lou, Nathan? I want you to tell me about her."

Nathan smiled. He watched her squirm in the hard plastic seat, fed on her uncertainty, and decided to let her sweat. "You be knowing her real good-like. You could even be twins."

"This is crap, Nathan. I'm not going to let you keep playing this your way, fuck-boy."

The words stung. He remembered someone else who had called him that and strained against the chain until his face swelled red with fury. "Don't you call me that, bitch. I ain't nobody's fuck-boy, you got that!"

"Yeah, then you tell me straight up what is going on here. Stop with the games, Nathan. I ain't playing no more."

He waited until the voices crawled behind the shadows and the blood stopped congesting his thoughts. Roberta was finished and started to leave. "You be leavin' me again? You be real good at leavin' me behind, ain't ya, Ricky-Lou? All you had to do was hold on for a few more seconds, and we wouldn't be havin' this here little chat."

Roberta did not stop. She was no longer listening to him and only snickered. The sound sliced through Nathan like a hot knife through butter, and he screamed, "Betcha wanta know all 'bout how I enjoyed myself with sweet little Becky-Ann, don'tcha, bitch? Course, it don't make no never mind to that big dumb sheriff no more."

Roberta paused at the door, turned slowly, and looked at Nathan. "This is the last game, Nathan. You tell me where we can find the Thornton children. I want to be sure those kids get buried proper, and then you'll tell me about Buddy."

"Ya'll ain't runnin' this sideshow, bitch. You best be calling yer big black boyfriend back in here and then call that lawyer of mine. We are gonna make a deal. You see bitch, I am crazy—I can guarantee that— but I ain't stupid."

Vazquez, May, Roberta, and Nathan were finishing the details of a binding agreement that would require the endorsement of an on-duty state attorney and a judge. Roberta had already made three phone calls to Georgia, seeking advice and guidance from members of her own staff. Nathan had consented to reveal the site of the burial pit containing the remains of the Thornton children, but he withheld vital information that would help a search party discover the whereabouts of the pit. Nathan stated that he could not remember the exact location and wanted to take Roberta on a personal tour to find the spot.

She also asked about Buddy and told him that neither the State of Florida nor the State of Georgia was considering prosecution as an option. The authorities in both states only wanted to close out several cases. Nathan refused to discuss anything else with May or Roberta. He had already given them information on the murders of Sarah, Deirdre, Junior, and six other children. May tried one last time to ferret out a little more information and asked about Sharon Hughes. Nathan gave him a funny look for the effort and said only "Who the fuck is that?" Roberta and Stan exchanged looks, but if Stan had looked closely, he would have seen fear, not confusion, in Roberta's eyes.

All the papers were signed before the end of the day. Nathan had won the game that day and would be on a flight back to Caulking, Georgia, before the end of the week. May was obviously annoyed, but he never said a word to Roberta about the agreement. He drove her to the hotel in silence and sped away. She tried to call several times between conference calls with her office, the sheriff's department and the FBI. There were so many details left to link together, and she wanted to bring the case to an end. Roberta doubted Nathan would tell her what had really happened to Buddy, but in her heart, she knew that Buddy was dead, and that was the only revelation that actually mattered for her anymore. In short, this entire twisted and manipulated affair had been orchestrated solely for the purpose of finding closure, to heal wounds by lancing the pain, bringing forth the infection deep within, to bring light to the dark and morbid places lurking in the fetid traps of sorrow. She had gambled all on a game of chance in which the outcome had been decided years ago. Roberta could do nothing more than accept defeat and the fact that closure was, in reality, a fleeting fantasy.

The following morning, John Vazquez had breakfast with Roberta and Stan. He came not only with a ferocious appetite, which explained why the man appeared to be triplets, but also with a pale blue file containing a single sheet of paper. The attorney was already at the table munching on pieces of toast and working on his third cup of coffee when Detective May and District Attorney Austin arrived. He watched as they exited the car, Stan holding open the door and helping Roberta step to the street, and he thought, "*Oh, how quaint, forever attentive to the ladies.*"

John waved as the two of them appeared by the hostess's podium and dragged himself from the seat, showering the table with crumbs. "Good morning, one and all. Isn't this a beautiful morning?" he announced cheerfully, extending a hand.

"John, it is raining outside, the temperature is dropping, and it is only seven o'clock. What is beautiful about it?" snarled May.

John turned his attention toward Roberta and asked, "Is he always this cheerful in the morning, Miss Austin?"

She smiled slightly, responding, "I am not accustomed to seeing Detective May in the morning hours, Mr. Vazquez." She sat down at the table.

Vazquez motioned for Stan to join them and wondered if the detective and the district attorney were sleeping together. Roberta could see the question hanging over their heads and decided that it didn't matter. John was just showing his jealousy, and she knew if he had the chance, he would sleep with her too.

"Take a look at this before you order. I recommend the egg-white omelet with spinach. It is a specialty and absolutely delicious," John recommended, handing the folder to Detective May.

Roberta tried to read upside down but soon returned her attention to the menu. She tried to interpret Stan's reaction, but his face remained expressionless. John Vazquez knew that this was merely a formality, something mandated by Judge Henry, a standard order requiring an officer of the court to travel with the prisoner. If May signed the form, he would take responsibility for Nathan Pomeroy until Pomeroy's return to Miami. Vazquez shoveled a fork full of egg into his cavernous mouth and motioned for the server to refill his coffee cup.

Stan finished and slid the blue folder across the table to Roberta without giving her any indication if he found the information agreeable or not. He merely shrugged and ordered a western omelet with a side of bacon, whole-wheat toast, and orange juice when the waitress came back to the table with a fresh pot of steaming coffee. Roberta decided to take John's suggestion and flipped open the folder's cover. She read the order carefully and, after finding nothing hidden in the language or intent, closed the file.

"Well, this is not for me to decide. I think Detective May, or whoever is assigned by the Beach, will have to deal with it."

May retrieved the folder, signed his name to the bottom of the page, and asked John to make several copies and have someone drop them off at his office for the official file. He did not look at Roberta as he began a discussion on the price of gold. Roberta was mildly disturbed, and although she knew Stan had the authority to make the decision, she knew he had reacted only out of spite. He hated this idea of taking Nathan back to Georgia and hated even more that Nathan was slowly gaining control.

Nathan Pomeroy was behaving exceptionally well this morning. Max was wary and ready for a repeat of the normal episodes, but Nathan refused to entertain the guard. He accepted without a remark the tray of tasteless gruel that only marginally passed as edible. Max concluded that Nathan must have been catching a cold or regressing into the catatonic state he had exhibited when he had first been brought to the institution. Max remembered how Nathan had oscillated between violent aggression and passive resistance, something the doctors called bi-polar disorder and something he simply called another day in paradise. He dealt with the violent mood swings by strapping the prisoner in a leather harness and securing it tightly to the wall with a short chain. Nathan responded with biting and more than once had sent Max to the infirmary for medical attention.

The harness brought back pleasant memories for Nathan. The voices shouted hello, and he dreamed of Sarah Thornton. A good deal of effort had gone into designing that special gift, and had he thought of it, Nathan would have apologized to the big guard for the nasty bites, but his mind was lost in the past, watching the little girl swing, hearing her cries of fear, tasting the blood in his mouth when he bit her hard on the buttocks—and he never knew he had taken a piece from Max's arm. Thus, a routine had been established by accident, and Nathan looked forward to the little moments of intimacy like a junkie craving another fix. He would scream and lash out at the guards, attacking a fellow inmate and being rewarded with a few hours in the harness with Max abusing his restrained body. The true secret of a joyful, happy life lay within the small pleasures, and those could be sought in the most unexpected way.

Max was concerned for the health of his charge. After all, this crazy killer represented a paycheck and demanded full-time attention, which meant Max was excused from some of the routine aspects of the job.

The other guards complained about Max not taking part in the mundane tasks of cleaning, painting, and preparing food, but the supervisor wanted to be sure that Nathan Pomeroy did not remain front-page news. They did not need the Department of Prisons reading accounts of violence or murders committed on their watch. No one needed extra inspections and all the hassle. Max had been given the special assignment of only taking care of Nathan, of guaranteeing that the prisoner would be molded into a model of compliance.

"What's up, Nathan? You come down with a cold or something?" Max had to ask.

Nathan did not answer him. He did not hear Max, because he was dealing with other conversations. Nathan was winging high above the security gates, watching the naked bodies of neighborhood children lying spread eagle across the brilliant green grass and waiting for him to arrive. He was lost in a fantasy and staring out the window, straining to see the rooftops of the houses across the grounds, hearing bits of conversations carried on the wind.

"Nathan, you need to see a doctor or something?"

Nathan turned his eyes away from the window without moving his head and answered, "Y'all are askin' me if I should visit the doc? Who's in charge here, you fuckin' baboon?"

Max smiled broadly, because this was the old Nathan, the one he had come to know, and everything was right once again with his world. He could relax and let the crazy bastard do whatever it was he did when he stared off into space. Max did not want to know what thoughts ran wild through this man's mind. He already knew what acts Nathan had committed to get here, and that was more than enough. Max settled into the metal chair by the door and began to read the sports section of the newspaper. Everything was as it should be, and Nathan soared far away, dreamin' special dreams about Georgia.

Final arrangements were made, and a hundred trees gave their lives for the hundreds of pages of reports, orders, and affidavits that had to be signed in triplicate, one copy for court and one for each of the state agencies. Roberta collected her copy and threw the thick envelope into her suitcase without bothering to read the final copy. She'd had enough of the bureaucratic nonsense, even if she was one of the bureaucrats. She just wanted to get along with the business of ending this case and living life again.

Stan May meticulously read each word, checked each clause listing individual and collective responsibilities, and made another copy of the paperwork for his own records. May had a habit of maintaining two filing systems, one for the department and one for himself, and most often, his was the more precise of the two. He'd had a partner years before who had taught him that saving his own ass was top priority and to make extra copies of everything. May had learned the hard way that file copies had a way of disappearing, memos a way of not being remembered, and memories a way of growing vague when needed the most to be sharp.

John Vazquez was amazed at how fast the system worked when it worked in its own best interest. The State of Florida, particularly the Division of Prisons, was very eager to rid itself of Nathan Pomeroy. The only person mourning the departure of Nathan was Max the guard. He was going to have to go back to being just another employee, no longer the keeper of the most famous crazy in this loony bin. He would have to go back to the menial tasks shared by one and all. No longer would he be considered a celebrity and someone envied with special status.

Nathan survived by honing his life to a singleness of thought, deed, and action. He lived to feed the desire, the desire gave him purpose for living, and the voices told him how to satisfy the desire. He never had been able to define the limits of his desire, because he had never been able to reach a point when the voices told him it was enough, to stop. They only grew quiet for a while, savoring the moment. The voices were telling Nathan that the desire was growing again, and he told them to be patient, that he had a plan, but the voices were loud, demanding, and it was a very good thing that the call of nature gave Max a reason to leave the cell.

A good plan had to have time to develop, and Nathan had been working hard. He had nothing but time inside the institute, and he knew the time had been well spent. Little did everyone know, especially that stupid bitch, Roberta, that he was here because he wanted to be here. He had not planned on killing Delores so soon. *She* had forced him because she could not control her appetite, her desires. He'd had to kill Delores after Roberta fed her desires but stopped short of finishing the job, leaving the woman alive, able to talk and identify the perpetrator. Nathan was safe; he had assumed that any court in the nation would find him insane, not responsible for his actions, and would just bury him away in some asylum to bide his time, and he was right. Roberta would have been crushed beneath the wheels of justice, institutionalized in a maximum-security prison until she was dead, and that was the part that concerned Nathan the most—because only he could be responsible for her death, and he would not allow anyone to take her or that pleasure away from him. Roberta had jumped the gun, come out of the closet with a bang, but he had known she had it in her all along, that it was just a matter of time, and timing was everything.

Roberta had decided to return to the institute alone that afternoon. She did not understand the reason but had to satisfy a nagging preoccupation. During her breakfast with May and Velazquez and for several hours afterward, she had been unable to dismiss a concern that Nathan Pomeroy was connected to her childhood. The thought was terrifying, but no one could explain to her satisfaction why and how Nathan knew the name he had called her, the name from her dreams, and how she had known what happened to the parents of this animal and what age he had been when he had killed them both. She had graphic recollection of the act, of screams of pain, the glint of a knife much like the one she purchased in Alabama, and she knew where the bodies were hidden. But how did she know, and how did he know the name of the little girl in her dreams? Roberta decided she had to confront Nathan again and ask him about Ricky-Lou.

Max was concerned about leaving Roberta alone with Nathan, just like he had been concerned before, but really, there was nothing Nathan could do to her. Max checked the harness and the chain and left the room saying, "I can watch every move in that camera up there.

If you get in trouble, I'll be here in a flash." He gave Roberta a wink as he walked out the door.

"That is very reassuring, but I believe Mr. Pomeroy will be a perfect gentleman."

Nathan sighed and leaned his head back against the wall. This was indeed an unexpected pleasure. He watched Roberta sit on the edge of his bed, and the voices started whispering. There were a few new ones this time.

"Nathan, I need to ask you a few more questions, personal questions that have nothing to do with our agreement. Is that okay with you?"

He did not answer because most of his conscious mind was hankering after the smell of her body. There was something irresistible about freshly scrubbed skin. He half closed his eyes and inhaled deeply. Yes, his mind was buzzing across her skin, between her legs, and licking not so gently at the most coveted recesses.

"Nathan, is it all right to continue now?"

He felt the sound of his name slide across the center of his brain and lodge somewhere by the back of the skull. He lost concentration, and his thoughts raced hot on the heels of the voices receding back to the safety of his subconscious. His eyes opened wide, staring as if he saw Roberta for the first time and found it odd for her to be sitting on his bed.

"You can ask any damn thing you want, bitch, but I'll be decidin' what to answer, got it?"

Roberta spoke for several minutes, and Nathan seemed to pay attention. She asked about Ricky-Lou, and she told him what she knew about the death of his parents. He sat and listened, drool running from the corner of his mouth, and Roberta wanted to wipe it away. She had asked every question that had been of a concern to her and waited to see if Nathan had any intention of answering.

"Well, that's a tall order. Betcha a buck you know the answer to every one of those questions, don'tcha, bitch? You just wanted to come back and fuck with me," he told her in tones that did not conceal the seething hate boiling behind his eyes.

"I don't know, maybe, but I need you to answer me, please." She was begging.

"I have—watcha call it—a riddle to be tellin' first. Let's see how smart you are, bitch. I be talkin' about a young woman, looking lots like you, little titties, just a patch of fur above her sweet meat like fuzz on a peach, all ready to bust into blood of woman stuff. You catch my meanin'?" Nathan hesitated. Roberta understood that he was talking about a girl about to start her period, and he continued.

"This girl-woman be havin' these feelin's about bein' poked. She be missin' it, if ya know what I mean. Course she ain't be havin' no one 'round, so she be down there with her fingers dippin' in the puddle," he told her, grinning, and with eyes bouncing wildly around the room. He was enjoying himself immensely and more so when Roberta had to look away.

"Now, this here little woman would be 'bout thirteen or so, and sittin' all snugly in a nice warm room, with a nice warm rug runnin' from wall to wall, with a nice big ol' bed to go a sleepy-bye in. She be down there gettin' herself all excited when the dreams start a comin'." He stopped and watched Roberta's face. This time, she could not look away, and her eyes locked into his.

"She dreams, Roberta, with the voices screamin', with the want of bein' there, runnin' her fingers through somethin' else, ain't she? She wants to be there when the watchin' and the cuttin' and the pullin' is bein' done! Yeah, she be pantin' real hard and listenin' to them voices. The screams dance in the air, and she can hear the rippin' apart of the stomach sack carryin' 'round all that blood and guts." His voice sank to a whisper, and Roberta strained to hear every word, drawing closer to him, almost feeling his rapid breath against her skin.

"And then looky there, the blood clot be comin' and she licks the red juice from the tips of those already wet fingers, while the screams grow louder. Don't you remember, Ricky? I do." He stopped talking, and Roberta pounded on the door for Max. Nathan was howling, jerking against the chain, and spittle flew against the wall. He screamed and called after her, "Where you goin', Ricky-Lou? You can't leave me again. I am a part of you, bitch!" Then Nathan burst into sick laughter.

Max jerked the door open wide, and Roberta fled from the building. She did not stop running until she found her rental car in the visitor parking lot. She was sobbing, her mind reeling in bright colors and filled with voices yelling to one another. She slid down the fender to the black asphalt and heard herself ask, "How did he know? How could he possibly have known?!"

Nathan had described perfectly the night long ago when Roberta had started her menstrual cycle. The cramps had excited her, and her young fingers had given her pleasure as her mind had dreamed of other things. She remembered that night, the taste of blood on her fingers, the smell that had engulfed her desires and the thoughts of blood flowing as the knife dug deeply into the dying flesh. How could he have known what she was thinking as she licked the blood from her hands? How could he have known that the blood mixed with the wonderfully violent fantasies had given her incredible sexual pleasure?

CHAPTER
TWENTY-TWO

THE ONLY WAY an airline would accept a passenger like Nathan was if he was sedated. He was allowed to board the airplane, along with Roberta and Stan May, before any other passengers were seated, and they were seated in the last three seats by the tail exit. Nathan snored peacefully as he drifted in a sea of colors with the consistency of soap. He wore custom restraints on his ankles made from a reinforced nylon strap and handcuffs. The flight attendant reluctantly served the drinks and peanuts. They considered both Roberta and Stan to be police officers and considered Nathan to be number one on the most-wanted list.

"I guess this must be rather peculiar," Detective May said to one of the stewardesses.

"We aren't particularly prepared for this type of service," she replied politely and asked, "Can he eat or drink anything?"

"No, he's fine right now, and I don't think he'll be in the real world until long after we land in Georgia," answered Roberta.

The tall brown-haired woman gave Roberta a side-glance and smiled. "I sure could use whatever he's on during some of these flights."

"Things get rough, huh?"

"People can be such assholes. They think just because they fork out a couple of bucks for a no-frills flight, it means steak and champagne anyway."

"You mean this is not champagne?" asked May, but the stewardess ignored him.

A small army was on hand when the plane touched down, and Nathan was transported through the terminal strapped into a wheelchair. The special ankle strap was bolted to the frame, and three uniformed officers made sure security was maintained. Nathan was beginning to come around by the time he was loaded, chair and all, into the back of a marked police van. He found all the attention fascinating and smiled like a child on Christmas Day.

"Y'all are sure goin' to a lot of trouble just for little ol' me. Can we turn on the siren?"

"Shut the fuck up, you crazy piece of shit. I remember all about you from the papers. You screw up one time and I ain't gonna wait for a second time," growled one of the officers. Nathan just grinned, thinking how good it was to be back home in the warm embrace of old friends and with the opportunity to make new ones.

The drive from the airport in Albany took longer than the flight up from Florida. Roberta was busy covering last-minute details with her office, checking the time for the press conference and making sure that all necessary accommodations to house the special prisoner had been arranged. Nathan was big news, which meant a photo opportunity and career enhancement for Roberta. Stan sat in the back of the van and talked cop-talk with the deputies. They all were anxious to hear about Miami, the crime there, and if it was true that drug dealers owned the streets. Stan had to listen carefully because of the heavy southern accents, but he was enjoying the camaraderie.

Nathan started complaining about being carsick and that he had to go to the bathroom. The driver, a sergeant with the Georgia State Patrol, had little compassion and threw Nathan an empty paper bag. "Do what you got to do, fuckhead. We ain't stoppin' until Caulking. *They* can wipe your sorry ass, not this old boy,"

Nathan was still grinning. He liked the sergeant. The man reminded him of Max, and while he laughed, he vomited all over the cargo space.

"What the hell!" shouted one of the deputies who had been treated with a splash.

A second deputy could not stand the smell or the sound and soon joined Nathan in decorating the inside of the van. The sergeant was cussing and trying to hold his breath at the same time. The van swerved from lane to lane until the tires grabbed the shoulder of the road and lost traction, careening the vehicle through the weeds and scrub-brush.

"Shit! Shit! Shit!" Roberta screamed, bailing from the passenger door the moment the van came to a stop.

Detective May was holding on for his life, glad he'd had the common sense to buckle the seat belt, and trying not to hyperventilate. He waited until everyone had shoved him out of the way and crawled from the side door, pale and wide-eyed, trying to muster as much dignity as the moment deserved. Nathan was giggling and crashing the wheelchair against the sides of the van.

"Get that crazy bastard out of there before he destroys state property," commanded the sergeant, and two of the deputies walked slowly back to the vehicle. The third man was on his hands and knees, trying to gain control over his stomach. Stan May found Roberta by a small stand of oak trees and walked up beside her.

"Next time, see if you can persuade our fearless leader to stop and let Nathan answer the call of nature," he suggested.

"I suppose this is my fault? Shit, look at that stupid fuck," she sneered as Nathan was being removed.

The rest of the journey continued without incident, with all the windows opened and the air-conditioner cranked as high as it would go.

A large crowd of people awaited their arrival, several news stations had sent camera crews. Thick electrical cables criss-crossed the parking lot outside city hall, and a small contingency of government officials stood under a tent erected by the front entrance. A hundred or more townspeople collected along the street, and several were carrying signs with the names of alleged victims. Nathan was craning his neck to look out the window. He was very excited that everyone would go to so much trouble just for him. This was his day, the prodigal son returning to the city.

The politicians tried to capitalize on the moment, offering whimsical speeches, praising law enforcement, and trying to take credit for anything and everything connected with this investigation. Roberta was stoic and her mannerisms stiff in front of the cameras, but her three-minute speech was precise and eloquent and left no doubt who was in charge. Stan stood back in the crowd, just another tourist trying to figure out what the hell was happening. The trooper and the three deputy sheriffs smiled for the cameras and paraded Nathan around in the wheelchair like a circus act.

Sheriff Ward made a sudden appearance and attempted to join Roberta on the courthouse steps. One look immediately informed the sheriff that he was not welcomed, and, being politically ambitious, he decided to take advantage of the flashing cameras. He stood next to Nathan and played the part of the stern, tough sheriff on duty to protect the citizens of his town. Nathan found the entire affair hilarious and played the wild-eyed crazy killer. He spit at anyone within range, snarled and snapped his jaws like some deranged alligator looking for dinner. The act could not be maintained for very long, and soon, he found himself unable to stop giggling. It was during moments of humor that Nathan appeared most dangerous and photographers forgot to take the shots, the cameramen failed to follow their cues, and Sheriff Ward distanced himself.

Three men in nearly identical suits, wearing the same ties and carrying the same briefcases, appeared from nowhere next to Roberta. One whispered in her ear. She listened intently and said something back before disappearing inside the building with the men close behind her.

"Miss Austin, the Bureau has been involved in this investigation from the beginning. We have the final authority, and we have other cases that eclipse your problems here in Caulking," stated Special Agent Lou Frost, agent in charge of a newly formed task force designed to solve cold cases involving the suspicious disappearance of children. The group had been created by a senator from California and spearheaded by several prominent families that wielded influence through substantial campaign contributions motivated by grief. The families shared the emptiness left when a child is abducted, when the laughter and joy are gone forever, replaced by an immobilizing fear and helplessness. These families had turned their grief into political power and vengeance—they had bought a piece of the Federal Bureau of Investigation.

Agent Frost introduced himself, trying to appear friendly. Roberta responded, "Like hell, sport. If you wanted to clear cases, why didn't you climb your ass aboard Air Force One and fly down to Florida yourself?!"

This stopped the conversation, and the FBI agents stared at Roberta. They suddenly remembered why no one wanted to deal with the Caulking authorities and each one wanted the other to talk with District Attorney Austin. Roberta glared them down individually, daring them to pursue this line of thinking, and when no one challenged her position, she spun on her heel and went to find Stan.

He had seen her followed into the courthouse by the three men in suits, and now he watched her storm out the door with fire flashing in her eyes. He waved her down. "Who are the suits?" he asked.

"You mean the three stooges. Take a wild guess," she replied.

"Well, let me see. Same Brooks Brothers dark-blue double-breasted suit, brown wingtips, baby-shit–colored yellow tie, and holier-than-thou attitudes—must be the feds."

"Give the man a cigar." Roberta growled, "Get ahold of the sergeant and tell him to move Nathan. I don't give a shit what the FBI thinks they can do."

Nathan was wheeled away down a back alley and into the Caulking jail by the service entrance before anyone discovered that the main attraction had left. The politicians continued patting each other on the back, and the camera crews decided to move on to other stories.

"Sheriff Ward, we need to talk about security, especially about who does not have access to Mr. Pomeroy," Roberta announced on the telephone.

"Hello to you too, Roberta. Welcome back. Listen for just one minute before you start screaming. I have three agents in my office demanding to talk with your boy. They have dropped a court order mandating my office to comply immediately," Ward told her, and then he waited for instructions.

Roberta chewed her lower lip in deliberation, motioned for Stan to come closer, and spoke to him with a hand over the receiver. "We need to buy some time. The feds have dropped a subpoena on Ward for possession of Nathan."

"That's nice. Don't forget that I'm just a visitor here and this ain't my problem, ma'am," he answered with his best southern accent.

"Fuck you too, sweetheart," she told him, and then she told Ward, "Did you know that Nathan is headed for Albany right now? We were instructed to have him checked at the hospital before any interviews."

Ward smiled. He knew she was lying through her teeth. He glanced at the nearest agent and smiled again, motioning the man to his desk.

"Yes, Sheriff. Do you know where the prisoner is now?"

"Sure do. Albany, or he will be in about forty-five minutes. They had to have him examined by the shrinks first, something to do with the original court orders."

The three men exchanged looks somewhere between disbelief and anger. "I need to borrow a phone, Sheriff. May I use yours?" said the agent in charge.

Ward vacated his desk, told the agent to have a seat, and strolled out of the office. He casually chatted with a deputy, smiled at the agents, and bolted down the hallway when no one was looking. He took the stairs two at a time and made it to the jail before Roberta had time to blink.

"Just what the hell are you doin'! This borders on conspiracy to violate a dozen federal, state, and even local laws concerning mutual aid, assistance, and something you don't know a goddamn thing about, cooperation," he spurted, and then he burst out laughing.

"We need a day at the most, and then I don't care what the feds do with him," Roberta explained.

"Think y'all can run those federal boys in circles that long?"

"Don't care. I just need some time to do what I have to do to close cases here in Caulking—that is my main objective.'

Ward noticed Detective May for the first time and introduced himself. May told him he was just here for the ride, that a judge down in Miami had wanted to flex a little judicial muscle by having him make the trip.

"Where is Mr. Pomeroy, anyway?"

"We put him in cell C. He's having a grand ol' time."

Ward walked to the front of the bars and looked in at the familiar face. Nathan smiled, but his eyes expressed anything but warmth. He had grown bored with this game. The voices were becoming belligerent, badgering him to feed the desires, and he wanted to suck the eyes from the good sheriff's head. Nathan stopped smiling. He stopped dreaming, and the world unveiled itself in real time. It was the present time, no longer fifteen or twenty years before. A strange silence echoed inside his head, and for the first time in a long time, the voices were not there, but Nathan did not mind being alone.

Ward was uncomfortable looking into Nathan's eyes. He felt like the man was stealing his soul and teaching his fears new tricks. The sheriff turned and walked away, never saying good-bye and not looking back.

"Thanks for the help, Sheriff. I'll swear we never had this conversation," shouted Roberta at the exit, but Ward had already left the jail.

"What's first on the agenda?" asked Stan.

"That is going to be entirely up to our guest."

Nathan was free of the voices, the first sign of a personal epiphany, and it was as if he had awakened from a long deep sleep that had not agreed with him. Time and motion lurched forward slowly in the beginning, but as momentum was gained, the acceleration of understanding grew with vitality, and he savored his newfound abilities. The giggling had to go. It was nothing more than a weak memory. Soon, cruel laughter full of manly strength boomed from within the cell. Roberta and Stan stopped talking in the middle of a sentence. The voice was unfamiliar, and Roberta called down the hall anticipating a deputy to respond. "Hello, who's there?"

The laughter stopped with a heavy sigh, and a rich baritone answered, "We need to talk. How 'bout if we start with cuttin' these straps?"

Roberta was the first one to head toward Nathan, and Stan followed cautiously behind her. They stood before the bars in the same spot Sheriff Ward had stood nonplussed and nervous just minutes before.

Nathan gave Roberta a wink, and the corner of his mouth curled into a shy smile. "Hi. This ain't the most comfortable position. How 'bout if we make us a new deal?"

Roberta stared at the man in the cell and resisted the urge to pinch herself. This was not Nathan's voice. Something was wrong. She looked to Stan for help in understanding what was happening here.

"I know this ain't been no picnic, but for the moment—and I don't know for how long, so y'all will have to work fast—you can be talkin' to the real Nathan Pomeroy."

Stan had read about multiple personalities but had never before confronted one in person. He did not believe that a person could have more than one personality, and he had considered the whole idea nonsense—but he now realized that he could be wrong. "You say that you are Nathan Pomeroy. Then with whom have we talked before?" he asked.

"I guess y'all could say that was Nathan too, but things are different right now. Just leave it at that, okay?"

Roberta shrugged. She was way out of her element and wished they had actually gone to the hospital in Albany. "So tell me, Nathan, do you know why you are in this cell and wrapped up like a Christmas gift?" she asked.

"I ain't no present, sweetheart, and I ain't partial to playin' games. Y'all are the police. I'm locked up and you are expectin' me to tell you family secrets," he told Roberta and strained hard to keep himself under control. This was going to be harder than he had thought. The pressure from the rage split the seams of his skull.

Stan smelled a trick and motioned for Roberta to follow him out of hearing range. He walked around the corner, hesitated at the desk, and decided that in the stairwell was better.

Roberta followed and waited until the door clicked closed. "What the hell do you make of this shit?" she asked.

"Just that, bullshit. He wants something real bad, like freedom, and is mustering all his control to appear somewhere near normal. I say we let him sit in there alone for a while and wait," suggested Stan.

"Wait for what?"

"The boom when he loses it. That can't be too much longer if we don't play the game with him."

Stan stepped back into the jail and listened. He heard only the buzz of the overhead fluorescent lights and Nathan breathing. He questioned himself, leaned back against the green wall, and pondered the rationale of provoking Nathan. Roberta placed a cautious hand on Stan's shoulder, gave it a little squeeze, and nodded toward the cell. Stan shrugged, scowled, and figured, "What the hell—let's play ball."

Roberta walked within several inches of the bars, and Nathan heard her approach. "Y'all finished jawin'? Don't be worryin' none. I ain't listenin'. But if you want to ask me anythin', I'm tellin' ya to get your butt in gear."

Stan lingered out of sight and motioned with his hand for Roberta to wait a while before saying anything to Nathan. He wanted to test his theory that Nathan could not stay out of character for long. Nathan sighed deeply and said something neither could hear. Stan could sense that Roberta could not resist the temptation of talking any longer.

"What y'all be waitin' for? I thought you had all these important things to ask, like where all those little kids are buried, where our, my, parents' graves are at, and then the biggy of the month, what happened to Sheriff Chandler." He let the pause stretch around the cell, engulfing all light and sound, extending beyond the bars until it wrapped black, leathery tentacles about Roberta. The effect was immediate, and she grabbed the bars with white-knuckle force, demanding to know where he had left Buddy's corpse.

"Tell me, you fucking bastard! Where is Buddy, what did you do with him..." her voice faded into a hoarse whisper as she stared into Nathan's calm and waiting eyes.

Stan tried to stop her. "Damn it to hell, you couldn't wait!" he screamed to himself. This was the moment, and she had blown it. Nathan had won again. Stan waited for Nathan to play the trump card. The wait was not long.

"I ain't sayin' as long as I remain strapped down, treated like some wild animal. Y'all get me out of here, somethin' decent to wear, and I'll start talkin' straight, no games, no more bullshit."

Stan shouted, "No!" and yelled at Roberta to keep the cell door closed, but before he could prevent her from inserting the key, other voices sounded from the elevators. The three federal agents, along with a dozen other people, suddenly filled the area between the desk and the cells.

"Ms. Austin, we need to talk now," instructed the agent Roberta had spoken with inside the courthouse. Stan slowly shook his head and lost all hope that Nathan would reveal anything other than lies and deception. Nathan was the victor, and he was the only one who knew the rules to the games that were being played out in this circus of authority. The federal agents would play his game without a second thought, and Nathan would reach new plateaus of fame.

Roberta had gambled and lost, and now she was praying the FBI did not flex more muscle than necessary and jeopardize her job. "No, we don't need to talk, Special Agent Frost. Sign the release form on the desk, which indicates you are assuming full responsibility for the prisoner, and he's all yours."

"Negative, you sign ours. It indicates that you have delivered Nathan Pomeroy to us and that we assume nothing more than that, and if you have a problem with this, Ms. Austin, I will then assume a telephone call to your boss, the attorney general, will be necessary."

"Is this how you boys play hardball? What are you, a bunch of rookies?" asked Stan.

"And just who the hell are you, boy?"

"Not your *boy*, I assure you, and I go with Pomeroy. My name is Detective May from Miami Beach Police Department. This prisoner is my responsibility, so ordered Circuit Court Judge Martha Stevens. So you can take your stiff-assed authority and stuff it, *BOY*. I got you outgunned," Stan told the agent, squaring off for a fight.

"Can I read your order, Detective May?"

"It's on the desk with the other papers."

Frost examined the orders, found everything to be as May had told him, signed the release form for Roberta, and told his men to unlock the cell. Nathan had been absolutely quiet during the verbal contest and waited patiently for the winner to collect the prize. His heart cheered when the cell door snapped open and the straps were untied, releasing him from bondage and the chair. His legs muscles were cramped, and he swayed like a drunk. The circulation had been reduced to a trickle, but this did not deter him from trying to spring to his feet. He asked about a change of clothes and smiled pleasantly at his new keeper, Agent Frost.

"You really shouldn't untie him. He's dangerous. Don't you know what this man has done?"

"He's just a man, Ms. Austin, and you'll be lucky if this guy doesn't sue the pants off this city, if not the entire state, for the way you have treated him. He's a prisoner, Ms. Austin, not some wild animal. He has rights, you know," Agent Frost chastised.

"That's where you are wrong, Frost. You'll be the lucky one if he doesn't have your balls for dinner, and calling him a wild animal is an insult to animals everywhere. You better watch your ass, sport, and realize what you're dealing with here." Her voice was like ice.

Stan took her to the side and said he would let her know what was going on, that finding Buddy's remains was his first priority. He looked over at Nathan, still amazed by the change in the man's demeanor. Nathan was joking with the agents, having a real conversation, but Stan knew it was just a matter of time before these idiot agents would see the true nature of their prisoner.

Twenty minutes later, Nathan was sitting in the backseat of a government car, wearing new, clean clothes and eating a cheeseburger, extra rare, just like he had asked for. May refused to ride in the same car and slid into the backseat of the second vehicle. Roberta was on the phone with Atlanta to demand that the governor intervene, and she was waiting for Judge Stevens to call back from Miami. She would not just roll over and play dead. This case was personal on many levels, and there was too much at stake to let the federal government waltz in and ruin it all. She watched the cars disappear at the corner and wondered how Stan was going to explain all of today's events to his boss.

The priority on the FBI list was four cases linked with three other states, none of which Nathan expressed having any previous knowledge about. In fact, during the alleged time frames for all the murders, he had airtight alibis.

Stan tried diplomacy with Frost, and when that did not work, he demonstrated how real cops played hardball. The convoy stopped for gas and cold drinks about two hours after leaving Caulking. May decided he would have a discussion with the man in charge. "Listen, Frost, I don't give a shit about politics. This has got nothing to do with me, and I am not a pawn in this private war between you guys and the Caulking Sheriff's Department. I came along for the ride because Pomeroy has information about a friend of mine, that's all, and I won't let you fuck this up," he announced without emotion, but his words were filled with the promise of violence.

Lou Frost removed his glasses, rubbed his tired eyes, and sniffed. He did not look at Stan, but he did consider what the detective had just said. The agent took a long drink from his soda and sniffed a second time. He told May without looking at him, "I know all about the disappearance of Buddy Chandler. You local guys don't give us feds much credit, or even consider us to be real cops, so you don't think we have those warm and fuzzy feelings inside when one of *yours* goes down." After a few moments of silence, he turned to look at May and said, "But we do, Detective, and Chandler is one of our priorities also, so don't get your Calvin Kleins in a bunch, all right?"

May nodded and walked away. He did not have anything else to say, and he figured Frost had said everything he planned to say also. Nathan was still smiling, talking and joking with the other agents, just like a regular person would do. Stan watched him carefully from the shade of an awning. He drank his soda and wondered when the old Nathan would rise from the dead. Nathan was cunning, playing these fed boys like a fiddle, and Stan wanted to be sure he was not in the line of fire when the shit hit the fan.

"I am sure grateful y'all got there when ya did, yes, siree, I am. That district attorney lady done gone nuts. Y'all seen the way she done had me strapped down in that chair like a mad dog. Yes, siree," he announced like they were talking about the weather. The agents were slipping further into a state of complacency. They considered Nathan not such a bad sort, as far as serial killers go. He was no doubt demented and not operating with both oars in the water, but he was not foaming at the mouth or biting and spitting. He was almost pleasant. The agents were all seasoned field operatives with years of experience, trained men accustomed to dealing with hardcore criminals. They had just never had the opportunity to deal with someone like Nathan Pomeroy. Nathan viewed himself as a career enhancement, a learning experience not offered in the lustrous academy in Virginia, and he wanted to be a well-remembered teacher.

The agents delivered Nathan to the holding facility in the FBI headquarters in Atlanta. The psychiatrist was summoned, but Nathan refused to speak with him, and just as Stan had suspected, the whole trip was a waste of time and effort. Nathan requested to speak to the agent in charge and rattled off how nice the fed boys had been to him and said that he would only cooperate and talk to his friends.

Nathan listened to the agents describe the four missing children, evidently all from prominent families with parents who desperately wanted to find the truth—families who apparently had the influence to force the largest law-enforcement agency in America to develop a task force just for them. Frost worded his sentences carefully, spacing evenly the simple words designed to bore a five-year-old, and he managed to provoke Nathan to the point of creativity. Dipping into his vast reservoir of experience, Nathan decided that a recollection of a more pleasant time was appropriate and closed his eyes, drifting far away and above the droning voices strafing his sensibilities with irrelevancy. Cries and whispers, moans and pleas joined other recollections swirling in a stew of special memories of the Thornton children. Nathan heard Frost tell him the names of the four missing children, the information sliding at the edge of his hearing, and he called to the voices to bring back Sarah, Deirdre, and Junior; but there had been only three of them. They needed a fourth to play bridge! Nathan dipped a little further back in time and found an angel riding a bicycle.

"Can you help us, Mr. Pomeroy? Can you help the grieving parents? They need desperately to close the chapter on a painful and disabling event in their lives," implored Frost, presenting a well-practiced delivery and looking for any sign that Nathan would crack.

A tear slid down along Nathan's cheek, and Nathan hung his head and bit his tongue to keep the giggling from spoiling the effect.

Stan May stood in the corner of the room and waited. He knew it was coming. The feeling was like electricity dancing in the air all around him, and he looked for a place to hide when the storm hit.

"Yes, sir, Mr. Frost, my friend, I understand." Nathan's voice was barely audible, coated with sincerity, and he thought, *Damn, I'm better than them fancy television guys.* The laugh started first as a small knock on the door of lunacy, building like a thunderstorm on the edge of a hot summer's day, and finally exploded with all the fury of Hell itself. Nathan shouted, pounded the sides of his head with balled fists, and brought the fear of God to the federal agents. He was screaming to dead relatives, demanding attention, as he proceeded to call roll.

May was the only one in the room unruffled by the sight. He had been through such an episode before, and he found himself mildly humored by the show. Nathan settled in the middle of the room, face down on the floor, still laughing, slowly grinding his teeth, catching his breath, and a meager part of his mind fingered casually at the threads of sanity.

Later, Nathan explained that there had been a special place deep in the swamp and not far from his house before it had burned to the ground, but he swore he had nothing to do with that, that would have been illegal. He promised that he would take them to the spot, probably nothing more than a patch of weeds by now, but he could find it, and he would show them where to dig, yes, siree.

Stan listened to Nathan ramble about the splendor of the swamp, the peace and quiet insulated from the modern world, and he remembered the fax Buddy had received about the skeleton discovered in the Pomeroy house after the fire. He decided to ask Nathan about it. "I have a question for you, Nathan," Stan began. "Tell me where you got that skeleton from, you know, the one that fooled us, the one we thought was you; and what about the teeth we found, those were your teeth, right, Nathan?"

Nathan's face twitched. He unconsciously ran a smooth hand along his lower jaw and remembered the pain. He remembered Carlos also, but the pleasure of the memory was spoiled by the smirk on the detective's face. Yes, he would have to deal with this asshole. He has more on the ball than these feds—he could be trouble. Nathan contemplated an answer, something smart, and then he thought again and decided that he should just shrug his shoulders and smile. "How am I to know? Maybe them bones belonged to the thievin' varmint that burnt my house," he told May, staring at him, waiting for the reaction.

May registered no indication that he had even heard the words, and Nathan could not stop the voices from invading his mind.

"No, Nathan, that man died about two years before the fire. Wonder where he had been buried all that time? I don't suppose you know, do you?" The question was rhetorical. May did not expect an answer, and he really did not know why he was pursuing the point with this idiot.

Frost listened to the conversation, decided it was counterproductive, considering that they still needed Nathan to cooperate, and said, "This is all very interesting, Detective May, but can we continue this some other time?"

"Sure, Frost. I have all the time in the world to ponder such things. Don't I, Nathan?"

Frost let out a deep sigh of exasperation and shook his head. Stan dropped the subject and smiled at the agent. Nathan was no longer giggling, and May watched the man rub his tongue across his teeth. He wondered about the thoughts causing the flames to shoot from the corners of Nathan's eyes and could not immediately dismiss the concern.

Early the following morning, Frost, the other agents, and Nathan collected Stan at his hotel. Nathan looked rested, bubbling with childlike anticipation. Stan was waiting in the lobby, eating Danish and enjoying a steaming cup of coffee. The weather had turned cold, the sky gray and forbidding with thick patches of fog obscuring the road. The men pulled on heavy jackets over thick sweaters and wore warm wool socks inside their hiking boots.

"I guess you don't get this type of weather down in Miami very often," said one of the agents.

"No, sir, and it's just fine with me. I remember it snowed one time, and that was the last time I saw the white stuff. You guys can keep it."

"We guys? Hell, I'm from Los Angeles, and the only snow there is the kind the Colombians make."

"Yeah, I hear that," May told him, and they both laughed with their breath turning to mist in front of their faces.

The drumming of fingers on the fender and the soft voice singing had been going on for some time. "You can go and you can hide, but please don't tell me that ya died, oh Ricky, oh Ricky-Lou." May was seated behind Nathan and was not paying attention to the little ditty the man was whispering, but if he had heard the name Ricky-Lou, the detective would have been most interested.

Nathan searched the landscape around him. After several hours of riding, it all started to look familiar, and, throwing his head back, he sucked in the aroma of wet clay, the fetid odor of swamp and stagnant water, and smiled. Yes, Nathan was home, and he noticed the sky was a pleasant shade of gray.

A fourth vehicle was waiting at the end of the paved road. The large tires and four-wheel drive capabilities would make it easier to travel across the forbidding terrain. Nathan giggled and danced, clapped his hands like a child at the sight of the truck, and pointed a long finger at Special Agent Frost, saying, "It won't be long now, sport!" He gave Stan a wink and a nod of the head toward the lake and the marsh that seemed to stretch forever beyond a line of trees. A moistness was in the air, and the wet anticipation of rain gave the woods a riparian feel. "Hope you don't mind gettin' them fancy leather shoes all muddy and wet, boys. We gonna be dancin' in the Devil's backyard soon!"

Stan watched Nathan's eyes smolder and boil. The hate was back. The forces of evil could not be kept at bay any longer.

A tall, lanky man crawled from the truck and leaned against the front tire, watching them approach. His name was Hank Daily, a local guide from Caulking hired to help the agents with the search. The federal car came to a stop behind the truck, and Frost walked over to the guide. There was brief conversation that Stan did not hear.

"Mr. Pomeroy, jump up front here and direct the driver," instructed Agent Frost. He introduced Hank Daily to everyone and crawled into the bench seat directly behind Nathan. Stan noticed the agent check his service pistol twice. The action was more than just a learned reflex. The act was purposeful, and the sudden concern for security doubled May's anxiety. He slid his own 9mm to a concealed position at the small of his back and wondered if the feds cared that he did not have the authority to carry a concealed weapon in Georgia.

"Detective May, why don't you jump up here in front with me? I betcha ain't never seen a more pretty lake. It is beautiful," Nathan boasted as he patted the seat next to him. He continued, "Come on, there's plenty of room," as he gave Stan a wide grin.

"That's all right. I can see just fine from back here."

The truck roared to life and bounced over a series of potholes before colliding with the remains of a fallen tree. Nathan squealed with delight, and the driver shifted into low gear to maneuver through the mud.

"You think we're nuts, don't you, Detective?" inquired Frost, straining to keep his balance and to keep his voice low.

"Well, maybe."

May did know exactly how crazy this was, but how could he answer Frost without sounding paranoid or, worse, without appearing afraid to handle one man? His mind was divided evenly into halves, each diametrically opposed concerning Nathan Pomeroy, the ability of the FBI, and his own fear. Nathan was just one man, flesh and blood, prone to death and pain just like they were, but knowing what this one man was capable of doing, what he had done, allowed the imagination to transcend to other levels.

"I figure that this will take the balance of the day and we'll be tied up on reports tomorrow. The day after, we can concentrate all our efforts on finding out everything we can about Sheriff Chandler."

Stan appeared to ignore the agent, staring out across the endless stretch of grass and trees. For some reason, Stan could not envision tomorrow. He was too busy trying to make it through today. He looked across the wasteland surrounding the lake at the copse of hardwood trees beyond the dirty gray water. This was Nathan's playground, a desolate, raw scar of land that could be easily misconstrued as beautiful. He saw a flock of white wading birds taking flight and followed their escape through the towering pines.

"Tell me about the four children," Stan said and continued to watch the birds.

"Why do you want to know? They're just four missing kids that we believe our mutual friend knows something about," Frost answered deceptively, and Stan smiled.

"Cut the crap, Frost. Stop stalling and try to do something totally out of character, be straightforward."

The agent was quiet, pondering the effect of what he was about to say, wondering if he should tell the detective everything or if he should tell him only enough to give the appearance of trust. He knew what to say. "Okay, let's start from the beginning, May. Once upon a time, there were four beautiful children from loving homes, with a mommy and a daddy, and then, along came some monster and stole them all away."

"Fuck you, Frost. Let me tell you a story. Four hundred children disappear every year because some perverts just like to fuck with little kids. I don't see the FBI getting all excited about them. I think this monster of yours just happened to fuck with four little kids with a very important mommy and daddy."

The agent's shoulders sagged slightly in defeat. This was going nowhere, and May was not going away any time soon. Frost studied the passing scenery with newfound interest and told the detective about the four children. May had correctly assumed that there was more involved here than a routine investigation of a possible serial murderer with a pedophile tendency, and he asked the agent if there was any real evidence linking Nathan Pomeroy to the federal investigation.

"No, not really. It's a long shot, but like a wise man said, it is hard to remember that your job is to drain the swamp when you're up to your ass in alligators, and I have a lot of alligators after my ass."

The sun was high in the sky, but the low sections of the swamp and the canopy of trees were still covered in dense fog. The temperature was not expected to rise above forty degrees, and the chill caused old bones to ache. Nathan recognized the immediate area and grew excited. It would not be long now, he told the voices. He asked the driver to stop for a moment so he could stretch his legs. The truck stopped inside a clearing on the far side of the lake, and everyone took a break. Nathan relieved himself behind a bush and was largely left alone to conduct his business. He entertained the thought of walking away and knew no one would be able to track him in his swamp. The voices began humming, and Nathan started grinning—there was time for small pleasures, and he told his friends to be patient.

Stan took a quick inventory of manpower, noted where everyone was standing, and ran a hand under his jacket until his fingers wrapped around the grip of the pistol. It would not be long now. Stan felt the electricity in the air. There was a pulse, a heartbeat hammering the calm, and a cold sweat ran down the center of his back. It was forty degrees, and Stan felt the back of his shirt sticking to his skin. Emotions drifted across the fog, swirled in the steam caused by their breath, and Nathan reached a cautious hand behind an oak tree. He found the cloth bundle hidden in a hollow. His fingers tore the knife away from the rotting material, and he felt the blade. Rust covered the exposed metal, but there was still an edge—it would do just fine. "Don't think these boys are gonna be a-worryin' 'bout no infections," he said and snickered.

Everyone was moving in slow motion. The fog was as still as frozen water, and Stan noticed the mark on the trunk of the tree by Nathan's head. He blinked twice, turning to see it clearly, and then Nathan was gone, a vapor blending into the fog. He heard screams of pain and shouts of surprise, and the report of a single gunshot shattered the air. Stan was spinning, pointing his pistol in all directions, trying to find a target, but it was like trying to take aim against the wind. He ran back toward the truck and tripped over the body of Agent Frost. The driver was slumped to one side, his arms dangling out the window and a pistol in the mud. May heard footsteps running away, sounding linear to his position and then silence. The detective had his back to the truck, but the feeling offered little comfort.

"Nathan!" he screamed, and the sound of his voice echoed. "Kill me now, you sick bastard, or I'll track you down and cut off your balls!"

"That's what I was a-plannin' on. There may come a time when I'll let you get me, but you best not rest and you best not be sleepin', 'cause if you fuck up again, I ain't gonna let you be the only one left breathin'. I'll be comin' for you soon. It just ain't your time, monkey-boy. It just ain't your time," Nathan answered.

"What's this all about, Nathan? Why did you want to come back to Georgia?"

"That be my business, but why don't you be asking yer girly friend Roberta? Betcha she can tell you."

"Why would she know what you want? What's the connection between you two, Nathan?"

"You are a dumb fuck, ain't ya, boy? You just better start payin' closer attention. Believe me, your ass is gonna be dependin' on it," Nathan warned, and then his voice in the fog was gone.

Stan heard a splash of water and a few hollow footsteps, then silence. "Nathan!"

All four agents were dead. Their throats had been slashed clean. Each kill had been silent, efficient, and delivered for the sole purpose of making good Nathan's escape. The agents had bought him time, delivered the beast to the jungle, and expected him to sit idle, cooperate, and behave as if he were a well-adjusted man trying to do the right thing. Stan knew that Nathan did the only thing his instincts would allow and that the voices were still welcoming him home.

Stan discovered after catching his breath that Nathan had kept a couple of things as souvenirs, mementos to remind him of this special occasion and to buy himself time. The first item was the keys to the truck, and the second was the microphone for the radio. The detective tried to get a fix on his location, collected a 9mm handgun and several extra magazines of ammunition from a dead agent, and started following the tire tracks back toward the road. May reminded himself that it had taken those most of the day to get this far in a motorized vehicle, and he hoped that he could find the road by daybreak.

The landscape before him illustrated Dante's description of Hell, and the smell of the rotting vegetation and stagnant water stung his eyes and brought bile to his throat. Never had he seen such a contrast with the thick, lush copse filled with dense growth and towering trees surround by endless stretches of yellow-brown grass, dead trees sticking up from the brown water that reminded Stan of emaciated scarecrows. The water seemed alive, constantly moving, filled with unseen things just beneath the surface, causing the swirl around his legs.

His first few steps away from the truck landed him in waist-deep muck nearly sucking the boots from his feet. Each step was a struggle, and the mud pulled him down further into the water until the water reached his chest at times. He remembered a Tarzan movie from many years before and a line of natives balancing boxes on their heads through a similar swamp. The natives had started to disappear one at a time. Stan was holding his breath, waiting for his turn to be sucked down beneath the water by some diabolical creature. His teeth were chattering. The cold had soaked deep into his bones, numbing his limbs. Stan wondered if Nathan was watching his pathetic attempt to make it out of the woods alive. He could hear the giggles bouncing off the trees, or maybe it was just the wind. Either way, Stan May was determined, and he pushed himself, even when his body wanted to give up.

CHAPTER
TWENTY-THREE

ROBERTA HAD SPENT the past twenty-four hours trying to salvage her career, her life, and her sanity. The snatching of Nathan by the FBI had stolen her thunder and left her office swirling in small-town gossip. Her budget did not supply enough funds for a press agent, and Roberta had to explain everything herself. The attorney general released a two-page statement explaining that it was the custom of the State of Georgia to offer cooperation in assisting any other agency, especially the FBI, in an investigation.

From her office, Roberta followed the wide hallway to the stairs. She passed an open door to the mayor's office and heard the steady buzz of a printer spitting out copies of another bureaucratic brainstorm. She could see the window of the interior office and the courtyard beyond. The building was not as large as the facade suggested but was hollow at its core. The offices were small and cramped, constantly in motion, and the number of people traveling the hallways reminded Roberta of roads in Atlanta during rush-hour traffic.

On the first floor, Roberta passed by an office she knew well. The polished brass sign on the door stated, "Sheriff Ward," and a pang of nostalgia gripped her heart. She hesitated, collecting her thoughts, hoping this was not a fool's mission.

"Come on in, it ain't locked," a voice boomed from inside of the office. Roberta shoved the door open and stepped through with a smile.

"Morning, Sheriff. Got a minute?"

I was wonderin' when you would get around to having a chat with me. I don't suppose you've heard the latest news 'bout your boy?"

The term "your boy" had more than a few possible meanings to Roberta. The first being Buddy Chandler, then, shifting gears, she wondered if the word boy was a racial reference to Stan May, and finally, she determined that Nathan Pomeroy must be making news again. She dreamed of the day she would read in the paper or hear on the afternoon news that Nathan had been executed or, better, killed in prison. Today was not going to be the day. "Tell me the latest," she said.

"Nathan escaped, killed all the FBI guys, and disappeared," Ward told her without a sign of emotion.

"That's real funny, Sheriff, but I have something important to discuss with you."

"God's honest truth, Roberta. A patrol picked up your Miami friend, and he's at Albany General bein' checked out. He crawled from the swamp like a gut-shot doe and damn near got squashed by a trucker on Interstate Ten."

Roberta thanked Ward for the news and headed back to her office to find out if May was able to talk. She had known the FBI was going to screw this thing up, but she had never thought Nathan would escape. Thank God, Stan had survived. That was a miracle in itself, and the only saving grace to the whole event.

Twenty minutes after leaving the first floor, Roberta was on the phone, talking with a staff doctor at Albany General. She was told that Detective May was suffering from hypothermia, exhaustion, and some minor cuts and bruises but for the most part had survived the trek across the swamp of southwest Georgia with few complications.

"The man is eating like a horse. How about giving us a break and take him home with you? We only have enough food left for four hundred patients. It won't last long with Mr. May around," the doctor joked, and Roberta told him she would be leaving within the hour to pick the detective up. In the car, she listened to the first reports of the agent's murders, which mentioned very little about Stan or Nathan. She did not have a plan, only to get Stan out of the hospital and hidden away until they could determine a real plan of action.

Nathan had spent the past day and a half hiding in thick hardwood trees miles away from where he had escaped. He had plenty of time to circle back, create false trails, and find something to eat. The helicopters were still searching the area, and one had circled directly above him once. Nathan resisted the urge to wave, and he listened to voices telling him to stay still. A heavy rain helped to destroy any traces of his tracks, and the temperature had dropped to around ten degrees. The hounds and men being mobilized for a search had little to look forward to, and their quarry was already on the move. He determined that he would be having dinner in a nice, dry place by nightfall and the dogs would be chasing a ghost through the cold, black water.

Nathan moved like a phantom, keeping to the shadows and cover of the tall canopy. He had left the swamp and picked up the pace on firm ground. The trees were thick in the forest, and he had not heard a helicopter in the last few hours. Three years, he thought, it had been three years since Nathan had filled his lungs with fresh, forest air and smelled the pine needles. The fog was returning with a vengeance as the sun went down and temperatures started to fall.

White clouds obscured his vision, and Nathan climbed to the top of a tree to gain a vantage point.

Roberta and Stan arrived in Caulking about the same time the search party was calling it quits for the day. Cold temperatures, fog, and fatigue had defeated both dog and man. Roberta helped the detective from the car and let him lean his weight on her to get inside the house. Warm air poured through the door, and their heavy clothes were suddenly a burden.

"Damn, woman, it must be eighty-five degrees in here. I'll bet your heating bill is double my electric bill in Miami."

"And you're complaining. Hell, I turned it up just for you. Stop complaining and give me your coat."

Stan removed his coat with a groan and a grimace. He had a deep cut along his right shoulder from colliding with a broken tree limb. The branch had cut through the thick coat like a knife and down his bare skin for about six inches. This was the worst of his injuries, however, and anything else he had suffered would be cured with a hot bath, a day's sleep, and a hearty breakfast. Roberta brought him a cup of coffee and a slice of sweet potato pie.

"This is great. You do not know how glad I was to see your face. I really appreciate this, Roberta," Stan told her with a mouthful of pie.

"The doctor said you were eating like a horse. I didn't know he meant literally." She laughed.

"You don't know how much you appreciate food, a glass of cold clean water, and even toilet paper until you spend what you think is the last hour of your life trudging through chest-deep brown and smelly swamp water."

"You ready to talk about what happened? I was going to ask you in the car, but you fell asleep before I could start the engine."

"I am damn tired, and I think I will be for a long time; but I need to talk about it or it will eat me alive."

Stan told her what had happened by the truck, everything that Nathan had said before he disappeared, and everything Nathan told the two FBI agents at the headquarters building. Roberta let Stan talk without interruption, and when he stopped to take a sip of coffee, she started asking questions, beginning with what he thought Frost was really trying to accomplish. Stan told her about the four missing children, and Roberta sneered. All this nonsense for politics, and now Nathan was free as a bird.

"Did Nathan tell ya anything about where the Thornton kids are buried?"

"No, but I figured that was where he was taking Frost and company. He saw an opportunity and took advantage of it. I don't think we were too far from wherever he dumped the bodies, but hell, in those thousands of acres, who would know?"

Roberta was particularly interested in the mark Stan had seen carved in the oak tree. She remembered reading something in reports about the search of the Pomeroy property that mentioned symbols carved in trees. They had found things buried around those trees. Stan described the symbol as resembling a sun with several flaming points, with one larger than the others, and theorized that the direction of the largest flame pointed toward something important.

"What did Nathan take out of the tree?"

"My guess is a knife, judging from the wounds on the agents. Each one had a cut throat or deep puncture. I never saw the knife, however. I only saw him reaching behind the tree, the symbol, and then the smile on his face before he vanished."

"You said you heard one shot. Think it hit him?" Roberta asked but already knew the answer.

"I doubt it. There was no blood, and nothing in the sound of his voice indicated injury or pain."

As the hours crept past and Stan's voice droned on about his experience in the swamp, Roberta felt the soft hand of sleep close around her mind, and soon she was dreaming. Her parents came to mind, and she shifted her position in her sleep. The Austins had afforded her the opportunity to grow, to expand to horizons inconceivable to her at birth, and yet there had always been something from her past, a mark not readily identified but nestled deep within her being—a bad seed, a deformed gene, the traces of lineage as indelible as a birthmark. Roberta could not escape who she was, only wrap herself in brightly colored clothes and pretend she was someone else. She drifted in a stormy sea, and the clear glare of enlightenment washed all color away, stripped adornment and wordy camouflage, and left her nothing to lend credence to the lies. Once bare, the flat, ugly message was delivered in a single, one-sided voice. She had only one fear left, and that was coming close to being revealed, but it was also the only exhilarating thing left to experience.

Nathan had discovered a park site along the far side of the swamp nestled between the highway and a fishing camp. He'd never bothered to explore this side of the swamp where it attached itself to the national forest. He watched a handful of trailers for signs of occupancy and smiled when the door of the oversized travel trailer opened with a squeak of the hinge. A man stretched and scratched absently as he stepped into the embrace of the late night air. Nathan shivered against the cold, and the pangs of hunger churned the acid in his stomach. The rest of the trailers were dark, except for the manager's wood shack by the highway, which had a light burning in the window. He wondered how many people were in the Winnebago, and he crept through the tall grass and edged within a few feet of the man. The odor of beer drifted from the door, and a shuffle of feet, a loud burp and cough answered Nathan. It was time to be neighborly.

The family of three was exhausted from hunting all day. The father was drunk from a case of cheap beer, and the wife had already tucked their daughter in bed. Nathan slipped the lock on the front door and crawled into the driver's seat. He had already made sure the manager would not be coming around to ask for the rental fee tomorrow and licked the blood from the back of his hand. The manager had merely been an appetizer. The voices were not satisfied, and he had to find better fare to satisfy his desires.

The snores shook the curtains, telling Nathan exactly where the man was sleeping. He decided to take his time with the father, but not until he had assembled the audience. The mother and daughter were secured quickly, their mouths and wrists taped tightly together. Nathan whispered between giggles for them not to move, showed them his bloodstained hands, and waved the blade though the air. It had been so long, and Nathan was enjoying this overdue pleasure.

"Who the hell are you, boy?" the father yelled, but the words were slurred and the movement of his massive body slow.

This was going to be better than Nathan had hoped. The old man appeared on stage right on cue—it was show time. Terror wrapped like a vise grip around the mother and daughter's shoulders. They could not look away and watched Nathan dance, twirl, and slash. The blade opened the man's stomach in a single pass. The man tripped on his own organs, and buckets of blood splashed across the women. A second pass, and Nathan swirled like a bullfighter, bringing the blade down between the shoulder blades with dramatic flair. From the father, Nathan moved to the mother, saving the tastiest morsel for last, and he cut the tape from the woman's mouth a little too deeply. The wound to her cheek caused blood to pour out like water, forcing Nathan to lose control, and he gorged upon the plentiful, tender flesh.

The eyes of the girl showed no response after the first ten minutes. She had stopped struggling and stopped trying to scream. The girl had realized there was nothing to be done, and her mind had quietly walked out the door. She was compliant when Nathan finished with her mama and came for her. Her eyes would not let her see the final acts of violence and perversion. Her mind would not let her feel. She had witnessed the first sexual assault and the stripping of the body, but it was doubtful that she was aware of it. Nathan placed a bloody organ into the girl's hands and told her not to drop it as he giggled and finished his task. The young girl never understood that she literally held her mother's heart in her hands.

Nathan never noticed that the girl was not screaming. The voices were loud enough to block all other noise. He went about his work with care and speed. The sun was rising on a brand-new day by the time he finished dragging the body parts to the manager's shed. He washed his clothes in the machine outside the office, took a bath under the hose, and waited until the dryer stopped spinning. There was plenty of food in the refrigerator and hot coffee on the stove, and the paper had been delivered by the time he dressed.

Stan had managed to pick Roberta up from the chair and lay her carefully in bed without disturbing her. He stood for a moment and stared down at the peaceful expression, but he would have turned his head if he had known the dreams that danced in her darkness. A ragged hole appeared in the center of her soul, left there by a shaft of black light to rot with infection while the Devil pissed in her mouth. Stan gently laid the covers across her body and turned out the light. He found an extra blanket and a pillow in the hall closet. The couch would do just fine. He had slept in worse places. At least this one was soft and warm.

After locking the doors and turning off the lights, he stretched out on the couch with the light from the television casting colors across the room. The stitches on his shoulder were itching, and he felt like someone had taken a baseball bat to the rest of his tired body. He swallowed two of the painkillers he had been given by the doctor and waited for sleep while thinking about the woman in the next room. She was one hell of a woman in so many ways, and just as strange in as many more. He could not figure her out, and he wondered if he really wanted to try.

Sleep overcame him before he had concluded, and the tired, battered muscles finally relaxed, having the chance to recuperate.

Stan heard Roberta cry out softly several times, disturbing his own sleep and bringing his own troubled thoughts to the surface. He quietly stood at the door to Roberta's bedroom and watched with sleepy, caring eyes as the dark torment engulfed her sleep. He walked to her side and gently lay down, pulling her to him, wanting to protect her and to chase away the demons that haunted her mind. Roberta snuggled close, her breathing calmed, and they slept peacefully in the comfort of each other's arms.

CHAPTER
TWENTY-FOUR

The Austin house was protected from the street by a high hedge surrounding a stonewall, allowing entrance only by the front, and that in itself was a feat. It did not take long before reporters began trying to contact Stan. Roberta had informed her office that the detective was recuperating at her home, demanding privacy and confidentiality, but he was denied both requests. The first assault wave arrived with the sun, and soon, a small encampment had sealed in Roberta's front yard, spilling into the street and the woods. Neighbors slowed down to stare at the crowd surrounding the Austin home and commented that there had been nothing in Caulking like this since the Thornton murders. If they had only known that the same man was responsible.

"Yeah, this had better not be another goddamn reporter," Roberta shouted into the phone.

"No, but I'm asshole-deep in them over here." Stan's voice was deep and irritated. Roberta had slipped out of the house earlier and gone to her office to try to assess the damage to her career. She had left Stan sleeping like a baby and had not questioned why he was in her bed and holding her.

"How about getting a few patrol cars to cruise by before I start shooting?"

"I'm talking to Sheriff Ward now. He claims a lack of manpower, and that a lunar eclipse and preparations for the invasion from Mars are interfering."

"At least you still have a sense of humor. That *was* a joke, right?"

Roberta knew how Stan felt. With all that was going on and all that had gone wrong, nothing would really surprise them at this point.

Two deputy sheriff units were sent to restore the peace of the neighborhood, with orders to clear the roads and public and private property. Roberta advised Stan to stay in the house, away from the windows, and not to answer the telephone.

"It'll take a few hours before I can get away from the office. If you're hungry, there's a few things to munch on in the cabinet above the sink. I was planning on fixing you a nice home-cooked meal," Roberta told him, and something in her voice, maybe in the easy way she was playing hostess, made Stan's imagination explode with interesting images.

Stan had survived a rough ordeal in his walk through thirty miles of muck and water filled with mosquitoes, thorns, and rattlesnakes, along with other wonders of the wild. Female alligators dug nests in the spring that were sometimes five feet deep, and the holes filed with water during the rains of the fall. Stan had managed to find three of the empty wallows, being lucky to have escaped with only bruises and without a broken leg while the dark water drenched him to the skin. He had lost one of the pistols in the last gully and filled the barrel of the other with muck. The holes were invisible in the murky, brackish water. Snakes as big as tree roots had slipped through the reeds, and water birds had waited until the last second to take wing, scaring Stan half to death with loud warnings issued in fright. Several times, he had come across the tracks of large animals in the soft mud around the woods, and though he did not have a clue as to the type of beast making the footprints, Stan had assumed the prints all belonged to some animal that would love to have him for a meal.

There were other times when he had discovered traces of man, telling him he was not alone and reminding him that Nathan was perhaps watching him from some secluded hideaway, enjoying his struggles. Evidence of recently abandoned campsites, limbs hacked away to open a path through the dense underbrush, and charred tree limbs turning to cold ash had given him feelings that, although there had been someone here recently, he was very much alone. Twice Stan had jumped herds of deer, as many as eight, a magnificent sight he would have enjoyed had he not grown weary of dragging himself through the mud and water.

Slowly, the bruises were fading, the cuts healing, and the sore muscles mending. He felt like a new man this morning. The lingering feelings left from the experience of the past few days had changed him in many ways. The images of the slain agents danced through his mind at odd times, and he often had to shake them free. A state of relaxation brought different opinions about life, created by having survived both the attack and the journey. It was a disquieting feeling, having been allowed to live when all others had died, as if he had been shown how precious and fragile life was. And as with other men given another chance, simple moments were magnified to prominent significance for Stan—merely because *Nathan* had decided it was not Stan's time to die.

Stan was pondering the sagacity of this observation when the phone rang and he automatically answered, "Hello?"

"Stan the man, well, well, well," someone said with a giggle. "I see you made it out, monkey-boy. Not bad, but you sure did look funny fallin' in all them gator holes." Then laughter filled the room.

The blood in Stan's veins turned to ice water, the beating of his heart hesitated for just a few seconds, and the wheels in his brain accelerated to hyper speed. He knew who was on the other end of the line, and dark shadows enveloped his mind. "You bet your sweet perverted ass I made it out, you sick piece of shit," Stan snarled.

"I see that a stroll through my graveyard did wonders for your disposition. I am very impressed, Mr. Fancy Pants. I thought for sure the swamp would've done what I just didn't feel like doin' yet."

"You don't have the balls to kill me, Nathan. You like butchering little children, harmless little babies, and incompetent assholes that weren't ready to kill you. Just come on back when you are ready to die, son. I'll be waiting on you."

"Brave words. Ain't got no punch to 'em, though, just filled with your stinky breath, and it tells me just how much you be fearin' this here good ol' boy. I was thinkin' 'bout telling you some new secrets, monkey-boy, but with that attitude, I ain't much feelin' like it no more. Fucked up again, Mr. Fancy Pants, 'cause what I was gonna tell ya was real interestin'. 'Member this, monkey-boy—if'n you gonna dance with the Devil, you best bring a new pair of shoes," Nathan said. The line went dead.

Suddenly, the world became a small and cold place. A thick, choking darkness reached across the threshold to grab all light and air from the room. The air was black, thick enough to swallow, complete and unchanging. Stan lost track of time, and he slid through a rapid series of emotions transporting him beyond mere wants and desires, those things that open doors to fear, uncertainty, failure, and guilt. He slammed the phone down, and it crashed from the table to the floor. He kicked it across the room, venting anger and meanness. He thought of calling Roberta, but what would he say to her? All he could say was that Nathan Pomeroy had called, that pissed him off and the bastard had hung up, but there was something else, yes, something he had just now thought about. How had Nathan gotten Roberta's unlisted phone number?

Stan decided to call Roberta anyway, and when he asked why Nathan knew her number, she became evasive, indignant at what the question implied. Her reaction greatly enhanced the detective's suspicion.

"Just what did he say to you?" The sound of her voice betrayed the shock, and without waiting for a response, she asked, "Did you ask him where he was?"

"Of course he did not tell me where he was," Stan shot back, and immediately, he regretted the way it sounded. He was angry only with himself. He should have been under more control, thinking clearly, trying to get information, not supplying it. Nathan had sounded surprised to find him, why? Had he been surprised that Stan was alive, or that he was at Roberta's house? Perhaps Nathan was jealous, upset, but not at Stan's comments, merely at Stan's presence in Roberta's house. Something strange was working here, something that Stan was missing, and he had damn well better work out the problem, or next time, he might not make it out of the woods.

A score of separate thoughts, each containing its own measure of emotion and anxiety, ripped apart Stan's thinking, each one counterproductive, generated from selfishness and insecurity. He chastised himself for losing sight of the objective and reminded himself that personal feelings did not belong in police work, the work was cold, indifferent, calculating. But the moment that reprimand took center stage,

Stan yanked it back and stripped bare the false pretense. Slowly and cautiously, he approached the subject of his feelings for Roberta, and he decided he didn't have time to take the long road—there had to be something down the middle. He wanted to slap his heart. He had already run the gauntlet with his mind. He had to get focused!

Nathan let the phone fall from his hand and let it dangle from the cord. He walked away from the phone booth and kept walking until he came to a bend in the road lined with mailboxes. The Winnebago was hidden inside an old barn down the road from an abandoned farm, surrounded with weeds growing several feet tall among dead corn stalks. Nathan had made certain to erase the tire tracks left in the dirt and dust. He read the names on the boxes and picked one he liked. Road dust and tired bones helped him decide quickly. He only wanted a place to nap and a glass of water.

"Pa, I see somebody comin' down the road. Ain't nobody I'd know." The voice of the young boy sounded above the sporadic cough of the old generator. He was calling to his father, the man covered in grease and trying to fix the temperamental engine.

"Who'd ya say was comin'?"

"Don't know. Some man. Look there. See, he just passed through the gate."

Nathan gave a friendly wave and walked directly toward the man and boy. "Mornin', y'all. Nice cold day, ain't it? Guess winter is settin' in early this year," Nathan said.

"Mornin' back. What business brings ya here?"

"Ain't got any business. My truck's busted down over yonder by that old farm. Saw them boxes out by the road and figured ya might have a phone," Nathan told the man, smiling and trying hard to look harmless.

The man introduced himself as Jake Taylor, and the boy was Abel. Nathan shook Jake's hand and said, "Most folks call me Nathan," then followed the man into the house.

Jake explained that the lines had been down most of the week, something to do with a snowstorm, but Nathan was welcome to try to call.

"Want a cup of coffee, mister?'

"That be mighty fine, Abel. I got a powerful thirst and chilled to the bone walkin' 'bout in this cold wind."

Jake watched Nathan talk with his son and could not shake a bad feeling running through his stomach. Something familiar about this man and the name Nathan was sending warning bells ringing in his head. He stood protectively next to little Abel and stared at Nathan. They were talking about the upcoming Hog Festival, which meant that Nathan had to be from around this area, because the Hog Festival was a local event.

"I guess y'all be plannin' on entering that big red sow. She sure is a beauty," Nathan told Jake, and despite his bad feelings, the man had to smile. He was proud of that hog. She was going to be a winner this year for sure.

"Where did you say you was from, Nathan?"

Nathan let the friendly smile slip from the corner of his mouth, and the expression in Nathan's eyes turned hard. He stopped laughing and waited until the voices settled to a low hum. The pause permeated the room. The delay was obvious, just taking up space and time. He had not planned on leaving so soon. Everybody was being friendly, and he had not finished the coffee. The house was warm, and the boy had just thrown a new log on the fire. There might have been time for a bite to eat, but no! This old boy had to ask personal questions. Nathan tuned to face Jake, angled his body away from the man, and let his arms hang limp. "Caulking, the other side of the lake. We—me and my family— have got a small farm. We be raisin' a little corn, some cotton, and melons. Ain't much, but we get by."

The man was remembering now, and his face could not hide his reaction. Nathan started to giggle a little. Jake grabbed his son by the arm and pulled him away. The voices were screaming as Nathan brought the knife across his body, driving the edge of the blade into the neck of the little boy. The father was confused, hesitating between helping his son and attacking Nathan, losing precious seconds. The blade came around twice, hitting the mark both times and sending Jake sprawling backward to the floor. Abel was dead before his father let go, and Nathan kicked the small body from his way to stand next to the dying man.

"Why'd ya have to go and ask them damn fool questions? A body ain't got no right bein' so nosey! Y'all could've had a bit more time had ya been a little friendlier," Nathan yelled, and the voices sang. He finally lost control, and the giggling took over his soul.

"Why'd you hav'ta kill my boy? We don't care none about your business, mister..." Jake sputtered a moment and then died alongside his son.

Two men standing next to a panel truck flagged down Trooper Jasper Smyth of the Georgia State Patrol. The truck had been pulled to the shoulder of the road, and Trooper Smyth flipped on the emergency light as he stopped the squad car next to the men. Both men started talking the moment Smyth cracked the window on his cruiser. He did not want all the nice hot air to escape.

"Man, you got to follow us back to the fish camp, up there on Route Ten! Something stinks to high heaven. Couldn't find Joe anywheres, and he ain't one to be leavin'. He been livin' at that site for near thirty years! It sure did stink, just like something died in there," the two men shouted together.

The trooper raised his dispatcher and asked if dispatch could call the camp by telephone. He explained briefly what the two men had told him. "Something 'bout a suspicious smell. Best send an ambulance, and I'll be headin' that way now."

What the trooper found at the fish camp became the evening news. A grim-faced reporter gave a graphic account as he stood before the camera and tried to interview Trooper Smyth. Smyth had been with the department for only a month, fresh out of the academy, proud and sure, and he had been unprepared to face his first death scene. The temperature had not dipped below freezing since the killing, so the cold weather had only delayed the rotting of the flesh. Veterans of the department were glad this was not summer, but the odor was still detectable for a hundred feet.

"Trooper Smyth, can you tell me what you saw when you opened the cabin door?"

"Are you fuckin' nuts? I puked my goddamn dinner all over the snow! There are pieces of bodies all over the place in there, and maggots crawling around and—"

The reporter jerked back the microphone, but it was too late. Thousands of viewers sat slacked jaw, staring at the television while their dinners got cold. The reporter wanted a story, he wanted sensationalism, and Trooper Smyth had given him both. A pretty, young female trooper wearing the dress uniform of the department approached the reporter with a prepared statement, but he just waved her away. He was laughing too hard at Trooper Smyth's response to deal with the business of reporting the news. She gave him a strange look, shrugged, and walked back toward the crime scene. Death had an individual effect on people: Trooper Smyth was appalled, but the reporter was a seasoned veteran and had seen and heard it all before. The concept of death was no less frightening to him, but he grasped the opportunity to laugh. He secretly wanted to keep the devils of trepidation at bay.

Nathan was crossing into Florida before the bodies were collected and removed from the fishing camp. It took investigators an hour just to determine how many victims they had, and even with a final guess based on the number of heads, it did not add up to the correct number. Nathan had kept a souvenir and laughed, saying, "Blow jobs don't count! Everybody likes a little head."

Nathan took his time, calculating that no one would be looking for Jake's truck until maybe the next day. Nathan found a total of two hundred and thirty-seven dollars in the house, a Remington double-barrel shotgun, a pistol, and a brand-new skinning knife still in the box. Nathan thought he had died and gone to heaven. A nervous expectation grumbled in the pit of his stomach. He took the knife from the box, ran a finger along the edge, and watched the blood flow down the polished steel blade. "You're just as pretty as a new red wagon, ain't ya!"

The forensic techs found fingerprints everywhere at the fish camp. The killer did not care about being identified, and soon, a new chapter was started in the never-ending saga of Nathan Pomeroy. Roberta Austin was called at three in the morning with the news of the fishing camp murders. Records indicated that the family had arrived in a 1991 travel van with Tennessee plates. A locate-and-notify message had been issued within the hour, but investigators on the scene did not expect to find Nathan with the vehicle. The victims had been dead for almost three days. There had been plenty of time for Nathan to make it to Florida, the Carolinas, or just about anywhere in any direction.

Stan immediately told Roberta that Nathan was heading back to Florida, probably Miami, and by now, he would be there. He called his office and had the duty sergeant release another bulletin. The last thing he needed was another body in his city with Nathan's signature. The chief of police considered giving Stan a reprimand and possible suspension for the prisoner escape, but the Department of Justice took full responsibility for events in the Georgia swamp, exonerating the Miami Beach detective and appeasing the chief. The letter of reprimand was replaced with a letter of commendation and a medal of honor for bravery in the face of danger. Stan hated it all. A shrine was being built for him with the unwanted assistance of Mr. Pomeroy.

Nathan had dumped the Taylor truck in the parking lot of a grocery store in southern Orlando and spent a few hours wandering through a K-Mart. He had sold the shotgun in Tallahassee for fifty dollars, the pistol in Tampa for a hundred, and still had more than one hundred and eighty dollars left from the money he had found in the Taylor house. He bought himself a new pair of jeans and a pair of boots. Just after sunset, he watched an elderly man walk toward an ATM window, leaving his new-model Lincoln by the curb with the engine running. Nathan would be arriving in Miami in style. The old man gave Nathan the finger and chased him for almost a block. His car disappeared down the street, racing south to the interstate that went to Miami. The car would be found abandoned within a few miles of the owner's neighborhood. The old man had been vacationing, heading home to Miami himself with a full tank and with a hamburger and fries in a bag on the front seat. Nathan appreciated the old man's generosity.

Roberta and Stan examined the crime scene at the fish camp. Investigators had already reviewed hundreds of digital images, and studying the photographs proved to them that no matter how often one was exposed to the craftsmanship of Nathan, no one could be prepared for the shock. They had seen the gutted bodies, the dismemberment and gruesome display, but the images still brought bile to the back of their throats and a nervous blinking to their eyes. Stan felt the heat of hate run barefoot down his neck. He swore a pledge on the graves of all who had died and would die at the hands of Nathan Pomeroy to kill the beast the second he found him again. Nathan would not stand trial, would not burden the taxpayers with long years on death row or in a cozy mental institution. The execution and burial would be quick, clean, and efficiently inexpensive—the price of one bullet and a plot in the county-owned cemetery.

Random thoughts drifted in and out of Stan's mind, filling him with righteous indignation, pity, sorrow, regret, and a demand for retribution. He felt as if he had already claimed the prize for poor effort and failure, and pangs of guilt assaulted him as he remembered Buddy Chandler's warnings. Stan called Buddy a friend, a man of action and honor, and Stan yelled at himself for having gone by the book and played by the rules of a civilized society when dealing with the Devil himself. Stan shed a silent tear for his friend and all the innocent people who had crossed and would cross Nathan's path. He made a promise to his friend to end Nathan's reign of terror and to even the score with Nathan's life.

Roberta had other thoughts separating in her mind as cream would from milk, flowing from the same source but destined for independence. The revulsion was redundant, and she cautioned herself on complacency. Part of her was appalled, demanding that she look away, that her stomach lurch, but there was still another part of her that was fascinated, examining with an eye for detail, picking out subtleties missed by the casual observer, admiring the artistic blend of color and texture. The diversity of thoughts met with a hodgepodge of remedies, all failing to satisfy the need, and her mind sought refuge in humor, a laugh, a giggle. Not much to do but let things run their course; she turned her head to keep Stan from seeing the smile. A certain degree of morbid humor was expected—anticipated actually—in police circles, but this was not an attempt to belong, to give the impression that she was just another investigator, hard and exposed to the raw realities of life. Stan did not look at her; he was occupied with his own inability to deal with the business of Nathan and he chased bright images down dark tunnels.

CHAPTER
TWENTY-FIVE

THE MEMORY OF her daughter's death was painful. She had spent weeks just trying to forget. The sorrow was devastating, and because her belief in God was strong, she could not commit suicide. She allowed other issues to cloud her mind as a bitter alternative, and sometimes she let chemicals and alcohol diffuse the thoughts across an endless chasm of nothingness. Each day began with a handful of prescription drugs and a vodka chaser. Friends tried to lend support but eventually drifted away. Relatives stood by her, but they offered the attention merely to assuage their own feelings of regret, and after some time, Nicole found herself very much alone in the struggle to survive without both Sharon and Buddy.

Earlier this week, a telephone call had brought a moment of illumination into the dark hole she had chosen to hide in, and she was very eager to meet the caller. He had told her many things that lifted her spirit in a way that transformed her into a nearly functional human being again. The man was polite, not full of false regret and pretenses, but actually talkative, and he brought Nicole out of her shell of self-pity. He had introduced himself as Jason Chandler, the son of Buddy, and explained that he had traveled to Miami to find his father and had learned of Nicole by accident. Jason had been away for a long time, and he and his father had not been close. Jason had not known that Buddy had retired and moved to Miami until he had attempted to call him at the Caulking Sheriff's Department.

"I'm awfully sorry to be just callin' right out of the blue and start askin' ya about my daddy," the young man apologized politely.

"No, it's fine, really. I would love to meet you and talk to you about Buddy. He is a great man, but I am sorry to tell you that he just disappeared," she told him and started to cry. She felt embarrassed, but

Jason told her he understood. He had determined for himself that Nicole and his father were more than just friends.

"Please, I understand. You and Daddy were very close," he said, attempting to make her feel more relaxed. She asked if he would please come to visit her home. Yes, he would like that very much, and he wrote down the address. She gave him instructions, but he told her it would be better if he just took a cab. The driving in Miami made him nervous—too many crazy people all in a hurry and not caring about anyone on the road but themselves.

"If it's not too forward of me to ask, where do you live?"

"Germany, fer now. I've been over in Europe with the Army," he told her.

"Oh, in the military. How nice. You're an officer, no doubt. What rank?"

"Lieutenant, ma'am. I'm what y'all call a flyboy," he said, bragging a little.

"A flyer? Oh, you are a fighter pilot. How grand!"

"It ain't much, but better than digging holes in the ground and livin' in tents," Jason joked, finding it easy to talk with Nicole, and he told her so.

"How long are you going to stay in Miami?" she asked, hoping it would be for a while.

"I ain't got but two weeks' leave, and I was hopin' to find my dad..." His voice trailed off, and Nicole heard him stifle a sigh.

"Well, you must stay with me. Come for dinner and we'll discuss it, please?"

Jason Chandler arrived just before eight. Nicole would have never recognized him as Buddy's son. The sheriff was tall and heavyset, with thick, graying hair. Jason was just a little taller than she was, with light brown hair and a slim, lanky frame.

"I take after my mom," he explained. "I always figured it was the reason me and Dad, well, the reason me and Dad never got 'long so good."

"Why? I don't understand."

"Guess every time he be a-lookin' at me, I be remindin' him of her. You see, she died young and all durin' childbirth, and my daddy always be faultin' me with it."

Nicole was silent for a while. That didn't sound like the Buddy she had grown to love, but then again, Buddy had never told her about a son or a wife other than Becky-Ann's mother. All of this new information coming at her at once was a little unsettling, but it did allow her to forget about Sharon for a time. Jason continued talking about Buddy and explained that he had not actually seen his dad for more than fifteen years. He had been living with relatives since high school. He claimed to have gone to a university in California and joined the ROTC, and after that, a career in the military had seemed natural to him.

"What did you major in during school?"

"Electrical engineerin'. Dull, but I love it," he explained further, and there was laughter in his voice as he joked about himself. Nicole was charmed.

"Are you hungry, Jason? I haven't had company for dinner for a while, not since—" Her voice cracked. She could not talk, and the tears came without reservation. Jason was confused, asked if he had done something or said something wrong. Nicole shook her head and excused herself from the room.

Jason waited until Nicole had ascended the stairs and he heard a door close before he strolled across the living room floor. He stood in the corner and closed his eyes. The dreams were magnificent, and the swelling of his erection caused him exquisite pain. He tasted the blood again, felt the soft caress of smooth skin against his face, and heard the voices demanding attention. He lay down on the new carpet and told himself, "The bitch musta gone fuckin' nuts when she found the little cunt all packaged and awaitin' like a present on Christmas Day!"

Nathan listened to the voices cheering but became distracted after finding the photo on the wall. He sat down in the chair that had replaced the one that Sharon had been left sprawled across and ran a finger over the glass of the frame. The urges were on the brink of taking control. His skin was crawling, digging into the muscle, and the room had extended miles in all directions. He heard Sharon's screams of pain—how special she had been. Roberta had wanted to lick and suck every inch of that body, bury her face between those silky thighs, oh, yes, siree!

"Maybe I should've let her have her way with the whore. Betcha good ol' Buddy poked it a time or two. Guess I'm just a selfish man. Ain't got no control."

Stan May had been back in Miami for nearly a month, and his memories of Georgia were beginning to fade. All traces of Nathan Pomeroy had evaporated once again, and the trail ended with the discovery of the stolen Lincoln. The car had been dumped in a southwest residential neighborhood just off the turnpike, undamaged, out of gas, and with the burger wrappers still in the bag. Investigators had determined that Nathan had driven the car until he had run out of gas and then had just left it by the road. Stan still had a copy of Nathan's wanted poster tacked to a bulletin board and all the files piled on the corner of his desk. A photo of each victim was taped to the front of the file, and a few of the more graphic crime scene shots appeared beneath each profile, a twisted before-and-after display.

"You thinking about going back to work sometime soon, May?"

Stan looked over his shoulder at the Miami Beach Chief of Police. "Hey, Chief, how's everything?"

"Just fine. I need a few minutes of your time," the chief said and walked toward the commander's office, not waiting for a response.

Stan followed the man, a little concerned about the tone of his voice and the polite attitude. The chief settled himself into the chair behind the desk and motioned for Stan to sit. The commander was not going to attend the meeting.

"I just got off the phone with Nicole Hughes. Ring any bells?"

Stan immediately recognized the name, the woman friend of Buddy Chandler, the mother of Sharon, who was suspected to have been another of Nathan's victims. He wondered why Nicole had called the chief. Her daughter's homicide had not occurred in their jurisdiction. Stan jokingly said, "Why did she call? Did Nathan come back?" It was meant as a joke, sarcastic. He immediately regretted saying it, but the chief did not respond. Stan searched the man's face for a clue and felt the blood drain to the soles of his feet. "Is Nathan back, Chief? Is Nicole all right? Am I right, is he back?"

"Yes, I believe you are right, and Nicole is as all right as she can be." His expression was one of sorrow as he continued. "Ms Hughes was not certain that it was Nathan. She called a mutual friend, John Patrick—it seems that Nicole and I have the same lawyer. John put Nicole in touch with me, and now I have a request." The chief explained to Stan that a young man claiming to be the son of Buddy Chandler had visited Nicole at her house. "The man called himself Jason, the long-lost son, living in Germany, said he was a lieutenant, a pilot, actually. This man said he had not seen his dear old dad for fifteen years."

"I don't understand. Buddy did not tell me much about his personal life, nothing at all about a son in the military. Maybe it is true. So why is Nicole so suspicious?"

"It seems that she excused herself, went upstairs to her bedroom after breaking down during a discussion that reminded her of Sharon, her daughter. Nicole spent a few minutes composing herself, came back downstairs to find Mr. Fighter Pilot gone, along with a photograph of Sharon. She said that this son looked nothing like his father, but what she described reminded me of your Mr. Pomeroy."

The chief told Stan he wanted Stan to visit Ms. Hughes—nothing official, just show her a photograph of Nathan Pomeroy. "Don't explain anything to her about Nathan or who he is, and just let everything stay on a casual level. If it turns out to be our boy, I'll arrange to put a watch on her house, okay?"

"Does she have any information about this Jason Chandler? Like, is he staying in Miami at a hotel, maybe an address in Germany, anything?"

"Nope, nada, except a cab company. Seems like Mr. Chandler does not like our style of driving in Miami and came in a cab." The chief reached in his pocket and pulled out a piece of paper. "Society Cab," he said, reading it out loud. "They are the ones used for the beach traffic. Check it out and report directly to me."

Stan nodded, still wondering why he was being involved. Nicole and Sharon Hughes were out of their jurisdiction, and technically, this should be checked out by the Miami Police Department. He was still pondering that thought when the chief added, "You understand that Nicole Hughes took the death of her daughter badly. She is out of it sometimes, and John thinks she may be hallucinating a little, okay? So let's not jump to conclusions. And I know it's out of our jurisdiction, but I would consider this a personal favor if you take care of it yourself. She has had a rough go of it lately. Anyone else might push her over the edge, and she deserves better than that."

Stan did understand now, and he did not have a problem with handling this for the chief. In fact, he considered this more of a personal favor for his lost friend, Buddy. The chief sighed and studied Stan for a moment, gave a slow shake of his head, and walked out of the office without saying another word. Amazingly, he trusted this detective completely and felt there was nothing more to say. What he did not feel necessary to reveal was that Nicole Hughes at one time had been a very important part of his life but it did not last, so they had parted as good friends. Nichole had not reached out to him, even though she could have, and the idea of calling him had been strictly John Patrick's because of the lawyer's concern for her. The chief knew Nicole was suffering, but he also knew that she would have to find a way to live again and no one could help her with that.

Stan made the telephone call and as a result received an invitation to lunch from Nicole. The voice on the other end was slurred and the conversation hard to follow. He tried to have an open mind and not be influenced by the opinions of others, but the chief may have been right about her mental condition. Stan completed a photo lineup card used to show suspects of crimes to victims. Nathan was honored with the center slot, surrounded with eleven other very similar photographs. Stan wanted to make this hard, but he doubted Nicole could find even her own face among a crowd, much less Nathan's.

Absently, a worker was going about mundane duties under the scrutiny of a manager. The worker was slow but deliberate, pushing a broom from one side of the aisle to the other with measured precision.

The type of work invited boredom and required the employee to have no more than three functional brain cells, and two of those routinely taking a break. The manager left the vantage point of the front desk and walked into the alley for a smoke. The worker smiled to himself, demonstrating ambition, a clear state of being overqualified, and carefully made his way toward the back office. He knew that making phone calls during work hours was prohibited but had timed the manager for a week. The man had never taken less than twenty minutes. The number was punched, and the worker checked his watch. Yes, she should be home by now, and it had been such a long time since they had talked.

The phone rang nine times before someone said "Hello?" and the peace generated by the simple greeting colored the world in tranquil shades of harmony.

"Hey, yerself. It's been a long time. Just wanted to say hey."

The rush of emotion was immediate. The voice bit to the very core of her soul, and Roberta was not able to answer.

"What's the matter, big ol' pussy cat done got yer tongue?" Nathan checked his watch—sixteen minutes to go. He had to get her talking, fast. The window of opportunity was closing. He wanted to hear her voice. In a whisper or shouts of anger, it did not matter. Just the sound was all that was necessary. Nathan would later replay the conversation in his mind, supplying his own words, and the voices would take care of the rest.

"Where are you, Nathan?"

"Long ways from home. Just hangin' out with friends, kickin' back, drinkin' a few. And you?"

Roberta tried desperately to calm herself, to avoid the same error she and Stan had both had committed before. She knew this was a game that Nathan was playing, trying to prove he could manipulate her emotions and reactions. She took several deep breaths. "My life is real good, Nathan. Work, mainly. Ain't got time for much else."

Nathan was growing suspicious. The woman was having a conversation here. No anger, no panic, no demands, or questions that required answers.

"I ain't been havin' too much time to myself, neither. Seen yer boyfriend, though. He's done gone to seed back home, porkin' out." He waited, but Roberta did not answer him. "Oh, y'all 'member a drunk ol' bitch named Nicole and her whorin' kid, Sharon?"

Roberta was trembling, her eyes blinking fast and her mind racing near the edge of the danger zone. She had to think fast, get ahead of the conversation, and ride the panic. One, two, three. "Yeah, I think she was a friend of Buddy's. You remember him, don't you, Nathan? Sheriff Chandler?"

Damn, she was not going to bite at the easy ones. He guessed he was going to have to go for the throat. "How 'bout Sharon? Great tits, tight ass, and with a pair of lips made for kissin' and suckin'? I know you 'member her. She was a great fuck! Oh, that's right. You didn't let it get that far, did ya?"

Roberta did not breathe or think. She just answered. "No, guess I chickened out, but you had a great time, didn't ya, Nathan?"

Fucking whore! Nathan wanted to crawl through the telephone and rip the smirk from her face. He knew she was laughing at him, playing him like a Friday-night fiddle. He lost all control, screamed at the voices to go to hell, and slammed the phone down. The manager was just coming back in the building when Nathan reached a climax of anger. Nathan checked his watch and noted that twenty-one minutes had passed. The man was right on time.

"What seems to be the matter, young man? Why are you in the back office? That is forbidden," the little man demanded.

Nathan spun on the balls of his feet, breathing fast and shallow, his pupils reduced to pinpoints, focusing, narrowing the target of opportunity. The manager felt the grip of fear, tried to create distance between himself and his employee, but his actions were slow and obvious. Nathan merely slapped him to the floor and stood menacingly over him but finally just walked away. The manager then made a fatal error and assumed he still was in control. Not recognizing that the threat was real and within striking distance, he greatly overestimated his position and shouted, "You're fired! You cannot go around beating up the manager!"

Nathan stopped, turning slowly from the door. He hesitated, allowing time to pass, emotions to enflame, and he grinned at the manager, smelling the sweat pouring from the little man. The manager was still sprawled across the floor, not trying to stand or invite more violence. Nathan locked the door and skipped back down the aisle, whistling, looking like a giant deranged child.

"Y'all really should learn when to zip yer lip. That's the trouble with you little guys. Ain't got nothin' but mouth. No balls at all, just bunches of words spittin' out all over the place," Nathan told him, and he towered over the terrified manager. "Words don't go meanin' diddly-squat in the real world, so you be jawin' fer nothin'."

"What are you going to do to me?"

"Don't rightly know. Somethin' special, though, somethin' real nice."

The answer came to Nathan as he raised his eyes and looked around the store. The hammer was within easy reach. No stretching, no getting up, just grabbing it. The first hit was nothing more than a dull thud, the second was softer but messier, and soon, Nathan was splattered with blood.

There was money in the cash register, a total of four hundred dollars from the daily receipts. He found another eighty dollars in the manager's pocket, and a search of the back office revealed a locked, zippered canvas bank bag. One slice with his knife, and he dumped the contents on the desktop—a week's worth of receipts, a company violation to stash money away, and a bounty for Nathan. He left the store with more than a thousand dollars, a new watch, and groceries for the month. The manager's car was in the back lot. Nathan left the front door open.

Nathan dumped the bags in the back of the manager's late-model station wagon, and the thought came to Nathan as he slid behind the wheel: what about the telephone call to Roberta?

He should have considered the concern before making the telephone call. Even though Caulking was Small Town, USA, modern communication services were available. Roberta had captured the number, written it down on a legal pad, and immediately phoned Stan May.

"Stan, this is Roberta Austin. How are you? I've got some news for you, Detective," she told him.

"This sounds like déjà vu, Ms. District Attorney. What is your news? Hope it's good. I need some good news."

"I just got a call from Nathan Pomeroy," she started. She had Stan's complete attention. "He called from a number in Miami. Are you ready for it?"

"You bet. Shoot."

She gave him the number, and it took Stan less than a minute to find the registered address as he continued to talk with Roberta. She told him about Nathan's mention of Nicole and Sharon Hughes, and Stan got more excited. He told her about the conversation with the chief, about Nicole's visit from a man claiming to be Buddy Chandler's long-lost son. He updated Roberta on the condition of Nicole and told her that he had poor hopes that the woman would be able to identify Nathan in a photo lineup.

"Hell, take the chance. I'll bet you a week's pay she'll pick out the bastard in a heartbeat. Think it's a good idea to keep her in the dark about Nathan? You could run the risk of pissing off a good witness down the road, and you may need her help," Roberta advised, and she felt the jealousy return. Suddenly, she felt like crying and ended the conversation with "Listen, I've got to run to court. The recess time has expired. I'll call you at home tonight, okay?"

Stan wasted no time in acting on the information from Roberta. Nathan had been right under his nose the whole time—the convenience store was only a few miles from his office. He first told his division commander and requested that a couple of marked units respond, which would get there quicker. As he headed out the door, he grabbed a few extra magazines and the city-issued bullet-resistant vest. The brochure accompanying the vest promised that the material would stop the penetration of a knife, and Stan prayed that he would not have the chance to prove the claim.

"Dispatch, this is Detective May, Homicide, unit seven fifty-nine," Stan said as he raised the police dispatcher.

"Go ahead, unit seven fifty-nine."

"Do you have two units responding to the Seven-Eleven, Byron and Seventy-first street?"

"That's a ten-four. Do you have any special instructions? I show the call as a routine check of a suspicious person, is that right?"

Stan grimaced. If Nathan was anything, it was not a routine call. He wanted to tell the dispatcher to send everyone, mobilize SWAT, and get backups from around the world, ask the Marines to stand by because they were dealing with the Devil himself, but he responded calmly. "Consider the subject to be armed and dangerous, not routine. The subject's name is Nathan Pomeroy. You should have a bulletin on him—everyone should have a bulletin on him."

"That's ten-four, unit seven fifty-nine. Will you be responding?'

"Yes, from the station, and tell the officers to be careful."

Miami Beach standard operating procedure stated that an unmarked police unit could not exceed the speed limit and could not operate as an emergency vehicle, but May threw caution and policy to the wind as the speedometer reached seventy miles per hour. He took the first five stop signs and hesitated for a nanosecond at the traffic lights. Stan May wanted Nathan to be face-down in his own blood by the time he got there—dying but not dead, because Stan also wanted to say good-bye and wanted his face to be the last thing the monster saw. He heard the units give an arrival. The radio was silent, everyone waiting for the officers to check the store and inform the dispatcher that they were safe.

"Dispatch, did you advise that a homicide detective was en route?" This was not a good sign. Stan held his breath, waiting for the air to clear and praying it was Nathan who was dead.

"That's ten-four, unit seven fifty-nine, Detective May, is en route. Unit seven fifty-nine, can you advise an ETA?"

"Just around the corner. Have them switch to a tact channel."

Stan waited for the units, and after a few moments, he heard his unit number being raised. "Unit seven fifty-nine, are you there?"

"Yeah, who is this?"

"Wilson and Rogers. Who is this?"

"Stan May. What have you got there?" Stan asked, hoping they would describe Nathan's dead body.

"Don't know who, but we got one. A little raghead with his brains all over the floor. Looks like someone beat him with a hammer. The hammer is still here. Did you copy?"

"Yeah, but what the hell is a raghead?"

"You know, a Pakistani, Indian, Arab, something from the desert somewhere—they wrap their heads in rags."

"That's real sensitive, Wilson, real sensitive," Stan answered, walking through the door of the store. He found the two officers standing over the body of the manager and watched a trail of blood snake across the floor. The body was still warm, but Stan knew Nathan was long gone. He began to issue orders, having the uniformed officers establish a perimeter around the entire building and requesting crime-scene officers to respond immediately. One of the uniformed officers started to use the telephone by the desk, and Stan exploded, "What the hell is wrong with you, man! You aren't some rookie, asshole! This is a crime scene! Don't touch anything!"

"Sorry, didn't think. I'll be out front, May."

Stan started taking preliminary notes. He observed that the cash drawer was open, the money gone, the manager's wallet and keys missing, and many items thrown to the floor around the store. He headed for the back and was hoping to find a schedule, an employee list, or emergency-contact telephone numbers. There was no identification with the body—he needed a name. Chances were good that old Nathan had taken the dead guy's car, and Stan needed a name to match with the vehicle registration. The more quickly he had the information, the faster he could tell the world. Stepping through the back door, Stan kicked the smashed telephone, and when he bent to see what it was, he found perfect fingerprints on the receiver.

The office had been ransacked, with drawers dumped on the floor, a canvas bank bag cut open, and paperwork strewn in all directions. The employee list was tacked to the wall and contained several emergency-contact telephone numbers. "Abdul Saddam" was penciled in beside the slot for manager, and Stan advised the dispatcher of the name and contact number. He could not find Nathan Pomeroy anywhere, but he did find "Robert Austin" scribbled next to the entry for daytime clerk. In fact, according to the schedule, Robert Austin should have been at work today and should have been here now. Stan shook his head at the name Nathan had used and immediately thought of Roberta's safety.

Voices from the front drew Stan's attention, and he emerged from the back to find a store full of people. Three crime-scene officers were carefully laying out equipment, one was loading a thirty-five–millimeter camera, and two other members of Stan's squad were staring down at poor Mr. Saddam.

"What do you think, robbery?" one of the detectives asked Stan. "I noticed the cash drawer empty."

"Anybody else here, any customers?" asked the other.

"No to both. It was an inside job, an employee by the name of Robert Austin, better known as Nathan Pomeroy. This is Mr. Abdul Saddam, the day manager. Mr. Austin is long gone, probably with Saddam's car."

The detectives exchanged sarcastic expressions and looked back at Stan. The first detective spoke. "You've got this Pomeroy on the brain, Stan. Give it a rest. You think he's responsible for every murder we handle now? Where do you get this crap from?"

Stan was becoming very annoyed and filled them in on his conversation with Roberta, explained about the telephone number, the trace, and the significance of the name Pomeroy was using. Once enlightened, both detectives understood and apologized to Stan.

"So where do we go from here?"

"I've got a call in for a records check of cars owned by Saddam. I was going to call his house. The phone number is on the wall in the back office," Stan told them, motioning with a thumb over his shoulder toward the back door. "God, I hate to do that, but I'm just waiting for the forensic boys to dust and photograph everything first."

Stan gathered the forensic team together and explained exactly what he needed from them. He took one of the technicians with him to the back and had her start working on the telephone. The last thing he needed was a crowd contaminating the scene, so he moved outside with the two other detectives and gave the uniformed officers instructions to allow no one to enter the store. A crowd of nosey neighbors began to gather around the parking lot, along with several reporters and a television crew setting up equipment. Stan grabbed the radio and asked for more officers and someone from media relations. A third unmarked car entered the front lot, and Stan walked over to bring the duty sergeant up to date.

A perfect match was lifted from the latent prints on the telephone, the cash register, and the head of the hammer. Nathan Pomeroy was the man, again, and a statewide bulletin was broadcast for his immediate arrest.

Stan called the home of Abdul Saddam and spoken with his brother, the night manager. Stan confirmed that the man on the floor missing most of his head was Abdul. The dead man's brother described Robert Austin; the description fit Nathan down to his redneck accent. The brother was driving to the station to examine some photographs, which was not necessary, but it made him feel better. The brother would also help determine how much money should have been in the store and if anything else was missing. The good news was that a firearm was never kept in the store.

On the other side of the bay, a quick drug deal was being transacted between a fast-talking, nervous-acting petty dealer and a giggling buyer. The dealer figured this country cracker had already fried his brain on crack, and he offered a hundred dollars for the 1994 Toyota station wagon.

"I ain't lookin' for a whole lot, ya understand. It's my uncle's car, but fuck him. What ya offer fer it, again?"

The dealer was nervous. He didn't like being in the open at three o'clock in the afternoon—in fact, not at all during the day—but he felt certain that there was no way this guy could be a cop. Nathan was having a difficult time concentrating on talking. The voices were singing out of harmony, shouting obscenities back and forth, and they were on the verge of ripping to shreds his very ability to think. The man watched Nathan grit his teeth and snarl at the air like a dog after a pesky fly, and he concluded that it was in his best interest to make the deal and leave.

"Okay, here check this out, and smoke your mother-fuckin' brains out man," the dealer said as he tossed a brown paper bag at Nathan.

Nathan bounced the bag in his hand, testing the weight, but never looked inside. He really couldn't have cared less if the dealer had paid him with walnuts. Nathan only wanted to dump the car and have the police grab some other guy who looked like him. *Stupid cops*, he thought. That would confuse the hell out of them, and he laughed out loud. "Sure, you ain't a-cheatin' me," Nathan said and tossed the dealer the keys.

The dealer handed the keys to another kid, maybe sixteen, and told him to take the car to a bank parking lot on the corner. They always let hot cars sit for a few days, waiting to see if the police were looking for them, and if it wasn't towed away, the car would be painted and sold.

Nathan chased demons and bad memories down the street, seeing no one in particular and everyone from the past. He tossed the bag of crack into an open car window and broke into a slow jog. The voices had not stolen his mind completely, and he laughed, thinking again about the police spotting Abdul's car with a skinny white boy driving. "Them stupid cops, they be lookin' fer me so hard that they might just shoot that boy, bullets flyin', thinkin' they done caught the big fish, and what will they have? Tell you what; they will have a lot of explainin' when it ain't me that be dead by their hands, yes, siree."

Flashes of bright light popped behind his eyes, and he lost feeling in both hands for a moment. Something was about to happen, he told himself. These were signs he should pay attention to, yes, siree. Something bad was going to happen. Nathan broke into a faster trot, and at the corner, he broke into a full run. People jumped from the sidewalk to avoid being knocked down, and soon, his clothes were soaked with sweat.

Stan drove back to his office after the body of the manager headed for the morgue and the crime-scene people had finished processing the scene. He left his two partners at the store to wrap up for him and went to meet the store manager's brother. Stan found the man waiting for him, and after a brief conversation, he produced the same photo lineup card he had planned to show Nicole Hughes. The brother identified Nathan Pomeroy as Robert Austin, a day laborer hired to clean the store and to do other menial tasks. The brother said that Robert was quiet and a hard worker who never gave them a problem and was always on time.

"Did Mr. Austin ever drive to work?"

"No, he always walked. He said he lived somewhere in the neighborhood. My brother would have the records at the store. There is a file for employee information in the desk," the brother explained, trying very hard to contain the growing realization of his loss.

Stan had searched the office and never located a file on Robert Austin. He wondered if Nathan had had the presence of mind to take the file with him or if Abdul had just never gotten around to documenting Robert Austin's information. He thanked the brother for his time. The interview was brief and ended with the obligatory offer of condolences, and the brother was shown to the door. Stan wondered how many times he had performed this ritual and how many times the bereaved family members had thought he was coldhearted. With a shrug, he dismissed the thought. There were other things to concentrate on. Nathan Pomeroy was still free and back in action in Stan's city.

Roberta spent the rest of the night sitting on the couch in front of the fire. She alternated between bad dreams, which brought on bouts of depression, and brief moments of elation nearing hysteria. The woman was certain her mind was sinking into a bewildering and devastating state. The absence of control eluded her normal approach to understanding the cause, and she spent hours failing to grasp an appropriate level of comprehension. The horizon turned a pale shade of blue, foretelling a beautiful day, and the fire reduced to glowing embers before some semblance of normalcy returned to her thinking. The telephone call had forced her to recall every minute of the visit with Sharon Hughes, and Roberta felt her skin become flushed with fever. The memory invoked passion and lust, and her urges forced her hand to manipulate the sensitive folds of flesh between her legs to a high state of arousal. She enjoyed at once the touch, the memory, and the satisfaction.

The ringing of the alarm clock brought her racing back to the present, faced with the realization that the entire night was a blank. She had stared at the television screen as if drugged long after the screen filled with static. A pounding headache and incoherence greeted her, and the memories of the sleepless night stayed just beneath her level of understanding. The hours were lost, the things she thought about gone, and the night a blur. Roberta had time for only a shower and a quick cup of coffee. She could not be late this morning. A meeting with all the division heads, which she had been planning for a month, was today, and there was a lot of work to be covered before lunch.

The water was freezing, and just as Roberta decided it might just be the thing to bring life back to her brain, the telephone rang. She dropped the robe to the floor and stood beside her bed naked as she answered. "Hello, this is Roberta Austin."

"My, how formal, even at home, Ms. Austin. Do you ever change hats and become a regular person?"

"Do you know what time it is, Stan? Do you ever go home? Do you even have a home?"

"Not this month. Hell, not this year, not since I have had the pleasure of meeting a few wayward citizens of Caulking, Georgia. I figured this would be about the right time to catch you. Is it a bad time?"

"Normally no, but there is going to be a group of pissed-off attorneys ready to hang me from the rafters if I am late because they had to get up an extra hour early for a meeting I ordered."

"We need to talk, Roberta. I spoke with Nicole Hughes last night. She identified Nathan. I told her everything—the truth, as you suggested—and after a while, she settled down."

"The poor woman. I can't imagine how she must have felt after realizing that she had invited her daughter's killer to dinner," Roberta whispered, talking to herself more than to Stan.

"Yeah, it got real ugly. When can we talk?"

"How 'bout late afternoon, 'round sixish. Good for you?"

"I'll be home. You know the number," he told her.

Roberta did not realize she had been staring at her reflection in the mirror during the conversation and letting her eyes linger slowly over her own flesh. She found her own body arousing. Her nipples were dark, hard, and demanding attention. Her eyes dropped lower across the slight curve of her stomach, which was not flat and athletic but still firm and sensual. Her eyes were hungry, devouring each new vision until resting at the edge of her dark pubic hair, and her mind sought fantasies that caused her imagination to blush. She forced herself away from the mirror, pulling her hands away with force, and stepped over the edge of the tub.

The water had had time to run hot, and the steam formed billowing clouds around her. Everything in the bathroom was hot and wet, the air thick and inviting. Her hands searched every inch of her flesh. Lingering fingertips spread wide the folds of her vagina, and she gasped out loud with pleasure. She was going to be late. The attorneys would be upset, but she was the boss, and the boss did not have to be on time. Roberta pictured her division chiefs while bringing herself to a climax. They were all nude, screaming and making wild love with each other on the conference room table. Blood ran down the legs of the women, and long, curved nails destroyed the skin on the backs of the men. It was going to be an interesting meeting, she thought, wondering if she would be able to avoid the memories. "No, I don't think so," she said aloud, and a giggle escaped her lips.

Back in Miami, the weather was warm for February, thunderstorms rolled in from the west every afternoon in time to wreck havoc with rush-hour traffic and to ruin vacations for snowbirds escaping the bitter cold of the north. The locals knew better than to complain. This was Miami—they knew to wait a few hours and the weather would change again. Temperatures could drop twenty degrees in a single day. Heaters might run full blast one day, and the next, the air-conditioners might strain to keep homes at a comfortable seventy-eight degrees.

Stan parked his car in the driveway and looked at the black clouds building fluffy, menacing mountains over the everglades. He liked the rain, especially at night when he was sleeping. A pounding storm with lighting and booming thunder made for beautiful dreams. He had barely made it to the front door when the first drops started to fall, and seconds later, the bottom fell out of the sky. The rain was good for the grass, and he prayed it would stay for a month and chase all the Canadians back home.

The telephone was ringing by the time he had checked the mail and turned on the six o'clock news. He had flipped through the channels, hitting the network stations first, looking for something about the 7-Eleven murder. "Hello, I hope this is my favorite district attorney," he said into the mouthpiece.

"Ain't you gonna be disappointed, monkey-boy," Nathan answered him.

Stan bolted from the couch. The sound of that voice sent electric shocks through his brain. He ordered himself to settle down. He didn't want to blow this chance like the last time, and he said, "No, not really. I just didn't expect you to be calling."

"What's all this nicey, nice shit, Mr. Fancy Pants? Y'all ain't tryin' to kiss up, now are ya?"

"Nope, just being friendly. Why did you call?"

"Now, that's better, bein' direct and cop-like. Did you find my boss-man?"

"Yeah, you still got his car?"

"Maybe I do and maybe I don't. I sure do like them big ol' cars, though, you know the kind," Nathan said, and Stan noticed the strain in his voice.

"You okay, Nathan? You don't sound like yourself." Stan was trying to maintain himself.

"You go fussin' 'bout yerself now, ya hear, and go on and get busy with the Georgia whore—you know, your favorite DA bitch—and leave this ol' boy 'lone."

"Can't do that, Nathan; you know that. I think that's why you keep calling, 'cause you know it too."

"What's that supposed to mean?"

Stan heard the concern in his voice now. This was a new Nathan, a less confident man. Maybe he was beginning to crack. Maybe the violent episodes were ending. Stan was hoping Nathan was starting to spin out of control and looking for a soft place to crash. He thought perhaps Nathan was reaching out for help, but he did not believe that for any longer than it took to pop up and disappear. There had to be something else wrong.

"It means you keep calling, wanting to play cat-and-mouse games. What? Are you getting bored, Nathan?"

"I ain't bored, Tricky-Dicky. You just watch yerself, ya hear. I ain't got no time to be playin' no games. I ain't playin' with Chandler's bitch, neither, just being neighborly. She does have a nice set of tits. Buddy always did like 'em big and bouncy. You ever sucked on your favorite DA's big juicy tits? Bet you like wrapping those big black lips around her nipples and slurpin' on them, don't ya?"

Stan had to be careful here, watch his words, and try not to upset Nathan again. He wondered why Nathan was so preoccupied with tits, Roberta, and Buddy. He gave a response slowly, "Yeah, she does have a nice set, and how 'bout that ass, nice and tight. It's a little too small for me, though. I like 'em with a little meat to hang onto," he said and waited.

"Well ya know what they say, the meat be getting sweeter the closer to the bone," Nathan answered. Stan was still holding his breath.

"So, I guess Nicole was glad to see you?"

Nathan was quiet. Stan could almost hear him thinking, hear the voices screaming across the telephone lines. The silence lingered for several minutes. Nathan was pondering the implications, wondering if the conversation had gone on too long. Maybe things had progressed in a wrong direction.

"I don't think I like a-talkin' with you, ol' boy. You be gettin' kinda smartassy 'bout things, start pointin' fingers at me likin' I done did somethin' wrong."

"Nope, just being cop-like, direct and no games," Stan replied, waiting to hear the phone go dead.

"That's you, ain't it? Mister Tricky Dicky himself. You ain't be try-in' to get me a-sayin' somethin' stupid, are ya now?"

"Nope, you can say whatever you like, or don't say anything at all. It's all up to you, Nathan." Stan was growing irritated with this nice routine, and then he remembered something. "Why did you use the name Robert Austin? It's a little obvious, don't you think?"

"Not unless you knew that dumb-ass fucker. He didn't know shit, just smilin' at folks and countin' his money."

Stan considered his next option. This was not going anywhere, and Nathan was not cooperating. He concluded that he liked it better and got more information when Nathan was pissed off. "Tell me some-thing, Nathan. Why did you really kill Sharon Hughes? Were you jealous, did you think that maybe Buddy was sucking on them young tits, and you didn't like the idea of having sloppy seconds from dear old Dad?"

"Go fuck yerself, asshole. You think I gutted that bitch. Ain't so, not really, and you best be talking with your district attorney bitch. Go askin' Roberta these questions. If I was sloppy second, it sure weren't from Buddy that day. You just ask Roberta what a nice piece of ass the little whore was. She'll tell you true what a delicious fuck she was, and while you be asking, find out how she liked fucking herself this morn-in'. You really should have been there, monkey-boy. She was wet all over."

Stan heard a slight giggle just before the line went dead.

Nathan found himself in a cold, dark place filled with wet walls of air, and he was floating face-down in the muck and mire of his own thoughts. Wild things were taking flight and drifting on unseen cur-rents of blistering hot air and floating before bursting into flames with pieces of charred flesh exploding across his skin. The air was thick and septic, saturated with the odor of rotting flesh. Nathan could do noth-ing but drift slowly in a circle around the invisible vortex, keeping pushed to the edge, away from the center and out of harm's way. He watched images taking form from the voices, incorporeal bodies struc-tured from words, ideas, and desires. The sight was hideous, affecting him at once, inspiring both terror and kinship. He had come home to a place he loved, and then he remembered all the reasons he had left and he relived the passions, fear and pain.

Stan stared down at the phone and shook his head slowly. He had to find an easier way to make a living. He called Roberta, who answered on the first ring. "It's 'bout time, ol' boy. I was beginning to think you didn't love me anymore," she teased, her voice deep and sultry, catching him by surprise again. She was always startling him.

"Yeah, well I've been busy. I've been talking to our friend," he told her.

"Is he still in Miami? What did he say? Is he all right?"

The concern in Roberta's voice stopped Stan from immediately answering, and he rapidly replayed the questions in his mind: Is he still in Miami? What did he say? Is he, the piece of murdering dog shit, *all right*?

He was talking about Nathan Pomeroy, the butcher of babies, old women, and good cops, and she was asking if Nathan was all right? What the fuck? Her concern indicated what? It sounded like she was talking about a close friend, a wayward relative who had failed to keep in touch, or a runaway child. The thought ran through Stan's mind at record speed until he exploded, "Who gives a fuck if he is all right! I'd be pleased as a pig in shit to find him face-down with a bullet in his head!"

Roberta caught herself, astounded at what her emotions were doing, and she squeezed her eyes tightly to block out the images as she pressed the palm of her hand to her forehead to stop the voices. She had to get everything under control. *Think fast*, she screamed to herself, but the whistle of the distant train was so loud and she could feel the vibration of the floor and knew they were getting closer. The little hand slipped from hers, followed by the shout full of fear and need, "Don't leave me, please don't leave me." But the desire for escape was too strong for her to slow down. The action was irreversible—escape was the only option.

"Roberta, are you still there? Hello!" Stan yelled.

"Yeah, I'm still here. Why the hell are you yelling?" She had to buy some time to think.

"Me? What the fuck are you saying? Asking if he is all right! Who gives a damn! Let's keep focused here. It's like you sympathize with this monster! He most probably killed Buddy. You do remember Buddy. And if that's too hard, maybe you need to revisit your files on his handiwork!"

The last words slapped Roberta hard across the face, psychologically knocking her to the ground, and she tasted blood in her mouth. The sudden jolt caused her mind to respond with a believable comeback. "Are you done, Detective?" Roberta knew that the best defense was a good offense, and she would have this asshole begging her forgiveness in no time. "When you said you had been talking to our friend, I thought you meant Buddy. Wishful thinking, I guess, since you so eloquently pointed out that he's most likely dead. Pardon me for still holding on to a little hope where he is concerned." The silence was loud enough to make a person go deaf. *Yes*, she thought, *it hit its mark big time*, and she waited for the response.

"Oh God, Roberta. I am sorry. I guess all of this Nathan crap is getting to me. Can you ever forgive me for being such an asshole?"

"Nathan has pushed all of us to the edge, Stan. He's like a cancer eating away at all that's good and infecting anyone he comes in contact with," she said with a thick whisper. "Let's just forget it, and we can both get focused on the issues. Deal?"

"I am sorry, and it's a deal."

Roberta wanted to know all the details and wrote down everything Stan had to say, asking questions, refusing to offer an opinion. She told him that the warrants and charges against Nathan were beginning to fill a three-drawer file cabinet. The joke around the office went "How many files does it take to kill a serial murderer?" Nathan Pomeroy was a legend, and articles appeared daily in the newspapers. There were even Nathan supporters who spoke out every now and then, and Roberta had been contacted by a national magazine for a feature interview and considerations for books about Nathan's life. Things were out of control. Her life was public, and the demand was wearing her down.

Stan knew nothing of the publicity, would not have cared if he had been told or not, and he wondered aloud to Roberta if they should let the matter be handled by the Bureau, suggesting that they wash their hands collectively in federal red ink.

"I can't believe you, Stan. Tell ya what, you do whatever you want, but this office is going to handle their own affairs. We don't go pawning off a job just because it gets tough."

"Real cute, Roberta, very small-town, but we here in the big city have other fish to fry. We don't gots what it takes to waste a-pissin' in the wind. Do y'all understand that?" Stan countered with an over exaggerated southern accent.

"That was very good, but I don't have time for this. Keep in touch."

The line went dead, and Stan was left to stare at the phone, again.

Nathan had escaped his private hell for a while, had swum the river Styx to a distant shore and sat for a few peaceful moments while watching the raging water reduce itself to a swirling eddy in dark pools. The voices could not compete with the roar of the water, and he was unable to hear himself. He wondered what he would do now. The end was coming fast, and the train whistle was growing louder. She was coming back for him. She would not leave him this time. He had a vision of a silver streak racing straight toward him, coming out of the darkness, born from the shadows and the stink, glimmering at the edges and distancing itself from the night, and a voice called his name. "Nathan," the voice whispered. "Nathan, baby, come to Mama; it's time to play."

The man yearned after the call, drawn to it like a moth to a flame luring the unsuspecting innocence to danger, sending out its treacherous message filled with love, promises, and lies. He called back, answering the lonely wail, but the others heard and forced their sound above the answer, blocking the reply, and soon, he could hear only the distant whistle of a fast-moving train.

"Damn ya to Hell," he screamed, and he pounded his head with the ball of his fist.

CHAPTER
TWENTY-SIX

ALL THINGS HAD begun to settle for Stan May, and he returned his attention to other matters. The world did not wait for Nathan Pomeroy, and there were others clamoring for his attention, desperate men and women trying to escape one kind of prison in exchange for another. The Bible says that the meek shall inherit the earth that we should turn the other cheek, and that good will always triumph over evil. Men like Stan May and Buddy Chandler had learned other lessons. They had been forced to witness other opinions and determine that the meek are mere targets inheriting nothing more than hard lessons, and that turning the other cheek merely invites a second blow. The business of good triumphing over evil was a tricky one, because sometimes men like Stan May did win, and sometimes they lost it all, like Buddy Chandler, but the ancient philosophers had determined that good is merely the mirror image of evil. This was something Detective May had known for a long time.

Stan had not talked with Roberta for weeks. There was no need, because Nathan seemed to have disappeared, again. Perhaps he had moved on to new horizons. The files sat in carefully measured rows on the shelves in the records vault, where they waited to turn yellow and covered with dust. Stan could not remove them from his mind, however, and although he had busied himself with other work, searching for other men and compiling notes on other cases, he could not forget. Memories would ease into his thoughts, unexpected and uninvited. He thought of Roberta often, recalling the day he had spent recuperating at her home after his ordeal in the Georgia swamp. And then, as if his memory refused to allow him to enjoy the past, jagged pieces of discord, black holes, and anger would thrust fingers in his mind's eye. He would remember their last conversation, other conversations, the events that had taken place at the institute, and memories would flow together like water and oil, leaving a bad taste in his mouth.

Today was one such day, and he sat in his office chair, feet upon the desk, coffee growing cold in the mug, and wandered in the wasteland. Everything was gray, fragmenting, exploding into a fine mist swirling helter-skelter around the room. Clear thinking was evading his sensibilities, and Stan was forced to examine the failures he considered connected with the Pomeroy case. He had allowed the investigation to become personal, a deadly sin, and now he wallowed in self-destruction. He had also let his heart dictate to logic, smearing the fine print of common sense. Perhaps it was because he had already passed a milestone in life, middle age, and he was heading up the hill toward being a lonely old man. Sure, the golden years lay light-years ahead, but that did not stop him worrying about arriving at the doorstep and standing there alone.

Few women in Stan's life had had any interest in a lifelong commitment to a dedicated police officer. Most had made it abundantly clear that they did not want to play second fiddle to his job. He had considered another alternative, to become involved with another police officer. Plenty of women were entering law enforcement, but most were just like one of the guys, tough, and foul-mouthed. Stan liked a woman to enjoy being female and to use attributes of femininity to enhance her appeal, but he did not care for Barbie dolls. He could not tolerate empty-headed company, regardless of the company's beauty. He had grown strongly attracted to Roberta Austin despite their first phone conversation, and for reasons he had never tried to sort through until today.

The first obstacle was logistics, and the second was the entire black-white issue, though that didn't seem to be much of a problem. Roberta was a very attractive woman, a little too manly sometimes, but feminine nonetheless. She was educated and cultured, and when she wanted to be, she was very vulnerable; she was as tough as nails when she had to be, which was quite often in her profession. Stan admired how Roberta had made it in an all-male world, not just doing well but also making it all the way to the top. There was also the cultural aspect. Southwest

Georgia was as southern as it came, complete with the KKK with grand dragons, burning crosses, segregation, and all other considerations affecting the rural south.

Prospects of success were few when considering a romance between himself and Roberta, but Stan could dream of nothing else. He had hoped she would spend more time in his neighborhood. Miami was a multicultural and multi-ethnic city and a town friendly toward cross-race relationships. The last time he and Roberta had spoken, he had wanted to invite her back down for a mini-vacation when shoptalk would be banned and they would have a time of quiet, intimate dinners, walks on the beach under a big Miami moon, a drive down to old Key West, just the two of them, together. But Roberta had never given him the chance. Things had gone wrong in the conversation, and the inevitable had occurred, Nathan. Stan pondered this thought carefully as he swirled the coffee in the mug and let the loneliness wash over him. Looking around, he discovered that he was the only detective in the office and it was after six. He heard the sound of someone pounding a keyboard up front, one of the secretaries trying to keep a deadline. Stan made a wet, sucking sound through his teeth and decided he would get drunk.

Dancer's, a favorite cop bar, was within walking distance of the police station, making it both convenient and dangerous. Alcoholism was not unheard of among law-enforcement agents, nor was the strong appeal of slipping out for a few hours early to enjoy the comradeship of brother and sister officers. The close proximity of the bar made it enticing for both reasons. The bar also attracted a large number of other patrons who just enjoyed the atmosphere. Cops always had a good time there, knowing how to step beyond the boundaries of polite society with flair and good-natured insanity.

Stan was not a regular patron of Dancer's. He dropped in only once or twice a month, depending on his mood, and tonight he wasn't looking for company, just a place to unwind. Stan would be among good friends, others who shared a common interest, people who understood no matter what happened.

He felt the pounding of the bass before he heard the sound of the music. The crowd spilled out the front door into the street. This was a good sign—hard to be lonely in a crowd like this—and he pushed his way inside, shaking hands along the way.

"Hey, May, what brings you to this fine establishment of debauchery?"

"That in itself answers the question," he yelled back at a tall, lanky kid who looked barely old enough to drive let alone carry a badge and gun. Someone else called out to Stan, but he could not find where the voice was coming from and ordered a pitcher of beer from the woman behind the bar. He slapped a twenty down on the counter and told her to keep it coming until that was gone.

Waitresses and bartenders liked working at Dancer's. Cops always tipped well, plus this was the safest bar on the strip. Who would hold the place up or start a fight in a bar full of cops, except the cops themselves, and those altercations were usually settled within seconds.

Stan had drained the last of the first pitcher, and the bartender replaced it with a full one. He was beginning to feel the effect of the beer. He was not accustomed to drinking, but tonight he did not care. Tomorrow, well, that would be another story. The room was beginning to thin out a little, and he was looking around for a friendly face for a little diversion when he heard his name.

"Hey, Stanley, grab a cue. We need a fourth player, you game?"

A dark-haired woman tossed him a pool stick with a laugh. Stan missed it, falling from the stool, and the room tilted to one side. The beer was affecting his balance, and the edge of the table offered support while he tried to retrieve the pool stick from the floor.

"You know, May, you really should pace yourself. Get out more and live a little or that body is going to self-destruct from boredom." The woman laughed and sent the colored balls rocketing across the green felt.

Hours later, a hundred dollars poorer and blind drunk, Stan staggered away from Dancer's. He fell through the door and into the night's wet embrace. It was raining, and the water felt good against his skin. "Damn..." was all he could manage while trying to determine the direction of the station. He had drunk enough beer to kill a horse and was seeing double. A powerful wave of nausea forced him to vomit into a garbage can in the alley by the corner. The beer had slowed down the world, leaving him dizzy and confused. Stan never heard the approach of footsteps across the wet pavement.

"Y'all should try and set an example for regular folk, you bein' a cop and all," Nathan whispered in his ear. It took several long, baffling moments for Stan's brain to send a signal to the rest of his body that he was in danger. Stan had been concentrating on a small slice of light between the shadows at the end of the alley. He had become fascinated with the disorienting effects of the bright, colored light, and all he said was, "What..." The rest was lost somewhere between his mind and mouth.

"Y'all have gots to be doin' better than that, Mr. Tricky Dicky. We have somethin' to talk 'bout, and I want you to remember," Nathan whispered. Stan could feel the hot breath. He was faced with the flight-or-fight syndrome taught about in the academy. To be plainer, he had to decide whether to shit or go blind. The blind part he had covered already, for he was blind drunk, and if he could determine if he was standing or sitting, the rest of the question might take care of itself.

Stan tried desperately to bring his brain under control. The parental part of his mind began to berate the child who had gone out drinking with the boys, and having a raving homicidal maniac breathing down his neck did not help him to relax. He stood suddenly with force, knocking Nathan backward and giving himself time to draw his pistol.

Nathan recovered quickly and screamed with rage. "You best be good, monkey-boy, or I might not tell you no secrets, and you know you only be gettin' one shot," Nathan spat in a flat, hard voice.

"How could I miss a big bag of dog shit like you? And I couldn't care less about your warped secrets. You're dead, fucker." Stan squeezed the trigger. Click. His heart stopped. Nathan began to giggle. "Fuck!" Stan screamed. He had forgotten to pull the slide back, to charge the weapon, and all the nice little bullets were stacked neatly in the magazine, just waiting for a call for action that never came.

"What a dumb-ass," Nathan said, and he laughed as he pulled the knife from his back, but before he could move, a group of late-night revelers burst through a back door. Stan fell to the ground and tried to find cover as Nathan stepped back into the shadows.

"Whoa, hey, what ya doin', pissin' in the alley?" said one of them, and the group howled with laughter.

"Yeah, you know what they say, you can only rent beer," Stan called back, and everyone laughed even louder. Stan was drunk, not stupid, and he quickly joined the group as he scanned the alley for any sign of Nathan. He tucked the 9mm into its holster and headed toward the street.

Back at the station, Stan downed several cups of cold black coffee. He was becoming more sober by the minute but still needed a few more minutes before he could intelligently talk with anyone about what had happened. A vibration rattled a beeper across his desk, and Stan found the noise irritating, as the effects of the alcohol were being replaced with a pounding headache. He recognized the number immediately as Roberta Austin's, and he realized that it was almost six in the morning, Saturday morning. That meant that he would not have to explain himself to anyone. The secretaries rarely came to work on the weekends, and the day-shift squad never made it before nine.

"Roberta? Stan May here. It's pretty goddamn early, woman. Is something wrong?" he barked immediately upon hearing her answer the telephone.

"You must work on your communication skills, Stan. It sounds like you have a sock shoved down your throat. Did you have a late night?" she asked him.

"Yeah, late, and great, with a shitty ending. What's up?"

"That's my boy, direct and cop-like," Roberta said and giggled.

There was that feeling again creeping over Stan like a cold wind. The giggle, the same comment Nathan had made, and she sounded just like Nathan. Stan could not understand. Maybe the phrase was nothing more than a colloquialism, but deep down he knew it was more than that, more than just a similar accent and local expression.

"I had a visit from Pomeroy tonight. It was a close call, but we are both still alive and well."

"What do you mean, alive and well?"

Again, he heard the concern, the wrong signal being sent—or was it the right signal, just the wrong receiver? He would have expected something different, maybe anger that Nathan had not been killed or put in jail, or something, but not the reaction she had given.

"It means the fucker tried to slice and dice my ass, and he got away, goddamn it," he yelled, no longer able to control his emotions. His head pounded with every word spoken above a whisper, and the acid in his stomach was doing the tango with the coffee. He had to throw up again and grabbed the trashcan.

"Stan, are you all right? That didn't sound so good."

"Thanks for the concern, but don't bother. Just answer one question, just one question, Roberta. What the hell are we trying to do here?"

"Do? I don't understand."

"Of course you don't, so let me spell it out for you. What are we, you and me, trying to accomplish here with this cat-and-mouse game and all the bullshit about Nathan—who is a very dangerous man, I might add. I want to know what the hell we are doing. This is supposed to be a police investigation, for God's sake, a manhunt for a brutal, sadistic son of a bitch, and you sound like you want to hang him half the time and protect him the rest. What the fuck is going on between you and Nathan, Roberta? And why do I feel like I'm running last place in a third-rate romance? Damn it, Roberta, I don't want to talk to you about Nathan, and I damn sure don't want to hear sympathy in your voice when you talk about him. I don't understand your connection with him, and I don't care anymore. I want to talk about us, just us!"

He had said everything he had wanted, finally blurting out most of what he was feeling, and he felt like an idiot for saying it. Stan waited for some reply, and for the moment, he was glad just to hear the soft, regular sounds of her breathing.

"What about us, Stan? You'll have to explain that part. And as far as Nathan is concerned, I do sympathize with him, and no, I don't know why, but I am trying to figure it all out. There is something inside me, deep inside, that wants to protect him. I don't know, Stan. I feel like I have failed him in some way that I don't understand yet, and all of this is scaring the shit out of me. I have nightmares every night of my life, dreams that take me to the edge of understanding and then leave me with an empty hole. Nathan is somehow a part of all of this, and I know that I can never have peace with him alive. He's eating at my sanity. He reads my mind. He plays with my senses, and I do things that scare me, because it's not me. He is inside of me, Stan, and only one of us can survive this. I'm scared. Sometimes I think I'm going insane," Roberta blurted out and started crying.

Stan had not been expecting an open and honest testimony of her fears. The devastating sound of crying made him feel helpless. He wanted to hold her, tell her that everything would be all right, but all he could do was listen. After a moment, Roberta was able to talk again, and she explained more about her feelings. She talked about the dream of the train, the nightmare of fleeing through the darkness while being pursued by men, and she said that one of them was her real father. She was holding the hand of a small boy, dragging him along, but she lost him and, without turning back, continued to run. The footsteps were getting closer, and from somewhere behind her, the boy was screaming for her not to leave him.

She waited for Stan to say something while she recalled every detail of the memories that flooded her mind, reliving all the horrible torture. Roberta was searching for a reason why she felt that Nathan and she were so connected.

Stan remained silent, fearing that any reaction would cause her to stop. He had investigated many child-abuse cases, and he understood the lasting effects the experience had on people, how it screwed some minds up so badly that the most morbid thoughts seemed normal to them. He began to understand the episodes that Roberta was having, and the blackouts.

"My God..." Stan said in a low voice, and then he asked her to come down to Miami. "Just leave, right now. I'll call the airport and make the arrangements. Please, just go to the ticket counter and I'll have the reservations finished by then. Please?"

Roberta agreed, thanked him in a small, little-girl voice filled with passion and gratitude. Stan's heart was singing, the blood racing hell-bent through his body, carrying tiny electrical shocks. Three hours later, the American Airlines jet touched down at Miami International Airport. Stan had barely had time to shower and shave, trying to make himself presentable after the previous night of no sleep and too much beer, before racing across the causeway to the airport.

He felt excited, like a lovesick teenager waiting at the front door for his prom date. The passengers had begun to emerge from the arrival gate, and he stretched to find Roberta. Only two aircraft had arrived at this gate and the crowd was small, but still, he could not find her. Then, suddenly from behind him, he heard a giggle and turned slowly to face the sound. "Hey, you lookin' fer me?" he heard a voice say. He closed his eyes tightly and opened them again.

"What, who? Roberta? I never saw you get off the plane!" Stan almost did not recognize her, but he hugged her hard, and she returned the hug passionately. The woman looked different, had seemingly grown taller, thinned out considerably, and developed hardness about her face. Stan felt the strength in her hug, and the shiver.

"Give me your stub and I'll collect the bags. The car is parked right out the door," Stan told her, pointing toward the right exit. Consider-ing it was Saturday during a slow travel month, Stan had not had trou-ble finding a parking spot near the entrance.

"This is it," she said, holding up a canvas bag. Then Roberta laughed, a strange, throaty sound reminding Stan of muffled explo-sions. He held her a second longer, not out of affection but because he wanted to look at her closely, determine the full extent of the changes, and then he let her go suddenly, almost pushing her away.

"What's wrong, Stan? You look worried or something," she said, giving him a queer look.

The drive back to the beach was quick. Traffic was light, and the conversation was strained and uncomfortable. Stan took her to his house, something he had not really planned, and Roberta did not seem to mind. He lived in a remodeled art deco-style home a few blocks from a stretch of beach with a fishing pier. He had spent many hours spent watching the waves and letting the tide carry his troubled mind to calm waters. The ocean was therapeutic for Stan, and he would always walk along the beach to find solutions to problems. He also went there to just sit and relax, to empty his mind and soul across the gentle waves.

"How about a drink, maybe a Coke or Arizona Tea?"

"No, thanks. This is a great house. I like the trim around the ceiling. Is it original?"

"Yeah, everything is original in design. Some things were remodeled during the restoration, but the ceiling has never been changed. The previous owner added the tiles and fixtures in the bathroom, something more contemporary, basically screwing up the house, and it has taken years to restore it," he explained, taking her on a tour. Stan was proud of his house, which had been built around 1950 and was solid, having endured more than a few powerful hurricanes. The oak tree in the front yard had been planted a year after the house was built, and its canopy covered the entire front yard. The only major changes to the original plan were the addition of the third bedroom, a pool, and a two-car garage. These changes doubled the value of the residence.

"Did you do the landscaping or did you hire someone?"

"Hire someone! I'll have you know that I, my dear, have a green thumb from way back. I did everything. It's a hobby of mine. All the plants are native to Florida. Taking care of them helps me to relax. I love to make things grow, watch them spring up from the ground and reach for the sky."

Roberta loved the backyard with the pool and privacy gardens. The lush vegetation allowed the pool to look like a lagoon rather than a man-made structure. She walked through the French doors and felt the sweltering effect of the humidity. The rain had stopped not long after the sunset, but the temperature was still over ninety degrees.

"Is it always this hot and sticky?"

"Most of the time, but it's worse this time of year because of all the rain," Stan said as he kneeled and ran a nervous hand across the water at the edge of the pool.

Roberta unbuttoned her blouse and sat on the edge beside him, reaching slowly to feel the wet coolness on her fingertips. "Wow, the water must be twenty degrees cooler than the air. It really feels great," she said, smiling. The next moments seemed to move in slow motion for Stan. Roberta leaned over, kissed him hard, and stripped completely before jumping into the pool with a big splash. Stan was still trying to catch his breath as he fumbled with his pants, trying to maintain his balance while shedding his cloths to join Roberta.

The intimate swim in the pool, filled with heated lovemaking, unexpected and uninhibited, led to wilder passion in the bedroom, the experience draining them both. They lay exhausted in each other's arms. This was far more than Stan had expected, but he was not about to complain, because this was exactly what he had wanted. Roberta was explosive, demanding and giving at the same time, draining Stan and forcing him to new levels of performance. She was relentless in seeking satisfaction, and she returned the pleasure with the same high-level energy.

Stan was the first to speak after a long, comfortable silence. "This was not what I had expected," he ventured.

Roberta rolled away and onto her back. "Yeah, me either, but I have wanted you for so long, and I wouldn't have had it any other way. We needed this, Stan, needed to get past all the dancing around each other and start a real relationship without all of the doubts."

Stan pondered the idea for a moment and could not find fault with it, but this was one hell of an icebreaker, one hell of a start. He liked the easy way Roberta was handling everything. There was nothing coy or reserved about her. She was bold and outspoken in both words and actions. Stan had no problems in communication with her, and she seemed to enjoy showing him exactly what she wanted.

During the quiet moments that followed the intense passion, her body felt natural lying next to him, her leg draped over his waist and her head resting on his chest. He ran his hand down her body and felt the silky smoothness of the skin, the firmness of her thigh, and he cupped her breast in a strong but gentle squeeze. She moaned and sighed, taking his hand and guiding it between her legs. She stretched slowly and kissed him hard on the mouth. A deep, satisfying sleep followed, filled with a rush of dreams that left them both drifting in a world of happiness until the early afternoon.

Stan awoke first and lay in bed looking at Roberta. He decided that breakfast in bed was in order, and he slipped from the covers carefully to avoid disturbing her. It wasn't long before he felt her arms embracing him from behind. He turned to find her sleepy expression a beautiful sight, and the sight of her body created a powerful hunger. Roberta recognized the look, smiled knowingly, and pulled him close to her, inviting him to satisfy them both. Breakfast would have to wait a while longer.

The telephone interrupted the scrambled eggs and toast they were devouring, and Stan answered, "Hello, May here."

"Well, ain't that special, monkey-boy." The familiar voice peeled the peace from his heart.

"You again, huh, Nathan? Hey, I meant to ask you last time, just how did you get my number?" Stan demanded.

"Ain't hard to get anything ya want in the Magic City. You should know that. That's what I like 'bout this town, anything goes!"

Stan was silent as Nathan talked. He watched the change in Roberta's face, her demeanor, and even the way she held her fork as she ate. "You feeling awright, Mr. Tricky Dicky? I didn't spook you like some big ol' scary cat, now did I?"

"What do you want, asshole? I don't feel like listening to all your shit today."

Roberta was making signs with her hands, shaking her head vigorously, wanting to take the telephone from him.

"You are special, ain't you, all tough and worked up? I do not suppose you know where the favorite bitch from Georgia is staying. You know she's back here in Miami, don't ya?"

"What do you mean, she's here? How would you know that?" Stan asked, getting that strange feeling again in his stomach.

"'Cause I feel her, asshole. Ain't you done figured it out? You be almost as dumb as her. She's close, though. I can smell her when I sweat. She be real close. And soon she'll be mine."

Stan closed his eyes and shook his head. Roberta was still trying to get his attention so she could speak to Nathan, and finally Stan gave in, shrugged, and tossed her the phone.

"Hello, Nathan."

Nathan's voice froze. This was a surprise, and he did not like being caught off guard. He waited until she asked if he was still there before he spoke. "Fuck you, bitch. What the fuck are you doing with that dick? You lettin' him dip his black dick in your white well, you whore?"

"Where are you, Nathan? I came back for you, to talk to you, to see you. Can we meet?"

It was now Stan's turn to make hand gestures and shake his head. "Are you fucking crazy, Roberta?" Stan hissed, trying to take the phone away from her.

She jerked back and shot Stan a menacing look, one that he had seen recently but not from her. "Let me be. I got to see him. I told you already. I ain't got no choice," she told him with a hand over the mouthpiece, and then she directed her attention back to Nathan. "Just tell me where the hell you are, damn it."

"Ain't you the pushy little bitch? What's wrong, monkey-boy can't push it in deep enough fer ya, or are ya just ready for what you been dreamin' 'bout all yer fuckin' life?" Nathan said with a giggle, knowing what the next question would be and waiting for it. The question came right on cue.

"What are you talking about, dreamin' and all?"

"You know what I'm talkin' 'bout, Ricky-Lou. I should have fucked you then and saved myself, but now I'll just have to make up for lost time. You ready to be digging up bones, Ricky-Lou? You know what's got to be, what should have been. Ain't no changing the nature of what you are, what you were born to be."

"Meet with me, Nathan, and we can talk about this face to face. Maybe we can explore some of your ideas, just tell me where," she whispered in a deep, sensual voice, causing Stan to shake his head slowly in disbelief.

Roberta made arrangements with Nathan. He instructed her to go to a pay telephone by a laundromat in a seedy area of South Beach. He would then call at a precise time, for timing was crucial, and he told her if she was late one minute, the deal was history.

Stan was vibrating with anger, unable to deal with the idea of Roberta meeting with a homicidal maniac, and to top it all off, she refused to tell him any of the details. Roberta insisted on going alone, settling this nightmare once and for all, but she had to do it alone.

"Are you out of your mind, woman? This guy is going to kill you. You do realize that, don't you? Honey, you have seen what he does to people. God, Roberta, please, we just found each other. I can't stand the thought of losing you, not now, not ever. I had rather die myself than to have a life without you. I love you, Roberta." Stan was almost yelling the words and was holding Roberta tightly, crushing her into him.

"I love you too, Stan. That's why I have got to do this, and I have to do it alone. Please understand that we don't have a chance until I can figure out what's going on with Nathan—what's the connection—and me. I have got to know for sure, and only he can tell me. Trust me, baby." Roberta reached out and held the handsome face in her hands, then kissed him softly. She could feel him tremble with anger at the thought of Nathan hurting her, and she enjoyed feeling the love surrounding her. "Calm down, sweetheart. How do you know he plans to kill me? I think he really wants to talk, to tell me all the things he has been hinting at for so long. Who knows, maybe I can talk him into giving up if we promise that he'll be treated right."

"You are insane, aren't you?" Stan took a deep breath. He knew that she had made up her mind and that nothing would change it. "At least let me arrange for protection for you, please?"

"How 'bout you trust me on this. I know him, Stan. Sometimes I think I know him better than I know myself. I tried to explain all this to you on the phone before I came down, and I thought you understood."

"No, Roberta, I don't understand all of this. Does it matter if he is the little boy in your dream? Does it change anything? He is still a killer, and if he is who you think he is, it still won't change that fact. You do not owe him anything. This is not your fault, the way he is. He will kill you, Roberta. He has said before that there could only be one of you, and he will kill you." Stan pleaded with Roberta for hours, trying different tactics to make her realize what she was walking into by meeting with Nathan. Nothing worked.

Roberta told him how much she loved him, throwing his thoughts and his arguments way off track, making an issue of their future and making everything grow beyond the safe zones of sanity. "Stan, with everything I have told you, you know that we will never have a chance unless this thing with Nathan is finalized. I have to know everything he knows. I have to find out who he is, and who I am, before we can have each other completely. Please trust me."

With her finishing words, Stan could no longer argue, and he pulled her close. Regardless of how stupid he thought this was, he realized that she was doing it to have a life with him, and that was good enough. Roberta looked up into the face of the man she loved, and Stan could tell there was something else she needed to say. Her hesitation scared him. What else could there be? "What?" he asked, waiting for more unpleasant revelations or suggestions and forcing himself to breathe.

"I love you, Stan. I mean, I really love you."

"I love you too, Roberta. But that is not what you wanted to say. What else is bothering you? After all this, you do realize that you can tell me anything, I hope."

"I know that, but I'm just not sure you are ready for this." She took a huge breath to build courage. "Stan, when all of this is done and Nathan is gone from our life—" Roberta took another deep breath and noted the look of concern on Stan's face before she continued. "Will you marry me, Stan May?"

Stan's mouth dropped open, and he stared at her, thinking that maybe he had misunderstood. She immediately pulled away from him and wished she could just crawl into a deep hole. "I'm sorry, I shouldn't have asked that. We, I, this, oh God....Don't even answer. I just... It's too fast for you. I—"

"Shut up before I think that you're trying to back out of it, now that you've asked," he said, a huge smile decorating his face. "Yes, Roberta,

I will marry you, and yes this is incredibly fast, and yes I want to spend the rest of my life with you. I love you so much that sometimes I can't believe it myself. I couldn't handle life without Roberta, not now." Stan pulled her into him, and they melted together. They smothered each other with love, talked about the future, and for a little longer, the world was warm and beautiful. The subject of Nathan did not surface again. Everything had been said, and Stan had decided to give in to Roberta's insistence only because he would be following her. He would make sure that Nathan did nothing to harm the woman he would share his life with.

Stan and Roberta had fallen asleep while holding each other and dreaming of old age and rocking chairs side by side. Stan awoke the next morning and rolled over, reaching out to feel the warm body next to him, but Roberta was gone. A note pinned to the cushion on the couch explained that she had gone to meet Nathan, that she wanted to get it over with so they could get on with their life together. Stan had overheard part of the location that Nathan had instructed Roberta to go to, and he knew that she was supposed to be there at eleven o'clock. The time now was ten-forty, and he would have to hurry. He ran for the car, carrying his clothes. He dressed in the car and shoved his pistol between the seats.

Roberta arrived exactly on time, and as she approached the telephone mounted on the wall, it rang.

"Hi, this is Ricky-Lou; talk to me, Nathan," she teased.

"You are a spunky little bitch, ain't ya?" he answered. "You see that telephone over yonder across the street? I ain't gonna call it, but you go over there, and by the way, I told you to come alone. What's the monkey-boy doing here?" he asked without showing any concern.

"I'm sorry, Nathan. He must have followed me," she said, searching the streets until she found where Stan had set up his surveillance on her. She knew that he was doing it out of love, but he was going to screw up everything.

"There's an alley runnin' between the buildings over by that other phone. You can slip down the alley and lose Mr. Tricky-Dicky," Nathan said as a little giggle escaped his throat.

"I swear I didn't know he was going to follow me, Nathan."

"I know that, Ricky-Lou. You seem to forget that I can feel what you feel. I can smell what you smell. I knows that you didn't know he'd be over there watchin', but that don't matter none. We are all that matters, you and me. We are one, Ricky-Lou, and there can only be one. Ditch the Mr. Tricky-Dicky and go to the back door of the third building. I'll be waiting with a hard on fer ya, darlin'."

"Well, ain't that special, shit for brains, but it ain't gonna be workin' that way," she spat into the phone. "Listen real good, ol' boy, I'm gonna start walkin' down this here road, headin' south, and you try and keep up. We'll ditch Mr. Buttinski along the way, and when I am ready for your sorry ass, I'll give *you* a signal," she hissed and slammed down the phone.

Detective May followed, sure that neither Roberta nor Nathan had seen him. He could not determine with certainty who was following whom at this point, and he did not allow himself to rush forward without certainty. He did not want to endanger Roberta, and considered time to be on his side. Patience was needed now. Just let the players of the game reveal their identities, Stan said to himself. Years of training combined with the experience of surveillance had caused him to become overconfident. He was confident that he would not be seen, just ambling along at a controlled, mock stagger to give the impression of a benevolent drunk merely trying to find the way home. Stan wondered if somehow Nathan sensed that he was following Roberta. He quickly dismissed the thought, slipping within the cover of the opposite side of the street, and feeling protected against detection.

As the stalker and his prey moved silently down the streets and alleys, Stan became increasing confused as to which one was Roberta. He had assumed that Roberta was following Nathan, but then he changed his mind and was convinced that Nathan was following Roberta. He could not be certain. The two figures moved in unison, one trailing the other by only a hundred yards. He hoped that Roberta would remember whom she was dealing with and never let her guard down. Stan blinked, and thoughts of a night full of love clouded his mind and interfered with his concentration as the two shadows made a turn. Stan had missed it and was going into a panic. *Dear God, let her be safe*, he prayed silently and started running down the streets, looking through the alleys and screaming Roberta's name. He no longer cared that she wanted to talk with this maniac. His only concern was for her life and for their life together.

Roberta had slipped into an abandoned building filled with cobwebs and rats. She made her way up to the third floor, with Nathan's giggles close behind. The room was dirty and smelled of decaying rodents. Roberta sat on the floor in the corner and waited for Nathan to join her. The door squealed as he pushed it open slowly and whispered, "Ricky-Lou, you in here?"

"Yeah, over here, Nathan," she growled with a childlike giggle.

"Well, well, Ms. High and Mighty, looks like you be findin' where you really belong, on the floor with the rest of the dirt." Nathan spat every word. "What do you want to know, cunt, before I do what you been dreamin' 'bout? You want to hear 'bout dear old Dad and Mom and how wonderful they were after you left me behind, or how for all these years I could smell you every time you had a bleedin' spell, could feel you when you squirted your juice over some asshole's dick? Maybe you just want me to say that I fergive ya leavin'. I don't. You were supposed to die that night, big sister, and now after all these years, nature will finally have its way."

Roberta watched him coming toward her and felt the need to reach out and hold the hand that she had lost in the race for her life so many years before. She stood and held out her arms to her brother, embracing him with the love that he had watched jump on the train and move quickly away. She started to cry and whispered in his ear, "I'm so sorry for leaving you. I remember everything now. I love you, little brother."

The motion came out of the darkness, born from the darkness and filing incorporeal edges with a fury, giving the image of both speed and form. Silence in the wake of such brutality transcended the terror beyond the limits of understanding, and only the sense of smell offered any hint that something hideous had happened. Slowly, imperceptibly, came the sound of breathing, not the heavy gasp expected after a great execration, for surely, it took strength and intense emotion to kill a person, but the slight rasping sound came in calm, evenly spaced intervals. Cold, reptilian eyes watched the life-giving blood ooze from mortal wounds delivered not in haste but in choreographed perfection across the floor. The delirium came rushing to fill the vacancy where celibate emotions had steered the acts of carnage. The hiss of expelled breath increased in volume, and soft murmuring distributed across the stench of death, resulting from savage, unrestricted blows delivered with both force and enthusiasm. The splatters caused by the slashing covered the walls and ceiling with blood, and the arms and the face of the killer ran red as the frenzy took on a new dimension of intensity.

Grunts and moans flowed faster, becoming sounds stretching limits into patterns of speech, filled with words and sentences bunched together until a conversation emerged. The dialect was odd, drifting away from recognition, keeping interpretation entirely to itself. If one took the notion to sit by the door and count the number of voices, maybe two or three at a time separated, perhaps as many as ten the next try, and finally, one would give up in failure. There were still other sounds, giving the noise a resemblance of the incoherent babbling of alley cats or hyenas sparring in the corner as trains, whistles, and squealing tires split the clamor.

"So, here we are, here we are. There can be no more of this. Nothing is as it sounds until all is *one...*" was repeated in a high-pitched whine as if the wind had taken aim at a split in time, stretching the edges to razor thinness, and the sound caused beasts to scream in pain. The giggling was uncontrollable, low and muffled, with a slight hint of sorrow not yet reaching the surface. The taste of blood was as it had always been, but different somehow. This was the blood of family, sweeter than that of strangers or enemies, and it caused a stir of excitement between the legs. The thread was pulled from the pocket and placed on the floor for later usage. The voices were singing, applauding the finality of this long-awaited event, and begging the performer to give an encore.

Stan found an open door to the abandoned building and easily followed the footsteps left in the dust and dirt on the stairs. The stillness throbbed with an eerie disquiet, and he strained to hear the slightest noise but heard nothing. One-step at a time, he ascended the stairs, trying hard to move stealthily. Abruptly, the slightest creak from a loose floorboard sounded somewhere above him in the darkness, giving Stan a start and a direction in which to continue the hunt. His heart was in his throat. It had taken him almost ten minutes to find the building, and his soul could feel Roberta slipping away. He had to find them. There could still be enough time, he told himself repeatedly as he ran up the stairs three at a time. He found two sets of footprints at the top third-floor landing. He breathed deeply in an attempt to stop his hands from shaking, and then he forced himself to continue, feeling defeat biting at his ankles. The silence, the darkness, the fear disoriented him, but he stumbled on blindly, motivated by instinct and desire to protect the woman he loved.

The wall supplied support and direction as Stan slowly made his way down the hall. He came to many doors, all locked and offering no indication of occupancy, so he continued blindly, hoping it would be as simple as finding the right door standing open. He strained to listen, but the building was as quiet as a tomb. Stan estimated that he had made it over halfway up the hall when he found a door slightly ajar. The rate of his heart increased twofold, the blood creating a high-pitched scream racing through his vessels, and he held his pistol in the ready position. Slowly, he moved into the room, pushing the door all the way open, unable to detect the slightest movement or sound. Moments later, he discovered this was merely a waiting room leading to a score of other offices.

The soft humming was almost undetectable, but Stan's senses were working overtime, and he followed the sound. Odors were drifting, long wispy strands of thin smoke, wafting, shifting direction with the slightest provocation, sticking to Stan like bits of ash, unable to steer clear of him. There were other distractions in the air as well, wet and heavy, saturated with the force to take hold, to shake his sensibilities, to cause his courage to waver like a flame before a stiff breeze. The voice was singing, and Stan was straining to hear, to figure out where it was coming from inside the room, and then the words reached his mind: "I am insane, or so I am told by those who speak so brazen and bold. With tongues that wag and chatter on, until all words are dead and gone. Bright eyes stare into my world, better to see dark corners of theirs. I'll let them in to occupy their time, and then I will break the rhythm of their minds. What fools they are to think black and white. I dream in color late at night. Like robots all standing so straight in line, they stare at me yet they are blind. But I am insane, or so I am told by those whose minds are bought and sold." The giggles and happiness he heard at the end of the poem told him that he was too late and the deed had been done.

Stan remembered that poem, remembered watching Nathan sing it while tied to the wall at the institute, seeing him lick his lips and relive the brutal torture his mind would replay for his pleasure. The sorrow was filling Stan up, strangling his desire to move, draining him of all feelings but one. This was the end of a hard road traveled, and he fought against collapse. Nathan had taken everything from him—his friend, his sense of right and wrong, his ideals of what life should be, and now Roberta. Thoughts were stacking themselves one upon the other, lying down to surrender, and among the settling and exhaustion, it became clear that there was just one more thing to be done. The law did not matter. The outcome did not matter. Only the requirement that it be done. Stan stepped inside the door, swept the room with his pistol, and waited for the moment to come.

The light bled through the gaps in the curtains, creating small stripes of yellow across the floor, capturing the dust in the air and allowing him to see two figures on the floor. He listened to appalling sounds of things wet and sticky slapping together and ripped apart. He heard what his mind told him was Roberta's crunching bones or gristle between grinding jaws, and he fought not to puke. He watched hands moving, causing the polished edge of the blade to pass through the line of light, and for a moment, a single eye looked up, blinked once, and turned away.

"Get away from her, you bastard," Stan screamed and took another step closer. Stan could feel his feet sliding, causing him to almost fall several times as he slowly inched forward. He looked down to see what was on the floor and shook his head, trying to help his brain to comprehend. The blood was everywhere, and the internal organs had been thrown all over the room, decorating it with red chunks of flesh. The bile in Stan's stomach jumped to his throat when he realized he was stepping on a kidney. "Oh God," he said out loud, losing himself in the horror. His mind was at war with itself. It needed to flee this place, to shut down, to protect its delicate balance, which was becoming increasingly in danger.

Stan could see the circular motion of hands as his eyes adjusted to the low light. The monster was stitching the blue thread through the stomach, drawn through the severed edges of flesh by a needle the size of a pencil. Singing and giggling accompanied each completed stitch. The singing voice was hypnotizing him, causing him to pause. "I am insane or so I am told—"

"No!" he screamed.

"Well, well, Mr. Tricky Dicky. Seems to me that you weren't invited to this little party." The words were almost a whisper, and Stan moved closer to hear. His mind was playing tricks on him. The darkness was swallowing his soul, and the smell crawled upon his skin, sucking the sanity from his pores. Stan stood in front of the blood-covered beast. He could not see the face clearly but noted the firm jaw as the light from the window danced on the red highlights hidden in the brown hair. His mind's desire to remove itself from danger was winning. He could feel the room growing smaller, the world growing dim. Shaking his head at one last attempt to maintain control, he inquired of the bloody horror standing in front of him, "Why?"

"It's in my nature, ol' boy. You can't be changin' yer nature. Can't be changin' what ya are. There can't be two of us. They can only be one, and that's me."

Stan watched in disbelief as the bloody figure walked toward him. He didn't see how nonchalantly the foot would kick the organs on the floor to the side or how the knife was being cleaned, with a hungry tongue darting around the edges, tasting the dripping blood. Stan was going into shock. He could not move, could not speak, and could not believe. A hand reached up to his face, and a bloody finger traced his lips, dipping inside his mouth so the taste of blood engulfed what was left of his sanity. The laughter brought him back to reality, the piercing howl of the Devil's demon at play. Stan raised his pistol and watched the surprised look run rampant across the face. The sound was deafening, the act was final, and the body fell to the floor with a thud.

CHAPTER
TWENTY-SEVEN

A YEAR AFTER the mysterious disappearance of Buddy Chandler, workers attempting to resurface the alleyways of a downtown section of Miami Beach discovered the forgotten grease pit that had unceremoniously served as Sheriff Chandler's tomb. The remains of the retired sheriff were returned to Caulking for a proper burial. Jefferson Chandler received a hero's good-bye, and his name was added to the list of law-enforcement officers killed in the line of duty.

Detective Stan May attended the funeral in full dress uniform, along with hundreds of rows of proud, grim-faced officers and Caulking residents. The governor of the State of Georgia gave the eulogy, and when the bagpipes produced their heartbreaking wail, the tears flowed freely and J. C. Chandler was officially laid to rest beside his beloved Becky-Ann.

No one claimed the body of Nathan Pomeroy, and eventually, buried in the county-owned cemetery with a brass plate cemented at the head of the grave. A clerk in Caulking discovered that taxes on the Pomeroy property were delinquent for more than two decades, and the property seized for foreclosure and resale. Not one person showed an interest in the thirty-odd acres of swampland labeled the Devil's playground.

After the funeral, Stan walked slowly back to the waiting van, his head high and shoulders squared. But he no longer felt the pride and dignity. He no longer desired to hunt armed men, and he no longer cared to understand the reasons why people did the things they did to each other. He no longer concerned himself with the inhumanity of man, with the violence, and with the disregard for innocence lost in the faces of abused and battered children.

"One more stop, please?" Stan almost whispered to the big man walking beside him.

"Come on, Stan. You know we ain't supposed to. Are you sure you can handle it?"

"Yeah, please, man. It might be my last chance to say good-bye."

The van pulled into a small overgrown lot on the other side of town. An old wooden church with a high steeple looked down on the grass that was persistently engulfing the cemetery. Stan stood for a while looking at the name on the stone, and soon, his body shook with grief. "Roberta Austin," it read, "peace is finally yours." Stan gathered wildflowers and laid a huge bouquet in front of the headstone. He ran his hands over her name as the tears flowed from his heart, and he felt the cold granite against his lips when he kissed her good-bye. The darkness was closing in again, his perpetual escape from this reality of loneliness.

The van door opened, and Stan obediently stepped inside. His companion helped him to the back and proceeded to buckle him to the sidewall, a necessary precaution when dealing with unpredictable patients, especially now when the medication was starting to wear off. Max felt sorry for the big man, and he remembered how strong and sure of himself Stan had been when they had first met many months before.

"Life sure is funny," Max said as the last of the buckles secured Stan for the ride back to the asylum. "What a pity," he whispered under his breath as he patted the detective on the head as if praising his behavior for the day.

Max was indeed very proud of Stan. He had been able to maintain his composure during the funeral and at Roberta's grave. Of course, the double doses of mood-altering drugs had been a huge help. But now the drugs were wearing off and the true nature of Stan May was on the edge, pushing his control into memory, where it would be eaten alive and spat out in acts of violence and disgusting displays of insanity.

Max had been assigned to be Stan May's keeper after several of the orderlies had complained about the constant mess that Stan would cause. Stan would often sit very still and quiet when the trays of food were brought in, and just before the attendant placed it on the table, Stan would scream or jump out at them and the tray would go flying to the floor. Stan would then burst out laughing in his insane way, then defecate, and rub the feces all over his body.

These acts of insanity were becoming a ritual, and often, Max would double the dosage of Stan's medication without the doctors' knowledge just to keep the big man so tired that he could barely stand. Max had had a long talk with Stan during one of his more sane moments and had told the former detective about the scheduled funeral of Sheriff Chandler. Stan had begged to attend, and Max had agreed help him get there if he promised to try harder to control his outbursts. Max had spoken to the doctors at the asylum and convinced them that attending the funeral would help Stan put closure on the Nathan ordeal. Max had pulled many strings, and the request had been approved with the encouragement of several sheriffs and police chiefs from all over the state. One of Stan's former coworkers had slipped an old uniform of Stan's into the hospital and left it for him to wear—it was the least he could do, considering that Stan had saved his life on more than one occasion.

Max knew that the voices were returning into the mind of the once strong-willed detective, whispering vile things that caused Stan to shake his head and pound it against the side of the van. Max watched as the man fought for control of his mind. Then he watched the man weaken and the voices finally consume him. The change was frightening and never ceased to send a chill down Max's back.

Stan could hear her voice inside his head, and he could hear Nathan giggling in the distance. His mind replayed the last moments of that day repeatedly, the wonderful love he and Roberta had shared just hours before, the anticipation of a future and the happiness surrounding them, and then darkness. His mind allowed every sense to be activated, allowed him to relive every smell, every taste, and every horror. He was back in the room, and he could see the monster stitching the blue thread. He could hear that dreadful poem being recited in the singsong tone, "I am insane or so I am told..." He could hear himself scream and feel the sticky blood and smell the death all around him.

He was there again. He went to this place several times every day and every night. His mind would not let him forget even the smallest detail, and the demons replayed them with rehearsed perfection.

Stan screamed and beat his head harder against the wall of the van, trying to drive out the memory. Max turned up the radio to block out the painful screams. It was always the same—the voices would come, and then Stan would become lost in a world of pain and suffering. Stan May prayed for death, prayed for the voices to end, for the memories to dull. The fight was over inside his mind as he watched the figure walk toward him. He tasted the blood as the fingers traced his lips and heard the giggles of Satan himself. The barrel flashed red and illuminated Roberta's face just before the back of her head exploded.

Stan sat in the blood-filled room for hours before he was found by a homeless man looking for a place to sleep. He held Roberta close until she was taken away. His mind had never accepted what he had seen and done. It just continued to replay itself day after day in its attempt to find an answer, all the while sending the detective further and further into darkness.

Max turned to look at Stan's rocking body strapped to the van wall. He turned down the radio to hear the singsong tone of the poem Stan was reciting. He remembered that poem, Nathan's poem. He always found it eerie how they both sang the same poem. He found it even stranger that, if he closed his eyes, it was Nathan he heard singing, not the broken detective. It was as if Nathan had crawled into the detective and taken over his mind. Max turned the radio back up, forcing himself to push those thoughts out of his head. It was just too weird and too spooky to think such things, and he had a long way to go before he got back to the asylum.

Stan continued to rock to the beat of his own drummer. He sang with a happy giggle as he pounded his head against the van and pulled at the straps. His voice became louder with every new beginning of the poem: "I am insane, or so I am told by those who act so brazen and bold..." And then silence. A chill ran through Max's body when the singing stopped. He swallowed hard and said a silent prayer. He felt the presence of evil, of pure darkness that made the air too thick to breath. Slowly, he turned. He let out a heavy breath when he saw Stan still strapped to the van wall, sound asleep. All of these crazy people were getting to him, he thought as he turned his radio back up and sang off key with every note.

Stan opened one eye and watched the driver as an evil smile played on his lips. The voices were back, but they were different now. *Yeah, things will be a-changin'*, he thought, and the voices agreed. Thoughts were causing needs and desire to run wild in his mind, and the smell of fear oozing from Max's body was intoxicating. "Yes, siree, things be gettin' back to normal," he said, and then he giggled and rubbed his hard-on with the hand he had managed to free from the straps.

If you enjoyed
FACE the SUN
Look for
WATCHING the MOON
book two of the story of evil
born from the Pomeroy legacy
By Robert and Tammy Davis

WATCHING THE MOON

CHAPTER
ONE

CASUALLY, THE CLERK picked up the cashier's check from the countertop and flipped it over to stamp the back. She checked the quality of the printed letters and blew gently through puckered red lips on the purple ink. The man who had given her the check watched the tip of her tongue protrude through the tiny circle made by her lips, which reminded him of a cherry Lifesaver. He counted the duration of each breath and quickly counted the number of pigeonholes on the wall behind her with darting, dancing eyes. He counted the plaques, the employee-of-the-month awards and framed eight-by-eleven photos of past chief property appraiser clerks before he went visually leaping down the green countertop inch by inch, taking note of every ledger, pencil, and paperclip. The man filed the useless information in a tiny, translucent box hidden away in the middle of his brain, a chamber kept wet and cold, and dripping facts into the worn surface of the cracked and pitted memory. Every fold and recess was stamped and dated, every memory coded. Every blink of his eyes captured and deposited still more little facts.

"Don't I get some kinda receipt for all that money?" The man grinned, and the young woman behind the green counter shivered but did not know why. Her shiver was obvious, and the man smiled again. His voice was light and airy, drifting around the clerk's head, giving her pause to try to understand the words. The words were small and bunched together as if trying to protect themselves from loud, more obnoxious noises. The words were carrying the challenge of a lisp, a delicate and gentle defect, which immediately demanded sympathy from most but outrage and anger from others.

"Sorry, gotta be a draft. I hate these ol' buildings with the cold draft; guess there ain't no young buildings in this old town." And she smiled back, mistaking the meaning behind the man's smile as an act of kindness.

"I suppose not," the man replied and impatiently looked at his watch. The clerk smiled back again and stapled the check to the inside flap of the folder. She filled out a receipt by hand and posted the amount on the inside page of a well-worn red leather ledger.

Sandy Palmer was the clerk's name. She had turned nineteen the previous week and engaged, for the second time, to a local boy working on her daddy's farm. Sandy worked as a clerk in the property appraiser's office in the old courthouse building. The new courthouse was still in the drawing stages and had not passed the Technical Review Board study. The plans had been submitted five years before, and the bickering had started the first day.

The man smiled and Sandy smiled, and he quickly counted the number of freckles across the bridge of her perfect nose. The information was important, and he stored it away in a little square box labeled "Sandy Palmer" deep within the translucent vault of his memory. This time he shivered, but Sandy did not notice, nor did she see him rapidly blink his eyes or dart his tongue back and forth. She did not hear the voices of the demon screaming inside his head, not the everyday garden-variety demon but a vicious, attention-demanding imp ripped away from its last host with great force, now using a selection of perfected voices chosen from the past and working well together to keep the pace of the game interesting—a game of smoke and mirrors designed to vault over the obvious and to slam pretense into the limelight while the real purpose tiptoed through the back window of the soul.

A single voice reached a pitch above all others, and the man grimaced from the pain as he heard, "Twitching emotion, empty smiles, empty eyes that stare at the face whispering beneath the mirror's edge. Tears kiss the surface, dance wet-side down between etched edges of milk-colored shadows dragging so slowly behind the lonely soul." He coughed to cover the tremor producing a twitch at the corner of his right eye, and the clerk stared at the clock.

"That's a whole lotta money for a burnt-down farmhouse and swamp land, mister," she told him, looking bored, and sighed.

"Yeah, you think so?" The man said in a low voice, in a loud whisper, and watched her small breast rise and fall.

"And ain't that the place where all them bodies and stuff was found? I 'member something 'bout the name." She paused and wrinkled her nose, thinking, but the thought remained elusive.

"Sandy?" a voice boomed from nowhere.

The clerk screamed. "Damn! Y'all tryin' to give me a heart attack!"

"No, sorry, Sandy. This has been a most tryin' day, child." The woman tried to smile but failed and continued. "If some freaky-soundin' guy comes in 'bout the old Pomeroy place, y'all give a holler. I want to see the person buyin' that horror show."

Sandy's eyes bulged, and she tried to give Chief Property Appraiser Dana Cullen every signal to stop her, but too late.

"What are you doin'? You okay, child?"

"I think she was trying to warn you that the freaky-sounding guy buying the horror show was already here and that would be me."

Dana Cullen let her eyes drag her emotions along the man's face. She fought back the urge to run, scream, or break out in tears, because there was just something unsettling about the way he watched her look at him. His eyes seemed to open wide and let her see directly into his mind. She looked him in the eye and thought she saw a hint of mascara on his eyelashes or a trace of blush on his cheeks, and he had the best manicure she seen in a long time. She decided to plow ahead—she had already stuck her foot in it—and said, straight-faced, "Ain't you somethin'. You just plain crazy, or am I goin' ta" wake up soon?"

Sandy Palmer gasped as she turned crimson and whispered very loudly, "My God, Dana," between clenched teeth.

Dana Cullen gave a curt nod and turned. She didn't wait for a reply because there was none coming, and the man seemed to snarl and smile at the same time. She walked out of the office, muttering to herself, "And he's a black man, to boot."

"I don't know what to say, mister; I guess she didn't know you was here."

"Really?" the man sneered and again asked for a receipt.

The silence lingered for the rest of the transaction. The man enjoyed watching Sandy stumble and fumble and refuse to make eye contact. The paperwork finished and stapled together; he paid the current year's taxes in full, and then the deed was signed, sealed, and carefully slid across the green counter toward the new owner. He looked at the deed and almost committed a fatal error when he looked at the name, a mistake that would have shattered all his years of preparation and all the careful maneuvering, the assembly of carefully chosen clandestine, choreographed acts. He bit his tongue and tasted the sweet salty traces of blood. He smiled and nodded slowly. "I think this about does it," he announced and turned to depart.

"Excuse me, Mr. Chandler?" The sweet voice rolled through the air in soft, thin layers toward the back of the new owner of the "horror show."

"Yes, did I forget something?" His voice was calm and level, not betraying the panic ricocheting in his mind or the sudden rapid increase in his pulse, and she did not see the waves of sweat squeezing from the pores in his skin.

"No. Just wanted to know what ya planned on doin' with that old place? It's a real wreck, if ya know what I mean? No offense."

He studied her face and saw nothing more than stupidity. "No offense!" His mind screamed, *You ignorant, straightforward, airheaded, blonde slut!* He was hoping there was going to be something more substantial, as if she may have taken one class at the junior college regarding real estate and property values as they applied to this financially devastated armpit of a county.

"Just going fishing, Sandy."

As he descended the rest of the steps, a voice counted the cracks in the concrete. He disappeared into the corridor and walked in short, measured steps to a leased car. The man stored away the number of blossoms on the tree by the street. *You stupid, fucking asshole!* he screamed to himself, and the voice wailed from the choir. "Daniel Chandler; hard to remember numb nuts, huh?"

Dana Cullen glared out the window and watched the new owner of the old Pomeroy estate driveway. She was on the verge of yelling out an obscenity as the car pulled away from the curb and out the rear exit, yet she controlled herself because she was a Christian woman and she did want to delay on getting back and questioning Sandy.

Daniel Chandler smiled to himself while thinking of the future. He just could not believe the dream had lasted this long, and now he was driving the very streets of Caulking. "Hot damn!" he screamed and drew a nasty look from an old woman in a pickup truck.

"Sandy!" Dana bellowed.

The poor girl screamed from being surprised again. "Will you stop that?"

"Yeah, of course. Whatever. It is just I am so stirred up over this Pomeroy thing! Tell me quick, tell me everythin'! What did the freak say, how much did he pay?" Dana was red-faced, her head about to explode as she slammed her palm on the desktop.

"What is wrong with you, Dana? The guy was okay, not real chatty, just wanted to take care of business and all."

Dana stared at the face of the young girl with a look beyond exasperation.

Sandy's eyes darted around the room, looking for a place to hide and praying someone would come in and rescue her.

"Child!" Dana yelled, the veins in her neck bulging. "Did that man have on makeup or not?"

"What? He was a black man, that's skin *color*, not makeup."

"C'mon," I saw he was a black man, but didn't ya see that red *color* on his cheeks? The little mascara smudge on his right eyelid, and I swear he had on lipstick! Plus them hands, I ain't seen a manicure like it since the funeral of the governor's wife!"

"Dana, you are startin' to scare me! You take a deep breath and have a drink of water or something."

Dana Cullen was infuriated. She glared at Sandy for a second longer before walking over to the basket and checking the details in the file herself. She read the top sheet and turned ashen. Her jaw dropped open, and she slowly turned her face back toward Sandy. "Is that all he paid for that place?" she whispered. "Sweet Jesus, what is wrong with this county?"

"Why? It's swamp land, Dana, and there ain't no house, no barn, no nothin' but all those rumors 'bout bones and such."

"Exactly! Just last week, me and Earl were a-talkin' 'bout opening a watcha call it—" Dana scrunched up her face, trying to remember. "Oh yeah, an amusement park, maybe makin' it a historic site or somethin'. Just because of all those bones and killin's and stuff! It's a gold mine, I tell you!" She watched the expression on the clerk's face alternate between fear and repulsion.

"You know, girl, me and Earl own the land on the other side of the river, right next to the Pomeroy place. Ya know where I mean. That place where that old, fallen-down Civil War mansion sets back in that old pecan orchard? Now that little freaky weasel comes in here and buys the best part right from under us!"

Everything about the town of Caulking died as the leased car bounced over the last pothole at the city-limit sign. The needle on the speedometer steadily chewed up the numbers and headed toward the triple digits. Daniel Chandler giggled and drooled as the white lines in the road became one and the scenery became just a blur. "Some days you're the windshield, some days you're the bug," he sang tunelessly as the needle hit the stop arm. Chandler was screaming with the song on the radio and giggling like a child while watching the blue lights twinkling in the rearview mirror.

"There had to be a speed trap along this ass-crack of a road!" He decided to let his foot off the accelerator and coast to a stop. He watched the Georgia State Patrol squad car fishtail and slide from lane to lane. "I thought all of 'them good ol' boys' knew how to drive."

The squad car slid to a stop with the tires screaming against the blacktop. Daniel quickly counted the number of blue lights flashing in his mirror and shoved the total into memory. The trooper looked down at something on the seat before his face exploded in anger. Daniel figured the look was not a good thing and anticipated that a good time was soon to be had by all. The door opened slowly at first, and a highly polished black boot hit the road. The Georgia Highway Patrol trooper slid out the door and stood up. The man just kept on going up until Daniel could not see him in the mirror.

"I hope y'all got a real good explanation?" The twang was classic. Chandler did not answer but merely handed the trooper all the necessary paperwork.

The state trooper carefully removed the neat little pile with two fingers and spat out, "BMW, huh?"

"Yes, sir, seven hundred series, and it's top of the line."

"Florida plates, Dade County address, huh?" The trooper continued to spit out the words, evenly spaced and full of intended maximum impact.

"Yes, sir, just like it states. Miami, Florida. Have you ever been there, trooper?" Daniel carefully counted the number of buttons on the trooper's shirt.

The trooper bent down until he could see Chandler's smiling face and carefully lifted the mirrored sunglasses he was wearing. The trooper reeked of tobacco, sweat, and some other odor not readily identifiable. He shifted the bulge in his right cheek over to the left and replied, "No."

"Oh," was all Daniel could think to reply. He watched the trooper cover the ground between the two vehicles in three giant steps.

Daniel waited patiently—What else was there to do?—but the voices in his head refused to stay quiet another second. They had given him time to himself, to sing and act foolish, yet all things must end. There is always a price to be paid, no pass, no get-out-of-jail-free card.

Daniel's eyes rolled up, exposing bulging white globes rimmed in moistened, sensitive layers of skin. His lips trembled, but no words fell out, yet there was a chorus of word-noise running amok inside his brain. His head fell to one side, and the eyes suddenly stared out at the woods beyond the road. Slick brown leaves and tiny eyes watched the human drama from the cover of slug-shit–filled dirt, snail trails, and cold rocks covered with lichens, moss, and crawling or winged things. A whole world watched back, and Daniel failed to see anything other than the layers of color coiled around his mind, the decay some foolishly mistaken for dullness. How those past visitors, now left far behind, had missed the point. Daniel was lost in a hallucination, watching smelly women waddling with large breast playing havoc with the earth's precarious spin through space.

Daniel let his spirits soar, to take wing and achieve the buzzard's view of things, a view that leaves behind the trials and tribulations of life, settling into a narrow perspective of waiting until the battle has been done. There is no need to become involved with the petty meaning of existence, just to wait until all efforts have been spent and then have a good meal of the spoils. The images slammed, blitzkrieg style, into the soft underbelly of his soul, and all came to an abrupt end when from the far end of pitch and tone, Daniel heard, "What is wrong with you, boy!"

The state trooper had returned with a stack of tickets containing the carefully compiled details of the violations committed by Daniel's driving. The trooper was wearing the same highly polished boots and mirrored sunglasses as he returned to the driver's side door of the dark blue 750IL BMW sedan. The trooper once again challenged gravity and several laws of physics by bending down, expecting to face the still smiling and innocent expression of Daniel Chandler, only to meet the dull-eyed stare of a man lost in his own mind.

The voices reached a fevered level were as they rocketed past the sound barrier, heading to a thundering crescendo. The trooper was shouting orders, and Daniel was merely watching the man's lips move. Words danced and vaulted across the stage as Daniel tried to drag them to his mouth, and he blinked in slow motion, leaving tiny droplets of tears outside on the skin of his cheek. The trooper was requesting backup and a medical response unit. He said something about a seizure, and the voice from the speaker asked about a fruity smell on the victim's breath. "Huh, no. I mean I don't know and ain't gonna get close enough to find out. Ten-four?"

Daniel felt the driver's door open. He was caught in the seatbelt, and the trooper had come close enough for him to determine the other smell oozing from the man—spearmint. The chewing tobacco had a spearmint odor to it. *How odd*, Daniel thought. He heard the Georgia State Patrol shouting. Finally, the words kicked holes in their captive spheres large enough to drip down the back of Daniel's throat and out his gaping mouth.

"I am insane, or so I am told by those who speak so brazen and bold. Whose voices wag and chatter on, until all words are exhausted and gone." Then the words created a bottleneck, stopping the flow and frustrating Daniel.

"What the hell is wrong with you, boy?" the trooper yelled as he jerked Daniel from the clutches of the seatbelt, twirling him around and onto the dust and dead grass at the side of the road. The sudden jolt broke the trance, and Daniel started screaming abuse.

"I need my medicine, you Neanderthal! What the hell is wrong with you, boy?" Daniel was allowed to retrieve a small zippered pouch from the glove box. The pouch contained various medications, which passed the inspection of the infuriated trooper. Daniel signed the tickets, four in all, and starts to proceed on his way, but he hesitated after reading the information at the top of the first citation. "This is not accurate, officer," he announced just as the trooper was hoping to be reunited with the sanctuary of his vehicle and be on his way.

"What's that you say? What ain't right?"

"I do not reside at this address any longer, sir; this is not correct."

"Listen, Mr. Chandler. I don't give a good dawgone where you live in Florida, if you moved into the governor's mansion in Tallahassee. Just figure out the total and send us a check." The trooper shoved the words out between the spaces in his teeth that he uses to spit tobacco juice.

"Don't live in Florida no longer."

"What?"

Daniel grinned, waited, and watched the face of the Georgia Highway Patrol trooper tiptoe around real, serious anger.

"And just where do you reside now, Mr. Chandler?"

"Why, right here." Daniel was still smiling, and the trooper was still holding his emotion at bay.

"Where? Right here? Right here is exactly where, Mr. Chandler?" The trooper's grip on his desire to snatch this man from the car raced dangerous close to the surface, but something stopped him from introducing Daniel to some real, down-home, Georgia hospitality, and that was the fact that he thought Daniel Chandler was crazy.

"Why, right here in Georgia, in Caulking County, right here as it says on the deed to this piece of property, right here." Daniel continued smiling, holding out the file containing all the paperwork Sandy Palmer had given him.

The trooper took only two strides this time to bring his boots back to the side of the BMW, and he read the file, rubbing a calloused hand across his face. The anger had slipped the leash and shoved a burning poker down his throat as he snatched the tickets from Daniel's hand. He tore the tickets into a hundred tiny pieces of yellow colored paper and threw them into the air. He cussed and glared at Daniel, ordering the smiling man to drive away immediately before "I rip off your head and shit down your neck, Mr. Chandler!"

Daniel finally made it to the old Pomeroy property just after dark. He had tripped the mileage indicator on the odometer when leaving the courthouse and learned he was fifty-three miles from town. It was further away than he had imagined, but he liked being far away from prying eyes. The town and the people had managed to live down to his expectations. The faces of Sandy Palmer and Dana Cullen popped into his mind. He painted them in red and shades of pain because Sandy was dumb and pretty and Dana was a miserable person, a hag. The image contorted and expanded until only pieces of their faces fit the frame of his mind's eye. First, he saw Dana's watery blue eyes and the sagging skin of her neck. Then it was Sandy's freckles and her red-gloss lips, but finally, the bodies merged, and Daniel barely had time to trap the vomit in his mouth.

The sky above was cloudy, and darkness surrounded the car. Daniel rolled down the windows to let the cool night air chase the fog from the windshield. Sleep was not going to be evasive tonight. The voices must have called it a day already, as his eyes started to close. Tomorrow was always another day, and there was so much to do, life had become so exciting. Daniel let the seat go all the way back and succumbed to the soft embrace of leather. He did not worry about the dreams because he took the pills and the pills always kept the nightmares from ripping a hole in his brain. The doctors had told Daniel he could live a normal life if he remembered to take his medicine, but no one had told the voices, and Daniel's attention was so easily drawn away.